BROKEN
DISHES

Berkley Prime Crime Books by Earlene Fowler

FOOL'S PUZZLE

IRISH CHAIN

KANSAS TROUBLES

GOOSE IN THE POND

DOVE IN THE WINDOW

MARINER'S COMPASS

SEVEN SISTERS

ARKANSAS TRAVELER

STEPS TO THE ALTAR

SUNSHINE AND SHADOW

BROKEN DISHES

BROKEN DISHES

Earlene Fowler

BERKLEY PRIME CRIME, NEW YORK

BROKEN DISHES

A Berkley Prime Crime Book
Published by The Berkley Publishing Group,
A division of Penguin Group (USA) Inc.
375 Hudson Street, New York, New York 10014

Visit our website at www.penguin.com

First edition: May 2004

Fowler, Earlene.
    Broken dishes / Earlene Fowler.—1st ed.
      p. cm.
    ISBN 0-425-19597-X
    1. Harper, Benni (Fictitious character)—Fiction. 2. Women museum curators—Fiction. 3. Dude ranches—Fiction. 4. Quiltmakers—Fiction. 5. California—Fiction. 6. Quilting—Fiction. I. Title.

PS3556.O828B76 2004
813'.54—dc22

                                                      2003063632

PRINTED IN THE UNITED STATES OF AMERICA

        10   9   8   7   6   5   4   3   2   1

To all the law enforcement
officers who keep us safe,
and
To all the quilters who keep us warm

Acknowledgments

Many, many thanks to:

Father, Son, and Holy Spirit—*Cristo rompe las cadenas!*—"Christ breaks the chains!"

Charlotte "Bunny" Brown—rancher and consummate Western woman—for your friendship, the many incredibly helpful e-mails answering all my horse, dog, and ranching questions, for some hair-raising horseback rides, for reading and critiquing this manuscript and for letting me borrow both your name and the real "MudRun." And thanks to her men, Richard, Reb, and Erick, for being such good sports and always being there to fix things (like hot-water heaters and generators) and for Richard's fantastic tacos!

Clare Bazley and Bonnie Haskell—fellow cowgirl friends and horse-lovers—for your friendship, encouragement, prayers, and doing such a great job critiquing this manuscript;

Tina Davis, Janice "Beebs" Dischner, Christine Hill, Jo Beth McDaniel, Carolyn "Mille" Miller, and Kathy Vieira—the kind of loyal friends of whom Dove would most definitely approve;

Melanie DeMattos—for the fun and informative barrel-racing lesson; and Linda Birdwell Anderson—for help with the names and descriptions of Central Valley flora and fauna;

Julia Fleischaker—who deserves a gold medal for planning and executing my book tours with the skill of a five-star general without once losing her cool;

Ellen Geiger—for being a most gracious and understanding agent, not to mention a real fun person to hang out with (we'll take that horseback ride yet!);

Margrit Hall—my quilting partner and friend, for sharing her quilting knowledge with me and designing such breathtaking quilts for our quilt book;

Jo Ellen Heil, Karen Olson, and Lela Satterfield—dear friends, spiritual upholders, and faithful believers of our Lord Jesus Christ—I thank God for your presence in my life;

Lisa and Chris Leverenz—for your hospitality during the three days I spent at the beautiful Paris Valley Guest Ranch;

Jack Mapson-Allison—for a quick, but thorough lesson on paramedic procedure;

Jo-Ann Mapson—who not only gifts me with support through her insightful critiques, but also through her loyal and loving friendship;

The Parkfield "Quilt Quake" quilters—Mary Russell, Pam Munns, and the rest of the ladies who allowed me to twice spend the weekend with them and observe their hilarious and inspiring quilting shenanigans (who *has* that rubber chicken?). I'm sorry, but I couldn't think of one of you I wanted to kill off;

Kristen Rager—assistant director, Riverside Forensic Lab—for answering all my crazy questions so promptly, the unparalleled tour of the lab and a special thank-you to Judy Rager for talking Kristen into e-mailing me in the first place!

Lynn Wiech—librarian, San Luis Obispo City Library, for help with Central Coast brands and history;

Christine Zika—whose editorial expertise and thoughtful insights make my books better and richer in so many ways;

In memory and thanks to two very special animal friends—Gumby, bridle horse of the highest order and Socrates, a goose's goose and friend to many. You were both precious and beautiful gifts from God;

And always, to my beloved husband, Allen, who after thirty incredible years of marriage, as corny as it sounds, is still my Huckleberry friend.

A Note from the Author

When I started the Benni Harper series in 1992, the first book, *Fool's Puzzle*, was written in "real time." It was 1992 in Benni's life as well as mine. Time in a long-running series is always a tricky thing. Since it often takes a book almost two years from the time the author starts writing it to the point when it is actually in the reader's hands, time sequences can become confusing. Each author deals with this dilemma in a different way. I decided from the beginning that I would age my characters more slowly than I and my readers were aging. With Dove being seventy-five in the first book, I wanted to keep her active and vital and I also wanted to explore the early stages of Benni and Gabe's relationship. Keep in mind while reading that the books, as of *Broken Dishes*, cover late 1992 to early 1996. Now, if we could just figure out a way for all of us to age like Benni and Gabe . . .

Broken Dishes

Broken Dishes is a simple pattern consisting of triangles arranged in a four-patch square. The squares are turned at different angles to create the broken dishes effect. It is a popular pattern with examples dating back to the 1790s and is one of the most common, earliest recorded designs in quilt history. Though a charming name that could have been inspired by many things including household accidents or even shattered dishes along the rough and rugged trail West, like many quilt patterns, it cannot be traced directly to any one original source. Most pattern histories come to us through folklore, old magazine articles, and sometimes diary or journal entries. It is a wonderful pattern to utilize colorful scraps of leftover fabric, but can also be quite striking and modern-looking if made using only two colors. Other names for this pattern are Old Tippecanoe, Bow Ties, Hour Glass, Whirling Blade, and Yankee Puzzle.

The Broken DIS Guest Ranch

SAN CELINA COUNTY, CALIFORNIA

Enjoy our rolling oak-dotted hills, gentle horses, beautifully decorated cabins and lodge rooms, delicious home cooking, and genuine western hospitality!

The Broken DIS Ranch is located in the breathtaking Cholame Valley, part of the Diablo Mountain Range, near Parkfield, the "Earthquake Capital of the World."

With 5,000 acres of the most rugged and beautiful landscape in the coastal mountain range of Central California, our guests are treated to an authentic western experience. Hunting, fishing, trail rides, hiking, square dances, barbeques, and ranch rodeos are only some of the fun activities awaiting you!

Owned by the Darnell family since 1936, the Broken DIS is a real working cattle ranch with real working cowboys!

DELUXE CABINS AND LODGE ROOMS,
ROMANTIC HONEYMOON CABIN,
FIREPLACES, AND SWIMMING POOL
FULL AMERICAN PLAN—3 MEALS DAILY
HORSEBACK RIDING
GUIDED HUNTING TRIPS

Perfect for romantic getaways, family reunions, business, or religious retreats. Stay for a day or a week!

For information and reservations, contact:
Broken DIS Guest Ranch
P.O. Box 100
Parkfield, California

CHAPTER 1

"*J*OE DARNELL WAS MY FRIEND, BENNI," DADDY SAID, HITTING the floor of our ranch house with his maple cane. Under the carpet, the wooden floor vibrated causing my dog, Scout, a chocolate part Lab, part German shepherd, to whine from his place in front of the dying fire. "Friends help each other."

"I'll go in your place," I said sitting across the room from him in my gramma Dove's rose velour recliner. "The doctor says you aren't supposed to do any excess activity for the first two weeks."

While gathering cattle two days ago, Daddy and his horse were charged by a rogue steer determined to keep his freedom. The horse and steer came out of the scuffle fine, but Daddy broke his leg in three places, something he was taking with only a pinch of grace and patience. Especially when he believed his best friend's daughter needed his help.

"He was my friend," Daddy insisted, his voice cracking. He looked away, but not before I could see tears well up in his pale blue eyes.

My father, a no-nonsense, taciturn Western man despite his Arkansas roots, so rarely showed emotion that a lump thickened in my own throat. Daddy knew many people, but he called few of them friends. Joe's death from a heart attack four months ago had left us all shaken. He'd just turned sixty-one, only three years older than Daddy, something I refused to wrap my own mind around.

I stood up and went over to where he sat in his brown corduroy easy chair, his heavy cast propped up on the matching footstool. Scout followed me, nosing Daddy's free hand. I perched myself on the padded chair arm.

"I'll be your pinch hitter," I said. "Your pick-up man . . . uh, woman." A pick-up man was the person on horseback who rescued a rodeo cowboy if he got a foot or hand hooked to his bucking horse or bull. I touched his rough hand with my fingertips and laughed. "That doesn't sound quite right."

A half smile softened the worried look on his lined, sun-browned face. "I know what you mean, pumpkin." His fingers absentmindedly scratched the outside of the cast, as if the plaster itched "You're a good girl. But Shawna and Johnny need me. Broken Dishes needs me."

The Broken DIS Ranch, affectionately known among the locals in San Celina County as the Broken Dishes, had been in the Darnell family for almost sixty years. When my father and mother moved to the central coast of California from Arkansas thirty-five years ago, Joe warmly welcomed them into San Celina's insular agriculture community. Joe, then a bachelor, became Daddy's first friend in California.

"Anything you can do, I can do better," I sang softly, teasing him.

He ran his fingers through his thick, almost white hair. "You know I trust you, but Joe mortgaged the ranch to his last penny building all those cabins and the lodge. He was sure this dude ranch business was the key to saving his pa's place." His eyes grew misty again. Joe had died before the first set of guests had been scheduled.

"Shawna's a smart girl," I said. "And a hard worker."

"She's still wet behind the ears. And that wild young buck she married—"

"She's Joe's daughter," I interrupted. "And I'm *your* daughter. Don't you think that we two girls inherited a little of our daddys' good sense?"

Shawna Darnell Abbott was Joe's only child. I'd come to know her as an adult since she hadn't grown up in San Celina County. Joe and Shawna's mother divorced when Shawna was two years old and she'd been raised in New York with little contact with her father. Two years ago, when she was twenty-one, her mother died unexpectedly. Shawna came west to visit her father, trying to make up for the years they'd lost. She never returned to New York.

When Joe died, she'd been married only six months to Johnny Abbott, a local boy Joe had hired as a part-time ranch hand. Johnny, also twenty-three, had spent most of his childhood hanging out in his parents' bakery in Paso Robles or riding his skateboard in front of the public library. Like Shawna, Johnny hadn't grown up a rural kid so it was hard to imagine him with his smart-aleck smile and unruly auburn hair, running a five-thousand-acre guest and cattle ranch.

Daddy picked up his cane again, gripping it until his knuckles whitened. "I'm not saying nothing about what you two can or can't do. You just need me there in case there's a problem."

"We need you to get healed up," I said. "And I need you to stay here and watch Scout. You know he can't come with me to Broken Dishes." Like most ranches, the DIS had its own ranch dogs and they were naturally territorial. Dog fights were something we didn't need during the guest ranch's first session. "Besides, you know as well as I do that the ranch's sleeping arrangements are limited. All the cabins and lodge rooms are booked for guests so that would leave you in the bunkhouse with the wranglers. I don't think you'd find those narrow beds too comfortable right now."

Daddy frowned at his toes poking out of the cast and didn't answer. He knew I was right, but was still frustrated. I walked over to the picture window. It was late January and the hills surrounding the Ramsey Ranch, where I grew up, were the bright, unbelievable green common to the Central Coast this time of year. In the circular driveway, my husband, Gabe Ortiz, San Celina's police chief, was bent over the open hood of my semi-new purple Ranger pickup, working on the engine. My gramma Dove, who had raised me since I was six, lingered next to him holding a basket of fresh eggs against her blue-jeaned hip. Her white braid switched back and forth like a mare's tail as she told him some elaborate story, gesturing wildly with her free hand. Though I couldn't hear it, I could imagine his deep rumbling laugh, a sound that still thrilled me.

I watched Gabe's Levi's pull attractively against his muscled runner's thighs. My thoughts were an electric flash back to that December day in 1992 when he came to my dad's ranch with the intention of repairing the broken starter of my old Harper ranch truck. I'd only been widowed nine months, full of raw and uncertain feelings. When our volatile relationship caught fire that day, my life was never the same. Hard to believe that was over three years ago. I turned back to Daddy who stared into the fire, his expression troubled and brooding.

"I'll call you . . ." I started to say every day, then quickly amended my words, realizing that might be difficult. "As often as I can. I promise I'll keep you informed. You've worked hard this last year helping Joe get the ranch ready. You know he appreciated everything you did."

His chest inflated in a deep sigh and he didn't answer. I didn't know how else to comfort him so I went back to Dove's chair and picked up the list that had been my lifeline for the last two months. It was already Friday and there was so much to do before Broken Dishes' first guests arrived in three days.

Right after Joe died, Shawna, who I'd become close to during the last year despite the fourteen-year difference in our ages, had confided in me about her fears for the ranch. A few weeks after Joe's funeral, while I was helping her wade through some of the ranch's complex legal papers, she brought up its financial problems.

"We'll lose Broken Dishes unless this guest ranch starts operating soon," she had said, running her hand through her wavy, dark brown hair. Her pixie-like features sharpened with worry. "I . . . I don't know where to begin, what to do. Dad and I were going to have brochures made, call some travel agencies . . . his funeral cost so much . . ." Her young voice quivered and a single tear trickled down her freckled cheek. "I can't let him down, Benni."

"Don't worry," I told her. "I'll talk to Dove and we'll figure out something."

Using the experience and connections I'd acquired as curator to the Josiah Sinclair Folk Art Museum and Artists' Co-op, I conceived the idea of a quilt retreat combined with a western dude ranch experience. Or guest ranch as most now preferred to be called. Quilters could bring their husbands or friends and when they weren't taking quilting classes, could experience a taste of the Western lifestyle that was celebrated in somewhat glossy and unrealistic glory in many travel magazines. Shawna loved the idea.

I was surprised and thrilled when, after putting out the word among quilt teachers, the world-renowned Victory Simpson called me from the coastal town of Monterey, about four hours north of San Celina. But after reading the biographical information on her bestselling quilt books—Victory herself grew up on a ranch—her attraction to the rural setting made sense. After I told her a little about Shawna and Johnny's plight, she kindly cut her teaching fee in half. The eight class spots filled up in one day and we even had a waiting list for possible second and third sessions if Victory was amenable.

While I was arranging the quilt retreat, my gramma Dove sprang into action and talked the board of San Celina First Baptist Church's Women's Missionary Union into holding their yearly planning/work retreat at the ranch. That wasn't too hard considering Dove offered to pay for it herself. With four hunters already at the ranch, the Broken Dishes' first session was full.

I leaned back in the chair and studied my list. Should I call the folk art museum first, to make sure they have my time off covered, or Tina at The Fabric Patch in Morro Bay to arrange the pickup of the three sewing machines she was loaning me for those quilters who couldn't bring their own? I was supposed to be at the ranch tomorrow to help set up the lodge's biggest meeting room, called the Murietta Room after an infamous local robber, Joaquin Murietta. It was where all the quilting and quilt lecture sessions would be held. Three days didn't seem like enough time to get everything done.

Daddy cleared his throat and I looked up. He was staring out of our huge picture window. The sadness on his face made me catch my breath. Since my mother died almost thirty-two years ago, Joe had been someone, maybe the only person, with whom I imagined Daddy had ever shared his feelings. Why hadn't my father remarried? No opportunity, or no desire? It was something we'd never talked about. My conversations with him always centered around what needed to be done around the ranch, cattle prices, family chitchat, Dove's latest shenanigans, which invariably irritated him, or the never-ending gossip within the ag community. I envied the intimate relationship I imagined Joe had with my father. There were so many secrets my father held tight inside himself, something I found out a few years ago when I questioned him about the circumstances surrounding my birth. I loved my father, but it hurt me sometimes that so much of him, by his own choice, was hidden from me.

I laid my list down and went over to his chair, sitting down on the floor next to his bulky cast, laying my cheek against the cool white plaster showing from his split Wranglers. Scout, sensing the sadness in the room, tried to worm his way onto my lap like he was a puppy.

"I'll do everything you would do if you were there," I said, hugging Scout's warm body. "I promise I won't let you down, Daddy."

He didn't answer, but placed his hand on top of my head, stroking it gently like I would Scout, letting his touch say the words he either wouldn't or couldn't articulate.

CHAPTER 2

"*D*EATH TO BUNNIES!" SAID THE QUILTER THREE DAYS LATER when I walked into the Murietta Room, Broken Dishes' largest meeting area. Like the rest of the ranch's new buildings, it was a log cabin structure with high ceilings and wide picture windows.

A comment like that is enough to stop anyone in their tracks, which I did, giving a nervous smile. It was 10 A.M. on the first full day of the western quilt retreat and everyone was still getting to know each other. Most of the quilters had arrived late yesterday afternoon, a sunny, but chilly Monday.

"Excuse me?" said Bunny, the Broken DIS's lean, fiftysomething manager. She'd just walked into the room with the same no-nonsense authority with which she runs this ranch and rides her tough little bridle horse, Gumby.

A blast of cold, late January air followed her through the open double doors, ruffling the red and white gingham curtains. The five-point buck head hanging above the doors didn't move an inch, but the old cowboy hat stuck in one of his antlers gave a perky twirl.

The quilter, whose name tag read Karen Olson, pulled the quilt top from her sewing machine. It was a simple nine-patch pattern set on point using blue-and-yellow flannel fabric covered with wide-eyed ducks and dancing blue rabbits.

The rest of the quilters, their machines set up in a horseshoe configuration facing the table of their instructor Victory Simpson, just laughed, obviously understanding what she meant. After her first lecture, Victory had taken a short break. I'd passed her a little while ago walking through the lodge's long hallway looking for the restroom. The quilters were working on personal projects for the next half hour.

"Nothing personal, I'm sure," I said to Bunny. I'd dealt with quilters often in my job as a museum curator and I knew them to be a mostly friendly and peaceful bunch.

Karen smiled. "It's not. I'm from Iowa and the local rabbits have helped themselves to more than their fair share of my garden last year. I'm holding a grudge. Truthfully, I love bunnies. I *adore* bunnies. I wouldn't even mind *sharing* with bunnies, if they had left me a carrot or two. At least enough to make one cake!" She held up her half-completed crib quilt top. "This quilt is for my latest grandchild-to-be. Please note there is not one speck of snow in the landscape." She had traveled here with her husband, Dennis, from a snow-choked Midwest, so he could hunt the wild pigs so prolific in these hills and do some fishing at the local lakes while she participated in this quilt retreat.

The other quilters called out enthusiastic and extravagant compliments from behind their buzzing machines without missing a stitch, a necessary skill perfected by most experienced quilters.

Marty Brantley, a snowy-haired widow from Southern California, looked up at Bunny. Marty was working on an intricate, overlapping Texas Lone Star quilt she started yesterday, one of Victory Simpson's original and innovative designs. "How ever did you get the name Bunny?"

"Long story short," Bunny said. "My given name is Charlotte Hopp. My first Easter an aunt sent me a card that had a place in the bunny's face where you could slip in a child's picture, which my aunt did." She placed her hands on her narrow hips and grinned at the ladies. Despite her name, Bunny was as physically perfect for the part of ranch manager as if she'd been cast by Hollywood, with her long, Wrangler-clad legs, capable hands, and a back as strong and straight as a redwood trunk.

Marty gave a delighted giggle. "Your name is Bunny Hopp?"

Bunny grimaced and ran a hand through her short, silvery curls. "Obviously my parents didn't think my nickname all the way through."

"I know how you feel," said a tiny, fast-moving woman with salt-and-pepper hair. She was a quilter from Long Island, New York. "I told everyone last night my name is Katherine, but my parents always called me Kitty."

"Kitty's a darling nickname," said Karen.

"Not if your last name is Katz," the woman replied.

The quilting ladies were still groaning when I followed Bunny down the hallway into the huge commercial kitchen.

"They seem like a nice group," she said, heading toward the thirty-cup coffeepot kept filled all day for both the guests and the ranch employees.

"They are," I said. "They've come from all over the country, so that makes it especially interesting. I think this quilt retreat/guest ranch idea will really take off and become the next hot travel adventure."

"Shawna and Johnny would sure appreciate that," Bunny said, pouring cream and sugar into her mug of coffee. "Speaking of travel, who do *you* think The Secret Traveler is?"

An old high school friend who was now a local travel agent told me there was a rumor that The Secret Traveler, a columnist syndicated in 200 newspapers across the country, was one of our guests. A good column about the Broken DIS ranch would be like a royal flush in the poker game of destination travel spots. I didn't even want to consider what a bad review could do to this fledgling enterprise.

"I haven't a clue," I said.

"Hard to believe," Bunny said, her back to me as she poured her coffee. "You being such a famous detective and all."

When she turned around, I made a face at her, despite the truth to her words. It was a too well-known fact that I tended to stumble into crime situations, something that did not always endear me to my by-the-book police chief husband. "I'll figure it out. And it better be the only mystery we have these next two weeks because Shawna and Johnny can't afford a bad reputation."

"That's the truth," Bunny said, staring down at her coffee a moment before taking that first sip.

"The Secret Traveler could be any of the quilters," I said. I started opening cupboards and drawers around the military-clean kitchen looking for something to munch on. With so much to do this first day, I hadn't had time to eat breakfast.

"Maybe we should start a betting pool." Bunny pointed to the huge refrigerator. "Rich made some chocolate cupcakes earlier this morning."

"Great!" I opened the refrigerator just as Rich Trujillo, the ranch's temporary chef, walked in.

"Get out of there," he said, waving a large wooden spoon at me, pretending to be annoyed. "Those are for the paying guests."

I grabbed a cupcake and dodged out of the spoon's way. "What about the hardworking help?"

"There's a box of soda crackers in the pantry."

Rich Trujillo was a good friend whom I'd begged to take this two-week cooking gig. The ranch's regular chef, Lupe, was down in Mexico until the middle of February on a trip to see her elderly mother. Today, his usual uniform of a brightly colored Hawaiian shirt and starched jeans was covered by a clean white apron. He was an excellent chef, in his late fifties with a square jaw and thick, black-and-silver streaked hair. Before retiring to Morro Bay, he had been a Phoenix firefighter, actually the most popular one in the city because before he joined the department he'd worked as a cook at his parents' Mexican restaurant. He broke many patrons' hearts when he gave up his restaurant career to fight fires.

I looked right at Rich and took a huge bite out of the chocolate-iced cupcake. "Umm, good stuff, *Señor mocosa grande*."

My pathetic Spanish accent made him laugh.

"What did you call him?" Bunny asked.

"Mr. Big Brat," he said, picking up an extra large can of chilies and pretending to throw it at me.

Without flinching, I took another bite of my cupcake. "What's for lunch?"

He shook his head at Bunny. "How in the world does she get anything done when all she thinks about is eating?"

"I'll have you know I've been up since 5 A.M.," I said. "Helped Sam and Lindsey feed the horses. Then I groomed a couple of horses and mucked out a few stalls. After that I helped Victory set up for her first lecture and helped the quilters get their machines situated. All of this without any breakfast. What have *you* been doing?"

"You're eating part of it," he said. "It's chicken, rice, and green chile casserole for lunch. And chocolate cupcakes for teatime if you leave any for the *paying* guests."

I popped the last bite of cupcake in my mouth. "I've missed you, Rich. Thank you a million times for helping us out like this. I'll owe you forever."

"Missed you too, *mija*," he replied, opening the chilies can with an electric can opener. "And you owe me *nada*."

When he went back to work on his casseroles, Bunny sidled over to me and said in a low voice, "Are you helping serve lunch? I strongly suggest you do. Actually, it might be even better if you helped at *every* meal."

I hadn't been present at breakfast this morning because I'd been more intent on making sure the horses were groomed and ready. They were a big part of the ranch's lure. I gave a small groan. "What has Rita done?"

Rita is my cousin. I prefer to tell people we're barely related, but unfortunately, her grandmother and my grandmother are sisters, so that makes us some manner of blood cousins, close relatives if you are from the South. Which we are.

Rita Mosely Johnson. How can I explain my cousin Rita from Pine Bluff, Arkansas? She is the Dolly Parton equivalent of me—five-foot-one, long curly reddish-blond hair, hazel eyes. Our unadorned physical statistics are identical. We even wear the same size clothes. But where I wear plain old Wrangler jeans, she wears butt-crack-tight Rockies in colors that would blind a hawk at a thousand yards. I wear T-shirts with the occasional plaid snap-button western shirt. She wears navel-baring tops with cutouts in places where bra straps *should* be. I usually wear my long hair back in a simple braid. Her teased strawberry-blond mane gives the expression *big hair* a whole new meaning.

And she was the guest ranch's waitress for the next two weeks, a situation I still can't quite believe happened. Three days ago, when I was due to leave for the guest ranch, for the third time in three years, she appeared on my doorstep with her usual tale of an unfaithful husband, no money, and no place to stay. My choices were bringing her with me or letting her stay at our house in San Celina with my husband, Gabe. Him, I trusted, but her, that was a whole other rodeo.

"We could use a waitress," Shawna told me over the phone when I asked about Rita tagging along with me. "The two I hired just decided to hitchhike to Alaska." The soft whoosh of a tired sigh whispered through the phone lines. "I was just getting ready to call the employment agency."

"Rita worked for a Waffle House once," I said, hoping I wouldn't regret my recommendation. Shawna offered her room and board and one-hundred-fifty dollars a week. It would solve our waitress problem and give Rita a little start-up money, if she finally decided this time her husband, Skeeter, was history.

Bunny shifted from one booted foot to the other. "I don't mean to be telling stories out of school, but if this morning is any indication . . . let me put it this way, she'll probably get incredible tips from our male guests. That's *if* she isn't killed by the female ones first. They had to ask for butter three times and I finally had to get it for them."

I sighed. "Okay, I get the drift. Has Shawna noticed yet?"

"Noticed what?" Shawna said, walking into the kitchen. Her dark hair was piled in a knot on top of her head and her red-checked western shirt, the ranch's semi-official uniform, fit her trim, young figure perfectly. She smiled at me, her neat, tiny features as cheerful today as a Disney character.

"Don't worry, it's nothing serious. It's my cousin, Rita."

Shawna laughed. She was two years younger than Rita but a hundred years more mature. "Don't worry about it, Benni. So she's a bit of a flirt. I imagine any of those women could put her in her place if they felt like it."

"You're probably right. But I think I'll work the meals anyway so everyone gets fair and equal access to condiments."

I appreciated Shawna being so understanding, but she had no idea how flaky Rita could be. I thought I'd only have to worry about the ranch hands whose bunkhouse was spitting distance from the cabin where Rita, myself, and Lindsey O'Brien, the one female ranch hand, were staying. Not to mention we couldn't afford to annoy The Secret Traveler, especially on the first day we were open for business.

"You're already doing too much," Shawna said.

"It's no problem. Besides, two waitresses are better than one. There's no such thing as food service that's *too* fast. Don't worry."

"Easy to say, hard to do," she said, her gray eyes blinking quickly.

Shawna had taken over the responsibility of the ranch's financial problems since her father died while Johnny took charge of physically running the ranch, with a great deal of help from Bunny and Whip Greenwood, their head wrangler. To carry that sort of emotional and physical burden while also mourning your father was a huge undertaking for someone only twenty-three years old. So far, Shawna had handled it better than many people I'd known who were twice her age.

"How's Pokey?" I asked. One of their twenty horses had a sore leg that Whip had tried to doctor unsuccessfully with Absorbine wraps and Bute mixed into the horses' grain.

"I had to call the vet," she said, swallowing hard, trying hard not to let her anxiety show. "Our bill with Dr. Kreft is already so high. Thank goodness he takes payments."

"He's used to it," I said. "Most ranchers around here are barely surviving these days. On a more positive note, one of the hunters bagged a three-hundred-pound pig this morning and is thrilled."

"That's great," she said, with exaggerated enthusiasm. "So, when's Gabe coming out?"

"Friday," I said, glancing up at the Farm Supply calendar on the wall. Today was Tuesday, January 30. "If he gets all his paperwork done, he might stay three or four days. Before he went into the marines, he worked for a little while at the Santa Anita racetrack so he can be an extra wrangler."

"I'm sorry you two will have to sleep separately," she said. "Though I am glad that all the rooms and cabins are rented. I gave Victory the honeymoon cabin. I felt like it was the least I could do."

"And I agree," I said. "She's doing us a big favor."

Though Broken Dishes was bigger than many guest ranches, the response to the quilt weekend was so enthusiastic we filled almost every bed. There were eight log cabins, some two-, some four-person, a bunkhouse for the male ranch hands and wranglers. Shawna and Johnny lived in the original adobe ranch house and Bunny had a small cabin on the other side of the barn.

"I hope the bunkhouse is comfortable enough for Gabe," Shawna said.

Rich turned around from the bread dough he was kneading. "If Gabe can survive marine barracks and the Vietnam jungle, your bunkhouse will be heaven," he said. "Shoot, it feels like I'm a rookie again. Except I do miss my firm mattress."

"Oh, I'm so sorry, maybe we can . . ." Shawna started.

Rich held up a flour-dusted hand and gave her a wide grin. "I was just kidding. My old back is fine and I'm having a great time." His encouraging words didn't relieve the tension in her face.

I placed a hand on her back. "Moaning and groaning is part of jobs like this, Shawna. Just ignore everything we whine about in the next two weeks. Behind-the-scenes kvetching is what makes everyone work as a team."

Rich and Bunny laughed.

Shawna turned doubtful gray eyes on me. She was taking her role as boss seriously, just like a scared, hyper-responsible twenty-three-year-old would. "If you say so . . ."

"If anyone complains to you, run it by me, and I'll let you know if it's something you really need to worry about. Deal?"

She nodded, her tense chin relaxing slightly. "Deal." She turned to Rich. "How're things doing in the kitchen?"

"Everything's right on schedule," he said, wiping his hands on his apron. "The chicken casserole for lunch with sopaipillas. For dinner it's chicken and dumplings and cherry pie with homemade vanilla bean ice cream."

I placed my hand over my heart. "Rich, you are the perfect man."

"You could show your appreciation by washing dishes," he said laughing and gesturing at the gleaming commercial dishwasher across the kitchen.

"No way, I'll leave that for Sam. By the way, do you need any prep help for dinner? Sam's dying to work with you."

Sam was my stepson, Gabe's only child, who'd come to live in San Celina over two years ago trying to mend his troubled relationship with his father. He'd recently decided to pursue culinary arts with vague plans of becoming a chef. With his parents' approval, he'd taken this semester off from Cal Poly University to work full time. I talked my best friend, Elvia, into letting him off from the bookstore so he could help at the ranch. I also promised Sam that when he wasn't giving trail rides or mucking out stalls, he could work with Rich who was a self-taught, but naturally talented chef.

Rich nodded, his coppery face genial. "I could definitely use more help with the dinner prep, but as fast as he works, even Sam might not be enough now that all the guests have arrived." He turned back to his bread dough and continued kneading it.

Shawna's face grew troubled again. With such a full house and an almost skeleton staff, everyone was pressed for time.

"No problem," I said. "I can chop and peel during the quilter's lessons with Victory." I turned my palms up to Shawna. "See, problem solved. Now, I'm off to find Rita so we can start setting the tables for lunch."

"And I'm off to see about the water pump in the north corral up by Condor Pass Trail," Bunny said. "Whip said it was sticking the last time he took a group up there."

The pump was at the first stop on one of the ranch's five organized trail rides. Before he died, Joe had done an incredible job clearing and marking the trails and developing watering holes for the horses as well as outhouses for the riders at strategic spots along the trails. For the overnight cattle drives and hunting trips he'd been planning there was a pieced-together hunter's cabin they called MudRun about a two-hour horseback ride from the ranch.

Shawna gave a nervous smile. "Sounds like everything is running smooth for today. Only thirteen more days to go."

"This first session will be the hardest," I said. "By next year, this'll all be old hat to you."

"I hope so," she said, starting for the door. I followed her out to the long front porch of the lodge where we stood for a moment gazing out over the stables and the bunkhouse. Rocking chairs made of rough-hewn logs and fitted with red and blue paisley cushions lined the front porch. At the other end of the porch, a couple of quilters were taking a break and enjoying the late morning sunshine. They smiled and waved at us.

I leaned forward, resting my arms on the rough porch railing. Shawna followed suit, and we watched Sam groom a little mouse-colored gelding. His crooning to the horse almost sounded like a song, the words ascending and falling on the brisk, winter breeze. Loud and soft, loud and soft. Behind him rose the Diablo Mountain Range, a dark greenish-brown etching against the icy blue cloudless sky. A mottled, red-tailed hawk swooped low, riding a thermal, on the prowl for lunch, close enough for us to spot the narrow white bands on his tail. It was chilly today. The weather channel on our television in the cabin predicted the high in the Cholame Valley would be fifty-six degrees, not uncommon for late January, early February. I'd have to remind the quilting ladies to dress in layers for our trail ride.

After a few minutes of silence, I asked, "Is there anything else you need done?"

Shawna bit her lip and didn't look at me. "I'm worried about Johnny. He's taken the success of the ranch so much to heart, like it's some kind of test of his manhood or something. If it fails, he'll completely blame himself and that makes me feel awful." With a thumbnail, she picked at a clump of dirt on the unpainted porch railing. "And I know this sounds childish, but I want my mother. And I miss Dad."

"I know." She'd had such a short time with both her parents, but especially her father. Now she had this huge responsibility of trying not to be the generation who lost the family ranch. Not to mention trying to live up to Joe's beloved reputation in San Celina County.

She gave her head quick shake and said, "We'll just do the best we can and let the cow chips fall where they may. I know that's all Dad would expect of me."

I sent up a quick prayer for the strength she and Johnny would need to get through these first years of marriage and this business. "You're absolutely right. Don't forget, you have a whole heap of friends pulling for you."

She smiled shyly at me. "I cannot tell you how grateful I am."

"Benni!" A shrill voice interrupted Shawna's words. My cousin, Rita, stepped out of our cabin and started imitating a bugling moose. "Ben-ni!" She only wore two towels, one around her head, one barely covering the rest of her. One of the wranglers, a young man in his early twenties named Chad, happened to come out of the bunkhouse in time to catch her act. He stood, open-jawed, staring at my scantily-clad, screaming cousin.

"Hold off on that gratefulness for a few days, Shawna. The fact that I came with my crazy cousin attached at my hip may cause you to change your tune."

She giggled, sounding for the first time in days like a young, carefree woman. Maybe Rita would serve some sort of a purpose other than flirting with the men. Heaven knew we needed a little comic relief.

"I knew girls like her in New York," Shawna said. "The clothes may be different, but the persona is completely the same."

"Let me go see what she's hollering about. I'll tell her to try and maintain a little modesty in this very close environment, not that my words will matter one iota."

"Benni!" Rita yelled again, stepping down to the bottom step of our cabin. "Help!"

"Hold your mustangs, Rita," I called back, starting down the porch steps. She almost lost grip on the towel covering her. "And your towel," I grumbled.

Chad's mouth opened a little wider, his bottom lip wet, giving him the appearance of someone with less than a genius IQ. When I passed him, I raised my eyebrows and said, "Don't you have some horses to groom?"

"Uh, yes, ma'am," he said, closing his mouth and giving an actual, physical gulp, before turning around and heading for the stable.

"What's wrong?" I asked Rita, hustling her back inside the cabin.

"My hair dryer broke and I can't find yours. I've looked *everywhere*."

"It's right here," I said, pulling it out of the top drawer of the bathroom vanity.

She grabbed the dryer out of my hands. "Shoot, why don't you just hide it?"

"Putting something away is not hiding it," I commented dryly. Though from past experience I didn't trust her to maintain any type of modesty around my husband, maybe I should have taken the chance.

She switched on the radio, turned her back to me and clicked on the dryer. KCOW came in loud and clear, despite how far back in the hills we were. Hereford Hank boomed, "Happy Tuesday, buckeroos and buckerettes. Here's a smoky old tune from our favorite cowgirl of all time—Miss Patsy Cline. *'Three Cigarettes in an Ashtray'*."

Rita flipped her hair over and started drying her roots, her reedy soprano butchering Patsy Cline.

"When you're finished, we need to start setting the table for lunch," I yelled over the dryer's high-pitched whine.

She just gave me an upside-down smile, not hearing a word I said.

Outside the cabin, I stood on the porch a minute, inhaling the fresh, cool winter air. It was going to be a long two weeks.

As I rounded the corner to check on the horses, I bumped into David Hardin, the ranch's oldest employee. He'd worked for Joe's father, then Joe, and was now continuing the tradition by working for Shawna and Johnny. He was sixty-seven and knew more about ranching than all of us put together.

"Whoa, there, Benni Harper," he said, catching me by the shoulders. The ranch's two friendly cattle dogs followed him—a black-and-white border collie named Sugar; the other a half border collie, half Catahoula hound named Buck with whom I had a special relationship. "Where're you heading off to in such a hurry?"

A tall, big-chested man with a contagious smile, he was a life-long bachelor. He walked with a slight limp and had a snowy white mustache and beard, a broad face sun-cut with creases, and he always wore a tan cowboy hat with a jaunty little feather.

"Hi, David," I said, stooping down to pet the dogs. Buck nosed Sugar out of the way so she retreated back to David. Buck, who'd worked cattle with me many times in the past, reminded me of Scout, who I already missed like crazy. "I'm going to check on the horses Lindsey picked for the quilter's trail ride this afternoon. How's everything in the bunkhouse?"

The long, narrow bunkhouse provided beds for nine people with two rooms holding four beds a piece and a bathroom at each end. In the middle was a private room and bath, usually awarded to the ranch manager. Since Bunny lived in a small cabin on the other side of

the barn, David, by virtue of age and relationship to the ranch owners, scored the coveted middle room.

"So far, everything's fine," David said. "Whip's on one side, since
he can't stand Chad and Sam's music. So I've got that hip-hoppy
music on one side and George Jones on the other."

"At least Whip has good taste in music," I said.

Whip Greenwood was in his early thirties, a few years younger
than me. He'd lived on the ranch and worked for Joe Darnell for
about twenty years. I was a senior in high school when he'd come to
Broken Dishes as a young foster child. A social worker friend had
talked Joe into giving him a home. To me, Whip was as much a part
of Broken Dishes as the weathered black oak trees dotting the hills
like random drops of inky night sky. Quiet even as a boy, he'd grown
into a raw-boned, sun-darkened man who went about his work with
the reserved, few-words attitude of a typical rural Western male.

"This weekend the concert in the bunkhouse may be even more
complex," I said. "Gabe likes blues and jazz. Emory prefers books-on-
tape."

My cousin, Emory, and my best friend, Elvia, newlyweds themselves, were coming up this weekend to help with the big barn dance
on Saturday night. It was open to the public and was an experiment.
If it was profitable, Shawna and Johnny hoped to eventually hold
more dances as well as other events like weddings, company picnics,
and family reunions. Anything to keep the ranch solvent. We'd all
been promoting the barn dance heavily for a month.

"No problem," David said. "I've got me a whole package of top
quality ear plugs. The rest of them can just duke it out."

I laughed. "I'd better get cracking and see about those horses. It's
almost time to start setting the table for lunch." Buck leaned against
my leg and sighed. I reached down and stroked his silky ears.

"Saw you talking to Shawna on the porch," he said, his leathery
face suddenly getting serious. "How's she holding up?"

"She's a tough little cookie. If anyone can make this guest ranch
work, it'll be her."

"I know, but I worry about her. And Johnny too. This is a lot for them so young in their lives."

David and I walked through the ten-stall stable to the corral in the back. Whip stood inside the corral, his arms crossed over his chest, watching Johnny attempt to catch a goosey young quarter-horse gelding. When the horse danced away from Johnny one time too many, he started cursing and swinging the bridle menacingly. That only caused the jittery gelding to kick his heels and shy away more. The horse reminded me of Johnny, nervous and a little green. Whip finally couldn't stand the spectacle any longer and, without a word, walked up and grabbed the bridle out of Johnny's hands.

"I can do it!" Johnny held tight to the bridle a moment before giving in to Whip's obviously superior physical strength.

"You're scaring the poor thing," Whip said with a languid drawl.

Talking softly, Whip inched his way over to the horse, whose ears were pinned back in fear. After a few minutes, the horse allowed Whip close enough to touch him. Whip moved slowly up alongside the horse, crooning low, rubbing his hand across the horse's flanks and neck. Within a few seconds, he smoothly slipped the bridle on.

"You need to be a little slower and quieter, Johnny," he said over his shoulder. "The horse can feel your agitation."

Johnny mumbled something unintelligible, but definitely derogatory under his breath.

Whip turned and faced the younger man, his expression annoyed. "What did you say?"

Johnny stiffened his spine and flashed angry eyes at Whip. "I said I can do what I dang well please. I own that horse."

The two lines bracketing Whip's narrow lips deepened. "I reckon I know that, Mr. Abbott." He dragged out the last two words, mocking Johnny. "I reckon you own just about everything here." He took the horse's lead rope and looped it around one of the corral's bars. "Then again, I guess it's more accurate to say your wife owns it."

"It's *our* ranch," Johnny snapped.

"Ranch?" Whip said, his laugh sarcastic. "This ain't no ranch anymore. You all are turning it into a playground for rich folks. Guest ranch." He turned his head and spit on the ground. "Waste of good land."

"What do you know?" Johnny said. "You're only here because Joe felt sorry for you and now Shawna does too."

I gaped at Johnny, shocked at his cruelty. I had always liked Johnny but one thing hadn't changed about him since he was a boy, his mercurial mood swings. I'd witnessed them a few times at his parents' bakery and, recently, at a couple of the ranch's brandings and barbecues.

I knew Johnny's harsh words hurt Whip more than he would show. Whip had loved Joe like a father and, except for David, no one knew the Broken DIS Ranch and its horses, cattle, and land better than Whip. That included Bunny, whom Joe had hired a year before he died. With Whip's length of time at the ranch, I'm sure I wasn't the only person wondering why Joe hired Bunny as ranch manager rather than promoting Whip. Or why Joe didn't include Whip in his will despite the fact that he'd practically raised him.

"That's enough, boys," David said, moving toward Johnny. He grabbed his shoulder and started talking low in his ear while Whip glared at them. Johnny and David had hit it off the first summer Johnny worked there. Johnny looked up to him like a grandfather. Whatever David said must have worked, because Johnny kept his mouth shut and they walked away, not looking back at Whip, whose chiseled face was now rosy with anger.

He glanced over at me and scowled.

I did the only thing I could think of to ease the embarrassment of my witnessing their fight—change the subject. "Are the horses ready to tack up for my quilters' afternoon ride?"

He nodded, color still high on his sharp cheekbones. "Checked all their shoes and they are good to go. Bunny says you should ride Patrick. He needs the exercise."

"Thanks, I will."

He swung around and walked out of the corral, leaving the gelding tied up. I untied him and led him back to the pasture.

Inside the stable, Patrick recognized me and stretched his neck out so I could give him a scratch under his jawline where the chin strap usually fits. He was a smart little roan quarter horse I'd ridden many times. He was in the process of being trained by Bunny to be a bridle horse—a horse trained in complicated ranch work. He's a quick learner, she'd told me, and has such a light mouth that soon I'll be able to control him on stage during a kettle-drum concert. At the touch of my hand, Patrick blew air and snuffled in pleasure.

"Oh, Patrick," I said, rubbing his chest and thinking about what I'd just witnessed. "What is it with you men anyway, always pawing and snorting?"

I double-checked the horses Whip chose for the ride. They were all easygoing, old lesson horses who would give you your quarter's worth. That was exactly what we needed. With this group of inexperienced riders, Lindsey and I didn't want unpredictable horses who might easily spook at a wind-blown leaf or a butterfly. I liked my quilting ladies and didn't want to see them hurt. The ranch also couldn't afford any lawsuits.

Assured that my trail ride was set, I walked back to our two-bedroom cabin to search for Rita. She was nowhere to be found, though there was lots of evidence she'd been there. The western-decorated sitting room was acceptably neat, but our bedroom was a disaster. Her twin bed, covered with the same red bandanna-print comfortor as mine, was a tousled mess. Pieces of clothing hung on every post of her black iron head and footboards. Even my neatly made bed was strewn with Rita's fashion debris.

I picked up a dark-stained tissue and an open tube of blue-black mascara thrown on our pine-wood nightstand. The hair dryer and various hair combs occupied the brown-and-white cowhide chair in the corner. Next to the chair, a half-empty can of Red Bull energy drink balanced precariously on the lamp table's edge.

I was emptying the soft drink into the cabin's bathroom sink when Lindsey came out of the second bedroom. Until this Friday when Elvia would be sharing the room, Lindsey occupied it alone. Glancing back through the open door at the clothes, makeup, junk jewelry, and fashion magazines scattered around my and Rita's room, I flat out envied Lindsey.

"Are you ready for our first official ride?" I asked her.

"You bet," Lindsey said, smiling. She was the same height as me, five-one, but was broader in the shoulders and wore her dark red hair in a short, boyish cut. A spray of tiny freckles, random as buckshot, sprinkled her tanned cheeks.

"The quilt ladies are looking forward to it." I picked up a damp, crumpled towel from the sofa. Underneath was a pair of red thong underwear. Using the towel as a mitt, I picked those up too, grimacing at Lindsey. "Sorry about my cousin. Hope she's not irritating you too much."

Lindsey stuck her hands in the back pockets of her Wrangler jeans and grinned at me. "No problem. I'm not the one sharing a room with her."

I tossed the towel and the underwear in the woven clothes hamper in the bathroom. "No, just the cabin. I'll do my best to clean up after her."

"Maybe you shouldn't," Lindsey suggested, rocking back on her boot heels.

"I know it's futile, but she's like a dog who was never trained properly as a puppy. Her bad habits are probably too ingrained for me to change now. All I'm trying to do is make it more pleasant for all of us to cohabit."

"Believe me, I've had worse roommates than Rita. At least there aren't any strange men sitting in our living room when we wake up in the morning."

I stared at her in surprise. "Are you psychic?"

She laughed. "Not that I know of. Why?"

"It's exactly how I became acquainted with her possibly future ex-husband, Skeeter, bullrider not-so-extraordinaire." I glanced over at the boot-shaped clock over the fireplace mantel. "I'd better get moving.

Lunchtime is looming and I'll make a wild guess that cousin Rita's not in the dining room setting the tables early."

"What time should I meet you at the stables?"

"One o'clock. Rita will just have to clean up the tables by herself. Our ride is at two so that gives us an hour to saddle up the horses. Could you make sure there's bottled water for everyone? I might not have time."

"Yes, ma'am." She touched two fingers to her brow. "See you at one."

I followed her out of our cabin, but she walked toward the stables behind us while I headed for the main lodge. The air had grown even chillier in the last half hour, a cold front blowing through. The sun, which had been brilliant this morning, now hid behind swollen, luminous blue-gray clouds.

Please, no rain, I begged silently. Not for two more weeks. Although rain was never unwelcome out here in the dry Cholame Valley, it would be much better for the guest ranch if any late winter storms held off until this group of guests finished their visit. We'd had some fierce rainstorms the week before the guests arrived and things were just now starting to dry out. We'd have to be careful on some of the trails and watch for landslides. Though there was no way The Secret Traveler could hold bad weather against the ranch, it would be preferable that she or he had perfect weather to report.

I entered the lodge through what was essentially the parlor, a room named after Annie Oakley by Joe and Shawna in honor of their favorite cowgirl. It was decorated with colorful Pendleton blankets on the walls as well as old black-and-white photos of early San Celina County. The vaulted, open-beam ceiling was even higher than the Murietta Room, giving it a rugged, cathedral feel. The huge fireplace, made of stones gathered from the hills surrounding the ranch, was breathtaking, a true focal point to the room. Above the mantel carved with acorns and oak leaves, was a copy of a William Matthews watercolor showing a cowboy giving his horse a drink.

In the hall, on the way to the kitchen, I passed the closed doors of the Murietta Room. Even through the thick oak doors, I could hear the quilters laughing. It was the most gratifying sound I could imagine hearing right then. Just what the Broken Dishes needed—happy, satisfied guests. Curious, I slipped inside the room to see what was going on.

Victory was teaching a class on how to interpret the colors of nature by taking photographs or slides and studying the variation in tones on a rock, a tree trunk, or the sky.

"Do you look at things?" she asked. "Or do you *see* them? There's a huge difference. If you look closely at the photograph of the tree trunk I am passing around, you will not only see shades of brown and gray, but also pinks and blues and violets."

The women passed the photograph around, nodding their heads as they saw what Victory was talking about.

"To achieve those effects in your quilts, you also have to see fabric in a different way. Look at parts of the fabric, rather than the whole. For example, use mountain print fabric to represent the ocean by using the snow on the fabric as foam for your ocean wave. You can see what I mean here on this sampler quilt. If you look closely, you'll see that each fabric I used to represent something in nature is actually something else. Remember, things sometimes aren't what they first appear to be, in nature and in good design."

I slipped back out when the women got up to check out her quilt. I could look at it later.

In the dining hall, Rita was as visible as Casper the ghost and not one of the round eight-person tables had been set. A bell, that's what my cousin needed. A big ole cow bell hung around her neck so I could locate her when I needed her. Or maybe a shock collar.

"What's put that Cheshire cat grin on your face?" Rich asked, coming into the dining hall carrying a plastic tray of condiments.

"Just amusing myself thinking about ways to keep track of my cousin who is supposed to be helping me set these tables. No, let me rephrase that. *I'm* supposed to be helping *her*."

He set down the plastic tray and strode across the room to flip on the lights. "This would go a little faster if we weren't working in the dark."

Above us, the three chandeliers flooded the dim room with cheerful brightness. I looked up and marveled yet again at the intricately hand-carved, horse-head chandeliers.

"They take my breath away every time I see them," I said. "The details are just incredible." Every horse head had been carved in oak, a different expression on each showing their individual personalities.

Rich joined me in my scrutiny. "It is something. I wonder if the person who carved it actually used real horses as models."

"If he didn't, then he has a very good imagination or knew many horses in his life." I grabbed some red gingham napkins and started folding them like swans.

"Those are pretty clever," Rich commented as he placed a bottle of Red Rooster hot sauce and a jar of yellow peppers on each table.

"Shawna showed me how to make them last night. She's really knocked herself out trying to think of every little detail."

"Let's hope people notice."

Rich went back to his cooking and I was finishing the last napkin when my gramma Dove and two of the WMU ladies wandered into the airy dining room. The two ladies, Leonora and Blanche, were dressed in similar outfits, stretchy blue pants and flowered tops. Dove wore her customary Wranglers and a pink plaid cowboy shirt, her waist-length, white hair pulled back in a braid. Her soft peach complexion was weathered and her crisp blue eyes were honest and straight-forward. Just seeing her made the very cells in my body relax.

"I thought you were doing trail rides and quilt lectures," Dove said, eyeing the table-setting cart. "Isn't this—?"

I finished her sentence. "Rita's job. Yes, ma'am, it is. As usual, when there is work to be done, your great-niece does a remarkable imitation of Houdini."

Dove clucked under her breath, and I wasn't sure if it was at Rita's irresponsibility or my stupidity in covering for her.

"The guests expect lunch on time," I said, my voice a little defensive. "I don't want to let Shawna and Johnny down."

Dove gave my arm a gentle pat. "I wasn't pointing my clucks at you, honeybun. I'm just not sure that having Rita work here was the smartest idea you've ever hatched."

"What else could I do? Leave her home alone for two weeks with Gabe?"

Dove grabbed some silverware and started setting a table. "Your husband is perfectly capable of resisting Rita's advances."

"I know *that*." I picked up a stack of plates and started placing them around the tables. "But why put the man through unnecessary agony?"

"Do you two need any help?" Blanche asked.

"No, I think we've got it covered," I said. "There's still thirty-five minutes before lunch starts."

"Then Leonora and I are going to pop over and see what the quilt ladies are making."

"Okay," Dove said, placing my red-checked napkin swans in the middle of each navy blue plate. "After lunch we'll get back to work on the Women's Shelter quilts." One of the ladies' projects was stitching up simple patchwork flannel quilts for San Celina's Women's Shelter.

"Anyone want to go on a trail ride?" I asked. "We have plenty of horses. Aren't you all supposed to be having fun too?"

This outing at the guest ranch was something that Dove paid for out of her own money to reward her committee for their hard work all year as well as to help Shawna and Johnny. But Dove, being Dove, was not above prying a little charitable work out of them during the retreat.

Dove shot me an aggravated look.

I shook a butter knife at her. "Lighten up, General Patton. Let the troops have some occasional R & R."

"They can rest when they're sleeping," Dove said.

"Do you have a really gentle horse?" Leonora asked. "How long is the ride?"

"About two hours," I said. "An hour up to Luna Lake and an hour back. There's a very nice outhouse at the end of the trail and I promise you a horse that feels like your favorite rocking chair."

"Maybe I will go," Leonora said, her face brightening. "I haven't been riding in years."

"I'll pass," Blanche said. "But count me in for the domino tournament tonight."

The WMU ladies had begun the tournament last night in the Annie Oakley Room.

"Sissy's ahead again," Leonora said. "We think she might be cheating."

Sissy Brownmiller was the fourth member of the WMU board. She wasn't the most popular chicken in the henhouse because she was such a dang judgmental, know-it-all. It would be quite a coup if someone caught her cheating, though I wasn't quite clear how someone could do that at dominos, especially with these eagle-eyed domino queens watching every move.

"Thanks for stealing one of my best workers," Dove carped after Blanche and Leonora left the room.

"C'mon, Dove, you paid for this retreat so they could have some fun, didn't you?"

"Only after our work is done."

"Like I said, General Patton . . ."

"Hush, little missy," she said, slapping me lightly on the butt. "I'm only teasing and they know it. Since when have I ever been one to turn down a good time?"

"Since never. Actually, I think Rita might have inherited that trait from you."

She was reaching out to playfully swat me again when the dining room door burst open and Sam, my stepson, stumbled into the room

with Chad, the wrangler who'd ogled Rita, close on his heels. They
slammed the door shut behind them. A loud honking was muffled by
the thick wooden door. They faced us, their eyes wide and white-
edged.

"Getting attacked by poultry was not part of the deal," Sam said,
his breath coming in short, fast spurts.

CHAPTER 3

"*Y*OU'VE MET SOCRATES," DOVE SAID IN A PLACID VOICE, SETT-ing out the cobalt blue water glasses.

"Who's Socrates?" I asked.

A thunderous honk came from the other side of the door.

"That big white bird scared the crap out of me!" Sam exclaimed. He took off his worn black Stetson revealing his short, dark hair. Like his father, he was a handsome man though he'd inherited his mother's deep brown eyes rather than Gabe's startling blue-gray ones.

"Sam, save it for the barn," Dove said in an indulgent, scolding voice. Sam had lived at the Ramsey Ranch for the last couple of years, so he and Dove had forged an easygoing relationship that couldn't have been closer than if she had been his *abuelita* by birth.

"Sorry, Dove," he said, his young face contrite. "But that bird is *muy loco*."

A plaintive honk punctuated his sentence.

"When did the ranch get a goose named Socrates?" I asked. I'd been here three days and never saw any poultry except for what was in Rich's freezer.

"He's a little possessive," Dove said. "Since I was in here and he doesn't know Sam and Chad and they are men besides, he was just trying to protect me. For some reason he doesn't cotton to men." She shrugged. "He showed up at my cabin door yesterday afternoon and has been following me around ever since. We have no idea where his home is."

"How do you know his name?" I asked.

Dove's face turned a soft shade of pink and she turned her attention back to arranging silverware.

"*You* named him?" I exclaimed.

Dove was a born-and-bred farm woman who took good and loving care of her poultry and livestock but never, as long as I have known her, gave a personal name to any animal that might someday be food. She called all cows "sweetie" and all bulls and steers "mister." Her poultry was always "the girls" or "the grain gang" if roosters or ganders were mixed into the bunch. *You don't get sentimental about your supper,* she always told me.

"He looked very . . . wise," she said, looking up at me and narrowing her eyes, daring me to tease her.

"No comment," I said, grinning back, lifting up my hands.

"When I get time, I'm going to call the ranches in the area and find out where he belongs."

"He belongs in prison," Sam said. "That bird is evil."

"For sure," Chad agreed. "He bit me in the balls!"

Dove cleared her throat and gave him the eye.

He dipped his head in embarrassment. "Sorry, Mrs. Lyons."

"So, what's up, guys?" I asked. "You need anything?"

"No," Sam said. "Just coming in for lunch and wondering what we should do this afternoon. Bunny is out on one of the trails fixing a broken water pump and Whip's busy with a colicky mare."

"Oh, no," I said. "That's all we need. How's the mare doing?"

"Looks like she'll be fine," Chad said. "It's just time consuming."

"Sam, Rich could use some help prepping for dinner. And when was the last time you cleaned the bathrooms in the bunkhouse? You can't expect Maria and Luis to keep your rooms clean on top of their other duties. Gabe and Emory are coming out this weekend and it would be nice if the bunkhouse was in semi-livable shape."

Maria and Luis took care of the ranch's housekeeping as well as laundry and odd jobs. Like David and Whip, they'd worked for Shawna's dad for years, long before he decided to turn Broken Dishes into a guest ranch.

"What time is Dad coming on Friday?" Sam asked, obviously trying to figure out just how long he could put off the chore.

"I don't know, so you'd best be getting it done by Thursday. You know how persnickety your dad is about cleanliness."

"Who cares? He's clear on the other side of the bunkhouse."

"Nevertheless, he has a nose like a bloodhound. Just do yourselves a favor and get those rooms spit and polished before he arrives."

Sam and Chad exchanged sulky expressions. Cleaning bathrooms was obviously not macho enough ranch work for them.

"Suit yourself," I said, pointing a dinner fork at Sam. "Just don't come hiding behind my skirts when your once-a-Marine-always-a-Marine papa chews your butt out for being such a slob."

"You never wear a skirt," Sam said, smirking. "If you did, Dad would be so shocked that he wouldn't even notice our mess."

"Go eat your lunch and get back to work," I said, waving him away and laughing in spite of myself. I adored my stepson and tried to keep things smooth between him and my husband, but Sam enjoyed teasing and often, outright annoying his father. Fortunately, Gabe was becoming more easygoing as he aged and took Sam's poking with humor and grace . . . most of the time.

After they left the room heading for the kitchen, Dove and I finished up in five minutes. Outside, the mournful honking had ceased but, every once in a while, there was a sharp peck at the wooden door.

"Your fan club is getting restless," I said. "I want to see this wise-looking goose."

Dove opened the door and stepped out on the lodge's wide back porch that looked over the cowboy sculpture garden. A huge white goose rushed over to her, planted itself in front of her and slowly dipped his head. I'd been around enough fowl to know that he was flat-out flirting with her.

"Now, Socrates," Dove said, stooping down to stroke his soft, downy belly. "What're you doing scaring those boys like that?"

Socrates dipped his long, graceful neck, love oozing out of every snow-white feather.

I inched over slowly, knowing better than to rush a goose and stooped down next to Dove. Socrates stopped and turned to stare at me with hard, beady, yet somehow comprehending eyes. Dove's name for him was perfect. It did look like he was pondering some wise and deep matters. He dipped his head slowly in my direction. I let out my breath and reached over to smooth my hand down his silky front.

"He likes you," Dove said. "I'm not surprised. He seems to have a thing for women with long hair."

After fawning over her new friend for a few minutes, I stood up. "Maybe I'll call my husband before I tie on my waitress apron."

"You're serving too?" Dove said, standing up herself.

I nodded, waiting for her scolding.

"I'm telling you, you should have just given Rita fifty bucks and a bus ticket to Reno."

"Actually, I think Reno is where she came in from this time," I said.

"Any word from Skeeter?"

"No," I said. "And that's the way I hope it stays. We have enough hot cowboy tempers around here without Rita and Skeeter's marriage fireworks."

She raised her eyebrows in question, so I told her about the exchange between Johnny and Whip.

"That's all Shawna needs," Dove said. "Johnny is immature and Whip is bitter. Not a good combination."

"No kidding," I said.

"Thank goodness Gabe will be here this weekend, in case they come to blows."

"Don't even think that. Then we'd have to figure out a way to convince the guests it was part of the Western experience."

Dove laughed. "Which it is. Two bulls fighting over a heifer."

I laughed with her. "Speaking of my hubby, how about yours? When is Isaac coming out?"

Her new husband of less than a year, Isaac Lyons, was a world-famous photographer who'd come to town a while back, fallen in love with my long-widowed gramma, and swept her right out of her dirt-stained Justin cowboy boots. He'd joined wholeheartedly into this endeavor to save Broken Dishes by offering to teach a nature photography class that would be free to any of our guests, but would cost three hundred dollars for anyone else. And Isaac generously donated the whole amount to the ranch. The class was this Saturday, before the dance, and was limited to sixty students. The open slots filled up the same day the ad ran in the paper.

"He's coming up Friday with Emory and Elvia."

"So I'm guessing he'll be in the bunkhouse with Emory and Gabe. On their side, I imagine."

Dove shrugged. "Who knows? Isaac can be a pretty cool cat. Maybe he'll want to bunk with the youngsters."

I laughed. "A cool cat?"

"Okay, far out dude in your language."

"That hasn't been my language since 1978."

She shooed me away. "Oh, scat. I have work to do." She marched down the steps, her chubby old goose waddling after her, faithful as a hound.

"Can I start calling you Mother Goose?" I called after her.

"Not and expect to live," she called back over her shoulder.

I glanced inside the dining hall. The large wooden clock over the entrance to the kitchen, its face carved with acorns and pine cones, told me I had ten minutes before I needed to start pouring water and setting out the rolls and butter. Enough time to call Gabe. Since we'd discovered that our cell phones only worked sporadically out here, I called him from the pay phone on the porch. It was the only phone available for the guests except in case of an emergency. Using it made me feel like I was at summer camp.

Lucky for me, Gabe was eating lunch inside the office today. His assistant, Maggie, must have gone out because he answered the phone himself.

"Chief Ortiz," he said in his gruff, all-business voice.

"Hey, Friday," I said, the only endearment I called him. "Honey" or "darling" never felt right with Gabe. I'd started calling him Joe Friday in derision the first time we met because of his straight-arrow, by-the-books personality. As our relationship changed, it shortened to Friday and became my personal nickname for him. "*¿Qué tal?*"

"*Querida,*" he said, his voice softening. "*Mi esposa, mi corazón, mi vida. Te adoro, te quiero, te amo. Te amo hoy y siempre porque no hay nadie tan especial en mi vida como tu.*"

Heat warmed the back of my neck just as surely as if he'd lifted my hair and kissed me there. "Friday, I have no idea what you said, but if you were here right now I'd be dragging you into the barn and ripping off your clothes."

He gave a low laugh.

"You know, Mr. Smarty Pants, you could also seduce me with the recipe to menudo. It's just the Spanish."

"Okay, first take the lining of a cow's stomach . . ."

I laughed and said, "Oh, can it. Translate what you said so I can repeat it to myself tonight when I have to listen to Rita snore."

"Sweetheart. My wife, my heart, my life. I adore you, I want you, I love you. I love you today and always because there's no one in my life as special as you."

It sounded almost as good in English as it did in Spanish. "Back at you, chief. I miss you too." I'd spent half this last month out here at Broken Dishes helping get the ranch ready. This next two weeks couldn't go fast enough for me. I wanted to return to my husband and my normal routine.

"How're things going?" he asked.

"Too early to tell, but I think, okay. The food is delicious, of course. Rich is a gift from God. Except for a horse colicking, a broken pump, and a petty squabble between Johnny and Whip, their head wrangler, the first day's been pretty smooth."

"That's natural," he said. "I'm sure everyone's nerves are on edge. How's Sam doing?"

"The women adore him, of course. And he's thrilled about helping Rich in the kitchen. You know, *papacito*, you have yourself a very nice young man there."

"So far, so good," he said. He loved his son deeply, but was still not comfortable with Sam's more easygoing and haphazard way of dealing with people and life. There was a lot of troubled emotional history between them, which they were both attempting to overcome.

"Try saying, 'Yes, he is a wonderful man,' Mr. Hardass Cop."

"Try talking like a lady or I'll tell your gramma on you."

I took the phone and hit it sharply on the lodge's log wall. "Would-you-cut-your-son-some-slack," I said with each smack.

"Ouch!" I heard his tiny, far-off voice exclaim.

I brought the phone back up to my ear. "I bet you were the kid in school the teachers loved. The one that always sat in front and tattled on the kids blowing spitballs behind her back."

"Which, no doubt, would have been you, Miss Spitball Queen," he said, laughing. "If you really want to know, I was the one pulling the girls into the coat closet and teaching them how to French kiss."

"Please," I said, groaning dramatically. "Spare me the gruesome images. When are you coming on Friday?"

"Early afternoon, providing I can get away. *Adios, mi vida.*"

I leaned against the log wall. "See you Friday, Friday."

Feeling much more lighthearted after our conversation, I went back inside the dining room, ready to serve lunch. A few minutes later, the quilt ladies started wandering in and finally, Rita showed up.

"Where have you been?" I asked. "I had to set all the tables myself."

"Personal business," she said.

"What personal business could you possibly have here?" I'd been using the ranch's only pay phone so I knew she wasn't on the phone making up with her straying husband.

She ignored my question and walked into the kitchen, giving Rich a huge smile when he turned around. Being a red-blooded and still breathing male under the age of one hundred, he gave her a subtle up-and-down, and returned her smile along with an appreciative look.

She was definitely dressed to impress, although since most of the men were hunting or fishing today, it was falling on blind eyes. I doubt the quilt ladies would be swayed toward giving big tips by her tight, red denim skirt and stretchy, body-hugging top showing a sparkly, Vargas-style cowgirl sitting astride a bucking bronco. The bronco's plastic eyes jiggled every time Rita did. I took one of the ranch's red cotton duck aprons and handed it to her.

"Put this on, please. Next time, could you please wear the red-checked shirt I gave you? With blue jeans."

Rita gave a deep, dramatic sigh and tied on the apron, completely covering her bottom half. If possible, it looked worse. Now she looked naked under the apron.

"Since it's only the quilting ladies, you can handle lunch," I said, making a quick decision. "I'm going out to start tacking up the horses for our ride and check on that colicky horse."

"I have to do all this alone?" she squawked.

Rich turned back around. "You can do it, Rita." His voice was encouraging. "I'll help if you get into any trouble."

"You will?" she said, turning to him, her black-lined hazel eyes wide with gratitude. "What a sweet man you are. It's so nice to have *someone* who is willing to help out a beginner."

He smiled at her. "We're all rookies at some point in our lives."

I shrugged and said, "Fine, you two work it out between you. I have horses to saddle." I grabbed an apple and headed out to the stable, leaving Rich to deal with Rita. He might find her amusing now, but after doing her job and his for the next two weeks, I had a feeling his smile wouldn't be quite as wide and accommodating.

After tacking Patrick up first, then a few of the other horses, I put on my spurs and leather chaps. Patrick needed some time in the ring so he'd have the kinks worked out of him before our trail ride. He was a feisty fellow, who had a stubborn streak despite his highly-specialized ranchwork training. Bridle horses were special, sort of like college-level horses in a world of grade-schoolers. Though many horses could perform the complicated movements required in ranchwork with control, power, agility, and speed, bridle horses did it with style, grace, and on a very light rein. That's what made them fun to ride. They challenged the rider to be alert and at their very best. Looking at Patrick, you'd never think he was special. He was small, a mud-puddle brown, and had a head as plain as desert dirt. But when he walked, he was as smooth as a panther. When he moved, even non-equestrians could see he was something special. After a half dozen turns, a couple of large circles, some backups and sideways maneuvers, Patrick was just tired enough to be a good lead horse.

When lunch was almost finished, I went back inside the dining room and informed the ladies to be down at the corral by 1 P.M.

"Oh, neat," said one of the four, big-haired cousins from Georgia who'd been the first group to book this trip. I think her name was Reba. "Do we get spurs?" All four cousins were dressed in expensive Lucky brand jeans, brightly-colored cowboy shirts and cordovan cowboy boots that I'd bet my Stetson were custom-made.

I smiled at them. "Your horses will do fine without them. Spurs can be a problem unless you know how to use them properly. You might get a bumpier ride than you'd like." After seeing their disappointed looks, I added, "You can try mine on later and take pictures, if you like." They flashed big smiles and nodded. That was all they really wanted.

By one fifteen we had all the ladies mounted and walking their horses along the slight upgrade to Luna Lake. Both ranch dogs accompanied us with Buck dashing ahead of the horses and circling back to check on us and Sugar, with her sweet, motherly personality, sticking close to me and Lindsey and always watching our faces with a slightly worried expression.

The ride meandered up the trail, with gentle switchbacks, toward the small lake called Luna because at certain times of the month, when the moon was full, it reflected the moon so perfectly that it looked like you could walk across the glassy water, pick it up, and toss it like a Frisbee.

I led the way pointing out wild flowers and local fauna.

"What we're riding through is sage brush," I said, pointing out the dark green bushes with long white shoots of flowers. "Your jeans will smell heavenly by the end of our ride. Buckwheat is the smaller bushes, the ones with the mauve flowers. Bees love it. I don't see any buck brush yet. It's in the lilac family and has small white flowers that smell like potatoes. Those bushes to our left with the dark, glossy leaves are coffee berry. In the fall it has dark red berries that taste bitter, but when we were kids we used to smear the juice on our faces and horses to play 'Indian.' " I pointed to a grayish bush with velvety leaves. "That's one of the varieties of yerba santas. It's also called miner's toilet paper. Check out the leaves. Almost as good as your most expensive two-ply toilet tissue."

The quilt ladies chuckled at my last remark. I continued pointing out various types of birds and trees, telling stories about early settlers of Cholame Valley including the tales about our county's most infamous bandit, Joaquin Murietta, the same man whose name identified their quilting room. In the middle 1800s he was rumored to have hidden out here in the backcountry of northern San Celina and southern Monterey counties. He was considered by some to be a bit of a Robin Hood character, though many old time lawmen would dispute that portrayal. My history studies from Cal Poly and my voracious reading of early California legends were finally coming in handy.

"Take most of what you hear about good old Joaquin with a huge bucket of salt," I said. "Don't forget that Señor Murietta was like a lot other famous western outlaws. If he'd actually been to as many places as claim him now, he would have never had time to rob any banks. It was pretty hard to rob a stagecoach in northern California and southern California on the same day. And more than one place in California claims the tree where he was supposedly hanged."

When we reached Luna Lake, Lindsey and I helped the women

down and handed out water bottles. I pointed to the small outhouse set back in the scattered bush pines. "All the amenities," I joked. "Including, if I remember correctly, a Sears and Roebuck catalog for perusing."

"You'd better not have corn cobs," one of the older quilters joked.

"Or a pile of yerba santa," Karen said.

I laughed and checked my watch. They'd be happy to find in the outhouse that there was a coffee can holding a roll of real toilet paper. "We have about a half hour, then we need to start back. It gets dark early and besides, there's a rumor that Rich made chocolate cupcakes for teatime."

"Race you back," Victory Simpson replied, sitting next to me on a bench carved from an old log. She'd decided to take the ride with us and this was the first time we had been able to talk since she arrived. Before this, we'd only spoken by phone when I arranged her sessions and in passing when we both were busy getting settled on that first day.

"From what I hear you're a very good rider so I'm not sure I want to do that," I said, leaning back and lacing my fingers around one knee. "Besides, it might give these ladies more of an exciting time than they'd anticipated." If one horse ran, it was a given that the others would follow. Like humans, they were undeniably influenced by what the rest of the herd did.

She was a lanky, handsome woman with silvery-white, shoulder-length hair pulled back with a black-and-silver clip. She was dressed in simply tailored jeans, a black turtleneck and a well-worn brown leather jacket. The only jewelry she wore was a wide, gold wedding band and a silver signet ring with the letter V. Though I knew she was in her early sixties, she could have easily passed for fifty. She definitely looked like a sophisticated artist, but she turned out to be very approachable and immediately charmed all the nervous quilters with her open and accepting style of teaching. There were other quilt teachers not quite as famous or as talented who had a more rigid method of teaching. Victory's books always stressed the idea that she didn't teach people how to quilt, she taught them how to create personal art with fabric.

"Craft has rules," was one of her common axioms. "Art doesn't. So *anyone* can create art."

"I try to ride when I can in Monterey," she said. "The only exercise I seem to manage regularly is walking." She gave a wistful smile. "My work keeps me busy these days. You know, quilting started as a hobby for me when my husband was sick. What was wonderful was the power I had over it when I had so little power over anything else. Matching points and pressing seams was so controllable, so predictable. The colors of the fabric, the feel of it between my fingers was so . . . I don't know . . . comforting. It literally saved my life." She leaned forward, resting her elbows on her knees and gazed out at the calm surface of Luna Lake. "Now, it's my whole life."

Her story was widely known because of all the interviews she'd given, but it felt different hearing the details from her. Her husband died a slow, agonizing death from Lou Gehrig's disease, and she had been by his side the whole time. Right after his death two years ago, she threw herself into quilting with determination and fervor and in that short time became one of the most celebrated authors and teachers in the quilting world. She'd written an amazing six books and traveled almost constantly. It was truly a miracle that she had time to help Shawna and Johnny.

"Is everything okay with your cabin?" I asked.

"It's wonderful," she said. "Though I feel a little guilty for having the best cabin on the ranch."

"Please, don't feel that way. These next two weeks are only possible because you agreed to be here. You deserve a comfortable place to stay."

"That is kind of you to say." We chatted for another few minutes and I brought the conversation around to the story behind her unusual name.

"My given name is Victoria," she said. "But Victory seemed a better name for my books." Her face softened. "It was my husband's nickname for me. His name was Garland and he liked saying every victory deserved a garland." Her cheeks turned a pale pink. "Silly marriage humor."

I smiled. "I understand."

I glanced over at the lake. A thin fog was starting to form across the top of the water. It was almost two thirty and we needed to start back. I stood up, brushing off the back of my jeans. "If you need anything, let me or Shawna or Johnny know. We want this to be a fun and relaxing time for you too."

She stood up and shook her silvery hair. "Thank you, though I can't think of a thing you haven't provided."

It took about fifteen minutes for Lindsey and me to round up the women and get them situated on their horses. I whistled for the dogs and we started back down the hill. Lindsey was riding point and I was following behind the group. The conversation between the women had become more muted and sparse. They were probably starting to feel the unaccustomed effects of being on horseback. I worried that maybe I should have opted for a shorter ride this first time.

We came to a place in the trail where it crested the hill and we could see the ranch about a half-mile away. The view was incredible, with pockets of early California poppies, wild mustard, and deep blue lupine making the hills look like God's own quilt. The women asked if we could stop a moment so they could snap pictures.

"Sure," I said. "If any of you want to dismount, feel free. We can help you get back on."

I was sitting on Patrick, keeping an eye on the horses as the ladies called advice to one another about the best angles to take their photographs when Buck came racing up with a long, muddy stick in his mouth. He came up beside me, his tail wagging like he'd just discovered a bag of dog treats.

"What've you got there, Buck?" I asked, resting my crossed wrists on the saddle horn. Sugar nosed around him whining, wanting to share whatever it was he held in his large mouth.

He wagged his tail faster. In front of me, Karen Olson, still mounted on her horse, glanced down at Buck. In a flash, a frown appeared on her face.

"What is it, Karen?" I asked.

"Do you think you can get Buck to give you the object he has in his mouth?" she asked in a tight voice.

I swung down off my horse. "Sure, he's a pretty well-trained dog, when he wants to be. Buck, down. Sugar, down."

They both immediately laid down. Buck gripped the stick with an assertive possessiveness that was not unusual considering his gender.

"Drop it," I said.

He hesitated, then obediently dropped the stick and wagged his tail.

I went to pick it up. Both dogs whined and wiggled in excitement, inching toward the prize.

"Wait," Karen said. "Do you have gloves?"

I gave her a perplexed look. "Sure."

Her expression remained troubled. "You'd better use them."

I dug my stained chamois gloves out of my saddlebag and pulled them on before bending over to pick up the muddy stick.

"Hold it up where I can see it better," she said.

I walked over to her and held it up.

"We may have a problem," she said after a few seconds.

"Why?"

"I'd have to measure it to be absolutely sure, but that looks like part of a femur bone. A human femur bone."

CHAPTER 4

NOW I'M NOT NORMALLY A SQUEAMISH SORT OF PERSON, BUT my first inclination was to drop it. Buck's eager gold eyes, as well as the eyes of his canine colleague, told me they were hoping I'd give in to my feelings.

"Are you sure?" I asked, holding it a little more gingerly. "This has been a cattle ranch for a long time." Bones were a common occurrence around a ranch and the Darnells still ran between fifty and seventy-five head of cattle.

"I'm a forensic anthropologist," she said, her voice grim. "Or I was before I retired last year. I don't think that's a cow bone."

I bit my lip, thinking, why isn't my husband ever around when his commanding presence, which normally irked me, would be welcome? By this time, the rest of the women realized something was holding us up and had walked over to us, their faces curious. Lindsey circled around and rode up beside me, her black quarter horse snorting and nervous.

"What's that?" Lindsey asked.

I walked closely to her so only she could hear my words. "Apparently it's a human bone. Buck just brought it to me and the dirt on it looks fresh. He's stuck pretty close to us the whole ride so I'm guessing he found it in this general area. I don't want the ladies upset, but I'm afraid there might be more than this one bone."

Lindsey nodded, her young face serious. "What do you want me to do?"

"Help everyone back on their horses and go back to the ranch. Find Rich and explain about the bone. Tell him that Karen is a forensic anthropologist, so this probably isn't a case of mistaken identity. Have him inform Shawna or Johnny then come up in the Jeep. It can make it up the trail this far."

"What do I tell the ladies?"

I thought for a moment. Should I try to hide what was happening? What would The Secret Traveler think? I quickly decided it was ridiculous to try and hide it. These were grown women who could handle the news, and there was nothing I could do about keeping it from the travel columnist. "Explain what we found and that we'll keep them informed. But play it down as much as possible. Take Sugar with you. One eager dog is all I can handle." I reached down and placed my hand on Buck's head.

"Gotcha." She called to Sugar, turned her horse and started for the women standing about fifty yards up the trail.

"Stay," I told Buck, placing my hand on his head. His tail wagged slowly as if sensing something troublesome was happening.

I watched Lindsey dismount, give a quick explanation to the ladies, then helped them remount. Lindsey swung up onto her horse and started walking her horse toward the ranch buildings, followed by the now quiet women.

"What would you like me to do?" Karen asked.

"Why don't you stay with me?" I said. "At least until the authorities get here. They'll probably want to talk to you."

"Absolutely," she said, her cheeks pink from the cold wind. "Though if I get down off my horse, I may have a bit of trouble getting back on without a mounting block."

"Go ahead and stay mounted. I'm just going to see if Buck can lead me to where he found this."

I held out the dirt-crusted bone for him to sniff. "Buck, find."

He barked and took off toward a clump of brush, thrilled to finally have some work to do.

"Here!" I set the bone down and shoved my reins into Karen's outstretched hand.

Luckily I was wearing gloves, a long-sleeve cotton shirt, and leather chaps. They were the only things that kept me from being scraped to pieces by the thick, scratchy chamise undergrowth.

Minutes later, following his barks, I broke through the brush into a small clearing. Buck, head down, barreled straight for a small pile of rocks.

"Buck, down!" I yelled.

He immediately obeyed my shouted order and flopped down, his nose stretched out toward the pile of rocks next to a half-dead Valley oak tree. They looked hastily covered with old leaves and branches of scrub pine. In the trees above us, a jay screamed like a woman being attacked.

"Good dog," I said. He looked at me and hesitated, his stomach rising slightly off the ground.

"Down," I said again. His stomach touched ground again, his hind legs twitching, ready to spring ahead at my word. "Good dog."

I looked around for a long stick, found a thick, forked one and poked at the pile of rocks and tree branches. Around the pile of dirt were definite shovel marks. It looked as if somebody had been digging something up, then abruptly stopped . . . or was interrupted. When I took the stick and stabbed at a large clump of dirt, unable to control his excitement, Buck nosed his way, whining deep in his throat.

"Get back," I commanded sharply, and he reluctantly backed up.

I knocked a damp dirt wad off the clump and felt my stomach lurch. It now looked like the top of a human skull.

I peered around nervously, though it was obvious these bones had been here a long time. Something else was obvious. They'd recently been disturbed, either by a wild animal . . . or someone else.

"Buck, come," I said, turning around to go back to Karen and the horses. To complicate matters, the Broken DIS Ranch was located in both San Celina County and Monterey County. The sheriff's department would have to be notified, but which one?

When I reached Karen, I told her my findings and though she tried to hold it back, her face brightened. She was obviously eager to investigate the scene.

"I know you'd love to take a look," I said, "but let's wait here until Rich arrives. I don't have to tell you that we might be dealing with a crime scene. I'm married to a cop so trust me when I say that we'll get our noses bit clear off if we mess up the scene."

"You're right," she said, her face chagrined when she realized that her enthusiasm had been obvious. "Sorry to look so excited. In my business, you tend to forget that there's a human element to a body. To us, it's just parts."

I stuck my hands into my back pockets and nodded. "You couldn't do your job any other way."

In less than a half hour, we could see Whip come up the trail in the open Jeep. Riding with him was Johnny, Shawna, and Rich. Buck ran down to meet the vehicle, following alongside until it stopped behind Karen and her horse.

"I guess I'd better get down off this horse now," Karen said. "Though I'm not sure I can climb back on."

I went over to her. "Don't worry, someone can ride or lead your horse back. You can go back in the Jeep."

"Thanks," she said, gratefully.

"I called the San Celina Sheriff's Department first," Rich said, climbing out of the Jeep. "Apparently this is their jurisdiction. The sergeant was a little skeptical at first, but I told him what Mrs. Olson did for a living. That impressed him enough to send someone out. He said they have a detective who lives in the area, and that they'd send him up to assess the situation. He also told me to inform everyone that since it's a possible crime scene to stay away from it."

"Where's the deputy coming from?" I asked. "Paso Robles?"

"No," Rich said. "Apparently he lives around Parkfield. They said he should be here in less than an hour."

Parkfield, back at the beginning of the twentieth century, was a semi-thriving quicksilver and coal-mining town with a population of almost nine hundred. Its prosperity was short-lived and now it was a town of thirty-seven hearty souls. Every twenty-two years or so, the town experienced a fairly large earthquake, at least a 5.0 on the Richter scale, making it a natural draw for scientists. Because of that, as well as boasting the largest array of earthquake-monitoring equipment anywhere on earth, its nickname "earthquake capital of the world" was not a misnomer. It was about forty-five miles northeast of Paso Robles and a mile and a half from the Broken Dishes. Besides all of the earthquake-detection equipment scattered around the hills surrounding the town, it was mostly famous for the Parkfield Inn, a log cabin lodge that had six rooms and, across the town's only street, a cafe/bar where they served tri-tip beef sandwiches, barbecue ribs, and skin-on French fries that people from a hundred-mile radius came to experience.

"Where's these so-called human bones?" Johnny demanded, striding over to where we were standing. He was acting tough, but I could see the adolescent fear behind his aggressive behavior. "I bet it's just some old cow bones. Shit, this is all we need, one more dang thing." He slapped his cowboy hat on the side of his long leg. Dust flew off his tight Wranglers. Shawna came up behind him, her face fearful.

At that moment, our attention was diverted for a few seconds when Bunny trotted up the path on Gumby.

"When are the police getting here?" she asked.

"Where are these bones?" Johnny repeated, ignoring Bunny's question.

I hesitated, knowing that if I led him there, everyone would want to follow and we could possibly mess up some valuable evidence. I looked up at Bunny and said, "A San Celina sheriff's deputy is on his way. Apparently he lives near Parkfield."

"Really?" she said. "I didn't know we had a cop living out here."

"I want to see these so-called bones before the cops come up here and start screwing around," Johnny said.

Shawna walked over to him and placed a hand on his shoulder, trying to calm him down. He jerked away from her touch and walk up the path, causing her face to crumple like a child's, ready to burst into tears.

I saw Whip walk up beside her, touch her shoulder and whisper something in her ear. In a moment, she seemed to visibly relax. She looked up at him, her eyes wide with gratitude.

"I want to see the bones," Johnny insisted, his back to Shawna.

"It would be better . . ." Whip started.

Johnny turned and snapped at Whip. "It's my . . ." He took a deep breath. "It's mine and Shawna's land. We have a right to see what's on our property. *You* wouldn't understand what that's like, owning something of value."

"Johnny!" Shawna said, her hand flying up to her mouth.

The skin above Whip's upper lip turned white. At his side, his scarred hands convulsively clenched. I gave Rich a worried glance. He answered with a small shrug, not fazed by their pawing and snorting.

"Johnny, that'll do," Bunny said with the same tone and words she often used with the ranch dogs.

"Look," I said to him, keeping my voice level and calm. "I understand your frustration. If this was my land, I'd feel the same way. But, I've been married to a cop long enough to know that physical evidence at a crime scene is downright holy to them. If we disturb anything, the sheriff's department could make life really uncomfortable for the ranch."

His young face was still agitated, but he was listening to me.

"If you promise not to go any farther than I tell you, I'll lead you to the edge of the clearing where the bones are. Will you promise me that?"

He tightened his lips, both of his fists clenched at his side, unconsciously mimicking Whip. A lot was riding on these next few weeks and all the strain of getting the ranch ready for visitors and worrying about saving it had come to a head with this incident. He and Whip both were close to exploding.

"Johnny, please," Shawna said softly, placing a hand on his arm. "We should do what Benni says. She knows about things like this."

He took a deep breath. "Okay."

"Lead the way, *mija*," Rich said. "I'll follow in the back."

"Be careful of the underbrush," I told everyone. "I'm sure there's a better way to get to the spot, but this is the only one I know."

I figured this wasn't the way the person who disturbed the grave went so I didn't think we were wrecking any physical evidence. At least that was what I planned to tell the investigators when they arrived. When we reached the clearing, Johnny headed straight for the pile of rocks I pointed out. Rich darted past us and caught his upper arm.

"Johnny, this is as close as we go." The fatherly firmness in Rich's voice told the young man that he'd allow no arguments.

Johnny tried halfheartedly to pull away from Rich, but it was more show than anything.

I turned to Karen. "Make sure and tell the sheriff's detective what you did for a living. I bet you could help."

She nodded, but her genial face was skeptical. "I'll offer what expertise I have, but you know cops."

"Yes, I do." Most were undeniably territorial though if the officer investigating this was smart, he or she would take advantage of his good luck that Karen possessed the background she did. "I'd let you get closer, but . . ."

She smiled at me and patted my shoulder. "I understand. Let's just play this by the book and let the detectives decide what to do."

When we got back to the horses and the Jeep, Karen said, "From the looks of the scene, I'd guess that someone was in the process of digging those bones up."

"So the big question is why," I said.

"Why someone was digging them up?" Bunny asked.

"And why they were buried to begin with."

No one spoke after my sobering statement. Except for Karen and

Rich, we were all familiar with the nefarious things that often happened on our ranches after dark. This grave could have a connection to any number of situations, none of which would be good news for the Broken Dishes—drug labs or a drug deal gone bad, escaped convicts, gang killings, even cattle rustling.

"Can you tell by what you saw of the scene how long they've been there?" I asked Karen.

She shook her head no. "Not without testing it in a lab. There's a lot of factors to consider. I'd need more time and the right equipment."

I turned to Rich. "How long did dispatch tell you it would be before the investigator came?" Fog was starting to roll in and night was coming on fast. In a little while, it would be too dark to see anything.

He checked his large, diver-style watch. "It's already been forty-five minutes. The dispatcher said the deputy lived in Parkfield and was supposed to be home today. Apparently he has family visiting."

Minutes later, we heard a vehicle down at the bottom of the trail. In the next few seconds we saw the headlights of a Jeep the same age and style as the one owned by the ranch come around the corner. Unlike the ranch Jeep though, its top was up and since it was twilight, it was difficult to see the people inside. When it pulled up behind the ranch Jeep and Rich aimed his flashlight toward it, I immediately took a dislike to the occupants. A large red-and-white bumper sticker stated— *So you're a feminist. Isn't that cute?*

An older man with a full head of bushy silver-streaked hair stepped out of the passenger side. He appeared to be in his early seventies and still good-looking in a rough, old sea-captain sort of way. The driver bent down to retrieve something on the floor as the older man strode toward us, his stocky legs as strong and sturdy as two aged cedar trees.

"Howdy, folks," he said. *"Comment ça va?"*

They were obviously not from the sheriff's department. Hunters, more likely. Unauthorized hunters since I knew this man wasn't a ranch guest.

"Hi," I said, stepping up to meet him. "I'm sorry, sir, but we have a . . ." I stopped, realizing I shouldn't be telling this perfect stranger that he and his buddy were trespassing on what might be a crime scene. "I'm sorry, but you'll have to leave. This is private property."

"That's right," Johnny said, stepping forward. "And you definitely aren't one of the hunters signed up to hunt on our property."

The old man's amiable expression didn't change when he held up his wide palms. "*Escuse-moi*. I'm just here with my grandson."

The man behind the wheel finished whatever he was doing and sat up. He opened the Jeep door and stepped out.

"Oh, no!" I exclaimed in a voice loud enough to cause Buck's ears to perk up. Everyone turned to stare at my dramatic response, looking at me as if I'd just grown three heads.

"Oh, yes," said Detective Ford Hudson of the San Celina Sheriff's Department, the cocky grin on his All-American, Texas-bred, Tom-Sawyer face, wide enough to split a watermelon.

CHAPTER 5

"IS THERE SOME KIND OF PROBLEM?" RICH SAID, COMING UP beside me. He slipped a protective arm around my shoulders.

Hud took in the gesture, his eyebrows raising slightly.

I tried to glare at him subtly, knowing what he was implying without saying a word. Detective Ford "Hud" Hudson and I had what might be termed an uncomfortable history. In the last few years we'd accidentally been thrown together while being involved in a couple of murders. I saw him occasionally around town and we politely greeted each other, but mostly we didn't run in the same circles.

He was a half-Cajun Texas native who, besides being an outrageous flirt, had an annoying wisecrack for every situation. From the first time we met, he took an inordinate amount of pleasure in pulling my chain, and though I knew that, like a compulsive raccoon washing and rewashing my dinner, I too often took the bait.

"Rich is an old friend of mine," I said, sounding more defensive than I intended. "And Gabe's."

"What in the devil are you talking about, woman?" Hud said with a grin, reveling in the fact that he'd already gotten my goat.

Confused, Rich looked at me and then back at Hud. "I take it you two have met?"

"Oh, yes," Hud said. "Benni and I are *also* dear old friends." He crossed his arms over his chest. "I should have realized if there was some kind of odd murder scene, you'd be involved."

"Who says there's been a murder?" I said.

Hud reached into the Jeep and pulled out a fleece-lined denim jacket. "It's getting nippy out here. You need your jacket, PawPaw?"

"I'm fine, T-Hud." The older man looked at me, his lined face thoughtful, studying me in a blatantly curious way that made me feel like squirming. "Who's the *jolie bassette*?" the old man finally asked.

"She's an old nemesis," Hud said, settling his broad shoulders into his jacket.

The man's expression became confused. "What's this nemesis?"

"*Ennemi,*" Hud said.

"*Ennemi?*" he said, looking me up and down, then giving a great, booming laugh. "This *fillette?*"

"What did he call me?" I asked.

The first Cajun word I could grasp the meaning and enemy sounded pretty close to the truth. Was this man calling me a piece of meat?

"Calm your ruffled tail feathers," Hud said. "*Fillette* just means little girl in Cajun. PawPaw, this is my old friend, Benni Harper. Benni, this is my grandpa, Iry Gautreaux. He's visiting me from Baton Rouge."

Mr. Gautreaux smiled at me with long, beige teeth. Then he gave me a flirtatious wink.

The Cajun apple apparently doesn't fall far from the tree. Hud obviously inherited his audacious personality from his grandfather.

Only because I heard Dove's voice in my ear admonishing me to be a good girl and respect my elders did I force myself to walk over and hold out my hand. "Nice to meet you, Mr. Gautreaux."

"*Bonjour, madame.* Please, call me Iry," he said, taking my hand, still smiling. "I apologize for laughing at such a lovely lady."

"Uh, no problem," I said, then turned and quickly introduced everyone standing behind me.

"Great," Hud said. "Now that we're all best friends, can someone please show me what y'all have found that warrants snatching me away from me and my pawpaw's cutthroat game of bourrée?"

I beckoned Karen to come closer. "This is Karen Olson. She's one of our guests and a retired forensic anthropologist. She was the one who realized the bone that Buck brought me was human."

Buck's ears perked up again at the sound of his name and he trotted over to us. I reached down and scratched behind his black-and-tan ears.

Hud smiled down at Buck. "Nice-looking puppy. Part Catahoula, isn't he? Good old Louisiana swamp dog." Then he nodded at Karen. "I'll talk with you in a minute. First, where's the bone?"

"Over here," I said.

He followed me to the ranch Jeep where we'd placed the femur bone on top of a stained paper bag. Hud pulled a pair of thin rubber gloves out of his jacket pocket and picked up the bone. While he studied it, he said in a low voice, "It's good seeing you again, Benni. How're things going?"

I let out a sharp breath. "Why do you always walk into a situation and immediately act like a jerk?"

He looked up and grinned. "I only save those moments for you, *chère amie*."

"The dispatcher said an investigator who lived in Parkfield was coming. Why are you here?" The last time I saw Hud he was living in the caretaker's house next to the octagonal barn in San Celina, an historical structure he was helping restore.

"I do live in Parkfield. On my days off anyway. I have a cabin about a mile from here. Want to come by for dinner? PawPaw makes a mean crawfish étouffée."

"So, what's the deal with these bones?"

"Pull back on them reins, ranch girl. Give me some time to think."

"Well, think fast. Shawna and Johnny can't afford to have the Broken Dishes get a bad reputation."

His blondish-brown eyebrows moved together. "The Broken Dishes?"

"That's the ranch's nickname. It's actually the Broken DIS Ranch. Shawna and Johnny Abbott own it." I gestured back at the group. "They're the young couple standing next to my friend, Rich."

"Right, your *old* friend, Rich," he repeated, smiling to himself as he went back to studying the bone. "Good-looking guy. Dark and brooding, just your type."

"Quit having such a gutter mind. He's a friend of mine and Gabe's. I'm still happily married."

"Wasn't so happy the last time you and I worked together."

"We're fine now. Not that it's any of your business." I was still sensitive about what had happened so early in my marriage to Gabe, his doubts about his feelings for a former lover that had reentered his life. Leave it to Hud to dig up those old bones. His crassness at bringing it up so blithely made me more than a little irritated at him.

He set the bone down and turned to face me. "Okay, even though I know that I rub your fur completely the wrong way, I'm dependin' on you to fill me in here, darlin'. The more I know, the quicker I can wrap this up."

"That's exactly what I want. What everybody wants." Though I'd never tell him this, part of me was glad it was someone I knew who was investigating the bones. He could drive me nuts with his adolescent teasing, but he was also a tenacious and gifted investigator. If anyone could wrap this up quickly, it would be Hud. And I might, slim as it was, have a better chance finding out about the investigation from him than from someone I'd never met.

I told him about the rest of the bones, about Shawna and Johnny and how this guest ranch was her father's last ditch effort to save the Broken Dishes Ranch from eventually being sold to developers.

"Sounds like a grave to me," Hud said.

I nodded. "Though I can't imagine that anyone at the ranch would have had anything to do with it."

His normally smiling mouth turned down at the edges. "Maybe not, but we can't rule it out. Since, as you told me, Mrs. Abbott's family has owned this ranch for almost sixty years, that leaves open many possibilities. A lot depends on how old these bones are."

"What are you going to do next? Will it interrupt the guests? That's what we're really worried about."

He didn't answer and walked over to his Jeep carrying the bone.

I followed him repeating, "What're you going to do next?"

He opened the door, pulled out a large, police-issue flashlight and handed it to me. "Hold this."

I pointed the light in his direction as he took out a package of brown paper bags. He slipped the bone inside one and labeled it with the date, time, and place found.

"What're you going to do?" I asked again.

"Pipe down a minute, will you? I'm trying to think."

"Is that what that smell is? I thought one of the horses ate some bad grain."

He shook his head and continued writing. "You can be such an adolescent sometimes."

"Me?"

Bunny walked over to us and said to me, "What's going on, Benni?" She deliberately ignored Hud's curious gaze, probably finding his bumper sticker as amusing as I had.

"I was just asking that myself, Bunny," I said. "And not getting much of a response."

"Bunny?" Hud said. "As in rabbit?" His chuckle caused Bunny to stiffen her spine.

Before I could jump in and defend her, Bunny said coolly, "That is Ms. Hopp to you, detective."

Another laugh gurgled in the back of his throat, but he managed to swallow it. "Yes, ma'am, Ms. Hopp." He turned to me. "I'll need someone to show me where the rest of the bones are. Then I'll call my captain and see if he wants to okay overtime for the forensic team to do their thing tonight."

"Benni would be the best one to take you," Bunny answered. "She's the one who found it."

He buttoned the three bottom buttons of his denim jacket. "Why doesn't that surprise me? Lead on, Señora Harper."

As I led the way through the brush to the site with the flashlight, Hud carried on a running commentary behind me, his voice like a tractor on low idle.

"So, here we are again. I really have missed you. By the way, you just look as cute as the dickens in those chaps. I purely love a woman in chaps and spurs. Have you and the chief run your course yet? He's way too serious for you, you know. Don't you believe there is a reason we keep being thrown together? Don't you believe that, maybe, it's not just an accident? Don't you believe that maybe we're meant to be part of each other's lives? Don't you believe in fate?"

"I believe I'd give my left ear in exchange for you shutting up for two seconds," I finally snapped.

"Don't you believe there's a reason we get on each other's nerves?" he said.

I didn't answer, but just kept walking. A minute later we arrived at the clearing. I stopped at the edge and pointed to the pile of rocks and dirt about twenty feet away. "There it is."

He stepped around me and took the flashlight out of my hands, pointing it at the ground. "There are a lot of footprints here."

"I let everyone come this far and then stopped. We came the same way that I did, which is a bit passable now, but was initially forged by me so I don't think it's the way the person who did this came into the clearing."

He turned to look at me, aiming the bright flashlight at my face. "You shouldn't have even let them come this far."

"Hey!" I said, holding my arm in front of my eyes. "It was that or Johnny was going to barrel through the woods and possibly mess up the crime scene."

"Sorry." He turned it back down at the ground. "Well, thank you for that anyway. Young Mr. Abbott does seem a bit agitated. Any reason you can think of why?"

"Maybe because he is very young, newly married, his wife just lost

her father, this is their first set of ranch guests and everything depends
on this session going well, and the little fact that these bones might be
the thing that guarantees they lose the ranch? Other than those few
minor things, I can't imagine why he'd be upset."

"No need to get sarcastic."

"So, what are you going to do?"

"Let me take a look first and then I'll have a better idea."

The darkness was getting deeper with every minute. Wisps of tule
fog weaved its way through the scraggly pines and valley oaks giving
the clearing a distinctly creepy atmosphere. A chill started working its
way into my bones that wasn't entirely physical. I shivered, then
hugged myself trying to keep warm. When we'd left the ranch this
afternoon I'd decided that a long sleeve cotton shirt was enough. I
hadn't counted on being out here after dark.

Hud started taking off his jacket. "Here, take my—"

"I'm fine," I said, holding up my hand.

"You are a stubborn girl. Stay where you are. I don't want the
scene more disturbed than it already is."

He walked carefully toward the makeshift grave, pointing his flashlight down at the ground. When he reached the bones, he stooped
down and shined the flashlight on the disturbed grave.

After about five minutes, he came back over to where I was
standing.

"So, do you think maybe animals might have dug it up?" I asked,
hopefully.

"Doubt it. Forensics will be able to tell for sure. Looks to me like
someone was interrupted in the middle of their digging."

"What're you going to do?"

"I'm going mark the trail then follow y'all back to the ranch and
give my captain a call. I'm guessing he'll just tell me to wait until
tomorrow morning to call out the investigation team. They've been
real stingy lately with overtime, what with budget cuts and all, and
since this is obviously not a fresh homicide . . ." He shrugged and
didn't finish his sentence.

"So you think it *was* a homicide?" I asked, my heart sinking. This was all Shawna and Johnny needed.

"Don't really know. I'm just a worker bee. I'll leave that to the forensic people to decide. If it is, I'll probably catch the case, but I doubt the captain will want me to spend much time on it. We've got plenty of fresh crimes to keep us busy." He started walking back down the path through the brush, a path that was becoming easier to maneuver each time we used it.

"Why should that make a difference?" I said to his broad back. I shivered in my thin shirt, envying his jacket.

"Why should what make a difference?"

"How old a murder is. I've never understood that, why murders that are, as you put it, *fresh*, are more important than one that happened a long time ago. Either way a person is dead and someone killed them. The murderer should be punished no matter how long ago it was."

"Because that's just the way it is."

"That's a dumb answer."

He stopped abruptly, causing me to slam into his back.

"Hey, cowboy," I yelped. "You want to signal before you put on the brakes?"

He turned and looked down at me, his features indistinct in the dark. "I agree with you. How's that for a first? But the truth is fresh murders are easier to solve so they show up on monthly reports as a concrete number of cases solved. The sheriff likes numbers because he's a politician, and a politician likes numbers he can give to the newspapers. It makes it look like he's doing his job so he can get elected again and again until he retires and collects a full-salary pension when he is fifty that is good for the rest of his life while everyone else has to work until they are seventy-nine. We worker bees like making the sheriff happy because, as the old Southern saying goes, when the bossman is happy, we is *all* happy." His voice became mildly sarcastic. "Thought you'd be familiar with all that, you bein' married to a politician yourself."

"Gabe doesn't consider himself a politician. He considers himself a cop first, a chief second. Nice story, but don't forget, I know you aren't a real worker bee." He'd inherited ten million dollars from his father, a Texas oil baron from whom he'd been estranged for the last twenty-five years.

Hud shrugged, his expression still cynical.

"Will the trail to Luna Lake be usable?" I asked.

"Not for at least a day. Maybe two. Why?"

"It's one of the prettier trails. And you can't get to some of the other trails without using it."

"Well, your guests are going to have to find someplace else to sightsee for a few days."

When we reached the others, Hud told them what he thought might happen. Shawna asked the same question I did about the trail to Luna Lake.

"I don't know how long it will be out of commission," Hud said, "but I promise, we'll do our best to get our work done quickly. I'll need to question each of the guests individually tonight."

"Now, wait a minute . . ." Johnny started.

Hud held up his hand. "Just a quick few questions. Nothing intense."

"You can use the ranch office," Shawna said, jumping in, trying to make peace. "May the guests have dinner first?"

Hud nodded. "Absolutely, though I'd appreciate it if y'all wouldn't talk about this at all to the guests or among yourselves, for that matter."

"Detective Hudson, would you and your grandfather like to join us for dinner?" Shawna asked. "There's certainly plenty."

He looked over at his grandfather, who gave a quick nod. "We'd be delighted, Mrs. Abbott."

Great, and I was serving dinner. He could order me to fetch him more butter, coffee, a clean napkin. Then again, maybe I could pawn him off on Rita.

After a little bit of discussion, we agreed that Bunny and I would ride the horses back, with Bunny leading Karen's horse. Hud and his grandpa would give Karen a ride back to the ranch.

At the ranch, while Hud set up in the ranch office, Shawna pulled me aside. "Could you please tell the guests what Detective Hudson is going to do? You're more familiar with this investigation procedure than the rest of us are."

"Sure," I said, though I didn't think I was any more qualified to announce what would be happening than anyone else. I went into the Annie Oakley Room, where most of the guests had congregated on the overstuffed sofas and chairs, playing cards or talking as they waited for dinner. The room, in spite of its spaciousness, felt cozy with a crackling fire in the huge stone fireplace and the reproduction Remington paintings interspersed between the antique branding irons on the wall. The four-pane windows on either side of the fireplace had blue-dyed burlap curtains tied back with strips of rawhide. In the background, a stereo softly played Marty Robbins singing "The Streets of Laredo."

After informing them of what had happened on the ride and what little we knew, I assured them that the proper authorities were taking care of things and that dinner would be a little late, but definitely worth the wait.

"Detective Hudson would like to briefly speak to each of you," I added, trying to make my voice sound casual. "He has agreed to let everyone have their dinner first."

"Name, rank, and serial number only," joked Dennis Olson, Karen's husband. Obviously an ex-military man.

I laughed along with everyone else. "Maybe a little more than that, but he promised me it would be painless."

"Is he that cutie who's wearing the dark brown cowboy hat?" asked one of the Georgia cousins, the short-haired brunette. Reba, I thought her name was.

"Yes, that's him."

"Then bring on the bright lights and rubber hoses," she declared in her sugar-syrup Georgia drawl. She elbowed her red-headed cousin. "This ole girl will tell him anything he wants to hear."

Her teasing words left the group laughing, which cheered me slightly. Rich's wonderful food would put the icing on the cake, so to speak. That was provided they ever ate. When Rita wasn't in the dining room, I went back to our cabin and found her lying on my bed reading a *Glamour* magazine.

"Rita, we have to set the tables for supper," I said, plucking the magazine from her green-painted fingernails.

"Didn't these people just eat?" she moaned, throwing her arm over her eyes. Her tiny red skirt rode high enough to show her underwear. Where in the world does one find purple camouflage bikini under-wear?

"Hard as this is to believe, the guests expect three meals every day. If you want to get paid, you have to serve every one of them. That was the deal we made, remember?"

"My jeans are still drying."

"You had *all* afternoon to wash and dry your jeans."

"I wasn't feeling well. I had to take a nap and I forgot they were dirty."

I touched my temple, not trusting myself to speak. I was certain she didn't own one piece of clothing appropriate to wear and she'd die before she'd wear a pair of my faded Wranglers.

"Fine," I finally said. "Just wear *something* and get yourself to the dining room and help me."

She was still whining when I closed the door of the cabin behind me. I stood for a moment on the top step and looked over at the lodge. It had turned blustery and cold in the last hour and the frogs were out in full force, noisy as an L.A. freeway. The moist air tasted of rain and dust, but the golden lights of the lodge's dining room gleamed warm and welcoming. I tried to push aside thoughts about the person's remains lying up the hill a half mile away. Who was he? Or she? What happened? What had the evening been like when this person died . . . or was murdered? Most of all, who had started digging the bones up? Why did they stop? Were they interrupted? What kind of strange person would do that? And why? I just couldn't imagine any of the ranch hands and guests with a shovel in their hands, digging up old bones in the moonless night.

Bunny was in the kitchen pouring a cup of coffee, so I begged her assistance and we set the tables in record time. Menu cards were placed in the center of each plate with the Broken DIS's brand faintly etched in the background. It was a clever touch that Shawna thought up. She printed them on her computer every day for the evening meal. It gave the meal a touch of class and a souvenir for the guests to take home.

Butter lettuce and new tomato salad
Chicken and homemade dumplings
Fresh green beans with bacon bits
Flaky buttermilk biscuits
Cherry pie with vanilla bean ice cream
Coffee, tea, or lemonade

Rich, thank goodness, had informed Sam earlier about the menu. My stepson had taken it upon himself to start preparing the salads when Rich was up the hill. As people found their seats I glanced over the chattering guests—the quilters and their husbands, the hunters, Dove and her church ladies—trying to imagine any of them being killers. It seemed impossible. So instead I thought about The Secret Traveler. About half of the guests, such as Dove and her church ladies, I could eliminate as the incognito columnist, but that left several possibilities, mostly among the quilters. I hoped this meal delay didn't put a black mark on the ranch's report card.

Rita finally showed up, wearing a white denim miniskirt and a skimpy Dickies brand tank top. Bunny had to go help Chad and Whip groom and feed the horses since Sam was helping Rich, so Rita and I were on our own.

"I'll take the quilt ladies and the hunters," I told Rita in the kitchen as we were tying on our aprons. "You take Dove's table and the staff table." That way I would most likely get The Secret Traveler and, if it killed me, I was going to make sure this evening would provide the best dining service the columnist ever experienced. I hoped that would make up for the meal's tardiness and the troubling bones Buck discovered.

"Why can't I have the hunters?" Rita complained. "They leave the biggest tips. You're taking the best tables for yourself. I don't think that's fair. I need the money worse than you do."

I shook my head. Rita would never believe I couldn't care less about tips. She was obviously fixing to pitch a fit, so I decided giving in would be the most prudent thing.

"Okay, I'll take the staff table and quilters and you take the hunters and Dove's ladies. Just try and keep your mind on serving dinner and nothing else. Okay?"

She rolled her eyes at Sam who was putting the final touch, a radish rose, on each dinner salad. A big grin spread across his face. The first year Sam moved to San Celina and stayed with us awhile, Rita had also dropped in during Skeeter's first of many falls from grace. Being close in age and certainly, maturity, they'd formed a bit of an allegiance against what they perceived as unreasonable parental authority, that is, Gabe and me. Now, without missing a beat, they took up where they left off.

"Grab some salads and let's go," I said to Rita, frowning at Sam. He quickly turned around and started pulling pans of buttermilk biscuits out of the huge commercial oven. Though I'd been known to cut him way more slack than his father, he knew me well enough to recognize my don't-push-me-I'm-at-the-end-of-my-rope expression.

We were in the middle of the first course when Shawna, Johnny, Hud, and his grandpa walked in. I glanced at Shawna and Johnny's faces. Johnny's face was stiff and nervous; Shawna looked tired and still ready to burst into tears. They pointed Hud and his grandpa toward the employee table and went into the kitchen.

"Just the position I've always dreamed about," Hud said when I slipped his salad in front of him. "Having you serve my every want and need."

"What did your captain say?" I asked.

"Man, this looks good," he said, unfolding his napkin. "This napkin is impressive. Looks like some kind of bird. Who took the time to fold all these napkins? This sure is a high-class place, isn't it, Paw-Paw?" He smiled at his grandfather.

"Hud, would you please tell me what's going on?" I asked.

He picked up his menu card and looked across the table at his grandpa, who watched us with an amused expression. "PawPaw, did you see this? Chicken and dumplings. Your favorite. This was sure hospitable of them to invite us to supper."

I picked up his salad just as he was about to stick his fork into it.

"Hey!" he said. "Give me back my greens."

"Not until you tell me what your captain said."

"There goes *your* tip, Ms. Harper."

His grandpa shook his head, picked up the salad dressing pitcher, and poured some on his salad. "*T-Hud, si tu ferme pas ta guelle, elle va te foutre ein tape.*"

"*Oui,* PawPaw," Hud answered. "But it would be so worth it."

"What did he say?" I asked, still holding Hud's salad out of his reach.

Hud grinned up at me. "That if I don't shut up you'll probably slap me."

I looked over at his grandpa whose dark eyes twinkled. "You got that right, Mr. Gautreaux."

"Iry," he corrected.

"Yes, sir. Iry."

"Okay, okay, my persistent little *béte rouge.*" Hud said. "The captain told me to seal off the area down at the end of the trail and we'd have a forensic team come out tomorrow morning. Since the bones are so old, it's not something he wanted to waste overtime on."

I set his plate back down in front of him. "Thank you. What would you like to drink?"

"You're so very welcome. Coffee would be fine, even if it is that dirty dishwater y'all call coffee. If I'm going to be around here for a few days I'll have to bring in a pound of Community coffee or my taste buds will rebel big time. If your attitude improves, there might still be a generous little gratuity waiting for you at the end of the meal."

I ignored him, took the drink orders for the rest of the table and moved over to the quilt ladies. Afterward, I went back into the kitchen to fetch another tray of salads. Shawna and Johnny were talking to Bunny who'd just come in from the stable.

"Hear the news?" Bunny said when I walked up. "They're not sending for the bone pickers until tomorrow."

"Yes, I just pried it out of Hud. That's a good sign. Maybe the media won't feel compelled to make a circus of it either. I'm sure there's a perfectly good explanation for those bones."

"When Daddy was building the lodge," Shawna said. "The excavators found lots of old bones and pottery. Even some old calvary buttons. But he never reported it. Said that it would just have caused a huge bureaucratic tie-up that would have delayed construction and cost us more money."

I nodded. That was common among ranchers. It was an unspoken rule that whatever you discovered on your land, short of it being a fresh human body, you tended to keep mum. There were too many groups who didn't respect the idea of private property and loved to tell ranchers what they should do with the land that had been in the rancher's family for generations.

But this situation was different. Most of the time, it was just a bone or two found, ones that might not even be human and weren't worth a police department's time or money to investigate. What we had here looked like a completely intact human grave, maybe one that was not hundreds of years old.

When I was serving the quilt ladies their salads, Dove gestured for me to come over to her table. "What's going on with the murder scene?" she whispered.

"It's not technically a murder scene yet," I whispered back. "The forensic team isn't coming out until tomorrow morning. All Hud will do tonight is ask everyone a few questions."

With me encouraging her along like a balky calf, Rita and I managed to serve dinner in a reasonable amount of time. Though the meal wasn't exactly punctual, the quality of the food made up for it. Rich's culinary genius would no doubt save our butts more than once these next two weeks. I fawned over the quilting ladies, keeping an eagle eye on them, trying to discern who was observing the dinner and taking mental notes. Like the board game, Clue, I listed what I'd learned about each person in my head.

Marty Brantley of Tustin, California. Motherly, widowed, soft, pleasant laugh. Retired school secretary. Has a brown toy poodle name Teacup.

Karen Olson of Iowa. Retired forensic anthropologist. Now, there is a surprise. She looks like your favorite Home Economics teacher. Fluffy brownish hair streaked with silver, bright blue eyes that didn't miss a thing.

Katherine "Kitty" Katz of Long Island, New York. Silver-and-black hair and a bubbly personality. All I knew about her was that she has been quilting for ten years and has attended dozens of conventions and quilting retreats.

Donna Kaufman from Alaska. Didn't know much about her except she grew up in Florida where her family once owned an alligator farm. She said she works for the federal government as an accountant.

Then there were the four cousins. Reba, Gaynelle, Loretta, and Pinky Hamilton from Atlanta, Georgia. All only children. Their fathers are all brothers. Party girls to the core. I don't think they ever stopped laughing. They've been going on, as they termed it, "adventures" together since they were girls. All were in their late thirties, some were married, some weren't, two had children. I couldn't remember who was who.

After dessert and coffee, Shawna asked everyone to go to the Annie Oakley Room, to wait their turn to be interviewed. Hopefully, the TV room off the hall, the hand-carved pool table, and various board games would keep them occupied while they waited.

While they started meandering toward the hall, Rita and I started clearing the tables. She passed by me carrying a single ketchup bottle and waved a handful of five dollar bills in my face. "I told you the hunters are the good tippers." She smirked and tucked them in the back pocket of her tiny skirt.

Though I was tempted to tell her that we weren't actually supposed to accept tips, that this wasn't a Waffle House coffee shop, at this point, as poor as her waitressing skills were, we couldn't afford to lose her. If the hunters didn't mind parting with their money as payment for watching her strut her stuff, I wasn't going to argue. At least *they'd* give Broken Dishes high marks.

Underneath Hud's plate was one of his business cards. On the back he wrote, "Tip—stay out of this investigation if you know what's good for you." I crumpled it and threw it down on his dirty plate.

After getting the dining room clean and halfway set up for breakfast, I headed for the Annie Oakley Room. The atmosphere was surprisingly jovial and relaxed considering they were all waiting to be interrogated. Some of the guests played cards, the WMU ladies loudly continued their domino tournament and some ladies worked on their handquilting. Whip, Chad, and two of the hunters had a game of pool in progress and in the TV room a few of the guests were watching an old Roy Rogers–Dale Evans video. Hud's grandpa, Iry, fit right into the group and was regaling the quilters sitting in front of the fireplace with some Cajun tall tales. I listened for a little while, smiling in spite of myself at some of the silly punchlines.

I was relieved to see that everyone appeared to be having a good time. Hud had commandeered Rich to be the one who fetched each guest. For the next two hours, I surreptitiously watched each of their faces as they returned from being interviewed, hoping for a clue to what they were thinking. At around nine thirty, Hud came back into the spacious room.

"Just want to thank y'all for your good-natured cooperation," he said. "That's all I'll need for now, but please, don't leave Dodge for the next week without checking with me."

Everyone laughed politely, knowing that none of them would be leaving for two weeks, not with what they paid for this trip. Since it was almost ten o'clock and many of the guests had early days tomorrow, the room emptied quickly. By ten fifteen, only a few stragglers remained, chatting around the fireplace, having one last cup of tea.

Though I was tempted to rush over to Hud and demand to know what he found out, I held myself in check, sat in a red-and-green plaid easy chair at the back of the room looking through a *Cowboys & Indians* Western lifestyle magazine. I hoped my feigned indifference would cause him to come to me. This time, I read his personality right.

"All done," he said, planting himself directly in front of me.

Without looking up, I kept flipping through the glossy magazine. "It would be so great if we could convince this magazine to do an article on the Broken Dishes. It's exactly the kind of exposure the ranch needs."

"Aren't you interested in what I think?"

I looked up from my magazine and waited ten seconds. Then, knowing good and well he was probably baiting me, I bit. "Well?"

He countered my ten seconds with twenty, then said, "Very interesting."

I stood up, tossed the magazine in a basket and started for the door. "Have a good night, detective."

"That's it?" he said, following me outside, the few guests left in the room looking after us curiously. "You're going to give up that easy? Where's the old persistent-as-a-leech Benni Harper I know and love?"

"Wonderful image, Hud. Thanks so much."

"Aren't you the least bit curious about what I found out about your guests?"

I stopped abruptly and turned to him. "Are you going to tell me?" He just grinned.

"That's what I thought. I'm tired, Hud. I have to be up early to set up for breakfast and I have a full day tomorrow. See you later."

"*Bonsoir, catin,*" he said, touching the rim of his Stetson with two fingers.

Back at our cabin, Lindsey's bedroom door was closed and I could hear a radio playing softly. She had been one of the first people Hud talked to and I assumed after she was questioned she'd come right back to the cabin since she had to be up early to feed the horses.

Though I hadn't seen Rita after her brief time with Hud and she also wasn't here in the cabin, I determinedly kept my mind off where she might be. A couple of the hunters had definitely been giving her the eye, not to mention her flirting with both Sam and Chad. I took a hot shower and was drying my hair with a towel when Rita finally came in at a quarter past eleven wearing smeared lipstick and a smug look. Since I had no control over it, I didn't even want to contemplate what that was all about.

While she went through her elaborate getting-ready-for-bed ritual, which encompassed much banging around in our shared bedroom, I decided to take a walk over to the main lodge to the pay phone outside the dining hall. Gabe never went to sleep before eleven-thirty so I would call him collect to say good-night. I sat down on a small Adirondack chair and dialed our home.

"Hey, Friday," I said. "How was your day?"

"Busy," he said, his voice warm and low over the phone. "My bed is cold and lonely. I miss you."

"Miss you too. Guess what happened here today."

"You found a body."

I gave a quiet squawk. "Who told you?"

"It was supposed to be a joke." Then he groaned. "Benni, how in the world did you manage to do that?"

"Calm down. It's not actually a body. It's just bones. And Buck found them, not me. I was just the first person to see them. He found a bone when Lindsey and I—she's one of the wranglers here—were taking the quilters for a ride to Luna Lake. Buck came back with this bone in his mouth and, get this, one of the quilters is a retired forensic anthropologist! What are the chances of that? Anyway, she thought that the bone Buck was carrying might be human. I followed Buck to where he found it, and there was definitely a human skeleton. One that someone had recently started digging up. So Rich called the sheriff's department and they sent out an investigator. Apparently it's not enough of a priority to pay people overtime to investigate. The sheriff's forensic team is coming out tomorrow, but the detective questioned everyone tonight."

"Whoa, take a breath," Gabe said. "I'll call around tomorrow morning and see what's going on. Who did they send for the initial investigation?"

I was silent for just long enough for him to get suspicious.

"Benni, what's going on?"

He didn't have to see my face to realize that something wasn't kosher. Gabe's last encounter with Hud had been when Gabe and I were on the verge of breaking up a little less than a year ago. They'd met, in a way, at Emory and Elvia's rehearsal dinner at Daniello's restaurant in San Celina. Gabe had walked up on Hud kissing my hand in the restaurant's bar and we'd never verbally addressed the incident. At the time we had much bigger fish to fry in terms of relationship problems.

"It was Detective Hudson," I said, keeping my voice light. "He owns a cabin near Parkfield. He was the closest San Celina deputy to the scene. Apparently it's their jurisdiction."

It was Gabe's turn to be silent. Then he said in a tight voice, "Isn't that the guy in the bar last year?"

"Yes."

He didn't say anything else, but I had a feeling this wasn't the last time we'd discuss Detective Ford Hudson.

"I can't wait to see you, Friday," I said.

"Me too, *querida*," he said, his voice softening. "What are you wearing?"

"What?"

"You heard me."

"Uh, jeans, sweatshirt, moccasins. Why, what are you wearing?"

"Nothing." Then he laughed.

"Oh, I walked into that one," I said, laughing with him. "Guess that's what you want my last thoughts to be about."

"You might be blond, but you are definitely not dumb. *Buenas noches mi corazón*. Dream sweet."

"I will now," I said softly, hanging up the phone.

It was now almost eleven thirty and most of the cabins and lodge rooms were dark. Days started early here on the ranch and ended early as well. The only cabin whose light was still burning was Victory Simpson's. Since it was the honeymoon cabin, it was set on a small hill farther back from the rest of the ranch. She was probably getting ready for her classes tomorrow. Or maybe unable to sleep, something I could understand. The year Jack, my first husband, died, my sleep patterns went crazy. I felt like the walking dead most of the time, and survived mostly on coffee, donuts, and sheer nerves.

I was halfway back to my cabin when I noticed a dark figure walking through the cars in the parking area beyond the stables. I slipped around the side of the stables, curious about who was as restless tonight as me. I stood in the dark shadows of the stable wall, watching the figure until it came into a patch of moonlight. It was Whip. He walked through the cars and trucks toward the trail that led to Luna Lake. What was he up to? Should I follow him? Was he trying to get to the bones? Before I could make up my mind, a door opened up in the bunkhouse, distracting me. David Hardin stepped out on the bunkhouse stoop and lit his pipe. From inside the bunkhouse, I could hear the muffled boom of rap music and Sam's loud, explosive laugh. By the time I glanced back to where Whip had been, he was gone.

CHAPTER 6

$\mathcal{A}$T 7 A.M. THE NEXT MORNING THE FIRST THING I DID WAS walk around the back of our cabin and gaze up at Luna Lake trail. The forensic team was already there. Their white van, a San Celina sheriff's black-and-white patrol car, and a dark blue Explorer blocked the entrance of the trail. Next to the Explorer was Hud's bright red Dodge pickup.

Rita didn't arrive at the dining hall until almost 8 A.M. When she finally wandered into the kitchen I was filling pitchers with orange juice. From the dining room I could hear the sounds of guests taking their seats.

"What's for breakfast?" she asked, then gave a loud yawn. She was finally wearing jeans and the red gingham shirt today, a small improvement over last night's miniskirt. The jeans were tight enough to announce she was either wearing a minuscule thong or no underwear at all and she'd tied the gingham shirt in a knot under her breasts Daisy Mae-style. I was too tired from a restless night's sleep filled with dream images of bones to say anything.

"I need a cup of coffee or I'll never make it through the next hour," she said, going over to the big silver coffeepot.

Rich and Sam had their backs to us, busy slicing bananas. Rich gave us a quick menu update. "Banana-almond pancakes this morning with honey-cured bacon, strawberry-oat granola and fresh pineapple/mango fruit cup."

"Yum," Rita said, grabbing a plate.

"That yum will have to wait until the guests are served," I said, trading the plate for a cinnamon bagel. "This'll help you last. Grab some coffee carafes and start putting them on the tables. The guests are ready to eat."

"Well, pardon me all to heck for wanting to sit down and have a decent breakfast before I have to work my fingers to the bone."

"You could have gotten up earlier and had plenty of time to eat," I pointed out.

She frowned at me and flounced out, but not before flashing Rich and Sam an injured look. They rewarded me with accusing expressions.

"You two Lotharios just get back to work," I said. "And leave Rita to me unless you plan on taking over her job and serving the meals as well as preparing them."

Chagrined, they turned around, muttering to each other in voices low enough that I couldn't make out what they were saying. They reminded me of the horses at the Ramsey ranch when one was disciplined and went to the others to touch noses and complain about that mean ole human.

At breakfast the major topic of conversation was, of course, the bones and the forensic investigation. Everyone had noticed the vehicles at the trail head while walking from their cabins to the dining hall. I filled the quilting ladies and Dove's ladies in on what little I knew.

"It shouldn't affect our schedule today," I assured them. "We didn't have a ride planned for that trail."

After everyone was served, I took pity on my whining cousin and told her she could go into the kitchen and have her breakfast.

"I can handle the tables alone now," I said. The only thing they'd need might be more pancakes or syrup or refills of their coffee carafes.

"Finally!" Rita moaned. "I'm about ready to pass out from hunger."

I leaned back against the wall and surveyed the chattering breakfast crowd. I'd moved past wondering who The Secret Traveler was and started contemplating who, if anyone in this group, might have a connection to the bones up the hill. I hadn't seen Shawna or Johnny yet this morning, but David Hardin was sitting over with Chad at the staff table.

"Hi, guys," I said, taking over a fresh carafe of coffee. "Want any more coffee?"

"No time," Chad said, wiping his mouth with his napkin and standing up. "I've got some calves to inoculate this morning. Whip took a couple of the guests fishing up at Redtail Lake so I have to cover for him with the horses too."

"Neither the quilting ladies or the church ladies will be riding today. I'll need Tanya and Fred for a barrel-racing demonstration this afternoon, but that's it."

"Good. Need to shoe a couple of 'em anyway."

After he left, I turned to David. "Where's Shawna?" I asked. "I haven't seen her this morning."

"She's probably up watching the police," David said. "I'll be heading up there myself in a minute."

I nodded. "Me too. How's she doing?"

He took a sip of his coffee. "Hanging in there. She's a tough little nut."

"That's for sure."

After checking with Victory to make sure she had everything she needed to teach her class, I cleaned up the dining room, then headed toward the bottom of the Luna Lake trail, about a half mile from the ranch compound. Sure enough, Shawna was there along with Johnny and David. They stood behind the yellow-and-black crime scene tape stretched across the bottom of the trail. A uniformed sheriff's deputy stood in front of it, his round, sunburned face bored.

"What's going on?" I asked, walking up next to Shawna.

"No one will tell us anything," Johnny said, his voice raising in anger. Shawna put a hand on his forearm and squeezed it.

"They've been here since six o'clock," she said. "We can't get any-one to tell us what's happening."

"Let me try," I said.

I approached the young deputy whose clean-shaven face immedi-ately became wary. "Good morning, deputy. Is there any way you can contact Detective Hudson for me?"

He gave me a long look. "Why?"

"I'd like to speak to him."

"Like I told your friends, the detective will speak to them when he comes down and, no, I have no idea when that will be."

I sighed inwardly. Young police officers often took their jobs and the authority given to them so seriously, sometimes to the point of being rude and unhelpful when friendly would work much better. Something they'd discover as they aged was that the old folk saying about catch-ing more flies with honey than vinegar was a cliché for a reason.

"I know it's a lot of trouble," I said. "But Hud and I are personal friends and I'd sure appreciate it . . . and I know he would too . . . if you'd give him a call on your radio there and let him know I'm down here and have some information for him." I was hoping that would intrigue Hud enough to get him down here.

He hesitated, trying to discern whether I was giving him a line or if Hud and I truly were friends and he'd get in trouble by not heeding my request. "He said he didn't want to be bothered unless it was impor-tant."

"Oh, he didn't mean *me*," I said, giving my most reassuring smile. He still didn't look convinced. I'd have to use my ace in the hole. "I'm Gabe Ortiz's wife." Though the sheriff's department and the city police didn't always have a smooth relationship, they did respect and honor their "brotherhood" under the skin. That sometimes passed on to me by virtue of marriage to a law enforcement brother. "San Celina's police chief," I added.

His expression became a little less hostile, though he was still sus-picious. Gabe was, after all, city police, not sheriff. "Okay, I'll give

Detective Hudson a call." He walked away from us a good fifty feet and spoke quietly into his hand-held radio.

"Did you find out anything?" Shawna asked when I walked back over to them.

"I'm working on it," I said.

Johnny glanced impatiently at his watch. "Can't wait around anymore. I gotta go help Chad with those calves." He leaned over and quickly kissed Shawna. "Let me know what you find out, babe." He seemed a little calmer now, which relieved me.

"I will," she said.

Johnny was gone only a few minutes when the deputy walked up to us. His blue eyes were neutral. "Detective Hudson said he'd be down in a few minutes."

"Great, thanks."

About fifteen minutes later we spotted Hud striding around the sharp corner of the trail and head toward us. Next to me, Shawna gave a sudden shudder.

"Are you okay?" I asked.

"Not really," she said. "I can't help thinking . . ."

Before she could finish her sentence, Hud ducked under the crime scene tape, nodded at the deputy and came over to us.

"Good morning, Mrs. Abbott," he said. He touched two fingers to his dark brown Stetson. "My grandfather had a delightful time at your lovely ranch last night. Thank you again for your hospitality."

Shawna smiled at him. "You're both welcome any time, detective."

"PawPaw and I may take you up on that. I think he's getting a mite tired of my bachelor cooking."

Then he turned to me. "And it's so delightful to see my dear, *personal friend,* Benni Harper, this morning. When Deputy Jackson called me and said my *personal friend,* Benni Harper, needed to speak to me, why I just couldn't rush down here fast enough. What can I do to personally assist you, my dear, *personal friend?*"

"Oh, hush. I only said that to talk the deputy into calling you."

He raised his eyebrows. "You know I would have come down to speak with you without you throwing around your weight as a police chief's wife."

I avoided his eyes, embarrassed that the deputy had told Hud what I'd said. "You know I normally don't do that, but the deputy wasn't being very cooperative."

"Not true," he said. "You have done that exact thing a couple of times in my presence."

"I have not!"

"Remember Paradise Valley? The fire captain? And the time—"

"Okay, okay, so I use my pull when it's absolutely necessary. Sue me. Forget that and just tell us what's happening so we can get back to work."

"You know, you can go back to work anyway. I promise, the forensic team knows its job and doesn't need any supervision from you."

"Please, Mr. . . . uh, Detective Hudson," Shawna said.

"Hud," he said.

"Hud," she repeated. "I just want to know a little about what's going on. Everything my husband and I own is tied up in this ranch and he's . . . well, he's very upset about this."

Hud tightened his lips. "I'm sorry, Mrs. Abbott."

"Please call me Shawna," she replied, her smile tremulous.

"Shawna," he repeated, his face contrite. "Please accept my apology. I don't mean to make light of the situation. We've exhumed about three quarters of the remains. They'll be taking them to the lab in Bakersfield. I've asked them to put a priority on it and if they aren't too busy, they might be able to tell us something in a few days. The assistant director, Kristen Rager, and I are old friends. She'll get me some information as soon as possible."

"Thank you," Shawna said. "Then I guess there's nothing we can do but wait."

"I'm afraid that's about it." His face looked truly sympathetic. "I promise, y'all will know what I know when I know it."

She looked over at me. "I'd better get back to the ranch. There's a ton of paperwork to do. Please, join us for lunch, Detective . . . Hud . . . if you have time. It's meatloaf and mashed potatoes."

"Sounds delicious," he said. "I might if things are rolling along here okay. I'm the primary detective on this case so I need to keep a close eye."

After she walked out of earshot, I turned to Hud. "Okay, what's the real scoop? Don't give me any of that bull puckey you just fed her."

"It was better she didn't know," he said, his face suddenly serious. "At least not until she has to know."

"Know what?"

"By the size of the skull, the forensic people are fairly sure it's a man."

"What else?"

He looked at me, then cocked his head. "I could get in real trouble for telling you this."

"So?"

He stuck his hands deep into the pockets of his denim jacket. "I cannot believe what I put up with from you. You truly bring out the masochist in me."

I crossed my arms over my chest and didn't comment.

He pressed his lips together before answering, serious now. "The side of his head has indication of a severe trauma consistent with someone bashing it in. It looks like, whenever this happened, it's a good possibility it was a homicide."

CHAPTER 7

"OH, NO!" I HIT THE SIDE OF MY THIGH IN FRUSTRATION. "THAT'S all they need. Why couldn't the criminal have dumped the body somewhere else?"

He pulled his hands out of his pockets. "This isn't exactly a public park, Benni." His dark solemn eyes studied my face. "I'd rather you not mention anything about homicide to the Abbotts or anyone else. I'll tell them when I think they need to know. No offense to your friends or their guests, but we don't know who to trust."

I'd been thinking that very thing last night about the guests, but hearing it from his mouth made it sound both ridiculous . . . and frightening.

"Well?" he asked. "Can I trust you to keep quiet?"

"Yes, but I can't imagine anyone at the ranch having anything to do with it."

"I'm not pointing any fingers. Not yet. Though I do have to wonder why these bones were being dug up after all these years at the exact same time this exact group of people are visiting the ranch. I'll also be looking into the employment history of the ranch as well as its earlier owners."

What he said made sense, though I didn't like what it implied, that

Joe or his father might have something to do with those bones. I knew studying the situation impartially was Hud's job, but I didn't have to pretend to like it. "I hope you'll be discreet."

"Am I ever not?" he asked, feigning shock.

"I mean it. Shawna is very young and very vulnerable right now. Just try and be sensitive."

"Your words cut right through my heart like a rusty buck knife," he said, bringing both his hands up to his chest. "That you would have so little faith in me, a man of integrity and heart, a man—"

"Would you just shut the heck up?" I asked. "Or if you absolutely feel the need to move your mouth, just tell me what the forensic people say about the bones. Do they know how old they are yet?"

"No, and trying to get those forensic people to even venture a guess is like pulling a bull's tooth. Let's just say they're gun-shy after all these years. Don't want to commit themselves until they have scientific facts." He started to say something else, but was interrupted by Karen Olson's voice calling out to us. She walked up, puffing slightly from the climb. The four quilting cousins from Georgia followed her, their perfectly made-up faces animated with curiosity.

"Hi, Benni," Karen said. "Any information yet?"

"Not yet," I said, glancing over at Hud.

"Would they mind if I . . . ?" She left the question open. Like most Midwesterners I'd known, she not only had a great respect for protocol and boundaries, she possessed impeccable manners. She wouldn't force herself on the investigation, but I could see she was itching to see what was going on.

"I'm sorry," Hud said. "The scene is restricted."

"Of course it is," Karen said with a sigh. "I've only been retired a year and I miss it, you know?"

"I understand," Hud said sympathetically. "I need to get back." We watched him walk back up the trail toward the site.

"I had to try," Karen explained to me.

"Believe me, I wish you could have talked your way in," I replied. "It would be wonderful to have someone on the inside."

"I'd sure love to be someplace on the inside with that cute little ole deputy," said Reba, whom I'd finally figured out was the brunette and the group's spokesperson. "Like the inside of a cozy little mountain cabin in the middle of Colorado. Oh, baby, that cowboy hat surely starts me ayearnin'. But, shoot, put a Stetson on any man and he looks a little bit sexier, don't y'all think?"

Her three cousins, two blondes and one with auburn hair, nodded enthusiastically in agreement.

I turned my head and winked at Karen. Then I smiled at the cousins. "What're you all supposed to be doing right now?"

They laughed almost in unison. Dressed today in matching gray plaid cowboy shirts, white cowboy hats, tight burgundy jeans and snakeskin cowboy boots, they could have been featured in one of Guess clothing's sexy magazine ads depicting the myth of the affluent West. From what I'd picked up from their conversations about stocks, bonds, and trust funds, they more than likely didn't buy off-the-rack Guess clothes, but had their dude ranch outfits handmade by the long-time family seamstress.

"We have a class with Miss Victory in exactly two minutes," Reba said, checking her platinum Rolex watch.

"Then you'd better get moving," I said, starting back down the trail toward the ranch. "I hear she makes you thread a hundred needles if you're late."

Behind me, another roll of throaty laughs commenced. "That Victory's a big ole squishy marshmallow," said Reba. "We just love her to death."

"I'll let everyone know what's happening up here," I called over my shoulder. "As soon as I'm clued into the facts."

"Forget those bones," said the shortest and blondest of the cousins whose name I thought was Pinky. "Just clue me in to Mr. Detective Hud the Stud's address." Another wave of laughs.

"You're on your own there," I said.

Karen laughed, just as amused by the cousins' antics as I was.

We parted ways at the main lodge where they went to Victory's class and I walked over to the ranch offices. Inside the cramped little room, Shawna sat in front of a calculator adding up a pile of checks. She looked up at me, her eyes squinting in worry. "Did you get any more information out of the detective?"

I hated lying, but I'd promised Hud. "He's waiting to hear what the forensic team reports." That wasn't exactly a lie, because he was. I sat down in the office chair next to her neatly arranged desk, trying not to look directly at her, afraid she might see in my face the one pertinent fact he did reveal to me. "Karen Olson tried to sneak a look, but he wouldn't let her. On the good side, I think this will be something that will certainly help her remember this trip and tell her forensic friends about." I gave Shawna an encouraging smile.

Her return smile was forced. "I hope she remembers more than that to tell her friends."

I pointed my pencil at her. "We can't guarantee a skeleton with every visit, but I'm sure that the food, activities, and wonderful hospitality of your unmatched professional staff will leave a favorable impression too."

Shawna leaned back in her chair. It gave a loud squeak that caused both of us to jump. We simultaneously laughed.

"We're not jumpy or anything," I said.

She grimaced. "You must admit, it is nerve-wracking. The thought that someone would use my ranch as a place to bury someone . . ." Her compact body gave a vigorous shudder. "I just hope whoever did it is long gone."

I realized then that it had not even occurred to her that the police would be taking a close look at the people who'd lived at the ranch before they'd start enlarging their search. Or maybe she was purposely avoiding that thought. I couldn't blame her. My mind went back to Whip and his lurking about the trailhead last night. He'd left early this morning to take some guests fishing so I couldn't watch him and see if he showed an unusual interest in the proceedings up the hill. Then again, what would be unusual? We were all curious as heck.

"I hear we're having meatloaf for lunch," I said, changing the subject. There wasn't much to be gained from talking too much about the bones.

"Yes, with garlic mashed potatoes."

"Hope that means cold meatloaf sandwiches tomorrow for the staff. My favorite."

"Mine too."

"I'm giving a barrel-racing demonstration this afternoon at two o'clock. Drop by the corral if you have time."

"I will if I can. I've still got a long list of phone calls to make finalizing the details about Saturday night's dance." She tapped a pencil on her front teeth, her gray eyes cloudy with anxiety. "A rainstorm is predicted. Sure hope it holds off at least until Sunday."

"Haven't early sales been pretty steady?" Behind me, a small heater cycled and started to glow. I could feel the heat start to permeate the back of my flannel shirt.

"Yes, but we're counting on a lot of last-minute people. We're selling the tickets at the Boot Barn in Paso Robles as well as all the Farm Supply stores in the county. And your friend, Elvia, has been an angel. Her store sold thirty-three tickets last week!"

I pointed a finger at Shawna. "I'll take a wild guess and say Sam's winning smile had a lot to do with that."

She almost smiled. "I'm sure it did. Still, the barn can hold about two hundred people and we've only sold a hundred tickets. A lot of people might be holding off to see what the weather will do. That forty-five-mile drive from Paso isn't easy if it's raining."

"Maybe we should all do a rain dance tonight. I bet your guests would love it."

"Aren't rain dances done when you *want* rain?"

"Okay, then we'll call it an anti-rain dance. Or a negative rain dance."

"An unrain dance?"

"That's the spirit!" I said, reaching across the desk and touching the top of her hand. "It would also be something completely original for The Secret Traveler to write about."

She leaned back in her chair. "It sure would. Do you have any thoughts on who it might be? I'm trying not to watch every guest like a hawk, but I find myself sneaking glances at them. So much . . ." Her voice caught for a moment. "So much is riding on that one review. How can one person have so much power?"

"I imagine there's a whole slew of singers, actors, writers, chefs, and artists who would ask that same question. I'm leaning toward the lady from Long Island. She's close to Manhattan, seems at ease with new situations, goes with the flow. All that adds up to someone who travels frequently."

She nodded. "But isn't it always the person you least suspect?"

"Or sometimes it's exactly the person who is the most suspicious. Guess we'll just have to keep our eyes and ears open," I said, standing up. "And be nice to *everyone*. Actually, that's not a bad philosophy anyway. Is there anything you need me to do before lunch?"

She shook her head no. "Unless you want to volunteer to add up all these checks, not a thing except make sure the ladies have a great time riding the barrels."

"You got it, boss."

"What's the program for tonight?" she asked. "Where is that schedule? I keep losing the doggone schedule." She pawed through the stacks of papers covering the desktop.

I tapped her shoulder and pointed to the neatly typed schedule thumbtacked to the bulletin board behind her.

She closed her eyes and took a deep breath. "Thank you. I swear, I'd be walking around without my nose if it wasn't stuck right to my face."

I patted her shoulder. "You are under a lot of stress and, in my opinion, you are handling it superbly. Don't worry about tonight, it's all set and there's not a thing you have to do. The church ladies are continuing their domino tournament despite the fact that there's rumors that *someone* is shamelessly cheating."

"Oh, no," she said, a genuine smile finally relaxing her worry-sharpened features.

I smiled back. "Yeah, it's quite the scandal. Dove and couple of her friends think it's Sissy Brownmiller, but they can't figure out how she's doing it. I'm supposed to discreetly monitor tonight's game."

She turned her chair and peered at the schedule. "What else is going on?"

"After my talk on pioneer quilts, it's a free night. I'll try to get some action going if people seem to be bored. Trivial Pursuit or Pictionary are always good games. Most likely the hunters will either play poker or pool. And there's always the TV room. I noticed that one of your satellite stations is playing *Annie Oakley*. Very appropriate."

"I love that movie," she said, her eyes growing soft. "When I was eight years old Dad sent me a red, felt cowgirl hat and a book about Annie Oakley." Her bottom lip trembled slightly. "It was one of the few presents he sent that my mother allowed me to keep."

"I'm sure there are other movies we can watch," I said softly.

"No, he'd like it. He used to call me Miss Oakley when he and I would practice shooting his old pistols." Her face hardened in anger. "He'd hate it that someone dumped a body on his ranch. He loved this place as much as he did me."

"I doubt that he loved anything more than you, but I do know he'd want you to cowgirl up and not let this get you down."

She nodded, her eyes shiny with tears. "Yes, he would. Thanks for reminding me."

A few minutes later I walked into the kitchen where Sam was elbow deep in a gargantuan stainless steel mixing bowl. Rich moved down an assembly line of cream puffs, spreading the tops of them with dark chocolate frosting. When I started to reach for one he said without looking up, "Keep going and lose a finger, *mija*."

"Oh, c'mon," I said. "What's one lousy cream puff? You have dozens."

"You can have one after you serve lunch," he said. "We need to make sure there's enough for the guests. Remember them? Like you've been reminding your cousin, Rita. The ones who actually *paid* to be here?"

He'd caught me dead between the eyes. Still, to save face I put up a feeble protest. "If I knew how to call you a big meanie in Spanish, I would." I leaned against the glass and stainless steel refrigerator. "Need any help, or is Sam enough?"

"According to most ladies, I'm more than enough," Sam said over his shoulder, his hands covered with ground beef, pork, oatmeal, and tomato sauce.

"Ah, he's inherited his father's Paul-Bunyan-of-an-ego," I announced to the room. "How nice for us all."

"Paul Bunyan?" Sam asked. "Wasn't he like a singer in the seventies? The one who dressed up like Benedict Arnold or something? I read about him in my History of Rock and Roll class."

I looked over at Rich and rolled my eyes. "What do they teach kids in school these days?" I turned back to Sam. "That would be Paul Revere and the Raiders and he dressed up like . . . uh . . . guess?"

Sam looked at me blankly.

"Think about it," I said, glancing up at the kitchen clock. It was a little before 10 A.M. "If you all don't need my help here, I'll come back at eleven to set the tables. I think I'll go over to the corrals and set up the barrels for my demonstration this afternoon."

I was rolling the third blue-and-red-painted barrel out to complete the triangle figuration when behind me, Buck gave a sharp bark of recognition. I turned and saw Gabe striding across the soft dirt toward me.

"Hey, Sergeant Friday," I said, running right into his open arms. I inhaled his comforting gingery scent and felt immediately safe and secure. Then I pulled back and looked up at him, suspicious. "It's Wednesday! You're not supposed to be here until Friday night. What gives?"

"Can't I just miss my wife?" he said, grinning at me. "Aren't you always nagging me that I work too hard, that we don't spend enough time doing fun things? Here I am, ready to have fun."

I stood on tiptoe and kissed the bottom of his chin. "I know you, Chief Ortiz, king of the workaholics. You never do anything without a reason. Spontaneity is *not* your long suit. You're curious about the bones, aren't you?"

"Not my jurisdiction, not my problem," he said without hesitation.

"So, why are you . . ." Then it dawned on me. "Gabriel Thomas Ortiz, shame, shame, shame on you! You are here to guard your woman. You should trust me more than that."

Like an addict who'd been caught with a dime bag in his pocket, he looked me straight in the eye and lied. "I trust *you* implicitly."

"Oh, honestly," I said, but nevertheless, felt flattered by his jealousy. Detective Hudson did occasionally serve a good purpose. "You're worse than a high school kid." I slipped my arm through his. "You're going to regret coming early because I'll put you to work. I have a trail ride scheduled tomorrow, but I also need help decorating the barn for the dance Saturday night. I'm hereby commandeering your time. You are officially on the decorating committee."

He groaned.

"C'mon, it'll be fun. Maybe the untangling of the tiny white Christmas lights we want strung around the barn won't be, but after that, I swear, you'll have a ball."

He brought my hand up and kissed it. "I'm just glad to be here with you. I'll hang lights all weekend if that's what you need."

"Spoken like a well-trained husband. I promise, I'll eventually make it worth your while."

"I'm going to hold you to that promise."

"As Dove would say, I'll owe you forever before I beat you out of it. Say, when you parked, did you notice if the forensic people still have Luna Trail closed off?" The trailhead was visible from the parking lot, but not from the lodge or the corrals.

"No, as I said, it's not my jurisdiction or my bones. Let the sheriff's department have that headache."

"I'm surprised the *Tribune* hasn't sent someone down to nose around."

"Probably still picking at the carcass of some other unfortunate victim. Give them time." Now that my cousin wasn't working at the newspaper anymore, Gabe didn't even try to politely hide his disdain for journalists.

"You old bear. A lot of good has been done by journalists."

He just grunted in reply.

"Well," I did have to concede, "this time I hope they have other fish to fry, journalistically-speaking. Otherwise, Saturday's dance might be packed, but not with potential ranch guests."

When we reached the lodge, I took him on a quick tour.

"This place is incredible," he said. He'd been at the ranch almost two years ago at a barbecue Joe had held when Shawna first came to live with him, but Gabe hadn't been back since. "Joe did a wonderful job. I imagine that it will be very successful once people find out about it."

"Let's hope so," I said. We ended the tour in the kitchen where we found Rich pulling individual sourdough bread loaves out of the huge stainless-steel oven.

"Hey, Gabe," he said, setting the pan down on the counter. "Nice to see you again."

Sam walked in carrying a box of fresh vegetables. "Hey, Dad, what're you doing here? Thought you weren't supposed to be here until Friday." He set the box down on the counter, then glanced back at his dad. "What happened? You get fired?" He flashed his father a teasing grin.

Gabe went over and stuck his hand in his son's black, spiky hair and ruffled it. "Very funny, *mijo*. I do take days off once in awhile."

"Hey, hey," Sam said, jerking away from his dad. "Watch the hair."

"You guys are so immature," I said.

"He's immature," Gabe said. "I'm right."

His son made a very gross, very graphic physical response with his lips.

Gabe held up his hand. "I rest my case."

"I need to fold napkins," I said, shaking my head. Gabe followed me into to the dim, quiet dining room.

"What are you doing this afternoon?" he asked.

"The barrel-racing demonstration you saw me setting up for. Then it's back to the dining room to get ready for dinner. Then a talk on pioneer quilts tonight. You want to be my wrangler for the demonstration? You can help the women on and off the horses."

"Can't. I saw Whip when I came in and I promised him I'd give Jet a workout. He hasn't been exercised much since Joe died. Whip said he and Bunny just don't have time."

Jet was a stallion that Joe was training when he had his heart attack. Three quarters Thoroughbred, one quarter Morgan, he was sixteen hands high and, except for one thin white stripe down his nose, black as a cup of double espresso.

He checked the clock on the wall. "I'm going to run over to the bunkhouse and unpack before lunch."

"You have plenty of time. Lunch isn't for another hour."

"Save me a cream puff," he said, kissing me quickly on the lips.

The dining room door had barely shut when it burst open again and he darted back into the dining hall, slamming the door behind him. His face was a mixture of surprise and shock. "Son of a . . ."

"What?" I said, alarmed.

"A bird just attacked me!"

A loud squawk sounded from behind the door which then opened revealing Dove and her WMU ladies. Their giggles sounded like a flock of chirping sparrows.

"What's wrong, Chief Ortiz?" Dove said. "Afraid of a little fowl play?"

"That . . . that . . . thing went right for my ba . . ." He abruptly stopped, realizing that all of the four elderly ladies' eyes automatically went right to the place on his Levi's where he was referring. He looked at me, his red face pleading for assistance.

"That's Socrates," I explained. "He's in love with Dove."

The ladies burst into laughter again.

"What?" Gabe said.

"You must have looked like you were going after Dove. He's her trained attack goose."

"For heaven's sakes," Dove said. "He is not."

"I was just going to give her a hug," Gabe said.

"How was Socrates supposed to know that?" I asked. "He doesn't like men very much."

"That part I figured out," Gabe said, glancing around. "Is there a back way out of here?"

I pointed at the kitchen. "Go through the kitchen which will take you to a hallway that leads to the Annie Oakley Room I just showed you. There's double doors across from the stone fireplace that lead outside."

After he left, I turned back to the ladies. "So, what's up?"

Outside, Socrates gave a lonely, miserable honk.

"I'm letting them have an hour off before lunch," Dove said.

"Letting us nothing," said Blanche. "We rebelled. We staged a sit-down."

"Actually, a stand-up," Leonora added. "We just had to get some exercise or our old bones were going to freeze in place."

"How about you all come to the barrel-racing demonstration after lunch?" I asked. "You look like you could use some fresh air."

"We'll open the windows in our cabin," Dove said. "We have lots of work to do."

"I agree, Sister Ramsey," Sissy Brownmiller said, her bony nose twitching.

Dove's soft peach face blanched. When Sissy Brownmiller, a hard worker at First Baptist, but a well-known stick-in-the-mud, agreed with her, there was definitely something wrong.

"I taught Benni everything she knows about barrel racing," Dove said, trying to redeem herself.

That wasn't strictly true, but I wasn't about to argue with her. "Great! Be at the big corral behind the stables after lunch. I'll start around 2 P.M."

With that time frame, I was going to have to insist that Rita clean up after lunch and be on time to prepare the dining room for dinner.

Though the barrels were in place, it would take me at least a half hour to warm up the horses for the demonstration.

"But what about the essentials bags for the homeless?" Sissy complained.

"We'll have a nice afternoon out in the sunshine," Dove said, her face visibly relieved that she and Sissy no longer played on the same team. "We can work on the bags after supper tonight."

"But that's when Benni is giving a talk on pioneer quilts," Leonora said "We don't want to miss that."

Dove shot me an aggravated look that said because I was stealing all her workers away, hundreds of homeless people will never receive their essentials bags filled with toothpaste, comb, toothbrush, soap, and deodorant.

I shot back an innocent smile. These dedicated ladies needed to have a little fun. "I promise I'll come help if you get behind schedule."

"Oh, all right," Dove said. "But we're working until lunch then."

Rita wandered in when I was almost finished preparing the tables for lunch. She was wearing red Rockies jeans and a tight white T-shirt that said, "Every Cowboy's Dream; Every Mama's Nightmare."

"Since you weren't here to help me set up, you'll have to clean up by yourself afterward," I told her. I didn't even bother commenting on her outfit. Hopefully, The Secret Traveler had a good sense of humor.

"That's not fair," she whined. "I was on the phone trying to track down Skeeter, that low-life jerk. I just keep getting his cell phone's voice mail and my Wal-Mart phone card is almost used up."

"You know what they say, 'Fare is something you pay to ride the bus.' I have to get the horses ready for my barrel-racing demonstration. Which tables do you want?"

"Are the hunters back?" she asked, her face lighting up. I could swear dollar signs appeared in her eyes, just like on a cartoon character.

"Not until dinner, I think."

She cocked a hip and checked her nails. "Then I don't care."

"Go ahead and take the WMU ladies. I'll take the quilters and we both can serve the staff." My plan was to hang around the guests as much as possible and try to ferret out, in a subtle way, if they had any previous connection to the Broken DIS.

I was so busy concentrating on how I would accomplish that task that it didn't occur to me until everyone began arriving for lunch that I had another little crisis on my hands, one of a more personal nature.

Gabe and Hud would be eating at the same table.

Not so bad, I thought to myself. There were lots of other people for them to interact with.

Then Shawna sent word to the kitchen that she and Johnny were eating in the office. Good, I thought, they needed some time alone. Whip was still out with the fishermen and Bunny had grabbed a sandwich, too busy to sit down and eat. That left Gabe, Hud, Hud's grandpa, Iry, Lindsey, and the old ranch hand, David Hardin. If this kept up it would soon be a little intimate lunch between Gabe and Hud. Not a pretty picture.

Fifteen minutes later when I came out of the kitchen carrying lemonade and iced tea pitchers Gabe and Hud were just sitting down across the round table from each other looking like two goats ready to butt heads.

"Chief Ortiz," Hud said, nodding his head. "How wonderful to see you again. You're looking well."

"Detective Hudson," Gabe replied, his face not moving a muscle.

"Meatloaf for lunch," I said cheerily. "Garlic mashed potatoes. Don't remember what's for dessert, but knowing Rich it's going to be very good and . . . uh . . . very rich."

David and Iry laughed politely at my lame joke. Gabe and Hud just watched each other. Gabe looked wary, ready to pounce. Hud looked like he was ready to burst into laughter any minute.

"Anybody want coffee?" I asked.

"I'll take some," David said.

When I came back with his coffee, obviously some words had been exchanged because Iry was shaking his head and Lindsey looked distinctly uncomfortable.

"What happened?" I whispered to Lindsey.

"Why do your husband and Hud hate each other?" she whispered back.

"Long story," I murmured. Then I said to the table, "Food will be right up." I rushed into the kitchen and grabbed two filled plates.

I served Gabe first, then worked my way around the table to Hud.

"Oh, waitress," Hud said, when I set a steaming plate in front of Iry. "I think this fork is dirty." He held up a perfectly clean fork and grinned at me. I glanced over at Gabe whose fork was poised over his meal, his face moving from irritated to furious in five seconds.

I took the fork, looked at it, then wiped it on my jean-clad thigh. "All clean, Mr. Hudson," I said, handing it back to him, smiling sweetly.

"I believe that might be a health code violation," Hud said, winking at me.

"Oh, Hud, c'mon, I'm not in the mood to . . ." I started.

Gabe interrupted me. "Hudson, do you want me to take that fork and shove it up . . ."

"Gabe!" I said.

"And shove it where, Chief Ortiz?" Hud said, grinning.

"For cryin' out loud, you guys," I said. "Grow up."

Hud's grandpa picked up his fork and said, "Benni, *fait comme si tu les voit pas.*"

"Excuse me?" I said.

He said loudly in English, "Pretend you don't see them." He pointedly looked at Hud, then at Gabe. "Then the little boys will have nothing to fight about."

Hud gave his grandfather an annoyed look. "*C'est assez,* PawPaw."

"*Oui,* T-Hud, it *is* enough," he answered blandly. "Let the *fille* do her work in peace."

His words actually caused Hud's face to color. My husband's face looked triumphant until Iry, from under his bushy, white eyebrows, shot him a chiding look. Even Gabe had the grace to look chagrined.

"How's the investigation going, detective?" David asked Hud, wisely changing the subject.

"Fine," Hud said, not smiling. "We should be out of there by tomorrow. Unless we need to take longer."

David gave a curt nod. "Any information on who these bones belong to?"

Hud shook his head no. "Don't know much yet, Mr. Hardin. Say, you were going to get back to me on this. Did you make up that list of ranch hands who worked here at the DIS?"

David's eyes narrowed, disappearing into the creased lines of his face. "Still working on it. Been a lot of cowboys through here in the last fifty years." He cleared his throat and started buttering his sourdough bread.

"I'll need it as soon as possible," Hud said, his voice deceptively friendly.

"I said I'm working on it."

Hud stuck with it like a coonhound. "Can you get to it today, you think?"

Gabe kept silent and watched both David and Hud.

At this crucial moment, I was forced to leave and pick up Hud's food in the kitchen. When I came back with his plate, David was fiddling with his silverware and the table was silent. Lindsey glanced up at me and raised her eyebrows slightly.

I set the first plate down in front of my husband. "I expect a generous tip, mister," I said next to his ear, trying to make him smile.

"Oh, you'll get something, sweetheart," he murmured back.

During the meal, Iry managed to steer the conversation toward that age-old Central California debate about who's superior—the Dodgers or the Giants. I wondered what David Hardin answered Hud. Because he'd lived and worked at the Broken DIS for so many years, longer than anyone who was currently here, it did make sense that he would know things other people didn't. I just couldn't understand Hud's reasoning in putting David on the spot in front of the rest of us.

Throughout the meal, thanks to Iry's reprimand, Hud behaved himself and didn't make any more unreasonable demands, therefore Gabe was also calm.

"Thank you, Iry," I whispered, picking up his empty plate. "Extra dessert for the peacemaker."

"*C'est rien, chère,*" he replied in a low voice. "Don't mind my grandson. He is always, what do you say, the mischief kind, him. He means no real harm."

I glanced over at Hud, who watched us curiously. "I'm not so sure about that, but thanks again."

After lunch, I hurried out to the stable to tack up Tanya and Fred. Halfway to the stables I heard Shawna call out to me. I turned and watched her jog slowly across the yard toward me. Her cheeks flushed bright pink with some kind of emotion.

"How was your romantic lunch?" I asked, smiling.

She ran her forefingers under her eyes, as if she were wiping away stray mascara. The bluish-gray circles remained. "Not all that romantic. This thing with the bones is really upsetting Johnny. The detective . . . Hud . . . came to the office before lunch and said it was going to be another day before they'd let us use the Luna Lake trail. Benni, he asked about my father. And David."

"What did he ask about Joe?"

"About who his friends were, who worked here, what his personality was like . . . whether he had a temper." Behind her, the quilt ladies had come out of the lodge and were walking around the pots of flowers that decorated the back patio. I could hear Victory pointing out the range of colors, how random nature was and how that freedom from traditional color combinations is often a good thing in their own designs.

"What do you think?" Shawna asked, her hand plucking at her hair, nervous as a sparrow.

I looked at her for a moment without answering, because she wouldn't like what I was thinking. They had to look at the possibility that Joe knew the body was out there and at the even more horrible possibility that he was involved. Something I didn't want to believe any more than she did.

"What did you tell the detective?" I asked.

The color in her cheeks glowed brighter and her eyes filmed over. "That I never, ever saw him lose his temper with anyone! Then you know what he asked? Did Dad drink? I said, not any more than anyone else. Why are they concentrating on my dad? Anyone could have buried those bones."

I placed my hand on her trembling shoulder. "That's just what cops do, Shawna. They start at the center, the closest people to the . . . incident, then they slowly start enlarging the net, so to speak. Hud's just asking questions about your dad because he owned this ranch for so long. I bet Hud asked about your grandfather too, right?"

Underneath my hand her body twitched like a newborn colt's. "He did ask about Dad's father. I told him we never met. I think Grandpa Darnell died when I was twelve or thirteen, something like that, during one of the times when my mom and dad weren't speaking."

"Trust me, Hud is handling it exactly how Gabe would if it were his case. I seriously doubt that this body has anything to do with either your dad or your grandpa, but they have to ask. That's just their procedure."

She nodded and pressed her lips together. "You're right. I don't know why it just struck me so hard."

"Because you're protective of your dad's memory. He would be proud that you stuck up for him."

"Thank you," she said, placing a hand over her eyes. "Oh, Benni, I don't know if I'm going to be able to do this."

"You will," I said, giving her shoulder a squeeze. "You're your father's daughter. I knew your dad and he'd have two words for you. *No Sniveling.*"

My remark made her smile. "The sign that hangs in the tack room."

"I've had it pointed out to me more than once when I used to come here with my dad to visit. Once when I was whining that I was bored and didn't have anything to do. Your dad, with my own daddy cheering him on, sent me to muck out some stalls where the horses had a little, shall we say, digestive problem. I learned not to snivel real fast. At least not around your dad."

That made her laugh. "I lived with him for less than two years, but that sure does sound like him. You're right, I need to quit sniveling. I have a ranch to run."

"The cops will be long gone by Saturday night. That's the most important thing. And all the guests will have such a great time that they'll forget about this little bump-in-the-road and The Secret Traveler will give you five stars and your guest ranch will be on the cover of *Condé Nast Traveler*."

"The Secret Traveler's highest mark is four stars," she said.

"We're going to make sure the Broken Dishes gets five."

She impulsively threw her arms around me and hugged me hard. "Thanks, Benni."

Just as she was hugging me, Whip walked up.

"Am I interrupting anything?" he said, smiling at Shawna.

"Just getting a pep talk from my biggest supporter," Shawna said.

"Hey, we're all behind you, sugar," he said, putting a hand on her shoulder. She smiled at him gratefully, her cheeks flushed.

"Did you get lunch?" she asked him.

He shook his head no. "Just got back with the fishermen. Rich fixed them box lunches, but I didn't eat one. I'll go in and see if there's any leftovers." He squeezed her shoulder with his work-roughened hand. "Are you okay?" The expression on his face was much more than just an employee's concern.

She nodded. "I'm fine, Whip. Go have some lunch."

After he left, the nosy part of my personality overcame my manners. I cleared my throat and asked, "Shawna, I know this is none of my business, but, you and Whip aren't . . . ?"

She laughed, her face turning a soft pink. "Whip and I were a thing once. We aren't together *now*. We hooked up, had a good time, and then just went our separate ways. I love Johnny."

There was enough age difference between us for me to flinch at the words "hooked up." The picture it painted in my mind was a little too space age and mechanical. "Well, not exactly your separate ways. He does work for you." Not the smartest thing for a woman to do, I thought, having an ex-lover as an employee.

"He worked for my dad," she said firmly.

"What did Joe think of you two being together?" I asked.

She shrugged and just said, "You know fathers. Like I said, Whip and I were only together for a few months. Remember, when you and I first met? That's when we were together, though we kept it pretty quiet."

They must have because I hadn't heard one bit of gossip about it, a miracle in the San Celina ag community.

"He taught me a lot about the ranch," she continued, "and, you know, about my dad." She looked down at her feet, her face sad. "He knew my dad when he was young. He experienced the things with Dad that I should have."

Which made her being with Whip more complicated than a short fling, something I wasn't sure she realized yet.

She looked back up into my face. "It's been over between us a long time. We're both cool with it. We've moved on."

I didn't answer. She might believe that, but it was obvious Whip didn't. It certainly explained the tension between him and Johnny. I hoped that she knew what she was doing, though I could appreciate her difficult position. Whip had lived and worked here since he was a kid. It would be cruel to just fire him. Why hadn't I heard of her relationship with Whip before now? The first chance I could find some privacy at the pay phone I would call Daddy and see what he knew about it.

She gazed over at the ranch office. "I have a stack of paperwork to do."

"I'll leave you to it," I said, troubled by this new complication. Was it something I should tell Hud or should I just stay out of the whole mess? For at least the next few hours, I wouldn't have to worry about it because I had a barrel-racing demonstration.

At the stables, I found Sam and coerced him into helping me tack up Tanya and Fred since my conversation with Shawna left me behind. It felt like that no matter what I was doing, I was always fifteen minutes late. Both the quilt ladies and the WMU ladies were already sitting in the metal bleachers waiting for the show. Lindsey had arrived and helped me check the cinches. As I warmed the horses up, I gave the ladies a quick history of barrel racing.

"Barrel racing started in the 1940s as a way for rodeo queen contestants to exhibit their riding skills. It became extremely popular because of all-girl rodeos and informal get-togethers where cowgirls, apart from cowboys, could show off their horsemanship skills as well as proving they were every bit as nervy as their male counterparts. Early barrel racers didn't breed their horses specifically to run the barrels. By the way, that is the proper term—you 'run' the barrels, not 'ride' them. Anyway, what a cowgirl hoped for was a horse who, besides being trained traditionally in cutting or roping, also had a strong desire to run and was quick and sharp at turning. Horses like that not only made good cutting horses, that is, working ranch horses used to separate cattle so they could be branded, vaccinated, or sent to market, but they made excellent barrel racers. There weren't any special barrel racing saddles or equipment back in the '40s and early '50s. A cowgirl used what she had, ran the barrels as well as she could, and hoped for the best. Women really started competing in this sport in the late 1950s. Mildred Ferris, Wanda Bush, and Sammy Thurman were all early cowgirls who won world championships and National Finals Rodeo qualifications with their expertise in a variety of events including barrel racing. Without them and a lot of other gutsy cowgirls there wouldn't be a Women's Professional Rodeo Association. If you follow rodeo at all you've probably heard of Charmayne James and her remarkable horse, Scamper. She has won an unmatched record of seventeen National Finals Rodeo qualifications including ten world titles with Scamper."

The women murmured in appreciation, nodding their heads. Even if you didn't follow the sport, the numbers were impressive.

"Now, I'm going to show you all how to ride the course and if any of you want to try it, Fred's a nice old horse who'll give you a limousine ride around the three barrels."

I climbed up on Tanya, a tough little sorrel mare with one white foot, who Whip said once ran barrels and won a dozen or so ribbons for a high school rodeo champ up in Salinas. Her quivering skin and soft snorts told me she hadn't forgotten her rodeo days and was itching to take those barrels. I patted her on the side, whispered some encouragement in her ears and watched Lindsey who'd positioned herself to my left with a stopwatch and a raised hand. At the drop of her hand I spurred Tanya and took off. I ran the barrels, one after the other, the cloverleaf pattern, something I could have ridden in my sleep. Then I spurred Tanya again on the down stretch. When we crossed the finished line, a line we'd spray painted in orange on the corral's hard-packed dirt, a cheer went up from the bleachers. It brought back some fond memories of my own high school rodeo days and I couldn't help grinning.

"18.3 seconds!" Lindsey called out.

"Is that good?" one of the Georgia cousins called.

"Nah," I called back. "But then I haven't done this competitively for about twenty years."

"You looked great!" Marty, the quilter from California, said. "Wish I'd brought my camera."

"Lindsey has a camera," I said. "But it's not for me. It's for any of you who want to try this." We'd started taking pictures a couple of days ago after I came up with the idea that all of us workers should carry those throwaway 35mm cameras and that a day before they all left, someone could run into Paso Robles and do the one-hour photo thing so the guests could have photographs to look at while they were traveling back home. It was a lot of work, but it might be that final touch that would impress our mysterious critic. Personal service was the key to getting the Broken Dishes noticed.

"I'll try," Reba said. "And all the other cousins will too."

"Thanks a lot, Reba," they said, poking at their ringleader. But they all gamely came out of the bleachers and listened closely to my instructions.

"Sit straight, but relaxed," I said, as I helped Reba onto Fred. "Center yourself in the middle of the horse. Try and absorb the horse's movement by staying loose and supple. Keep your hips, knees, and ankles flexible. Try not to lean forward. That unbalances the horse. Keep a light touch with the reins. You want the horse to feel your control, but you don't want to tug at his mouth. Think about what you want to do. Look at the barrels as you turn. The horse will know what you want to do by your body language as you ride."

I adjusted the stirrups so they fit her long legs comfortably. "First we'll try walking the barrel course and those of you who want to try taking it a little faster can do that. Don't be afraid of old Freddie. He won't let you down."

"Then he isn't a true man," Pinky said, having opted to be the official photographer.

"Well, he has been gelded," I said, causing the women to laugh.

By three thirty everyone had a turn, and afterward we made sure that anyone who wanted their picture taken was accommodated. The quilters started back to the lodge for another quilting session with Victory. Dove's ladies also headed back toward their cabins, ready to work on the homeless shelter bags until dinnertime.

"I'll be there in a minute," Victory said to the quilt ladies. "I need a horse fix."

She walked over to where I was standing with Tanya.

"Want me to take Tanya back to the stable?" Lindsey asked.

"That would be great," I said. "Check her right front shoe. It might be my imagination, but I thought I felt her hesitating on that foot."

"Gotcha," she said.

Victory stood next to me while I unbridled Fred and pulled a soft halter over his head. "You're a good old boy," she said. He dipped his head down and she reached over and rubbed behind his ears.

"He is," I agreed, watching her rub the place behind Fred's ears where the bridle's crown piece goes. "Why didn't you give the barrels a try?"

Though three of the Georgia cousins, Karen, Marty and even one of Dove's ladies had trotted around the barrels, Victory had chosen to remain a spectator. Since I knew from her history that she'd grown up on a ranch, I was curious why she sat this experience out.

A slight breeze blew her silvery-gray hair into her face. She brushed it aside, a sad smile on her face. "I've certainly spent my time circling those barrels. Just didn't want to take time away from the paying guests."

"You do know you can ride any time you like, don't you? I'd be glad to saddle you up a horse whenever you want."

She nodded. "Yes, Shawna told me. I may go on a ride by myself before I leave, see all the hard work her dad, Will, put into it."

"You mean Joe," I said.

Her face flushed slightly. "Oh, dear, you're right. Joe." She gave a small laugh. "I used to blame menopause for my faulty memory. Now I just call them senior moments."

"Shoot, I'm in big trouble," I said, laughing with her. "Because I'm already having trouble remembering people's names."

"You know, I really do want this to be a wonderful, unforgettable time for these quilters. I want this ranch to succeed for Shawna and Johnny. It's the least I can do." She gave Fred's neck one last pat. "And on that note, I'd better get over to the lodge and see to my ladies."

I watched her walk away, impressed by her concern for Shawna and Johnny whom she'd never even met before this week. Her reputation in the quilt world for being an unusually kind and caring person wasn't exaggerated.

It was in the stable when I was unsaddling Fred that something niggled at me, something she said that didn't sound right. My mind replayed our conversation over and over, trying to remember everything she said. Then it struck me. I finished up with Fred and headed over to the ranch office to check.

Shawna was on the phone talking to a food vendor. She held up one finger to let me know she wouldn't be long.

"Our milk people are granting us another month of credit," she said after hanging up. "Thank God. And I do mean that literally."

"Is that the Worley family?" I asked. I'd been in 4H with Debra-jean, the youngest of the four Worley sisters. They had a small dairy operation near Cayucos and were one of the last dairy farms left on the Central Coast, once famous for its Swiss-Italian dairies.

"Yes, Lupe, our regular cook, has always loved their incredible butter and cream. Rich was impressed too. Said he was going to start looking for their stuff in his local market."

"They do have good quality milk products, not to mention that it's nice not to be supporting some huge corporation."

"Amen to that," Shawna said, tapping her pencil against the handle of her office chair. "What's up?"

I shifted from one foot to the other. How could I ask this without making Shawna suspicious? An idea suddenly blossomed. "I was thinking about making up a scrapbook of the ranch's history. You know, sort of a time-line book that you could keep in the Annie Oakley Room for guests to peruse. I was making a list of the names of your family. Your grandfather was Joseph John Darnell, right?"

She nodded. "My grandmother was Essie Ann. My dad was their only child." She smiled ruefully. "Guess that runs in the family. Apparently grandmother Essie was an only child too."

"And your mom's full name?"

"Isabel Suzanne Miller. Dad's name was Joseph William Darnell."

"That's right," I said, my heart beating fast. I was right. It was a story I remembered from my childhood, one I'd overheard Joe telling Daddy once on a ride. "Didn't he have a nickname . . . ?"

"He was called Will when he was a kid. Daddy told me that grand-mother Essie hated him being named after his father so she called him Will though his dad always insisted on calling him Joe. He went by

Will until his mother died when he was in his twenties. Then he just went by Joe. Probably to make his dad happy."

I nodded, trying to keep any expression off my face. "I can see why."

Victory Simpson *knew* Joe's childhood nickname. How in the world would she know something as personal as that if she hadn't ever met Joe Darnell, something she hadn't actually said, but did imply? What reasons could she have to hide their relationship? And could it possibly have anything to do with the bones Buck discovered?

CHAPTER 8

"Is SOMETHING WRONG?" SHAWNA ASKED A HALF HOUR LATER when she walked by me standing on the porch drinking a Coke. "You look worried."

I'd left her office in a hurry, afraid she'd see the confusion on my face. I took a long swig from my drink, buying me some time to think. "Just trying to figure out what I have time to do in the next two hours before I need to start preparations for dinner. Say, do you have any old family scrapbooks or photo albums that I could look through? There might be some interesting tidbits that I could work into my talk on pioneer quilts this evening. That would make it more personal for everyone and, hopefully, more memorable."

Her face lit up. "We do have some trunks full of papers and photos. Dad kept them here in the office. I've always meant to go through them myself and see if we could frame any of the pictures for that empty wall in the Murietta Room. I just haven't had time."

"Certainly understandable. If you'd like, I'll pull out the most western-looking photographs for you while I'm at it."

"That would be wonderful," she said, gesturing for me to follow her. Inside the ranch office she lead me to a door that opened to reveal a storage room. Inside, next to some boxes of office supplies, were about a half dozen pasteboard boxes, three old trunks, and a fly-specked metal file cabinet. "The history of my humble family," she said, holding out her hands.

A small window sat high on the wall and though the room was thick with dust, I decided not to open it. The room had a coldness that seemed to permeate the bare pine walls. Involuntarily, I gave a small shudder. Any body warmth I'd worked up while barrel racing was already being replaced by this bitter cold air.

"I have that portable space heater in the office," Shawna said. "You're welcome to use it."

"Don't you need it?" Her office wasn't very warm either. As common to a rancher, her dad had spent more money on the areas seen by the public and needed by the animals than the ones used by the owners.

"No, I'm through with office work for today. I'm going over to the north pasture see how Rawhide is doing." Rawhide was Joe's prize Black Angus bull. She told me that whenever she missed her dad, she went out and talked to the bull. "After that I'm going to help Maria with the rooms. She's been working awfully hard with this many people here. Then I'm calling the band about the dance Saturday night."

"Emory and Elvia will arrive sometime Friday afternoon. She's bringing a bunch of books with Western themes that she'll be talking about before Meg Matthews' poetry reading." Meg Matthews was a local cowgirl poet who'd published two books and was a popular performer every year at San Celina's Cowboy Poetry Festival.

"I love her poetry," Shawna said. "It was so nice of Elvia to contact her and arrange for this reading. So much is going on this weekend. I hope we can keep up." She started chewing the tip of her red pencil, her eyes blinking rapidly.

"We'll be fine. There's not much to do with Isaac's class. He's always organized, but I'll ask him if he needs anything. It starts at 8 A.M. on Saturday. Are we set for the continental breakfast we're serving his students?"

"Yes, that's what I was talking to the Worleys about. Rich is making cinnamon rolls and needed extra butter, milk, and cream. Though people were told to bring their own lunches, we're providing coffee, tea, or lemonade as well as apples and cookies for an afternoon snack. And there'll be coffee, punch, and cookies served at the dance."

I groaned with pleasure. "Rich's cinnamon rolls are killer. I'll get up early Saturday to make sure and snag one before they all disappear. The continental breakfast will be where?"

"Original plans are the Cowboy Garden unless it rains. Then we'll have to set up in the Annie Oakley Room."

"That covers all the bases then." I looked down at the trunks, unable to control my eagerness. "History beckons."

"Have fun," she said, her tone dubious.

"Are you kidding? Put a history buff in the middle of this and let her go? You'll probably have to send a search party for me."

After she left, I moved the space heater to a place in the center of the storage room, then closed the thick wood door between the office and the room. No use wasting what little heat it generated. I turned on the one overhead light and sat down on one of the trunks.

For the first time in days I was totally alone in a quiet place. I sat for a moment and just enjoyed the silence and the warmth radiating from the heater's coils. My mind went back to what I discovered . . . or thought I'd discovered . . . about Victory. It was too much of a coincidence that she'd accidentally call Joe by his old nickname. She definitely had some sort of connection or acquaintance with Joe Darnell. The question was what? And how would I find out without screwing up the quilt retreat?

Then there was that other dilemma—should I tell Gabe? Keeping things from each other had always been a sore spot in our still fledgling marriage. It was one of those places in our relationship where we still hadn't worked out the kinks, come to a satisfactory compromise that suited both of us. He wouldn't tell me about his work and I stubbornly, and I'll admit, sometimes childishly, held things back from him. So, what would it be this time?

After some thought, I decided to wait. Not because I didn't trust him, but because I truly didn't have anything of substance to tell him and I didn't want him to start looking at Victory as a potential criminal, something I knew he just couldn't help but do. Better to keep it to myself until I was certain about what I actually knew and what was just suspicion. After all, Victory's connection with Joe might be something perfectly innocent. And even if it wasn't, even if Victory and Joe had an affair, there was no reason to believe it had anything to do with the bones Buck found. Right now, Shawna didn't need any extra heartache in her life.

When I opened the first trunk, the pit of my stomach jumped with excitement. I'd loved history, especially personal, family histories, since the first time Dove read me *Little House in the Big Woods* by Laura Ingalls Wilder. And the history of San Celina County and its early pioneers was especially interesting to me, maybe because I envied them their lengthy connection with this land I loved so much. Since I only had a few hours, I decided to give a quick look through all three trunks, the file cabinet, and the boxes to see what was what. That way I could see if there was anything I could use tonight and if there was anything I could save for a future date.

Already I was getting the germ of an idea for an exhibit at the folk art museum, a photograph gallery of old pictures taken in San Celina County and the same places seen today through the eyes of the photographers and possibly other artists in our co-op. There were lots of old photographs in the historical museum we could borrow. It could even be a joint show with part of it at the folk art museum, part at the old Carnegie library which was now the San Celina Historical Museum. I'd run it by Dove this evening. If we could get Isaac to take some of the new shots, and I was sure we could, that would provide the celebrity factor needed to garner publicity in the Los Angeles and San Francisco newspapers.

I shook my head. Enough of planning the future. I had more current calves to catch. In twenty minutes I'd figured out that the metal file cabinet held the ranch's old records; the trunks a variety of knickknacks, clothing, and memorabilia from local rodeos including the annual Parkfield Ranch Rodeo; and most of the boxes held ancient spurs, bits, and worn pieces of bridle. Two boxes were filled with photographs. With the last box I really scored. It produced a musty-smelling log cabin quilt that had definitely seen better days, but would be perfect for my talk.

By the predominance of dark, small-printed fabrics—indigo blue, black with some bright overlay patterns of rust, dull mustard, and pink, deep cranberry reds and some geometric brown and pink prints—and an extremely wide sashing, I guessed the quilt was made before the 1920s. Could it possibly have been made by Shawna's Grandma Darnell? Or maybe even her great-grandmother, who I'd just read was originally from West Virginia? I set it aside and hurried through the photographs, trying to find one that pictured the quilt. I also put aside any photos showing people I recognized like her father or David Hardin. Everyone would get a kick out of seeing David when he was a dashing young cowboy. I was hoping he'd enjoy being the center of attention for a little while. While I was going through the boxes, a small part of me was hoping I'd find a photograph of Victory Simpson.

I struck pay dirt at the bottom of one of the pasteboard boxes, though not in terms of clearing up the mystery involving Victory. It was a crinkle-edged photograph of the original adobe ranch house, where Shawna and Johnny now lived. A line of people perched across the front porch like sparrows on a telephone wire. Hung over the porch railing, obviously getting aired out, was the same Log Cabin quilt sitting on the box next to me and another one made of dozens of small, five-pointed stars. Perfect for my talk.

Glancing at my watch, I realized it was past five o'clock and dark. I'd have to hustle to set the tables by six o'clock.

I gathered up about thirty snapshots and the quilt and turned off the heater. Closing the storage door behind me, it occurred to me that I had the office to myself. Why didn't I think of it earlier? This might be my only chance to call Daddy privately and see if he could shed any light on Shawna and Whip. If anyone would have known about Victory having a relationship with Joe, it would be Daddy.

❖

"HEY, PUMPKIN," HE SAID, ACCEPTING MY COLLECT CALL. "HOW'RE things going? Sure wish I could be there."

"I do too," I said. "How are you feeling? How's Scout?"

"Now, both me and your puppy are doing just fine. My leg itches like the dickens, but we're having a fine time eating Dove's casseroles and watching some of those shows where people fight on television, call each other all manner of names. Is it me or are people just getting plain nuttier?"

"You must be desperate," I said, laughing. Daddy had never watched daytime television for as long as I could remember.

"Nah," he said, chuckling. "I have been taking it easy, but I'm about ready to go nuts just sitting here."

"Just give it time," I said. "I thought I'd give you a call and let you know what's going on here at Broken Dishes." I quickly told him what happened on the trail ride, about Buck finding the bones, and about the sheriff's department's part in the investigation.

"Doesn't that beat anything you ever heard?" he said when I was finished. "They have no idea who it is?"

"Not yet. I'm not sure how long the forensic stuff takes."

"What's Gabe think?"

"He pretty much staying out of it. Not his jurisdiction so not his problem, to quote him directly. He came up today."

"Thought he wasn't coming until tomorrow."

"He missed me," I just said, leaving it at that.

"So, other than the bones y'all found, is everything else going all right?"

"Pretty much. I do have a question for you though. Have you ever met Victory . . . uh . . . Victoria Simpson?"

"Who?" His voice sounded genuinely confused.

That answered that question.

"How about Garland Simpson?"

"Don't believe I've ever met anyone with that name. Why?"

"Just trying to piece together some things here. I'll explain it all when I come back to San Celina."

"Okay," he said, not pressing me for details.

The one thing I'd always appreciated about my father was he never forced you to talk when you didn't feel like it. It wasn't that he wasn't interested, he was just extremely private and respected other people's privacy too. That's why I hesitated before asking the next question.

"Daddy, did you know that Shawna and Whip . . ." I paused a moment. I wasn't about to use the words "hooked up" with my dad. "Uh, dated?"

There was a long silence on the phone. Then he cleared his throat. "Joe might have mentioned it."

"What did he think about it?"

Another long silence. This type of talk was hard for my dad, especially now that Joe has passed away. "He wasn't crazy about it, but he stayed out of his daughter's love life. Mostly. Like I always have yours."

"Mostly?"

"He did mention it once to me that he spoke with Whip, told him that he felt Shawna was a bit too young for him."

"Did he say how Whip took it?"

"Said he didn't react. But they broke up soon after that."

"So did Joe think Whip broke up with her?" That's not the impression I got, even though Shawna implied it was mutual. It was obvious to me that Whip still had feelings for her.

"He didn't say. Guess I just assumed that he did. She started going with Johnny shortly after that, and Joe was thrilled. Johnny's young and brash, but Joe thought he was better for Shawna in the long run."

"Did he say that?"

"Didn't have to."

I knew what he meant. It was that nonverbal, but very pointed way that Western men and Western women had of communicating. It drove Dove wild sometimes because she still was a Southern woman at heart and thus wore her heart and all her opinions on her very prominent sleeve. In that way, I was a lot more like Dove than many of our taciturn ranchwomen friends, which often made it hard to communicate.

"One more question and I'll let you get back to your crazy TV shows," I said. "Why do you think Whip was left out of Joe's will? I mean, I know Shawna was his blood daughter, but Whip worked for him for a long time."

There was another long silence where I could tell Daddy was trying to decide how to word his reply. "Well, Joe bailed Whip out of a lot of financial situations. Maybe he thought that was enough of an inheritance."

"Was Whip known for being wild?" I pressed.

"Wild enough," was all Daddy would say. His voice told me that was all I was going to get on the subject.

"You take care of yourself," I said. "Hug Scout for me."

"You be careful. Tell that husband of yours to watch out for you."

I laughed. "No one has to tell him that, Daddy."

"I reckon not," he said with a chuckle.

I stood there a moment, looking at the phone. That took care of that end. Obviously, if Victory had been friends with Joe it was either before Daddy's acquaintance with him or it was a secret. Or, a nasty little voice said to me, maybe your daddy didn't tell you everything, not the first time that's happened. I shoved the little voice back, not wanting to consider that possibility.

Was Victory and Joe's relationship also a secret from Garland? How in the world would Victory and Joe had even met? They definitely didn't run in the same circles. There had to be a way for me to find out.

At least Daddy did shed a little more light on the situation between Shawna and Whip. Why would Whip torture himself by staying here? That had to be painful watching Johnny every day not only being with the woman Whip loved, but owning the ranch Whip possibly thought of as his own.

Outside the office, the weather had become misty with the coming rain scenting the air with that thick, earthy scent that every rancher and farmer loved, especially out here in the dry northeast section of the county.

On my way back to my room with the box of photographs and the quilt, I looked across the patio to a small vine-covered gazebo near the built-in swimming pool. The pool was covered for the winter so not many people lingered down near the gazebo. But a movement caught my eye and I stared for a moment, trying to see who was rendezvousing at the gazebo.

The figures moved and I caught a glimpse of them. To my surprise, it wasn't Rita, whom I vaguely suspected to be out there. It was David Hardin and, even more surprising, Marty Brantley, the widowed quilter from Tustin. Why in the world were they skulking about? How did they know each other?

I forced myself to stop staring and hurried toward my cabin. Except for my cousin, Rita, for whom I felt personally responsible since I brought her here, the relationships of the guests or the employees on this ranch were really none of my business. Still, with the bones of a likely murdered person up on the hill and now this question about Victory and Joe's possible relationship, I couldn't help but look at everything and everyone with a suspicious eye. I laughed to myself. Lord help me, the longer I was married to Gabe, the more I thought like him—that old cop belief, there are victims and there are criminals and nothing in between. I left the two manila envelopes of photos and the quilt on my bed then headed for the kitchen.

"What's cooking, Señor Trujillo?" I asked, tying on an apron and putting a stack of napkins on the serving cart stocked with glasses, plates, and silverware. "Where's my illustrious partner in waiting?"

He didn't turn around, knowing how I was going to react. "She said to go ahead and start without her. She had some phone calls to make."

I inhaled deeply, wanting to scream, but said instead with a false cheeriness, "Okay, is Sam around?"

"Right here," Sam said, coming out of the pantry carrying a big can of green peppers.

"You'll have to help me serve. Otherwise the guests won't get their food while it's hot. Speaking of food, what're we serving tonight?"

Rich turned around and gave me a rueful grin. "The menu cards are over on the counter." He pointed behind me with his spatula.

> *Traditional Caesar salad*
> *Swiss steak with mushroom gravy*
> *Herbed red potatoes with baby onions*
> *Tomato-cucumber medley*
> *Carnival cornbread*
> *German chocolate cake*
> *California fruit platter*

"Sounds fabulous, as always," I said, adding coffee cups to the cart. "You could open a restaurant."

"No way," Rich said. "This is fun, but by the time this gig is up, I'll be ready to turn in my spatula and eat someone else's cooking."

"Are we going to have a Mexican night?" I asked. Rich's Mexican food was famous among his friends, especially his white enchiladas.

"Tomorrow night, *mija*. I'll be burning chilies until midnight."

"I'll come help if I can. I'll try and rope Gabe into helping too. Right after my talk on pioneer quilts."

"Don't worry, Sam's helping me. Hey, what's Gabe really doing here early?" Rich said over his shoulder as he tossed the bowl of Caesar greens. "I thought he wasn't due until tomorrow."

I started setting salad plates on the serving cart. "Just decided to take a little extra time off to relax."

Next to me, Sam let out a loud laugh. "My dad? Did someone slip some downers into his nonfat latte?"

"No," I said, not elaborating and not looking at him.

Rich turned around, a spark of comprehension on his face. "Oh, I get it now. He's not relaxing, my dear little Samuel. He's here to protect his lady."

"What?" Sam said, his thick eyebrows bunched together in confusion.

I felt my cheeks turn warm. "Oh, hush. He's just being an overly jealous, macho Latino man, which both of you should understand without any effort at all."

"Who's he protecting you from?" Sam asked, still confused.

"No one." I flashed an warning look at Rich. His brown eyes laughed in reply. "Find an apron, Sam, and let's get these tables set."

Though I still felt awkward waiting on Gabe and Hud, I decided it was better for me to deal with them than Sam, so I assigned him the quilters and the hunters. Both groups would appreciate his congenial personality. If anyone could charm our secret travel columnist, it would be Sam.

And, I'd decided when I was serving the Caesar salads, whether Shawna protested or not, I was going to insist she start docking Rita's pay for the meals she missed serving.

The employee table was full and the conversation, thankfully, lighter than normal. Hud didn't show up, though his grandfather did. Iry kept the table laughing at his adventures running a restaurant with his cousin, Varise. Apparently Varise still owned King Varise's Cajun Palace and Dance Hall in Baton Rouge, Louisiana and personally greeted every customer who walked in the door.

As I served, I couldn't help wondering what had kept Hud from dinner. Something new about the bones?

"You look like you're plotting something," Gabe whispered when I served him dessert.

"Why, suh," I said in my most sugary, Southern accent. "Whatevah do you mean?"

"Whatever it is, forget it," Gabe said, automatically.

"Eat your cake, cookie," I replied.

After Sam and I had cleaned up the tables and he was starting on the dishes, I went back to my room to get my notes on pioneer quilts.

When I passed by the stables, I saw why Rita had missed her stint at dinner. She and Chad were in a very physically involved lip lock. I almost said something, but decided that if Rita wanted to get back at Skeeter by cheating with Chad, there wasn't much I could do about it. I would, however, make the point to her that she did agree to serve meals at a certain time and she should honor that agreement.

At the cabin I picked up my notes for my pioneer quilt talk as well as the log cabin quilt I found in the trunk. On my way to the lodge, I stopped off in the Cowboy Garden where I could sit for a moment on a bench under the oak tree at the back and gather my thoughts.

The ominous clouds had partially cleared away revealing a brilliant three-quarter winter moon. Stars crowded the indigo sky, like handfuls of diamonds casually tossed into the darkness. The Western sculptures in the garden, made by David Hardin using rusty horseshoes, tractor parts, old parts of bits and spurs, took on a stark, surreal look, almost like, any moment, they'd start moving on their own. I pulled my flannel-lined Wrangler jacket closer around me and stood up. Just as I did, one of the side doors to the lodge opened and Kitty Katz, the woman from Long Island, stepped out. Instinctively I moved back into the shadow of the trees so she couldn't see me. She wrote a few lines in a palm-sized notebook, looked back at the door she just come through and then headed toward the cabins.

Had I just witnessed The Secret Traveler? I'd suspected Kitty from the beginning. She seemed very self-assured and well-traveled. I prayed that whatever she wrote down was good. Though my first instinct was to tell Shawna, after some thought I decided it might be better if Kitty wasn't given special treatment, that doing so might actually adversely affect her review. After all, she was probably not just watching how she was treated, but how everyone was treated. I shook my head as I walked back to the lodge. There wasn't a full moon tonight, but everyone sure was acting like there was. There was so much unexplained skulking about this place that it was beginning to seem like a Mel Brooks movie.

Inside the lodge, the men were gathered around the pool table, some of the quilters were doing handwork and talking, some were working on a two-thousand piece jigsaw puzzle and the domino tournament was in full, very loud swing. Dove called a time-out when she spotted me and gestured at me to follow her into the hallway.

"Where have you been?" she said, her voice sounding like one of Socrates' hisses.

"Around. How's the game going?"

She glanced over her shoulder, her eyes darting like a lizard's. "I need you to be a guard. Sure as my name is Ramsey, that Sissy is cheating and I'm going to catch her at it."

"How do you know she's cheating?" I asked, glancing at my watch. I had fifteen minutes before my talk. Getting tangled up in trying to spot a domino cheat was not in my immediate plans. "And your name is Lyons now."

"Quit sassing me. She's winning too often. We know she's doing something, but we just don't know what."

"Maybe she's hidden dominos up her sleeve," I said, laughing.

She wagged her finger at me. "Missy, this is not a laughing matter. She's being a bad Christian witness and we need to call her on it. Why, she's a disgrace to Baptists everywhere."

"I've always wondered why it's okay for Baptists to play dominos and not poker," I asked, hoping to divert her attention.

"I play poker," she said.

"I know *you* do, but it's not okay generally speaking. Why is that? And what's with the thing against dancing? Didn't King David dance before the Lord? Naked, if I remember correctly."

She waved her hands in front of me. "Quit trying to change the subject. And he wasn't naked. He wore a loin cloth. Can you at least stand in the vicinity and see if she's doing anything fishy?"

"Ten minutes tops. Then I have to give my talk."

"Okay," she said, following me back into the great room, her hand firmly pushing me between the shoulder blades. "Keep those peepers open."

I watched Sissy like a starving hawk and, honestly, couldn't tell if she was doing anything remotely illegal. But, then, I was a novice domino player. If there was any problem it was that the ladies talked and laughed so much that it would be easy to slip an unwanted domino or two into or out of the bone pile, which was sitting closer to Sissy than I would have allowed under the circumstances.

"Anyone interested in hearing about pioneer quilts come on into the TV room," I announced. All of the quilt ladies and two of the men joined me and Shawna. Laughter from the pool table filtered across the room to us. It became ominously quiet among the domino ladies.

"FOR OUR PIONEER MOTHERS," I STARTED, "THERE WERE NO QUILT retreats or design schools or fancy books with colored photographs to teach them how to design and make quilts. Yet many of them learned to quilt and quilted regularly as part of their preparation for moving West. Most of them used simple, geometric patterns that had been passed down to them from their mothers and grandmothers. Sometimes, a particularly artistic quilter, bored with using the same, well-known patterns, would turn to her physical environment to create new pattern designs. She might use the flowers, trees, weather, or animals and birds seen along the trail West as well as the new ones she experienced after settling in the new land. Quilt historians speculate that these women's experiences and how they perceived them is how we got patterns like Wild Goose Chase, Hole in the Barn Door, Churn Dash and, of course, Oregon Trail, and Road to California. These pioneer quilters often didn't try to copy their physical environment exactly, but as budding abstract artists, they imitated the rhythms of pattern and color found in the markings of for example, a hawk's feather, petal of a California poppy, the rings of a fallen oak tree.

"Quilting was both a physical necessity for these women, since one of their primary jobs was to provide warm covers and clothing for their families, but also a means of artistic expression, something denied most pioneer women, especially those of modest means. The quilts owned and made by pioneer women were also a way of maintaining ties with loved ones they'd left behind at a time when photographs were not common for the everyday person. Letters could take months to arrive, so when a pioneer woman especially missed her mother or sisters or dear friends she could touch and gaze upon her quilts, often memory quilts made by her family and friends, and recall her earlier life.

"It really is amazing that any quilts survived the hard trip West. They were used as outside bedding, to line the insides of covered wagons and, sadly, often as burial shrouds. But obviously these quilts were cherished and, apparently, they were also very durable, much like the women themselves. Quilts were an intricate part of these women's lives touching every part: birth, marriage, illness, and death. Those early pioneers were often optimistic and adventurous people who embraced change and purposefully chose to break away from loved ones and seek a new life. But many of the women who traveled west did so reluctantly, following the men they loved, leaving behind with some regret, their extended families and beloved communities. Quilts helped ease that transition and also provided a way to become acquainted with other women along the trail and in their new home. By 1890 almost a million women had settled the trans-Mississippi West and many of them were quilters. Though men conquered the West by clearing land for farms, laying down railroad tracks, and literally building towns in the middle of nowhere, it was the women's expertise at quilting and sewing that clothed the men and kept them warm as they built the new land.

"Pioneer quilts are the most anonymous of the arts practiced by women throughout the ages. Not many were signed and even fewer had the stories behind their making recorded in a letter or diary entry. Most of the time we are lucky just to identify the period the quilt was made by comparing patterns and fabrics to other quilts of that era. The quilters' names and stories are lost to history. But their art and vision live on to inspire future quilters and encourage them to embrace their passion, their dreams, and their future."

After the talk, I showed some of the quilts loaned to me by the San Celina Historical Museum, as well as the Log Cabin quilt I found in the trunk. Shawna was especially touched by that quilt and was thrilled I'd found it. We all laughed at the pictures of a young David Hardin. He would, without a doubt, be in for some razzing from the ladies tomorrow.

Around eight o'clock Rich came through the kitchen door pushing a wooden tea cart carved with local cattle brands. It had become a nightly ritual that the guests really seemed to enjoy, hot tea or coffee and some kind of delicious delicacy. Tonight it was bite-sized peach turnovers and tiny oatmeal and chocolate chip cookies.

As Rich ceremoniously poured tea into thick, white mugs decorated with the Broken DIS brand, even the men at the pool table wandered over. Gabe sat in a corner easy chair reading a book on the history of branding.

"Hey, Friday," I said, going over to perch on the chair's padded arm. "What's cooking?"

He set his book down on the floor. "Not much. Sorry I missed your talk. Had to check in with Jim and catch up on what was happening."

"Anything exciting going on in San Celina while we're out here in the wild, wild west?"

"Everything's quiet. I have to be back Monday to interview two new dispatchers and I also have a lunch with the new sheriff."

"Should I be jealous?" I asked, laughing. San Celina's new sheriff was a woman, a very attractive woman in her mid-forties who'd worked for the Yuma, Arizona county sheriff's department for twenty years.

"Not a bit," he said.

Shawna came over holding two mugs of tea. "Right one's got caffeine in it," she said. "The other one is herbal mint."

"Caffeine," I said reaching for the right one. "And I'd better grab some of those cookies before this crowd inhales them all."

Shawna sat down on the chair across from us. "A reporter from the *Tribune* came by during dinner."

"Oh, no," I said. Shawna wasn't at dinner, but that hadn't alarmed me. I assumed she was trying to sneak a little private time with Johnny.

Gabe shook his head. "Never takes long for the vultures to arrive."

"What?" Shawna said, laughing nervously.

"He hates journalists," I said. "Who was the reporter?" Maybe it was someone I went to school with and could influence into softening the story, perhaps running it in the newspaper's back pages.

She thought for a moment. "It was a woman. Someone named Belle or Nell. Something like that."

"Belle Ryan," I said. "Dang." I had gone to school with her and we'd never liked each other. And she'd never forgiven me when my cousin, Emory, blew into town a couple of years ago and started work at the *Tribune*. Everyone had loved him, always the case with Emory, and she'd personally held it against me. She was never kind to Gabe in any of the stories concerning the police department. "She's a bulldog. What did you tell her?"

"Not much because I don't know anything." Her eyes blinked rapidly. "But she started questioning me about Dad, just like the detective. Why is everyone so ready to blame my dad for this?"

"It's not personal," Gabe said in a gentle voice. "At least not with the detective. He's just doing his job the way he's been trained."

I glanced at Gabe in surprise. He was defending Hud? That was a first.

"As for the reporter," he continued. "I've dealt with Belle Ryan. Just be careful what you tell her, answer yes or no, don't give long explanations. And *don't* give her free access to the ranch."

Shawna nodded. "I did ask her not to bother the guests. But when she left my office, she completely ignored my request and tried to go over to the dining room. Whip stopped her and made her leave."

"Good," Gabe said. "Tell her that if she wants to talk to you, she'll have to do it by phone. It's best to keep a tight rein on journalists."

"I'll do that." She looked over at me. "What's on your agenda for tomorrow?"

I blew on my tea to cool it. "Thought I'd see if any of the quilters were up for another ride. Maybe one not so filled with intrigue this time."

Shawna grimaced. "That's for sure. Have you heard anything else from Detective Hudson about the bones? I haven't seen him since lunch."

I looked down into my pale-brown tea. "The detective's keeping his thoughts to himself."

Shawna glanced at Gabe with a question in her eyes.

"Sorry," Gabe said. "He wouldn't tell me even if he knew something."

She sighed. "I just wish the whole mess would go away. Not to mention the detective himself. I mean, he's nice and all, and his grandfather is a real sweetheart, but just having him here worries me. I'm afraid the guests will start to feel like they're being spied on."

Which they are, I thought.

"If they have nothing to hide, it shouldn't matter to them," Gabe said in his practical way.

"I suppose," Shawna said, her voice doubtful.

"Was there anything you particularly wanted me to do tomorrow?" I asked.

"Actually, there is. Johnny and I decided this evening that we really need to sell Rawhide."

"Oh, I'm sorry," I said, knowing how hard it must be for her to sell the bull her father had prized.

"Dad spent too much money on him, but he was registered and has a great bloodline. We were hoping to improve the quality of our cattle, maybe advertise it as gourmet beef, make it a selling point for the guest ranch. But even though Rawhide's bloodline is good, he's too unpredictable, and we sure don't need any more unpredictable things in our life right now." She met my eyes directly. No tears this time. It was a choice between the bull her dad loved and the ranch he loved. "And we need the money," she said bluntly.

"You have a buyer?"

"He's coming tomorrow morning with a trailer. We've had offers ever since Dad died and I've fought them off, but now . . ." She let her voice trail off. Then she straightened her shoulders. "Rawhide's up in the pasture behind that bend on Condor Flats Road. You know, where the old man rock is."

I nodded. The profile of the rock looked like an old man with a fat bottom lip. "I'd be glad to help bring him down if Whip or Bunny needs my assistance."

"I'm sure they'll be glad to take you up on that offer. He's pretty rambunctious." She looked far more tired than someone her age should.

"Is there anything else we can do to help you?" I asked her softly.

She bit her lip, then gave a tremulous half-smile. "Solve this mystery and get rid of you-know-who."

"You mean Inspector Clouseau?" Gabe said.

"Gabe!" I said, gently smacking the back of his head. Still, I couldn't help laughing.

"Ow!" he said, with a big grin on his face.

"Who?" Shawna said.

"Dumb French detective in the Pink Panther movies," I said. "Long before your time."

She shook her head, not certain how to react.

"Everything will turn out okay," I said, though I wasn't sure of it at all.

"I hope so," she said. "Guess I'll go check with Rich and see if he's all set for tomorrow. Then I'll call it a day."

After she left, I leaned close to my husband's ear, nipped it and said, "Gabriel Thomas Ortiz, you are a bad, bad boy."

"Sweetheart, you don't know the half of it," Gabe said, taking my hand and kissing the soft inside of my wrist.

CHAPTER 9

"I HATE THIS," GABE SAID LATER, WALKING ME BACK TO MY cabin. "You are always getting us involved with things that keep us physically apart." Though it was not even nine o'clock and half the guests were still having fun, both Gabe and I decided to turn in early since we'd both been up since 5 A.M.

"Not on purpose," I said. "Keep in mind we're doing a good deed. I'm sure this is good for a rhinestone or two on your heavenly crown."

He grabbed my hand and pulled me around the corner of the cabin, out of the pale yellow porch light.

"*Mi amor,*" he whispered before covering his lips with mine.

"Friday," I said, after a few minutes. "You are definitely the best cop I've ever kissed."

"I'd better be the best man you've ever kissed."

I leaned back in his arms and ran my finger across his damp bottom lip. His thick black mustache tickled my skin. "Cool down that Ferrari libido, Chief. I have a busy day tomorrow and you do too, so we'd better get some sleep. Doesn't Bunny want you to work with Jet again?"

"Yes. It was great today. He's a beautiful animal."

"We'll see how you feel tomorrow. I bet you'll hurt in places you didn't know existed."

"I'll feel fine. He's just a horse."

I kissed him one last time. "That's the macho Mexican man I love and adore. To the bunkhouse with you, Pancho Villa. Take a cold shower."

"With how much hot water my son uses, that's a strong probability," he grumbled.

"Then you'd better beat him to it. See you in the morning. There's a rumor that biscuits and gravy are on the breakfast menu."

"Good, if I can't have sex, biscuits and gravy are almost as good."

"Well, that's a fine sentiment. I'm that easily replaced by flour, milk, and bacon fat? Whatever happened to that health nut I married?"

"He lives in manifest denial five days a week. The other two days he is wickedly and irresistibly influenced by his adorable junk-food-addicted little *esposa*."

I laughed and went inside the cabin.

It was fairly early, so I was surprised to find Rita snoring away. Why she was tired enough to be sleeping before 9 P.M. considering she hadn't even served dinner was something I didn't understand and didn't want to ponder for too long. Lindsey's door was closed so I assumed she'd turned in also since I hadn't seen her since she'd been questioned by Hud early this evening.

After puttering around for a half hour, brushing my teeth and straightening up the cabin's living room, I still wasn't sleepy, so I decided to take a walk, hoping the fresh air would relax me.

Outside, the three-quarters moon had slipped behind some clouds and except for the pale yellow lights on each cabin's porch, it was dark in that way it can only be this far away from civilization. The crickets and the frogs were playing dueling banjos tonight and in the distance, a coyote yip reverberated through the hills, a reminder that we were the intruders here, not them.

I walked out past the stables and barn to the shadowy parking lot. From where I stood, I could see the trailhead leading up to where the bones had been discovered. The hill was dark and silent. Obviously the sheriff's department had either left for the night or finished their investigation. I'd check with Shawna in the morning and see if the trail was open for use.

Back at the stables, I quietly let myself in. The familiar burnt-butter smell of damp hay, grassy manure, musty wood, and warm horses never failed to calm me deep in my soul. The horses snuffled and moved in their stalls, nickering softly to each other, aware that some-one had entered their domain. In a few minutes they would settle down, once they sensed that I didn't bring danger with me. But it would take was one horse to become frightened, then they all would panic, herd animals down to their very core.

Not so much different from humans when you think about it. If you kept the alpha horse calm, they all stayed calm. In a way, that's what we were trying to do at the ranch. Keep the staff calm and the guests would stay calm and have a good time. Hard to do, though, when those bones literally and emotionally lingered above us.

"Hey, boy," I said, reaching my hand into Gumby's stall. Bunny's nine-year-old bridle horse sniffed at my hand, looking for a cookie, then consented to let me scratch between his ears. He was a chestnut gelding, with a star and connecting strip of white on his face. Though sometimes snorty, he was mostly bluff. He had the kindest eyes of any horse I'd ever known. His personality reminded me more than a little of my husband. Next to him, Jet nickered and kicked his stall door. He also reminded me of Gabe in more ways than looks. The horse needed a good, long ride to work the kinks out of him. Gabe would certainly have his hands full with him tomorrow.

"Hey, darlin'. Couldn't sleep?"

My stomach lurched in surprise at the sound of Hud's throaty voice. I turned to see him standing at the stable entrance. The moon had slipped back out from behind the clouds illuminating his white Stetson and solid frame. Fragmented shadows hid his face until he stepped inside the stable, lit dimly by a single sixty-watt light-bulb.

"Just saying good-night to the horses," I said. "What're you still doing here?"

He walked up to me, his hands stuck deep into his fleece-lined jacket, his face shadowed again. "They finished work at the crime scene an hour ago. Went over to tell Shawna the trail could be used again."

"Good. What were the investigator's conclusions?" I asked in a casual voice.

"Nice try, ranch girl," he said placidly. "But it's confidential."

I frowned at him, frustrated. "You told me about your suspicions that it was a homicide. Why so secretive now?"

"I had a weak moment. Did you keep it to yourself?"

"Of course I did. Well, I told Gabe."

His mouth twisted into a half smile. "Of *course* you did."

"So what happens now?"

He pushed his hat back slightly, making his face more visible. "They'll take the remains back to the lab and start testing. We'll find out preliminary results in a few days."

I bent over and picked up a lead rope lying on the ground and laid it over a empty stall door. The horses snorted and complained, aware that there were now two humans invading their domain. "I just hope that the newspapers don't make a big thing out of it. Shawna said there was a reporter nosing around this evening."

He tilted his head. "You couldn't expect it to be a secret forever. Joe Darnell was a prominent figure in San Celina County. Quite beloved from what people tell me."

"He was a wonderful man."

"Maybe."

His cynical tone instantly made me angry. "Joe didn't have anything to do with those bones."

Hud's shoulders moved inside his jacket in what appeared to be a shrug. "We don't know that yet. Wouldn't be the first time a man showed one face to the world and was an entirely different person in private. I've met serial killers who would give their last bite of food to a stray dog."

"You don't know anything about Joe Darnell! He . . . he . . ." My voice stammered, which embarrassed me and made me even angrier. "He was a good man."

Hud's voice softened. "Look, I'm sorry, but you have to admit you aren't exactly impartial. Joe Darnell was your daddy's best friend and like family to you. To me, he's just another suspect."

"But not the only one," I said hotly. "There are other possibilities."

He stepped closer, his eyes interested. "Is that right? Like who?"

A chilly wind blew through the stable, causing me to shiver. Was I willing to point the finger at Victory simply because I wanted to protect Joe? She was likely innocent of anything except a clandestine relationship with Joe. Did I have the right to sic the police on her? Not, I felt, with what little I knew right now. As much as I wanted suspicion to move away from Joe, I didn't want to involve Victory until I knew more about their relationship. Besides, I hadn't even mentioned my suspicion to Gabe, so I wasn't about to spill it to Hud.

"I don't know," I said, throwing up my hands. "Just others. Maybe people who don't even live here anymore. Maybe those bones are a hundred years old."

"You're absolutely right," he said. "Or they could be ten or twenty years old. And it *could* be anyone. Take that Bunny lady. What do you really know about her anyway? Or how about David? He's lived here the longest. Or Whip. Or Chad. Or your friend, Rich. Or what about those quilters? They look like a suspicious bunch to me and pretty strong. If they can lift those heavy sewing machines, a man's body should be a cinch. Why, it could be Chief Ortiz, for all we know. I bet he has some nefarious things in his past. Or how about your own daddy? He was such good friends with Joe, how do you know he's not involved with those bones? How well do you know your own daddy, Benni Harper?"

Those last words froze me silent. It felt like a razor blade slashed my heart.

"You're an . . ." I started, then clamped my mouth shut. At that moment, if I'd been a man, I would have smashed my fist in his face.

He instantly became contrite. "Hey, I'm sorry, I didn't mean to open up any old wounds."

"You didn't," I said, my voice short.

"I know how fathers can sometimes . . ."

"Forget it."

He was quiet for a moment. In the darkness, I could hear my own breathing, a loud and thick thumping in my ears, a harsh, human sound among the horses' soft nickers.

"C'mon," he said. "Don't take it so personal. I was just throwing out ideas. All I want to find out is the truth. I thought the almighty truth meant something to you, what with you being so religious and all."

I took a deep breath and counted to five, knowing if I didn't, I'd say words I knew would come back to haunt me. "The truth does mean something to me. It means a lot. But so do people. Accusing people of crimes they might not have committed can ruin lives. You know as well as I do that some suspicion always sticks. Good night." I brushed past him and started for the doorway.

"Tell your cousin I had a fine time tonight," he called after me, obviously determined to have the last word.

I whipped around. "What?" Hud and Rita? What a frightening thought.

"I said . . ."

"I heard what you said and I can only hope you were kidding. One, because she is still a married woman, despite how she acts. Two, she's a lot younger than you and a lot more foolish, though that might be a incorrect assumption on my part. I would hope you wouldn't take advantage of her immaturity. And three, it would be highly unprofessional considering you're in the middle of an investi—"

"Hush, *chère*," he said, laughing. "I was just kidding. Just wanted to see you spit and hiss. Trust me, she's not my type, though she does resemble you more than a little. You on steroids, that is."

That stumped me for a moment. Was that an insult or a compliment?

"Look," he said. "As much as I'd like to, I can't make the killer be someone they're not. You must admit, Whip would look the most appropriate on a Wanted poster, but it would be more interesting if it were one of the quilters." He flashed me a big grin and held up his hands like he was framing a movie shot. "Picture the headlines. 'Brilliant Detective Sews Up Another Homicide.' "

"You know, this might be highly amusing to you, but everything Shawna and Johnny owns is tied up in this ranch. Unlike some people, they don't have a trust fund to fall back on." I was one of the few people who knew about Hud's abusive father who paid off his son with a ten-million-dollar payment.

His smiling mouth dropped into a frown as quickly as his hand fell to his side. "Low blow, ranch girl."

"Yeah, kind of like implying my father is a murderer."

We stared each other down, waiting for the other to crack.

"I was just kidding," he finally said, his expression turning neutral. "Where's your sense of humor?"

"I still refuse to believe Joe had anything to do with those bones." I wouldn't even talk about my father to him.

He settled his hat back down on his head. "That, Señora Ortiz, is your All-American, Mom-and-apple-pie, God-given right."

"Yes, it is." I started walking out of the barn.

"Benni," he called.

Though I wanted to keep walking, compulsively, I turned slowly around to face him.

He pointed at his cowboy hat. "As much as I irritate you, try to remember it's white, okay?"

AFTER THE MORNING SESSION, THOUGH THE QUILTERS WERE still a little nervous about taking another horseback ride, the Georgia cousins, bless their enthusiastic hearts, convinced everyone it would be fun. After promising them they'd actually feel less sore the more they rode, I also assured them we would be riding in the opposite direction of where the bones were found.

"Need another wrangler?" Bunny asked as she helped me saddle the horses.

"It's a flat, gentle ride so I think I'll be fine alone, though you're welcome to come if you've got the time. Also, Victory's coming on the ride and she's an experienced rider. We'll ride the mile and a half to Parkfield for lunch with a stop at the Parkfield cemetery. I thought they'd get a kick out of some of the old headstones."

She looked over at the ranch office. "Then I'd better stay here. There's still quite a bit of cleaning up to do on the barn for the dance this Saturday and I have to get things ready for next week's branding. I'm still of mixed feelings about whether we should actually brand or castrate any cattle while the guests are here. That might be a bit more of the wild west than they bargained for."

"You might be right. Maybe we should just do a cutting and reining demonstration. No blood and guts."

She wrinkled her brow and gave a half smile. "And no plastic kitchen bags of balls," she said, referring to the common method of sharing and taking home the infamous Western treat.

I grinned at her. "Yes, this group may not appreciate the finer culinary aspects of prairie oysters, though I imagine Rich would have no problem slicing them up, breading them, and frying them with a little salt, pepper, and Tabasco sauce. Did Shawna tell you I'd be glad to help you catch Rawhide?"

Bunny nodded. "We'll do it this afternoon after you get back from Parkfield. That easy ride should be just what Patrick needs to warm him up before some real work."

Our ride was decidedly less strenuous than a few days ago, giving me time along the way to point out things that I thought might interest them about this part of California, things they could take back with them as another memory of their ranch experience or even incorporate into their quilting designs. Victory rode Stormy, a good-natured sorrel gelding, and followed the group, something I appreciated since she was the only other experienced rider. Besides, if I was lucky, maybe I'd be able to manage to talk with her alone and she might say something that would substantiate my suspicions that she and Joe knew each other.

"Those fence posts are made of juniper," I said, pointing out the gray, scraggly-looking trunks strung with rusty barbed wire. "It might not be the most attractive fencing in the world, but it's cheap and it's strong, which is why ranchers like it. Some of those posts are probably a hundred years old."

The ladies murmured in appreciation. On the side trail to the Parkfield cemetery, I pointed out places in the brilliant green meadows where wild pigs liked to wallow, patches of early wildflowers like blue lupine, filiree, and wild mustard. We even spotted some flashes of bright orange poppies on a distant hillside.

"That's our state flower," I said, pointing to the narrow swatch of neon orange. "The California poppy. It's a very early blooming for it, but that place on the hill probably gets the morning sun and is protected from the wind."

At the cemetery, everyone dismounted and I tied the horses up to some cottonwood trees outside the rusty linked fence surrounding the grounds. I opened the gate fastener, fashioned from a rusty horseshoe.

"We've got about a half hour, ladies," I said, glancing at my watch. "We don't want to miss lunch."

After passing out the bottles of water and grave-rubbing supplies I'd packed in my saddlebags, I left them to wander around the weed-filled acres. Though I was tempted to go with them, I decided to stay with the horses, so I sat down under the biggest cottonwood tree. With my back against the cold trunk, I watched the ladies zigzag up and down the rows, throwing comments to each other over the crumbling, lichen-covered gravestones.

Karen and Kitty really got into doing the grave rubbings, while the others cruised the uneven pathways calling out to each other when they came across a particularly interesting stone.

"Listen here," one of the Georgia cousins called. "This one shows a cabin and some deer and it says, 'His Spirit is Free to Hike the Mountains. Mel Taylor.' His nickname was Bub."

"That's so sweet," another cousin called. "This one says, 'Leo B. Radcliffe—Saddler—1 Calif. Cav. March 27, 1939.' Wonder if that job exists in today's modern military?"

While they wandered, I checked the horse's cinches and saddles to make sure there wouldn't be any unforeseen accidents. Then I leaned against the trunk of the tree and checked my watch again. I could let the quilters linger another fifteen minutes, then we had to mount up again for the half mile ride to the Parkfield Inn.

"Oh, listen to this one," Karen called out. "It says 'He left the woodpile higher than he found it. Jerry Frederick.' "

"If that isn't the measure of a good man, I don't know what is," Marty called back.

During the spirited exchange Victory was strangely quiet. I watched her walk down the graveyard rows, her face intent, as if she were looking for something. Trying not to be obvious, I went from horse to horse, ostensibly checking their cinches and straightening their saddles.

Maybe it was my imagination, but she seemed pretty familiar with this cemetery. She didn't stop to linger over graves like the other women, but walked like she had a purpose, finally stopping at a stone surrounded by a dilapidated metal fence. She stared at it for a long moment, looked around and then moved on, acting interested in a gravestone that Karen and Kitty were photographing.

Who was buried there, and how could I see who it was without arousing her suspicion? Come back later after dark? That didn't sound appealing and I wasn't sure exactly how I could get away with it without arousing questions, especially from Gabe. But if I went over there right now, it would be too obvious. My mind started working on how I'd sneak away without anyone knowing. It seemed impossible. It was too far to walk in the dark, but if I saddled up a horse, Whip or someone would want to know why. I had to do it now. As casually as I could, I walked into the cemetery, pretending to mosey down the pathways, glancing at the headstones. When I reached the one Victory seemed interested in, I was a little disappointed.

"God's Precious Lamb" was all it said. It was obviously a child's grave. But there was no name, no date, nothing to indicate who was buried there. Why had she lingered in front of this particular grave? Maybe because she and Garland had never had children, this grave struck her more deeply. Was I just making the clichéd mountain out of a mole hill with Victory because I so desperately wanted someone else to suspect other than Joe? Or, remembering Hud's suggestion, my own father?

"Time to go, ladies," I called out. "Don't want to let the Parkfield Cafe give away our reservations."

My teasing comment made more sense to them once they saw the cafe. It was a rustic log-cabin structure whose casual nature would bring out the Western in any cowgirl, no matter how concrete her ranch. It was definitely not the type of place that took reservations.

The decor consisted of bear and deer heads on the walls as well as dozens of rusty brands and pictures of local ranches and the Parkfield Ranch rodeo as they looked back in the thirties. This was a popular spot for ranchers, car clubs, motorcycle enthusiasts, and anyone who loved a good steak sandwich and didn't mind a drive across open cattle country to buy it. The bar was the kind you could really belly up to, the wooden floor scarred by boots and numerous spurs. My own nickel-plated spurs made a clinky-clank sound that I still found appealing after all the years of hearing it. Good solid spurs and real leather boots makes any woman feel six feet tall. As Dove once told me, both should be a part of every woman's wedding trousseau.

After a spirited lunch, we took a quick peek at the Parkfield Inn. Then we took pictures under the BE HERE WHEN IT HAPPENS! sign referring to the mother-of-all-earthquakes they expected, as the scientists put it, "any time now." After the requisite time in the tiny gift shop next to the Inn, where the Georgia cousins bought enough geegaws to fill my saddlebags, we mounted up and headed back to the ranch.

After making sure the women were all doing okay on their mounts, I slowed down and rode beside Victory, casually asking, "Did you enjoy the cemetery?"

She kept her eyes on the trail. "Yes, I did. Cemeteries always inspire me. The designs on the gravestones often work their way into my patterns. Whenever I travel, I try to always check out the local cemeteries, especially the older ones."

"I know what you mean. I haven't spent a lot of time in the Park-field cemetery, but I know there are some interesting stones there."

She turned to look down at me, sitting slightly higher on Stormy who was a huge quarter horse with powerful haunches. His nickname was Jeep because he took hills like a four-wheel-drive vehicle. "I saw some patterns I found interesting today. They'll probably show up in a future quilt design." Her expression remained distant. Did she suspect I was watching her? Probably not if she was innocent.

Innocent. Guilty. Where was my mind? Internally, I shook myself like my dog Scout does after a bath. For cryin' out loud, I was reading too much into a simple excursion to a local cemetery. Even if Victory had been to this area before, had been to this cemetery, that wasn't enough to assume she had a thing to do with those bones up on the hill.

"It'll be beautiful, I'm sure," I said. "I'd better get back up to the front." I trotted around the ladies' meandering horses, giving Patrick his head. As we neared the ranch, he stepped up his pace knowing that dinner awaited. I shortened the reins a little, telling him to slow down. As lead horse, the others would pick up on his cue and I didn't want to end this leisurely ride with anyone unexpectedly tumbling off a horse overly-anxious to get to his or her grain bucket.

At the stables, I swung off, tied up Patrick and went over to help the ladies dismount.

"Would you like help unsaddling the horses?" Victory asked.

"No, thanks," I said. "That's my job. I see Sam over there. He can help me if I need it. You go ahead and do whatever you had planned."

She nodded and strolled off, her back straight and purposeful.

The whole time I unsaddled the horses I scolded myself. I was nuts to suspect this talented, personable woman of having anything to do with the murdered person up on the hill. Obsessive-compulsive. Pathetic, really. I mean, I really should concentrate on something else. On someone else. But what were my other options? Bunny, David? Hud's words echoed in my head. What did I really know about Bunny? I knew I liked her and that she was great with horses, plainspoken, and a good ranch manager. She was a widow. We'd talked about that. She and her late husband had owned a small ranch near Carson City, but medical bills caused her to have to sell it when he died. She had a son who sold tack for some company up in Reno. I knew she'd once ridden bareback broncs in the women's rodeo circuit. She and Joe met at a horse auction, not an unusual place for ranchers to meet.

Could she have come to the Broken Dishes with the plan of digging up those bones, covering up something in her past? If so, why wait until this weekend? She'd had a whole year of the ranch being almost deserted.

Thinking about David being involved was more than I wanted to put in my mind. He'd known Daddy as long as Joe had. Like Whip, he was as much a part of this ranch as the hundred-year-old juniper fence posts.

After finishing with the horses, I started toward the ranch offices, intending to report to Shawna about our ride. I was a few feet away when Johnny's angry voice bellowed out of the open office window.

"What else can go wrong?" he yelled, turning the air fifty shades of blue with his curses. "I can't believe that friggin' bull got out."

CHAPTER 10

"*J*OHNNY, PLEASE, CALM DOWN," SHAWNA SAID, TRYING TO pacify him. From where I stood, I could hear a thin tremor of emotion strangling her voice.

"What else can go wrong?" he repeated.

"It's that fence near Dead Horse Canyon," I heard Bunny say. "Whip and I fixed it a few weeks ago, but I've been telling you that whole quarter mile stretch needs to be completely replaced. It's good enough for the heifers, but I told you it wouldn't keep in a bull like Rawhide."

"We can't afford new fencing," Johnny snapped. "We can't afford shit." Bunny didn't answer, but I could imagine her irritated expression. Johnny had a long way to go in learning how to talk to people in a mature, business-like way.

Gabe came out of the back kitchen door and spotted me lurking near the office window. "What's going on?" he asked when he reached my side.

I answered in a low voice, "Rawhide has escaped and the buyer's coming for him tomorrow morning."

"Poor kids." He rested his hand underneath my ponytail, gently massaging my neck.

"We gotta find him today," Johnny said, his voice still loud. "We need that money and we don't need it tomorrow, we need it now. The feedman won't take our credit anymore. He wants cash."

"Don't you think I know that?" Shawna said, her voice sounding edgier. "There's the petty cash . . ."

"That's not enough!" Johnny snapped. "Dang it, this place is looking more like a circus every day. Why am I even wasting my time with this money pit?"

"Now, Johnny, calm down," David's firm voice said. I hadn't even realized he was in the office.

He was interrupted by Shawna, her voice hard and clear, the tremor replaced by a coldness that surprised me. "It might feel like a waste of time to you, but this is *my* inheritance, *my* history on the line. It means everything to me. *Everything.*"

"Everything?" Johnny said, his voice quieter now, but still hard. "More than us? More than me? *You* find the bull then."

He burst out of the office, ignoring Gabe and me and strode across the yard toward the parking lot. In minutes, he was in his pickup, barreling down the long driveway, trailing behind him a rooster tail of dust. Bunny came out of the office, her face stiff with anger, followed by Shawna, whose brown eyes were glossy with irritation and emotion. Behind her, David came out, his old face tired and troubled.

"Rawhide escaped from the pasture sometime early this morning . . . no one knew . . ." Shawna started. "We can't . . . Uh . . ." She gazed helplessly over at the tunnel of dust Johnny's pickup truck made as he drove away. "We . . . I mean, I need to . . ." She looked about ready to start sobbing. David came up behind her and put a comforting hand on her shoulder.

"Let's saddle up the horses," I broke in. "We can round up as many experienced riders as we can spare to hunt for him." I looked at my watch. "It's a quarter to three. We have a good two, maybe two and a half hours of daylight left. He couldn't have gotten too far." I crossed my fingers behind my back knowing that wasn't true. "We'll have him back here before dinner."

Bunny, Gabe, and David looked at me dubiously. But it was

Shawna's hopeful face that spurred my rash confidence. "If you can take my place serving dinner, Shawna," I continued, "this can be taken care of before Johnny comes back from town."

"You really think so?" she asked.

"Yes," I said. "But we can't waste time talking."

"No, we can't," Bunny said, her voice not enthusiastic.

We found Whip in the stable and explained the situation. "I'm game," he said. "But Chad's not here. Went to town for a dentist appointment."

"Okay," I said. "That leaves you, me, Gabe, Bunny, David, Sam, and Lindsey."

"Lindsey's not here either," Whip said. "She's driving Chad because his work needed anesthesia. Where's Johnny?"

There was an uncomfortable silence, then Gabe said, "He's a little upset. He needs some time to cool down."

Whip gave a disgusted grunt. "Better off without him then." He looked over at Shawna, his face turning gentle. "Don't worry, kiddo. We'll find that bull before the buyer gets here."

She nodded, her own expression grateful. "Thanks, Whip."

"Okay," I said. "That's six of us. Perfect."

"David shouldn't be riding. He pulled his back out yesterday," Bunny said.

David flashed her an annoyed look. "I can handle a piddling little bull."

Her voice remained firm. "David, we just can't afford to have you completely laid up. Besides, someone needs to stick close to Shawna and keep an eye on things." Since she was officially the ranch manager, he couldn't argue, though his agreement came with some unabashed grumbling.

"That leaves us five riders," I said. "Someone will have to ride alone."

"Not a good idea with this bull," Bunny said, her voice worried.

"I know," I replied. "But what else can we do? There's no time to wait for Chad and Lindsey."

While Bunny and Whip picked out the best horses for this situation, everyone strapped on spurs.

"We're going to have to use Jet instead of Pick," Bunny said, when we were all gathered together to receive our assignments. "Pick's favoring his left foot for some reason. Jet's not a trained cow pony, but he has more spirit than any of the pleasure horses. Rawhide would scare them into the next century."

"I'll ride him," Gabe offered. "I worked him a little today."

Bunny nodded. "That still only makes five of us. I don't like the idea of anyone going out alone." She glanced up at the darkening sky. "Especially since we're expecting a storm tonight."

When we were in the process of saddling our horses, Hud walked into the stable. "What's going on? Are all y'all going out riding? Who's going to watch the asylum while the interns are out whooping it up?"

Gabe narrowed his eyes and started to speak, but to keep the peace, I jumped in.

"A bull is loose, one that Shawna has a buyer coming for tomorrow, and we need to find him." Then I gave him a look that tried to say, I've been nice, now go away and don't cause trouble.

His face turned thoughtful. "Need another hand?"

"No," Gabe said, his voice curt.

Sam, who'd just finished readjusting Tanya's stirrups to fit his long legs, gave his dad a surprised look. Then a small smile snuck across his tanned face. Though Gabe and Sam mostly got along these days, Sam still enjoyed seeing his father thrown off balance once in a while and it was obvious to anyone with a modicum of sensitivity that Hud definitely had the ability to ruffle Gabe's feathers.

"Don't we need all the help we can get?" Sam asked, not looking at his father as he continued fiddling with his stirrups.

Gabe gave his son an uninhibited glare.

"He's right and it looks like there's only five of you," Hud said.

"He can count," Gabe said, sarcastically, tightening Jet's cinch. "Call the newspapers."

"Well . . ." Bunny said, glancing over at me, her face questioning. With Hud, it would make three teams of two riders. Definitely better when you need to cover a lot of ground quickly. It was never good to ride alone, especially when you're searching for a mean bull who doesn't want to be found. Then again, it was preferable to an inexperienced rider who would just slow his partner down.

"Thanks, Hud," I said. "But a situation like this takes someone who's experienced with horses and cattle. This bull is crafty and probably wouldn't think twice about charging you or your horse."

He walked over to where I was holding Patrick's reins. "May I?" He held out his hand.

I shrugged and handed him the reins. Patrick was one smart horse and if Hud wanted to make a fool of himself in front of all these experienced horse people, Patrick would certainly cooperate. A good bridle horse is patient, but also doesn't suffer fools gladly. Sorry, I silently apologized to Patrick.

Everyone silently watched while he made friends with Patrick, talking softly near his ear, running his hand down his neck and withers, letting Patrick sniff his hand. He adjusted the stirrups and cinch, then stepped him forward a few steps to see if he was cinch-bound. He mounted quickly and smoothly, told Patrick with a touch of his heel to step forward then backward. It was the gentle, almost imperceptible pressure with his heel telling Patrick to move backward that told me Hud had ridden bridle horses before. It was a cue for the horse to gently arch his back, sort of like a cat, so that he has the freedom to back up a long distance. He rode down the barn aisle, asking Patrick with subtle leg, toe, and voice cues to turn, stop, back up. All of this without spurs and with the lightest of hands. In less than five minutes. This was a man who knew horses. And he'd ridden bridle horses before. He was as well trained as the horse, a must for anyone who rides a bridle horse.

He looked down at Bunny. "My uncle Beau trained bridle horses for a living. I spent a few summers with him when I was a boy."

"Okay, you've convinced me," Bunny said, looking around at the rest of us. "He can ride Stormy and Whip can take Granite. He's old, but reliable and Whip knows his little quirks. Anyone else have any objections?"

I glanced over at Gabe. He readjusted Jet's chin strap and didn't say anything.

"All right, then," Bunny said. "Here's the plan. Sam, you and Whip ride together—take Tanya and Granite, they work well together. Gabe and Benni, you're a team on Jet and Patrick. I'll ride with Hud—we'll take Gumby and Stormy. That puts me, Whip, and Benni with those of you who don't know the ranch's property as well."

After everyone was saddled up, Bunny assigned us sections. "Whip, you and Sam go north of the corral up to Skunk Flats, it's flat and won't be too hard on Granite. Hud and I will check over by the old windmill. He might be headed over there for the water. Benni, you and Gabe take MudRun. We dropped a load of onions there a couple of weeks ago and Rawhide might remember that. Don't ride across that bridge over the creek. It's pretty unsafe. If you need to go as far as the cabin, then you'll have to wade through the creek, but it should be pretty low right now."

MudRun was about four miles from the ranch, up near the top of the ranch's highest hill. It was an old slapped-together cabin that Joe, Daddy, and their friends had often used during hunting trips. It was a basic shelter made of pine boards with two sets of bunkbeds, a couple of chairs, an old sofa, a round table perfect for poker, a fireplace, and an outhouse.

"We'll have that bull home and ready for the trailer before dinner," I said, with bravado. Everyone's response was a few grunts and some apprehensive glances at the dark gray storm clouds.

It was obvious the minute Gabe mounted Jet that the horse had decided he'd had enough riding that day. Even with his past experience exercising unpredictable racehorses, Gabe couldn't keep the stallion under control. Jet crowhopped and kicked like a wild mustang, baring his teeth at any horse who came close. He certainly wouldn't be any use to us right now.

"Dang piece of dog chow," Whip said, riding up beside me. "I told Joe to get rid of him, but he had a soft spot for the old dink."

"I don't know," Bunny said. "Maybe he's just feeling his oats. Let Gabe try a few minutes longer."

We watched Gabe struggle for dominance until it was obvious he was going to have to switch horses. I glanced up at the gathering rain clouds. Hopefully, the storm was still a few hours away.

"Take him back in," Bunny called to Gabe. "We haven't got time to mess with him. Let's saddle up Hoop and you can ride with me. Hoop's not good at hills since he got that bowed tendon, but where we're riding it's pretty flat. Hud can ride with Benni up to MudRun. Stormy's got the power for those hills."

"Uh . . . I think . . ." I started, glancing over at Gabe's dark face, rosy with exertion and embarrassment. He hated failing at anything, but doing so in front of Hud, that was the ultimate humiliation, especially after Hud's expert display of horsemanship.

"Fine," Gabe said, not looking at me, his body language saying *I'm embarrassed enough, don't add to it by making a scene.* He tightened the reins on Jet and spurred him back toward the stables.

A soft chuckle came from Sam. I turned to glare at him, but that didn't wipe the grin off his face. He was clearly enjoying his father's discomfort. Of course, he was smart enough to enjoy it after his dad left the area.

"Let's just go find that bull," I said, ignoring him. "The sooner he's back in custody, the sooner we can all have a good night's sleep."

"Gabe and I will take Sugar," Bunny said, calling for the dog. "Benni, you and Hud take Buck. He's younger and can handle running in the hills."

During this whole time, I didn't once look at Hud. But when we started out, I turned in my saddle and said, "Not one word. I don't want to hear one smart aleck word from you."

His face was completely without expression, but his brown eyes were definitely amused. "Yes, ma'am."

I spurred Patrick into a trot. "Let's go, Buck," I called to the dog and with a joyful bark, he darted out in front of us up the trail toward MudRun.

CHAPTER 11

WE DIDN'T SPEAK FOR THE FIRST MILE. THE ONLY SOUND WAS the horses sputtering and snorting as we settled into a long trot, a gait that would allow the horses to travel a good distance with less effort. We couldn't afford to tire them out before finding Rawhide since we didn't know how much energy they'd have to expend chasing him down. Hud kept up without problem. For a city boy, I had to admit, he was a darn good rider.

Buck would take off into the low sage brush and blue lupine, then circle back around to me to check for any commands before disappearing again. If Rawhide was anywhere near MudRun, Buck would find him.

Forty-five minutes later we were at MudRun's first gate. We'd climbed almost a thousand feet in elevation with still no indication of Rawhide. The terrain changed slightly as we went higher with more dusty gray pines and stunted cottonwoods. Juniper trees grew thicker, reminding me of my childhood. My friends and I would use the gin-scented berries as ammo in our games of cowboys and Indians. Halfway up the mountain, the creek that Bunny warned us about appeared at the side of the trail. Its cheerful tinkling mingled with the sounds of creaking saddle leather making me almost forget we weren't just on a pleasure ride. It was starting to grow colder, and with one hand I buttoned the front of my wool-lined Wrangler jacket. In the next half hour, we'd climbed another thousand feet and were in sight of MudRun's second gate. That was when Buck started barking. I held a hand up to Hud to stop. In the quiet moments between Buck's bugling, I could hear a faint snorting in the distance.

"Good boy," I said out loud. "Rawhide's up ahead. Let's go." I spurred Patrick to a fast trot. If the bull alluded us, he could either go higher up on one of the hills making it a real pain to catch him or, spirited young bull that he was, he'd head for one of the narrow canyons where we'd have to go off trail to catch him. With the waning daylight that would mean we'd have to give up for today. And that might be Rawhide's ultimate downfall. Even as big as he was, being alone made him a very real temptation to the always hungry mountain lions that roamed these hills this time of year.

I slowed down slightly with Hud right behind me, matching my gait. When I reached the gate, I cued Patrick to move sideways so I could spin the combination lock. After Hud and Stormy went through, I pulled the gate closed behind us. The bull's snorting sounded louder now and I could hear brush snapping and breaking. Buck was going crazy. Rawhide was likely not more than a hundred yards away though we hadn't spotted him yet. He had apparently jumped or pushed his way through a weak spot in one of MudRun's fences.

Hud turned in his saddle and asked, "Where do you want me?"

"See the cabin?" We were perched on a rise, looking down into a small valley. Through the scraggly pines and oaks, we could see the patched green-and-black roof of the hunting cabin.

He gave a curt nod.

"Go around the back of it and station yourself on the trail that leads away from the corral. It's right beside an old shack with a broken wagon wheel on the porch. If the bull heads up that trail, we're in trouble because there's a lot of little canyons back there. Open the gate of the corral and I'll see if Patrick, Buck, and I can maneuver him into the corral. Worse comes to worse, he can stay there overnight and we can come up here early tomorrow and trailer him down."

"Is the corral in good repair?"

"Let's hope so." If I remembered correctly, it was a three-inch metal pipe corral so I was pretty sure if we could get him in there, he was unlikely to escape.

The last quarter mile to the cabin was a steep climb down, a fairly good road, but narrow. Only one pickup at a time could make it down this old road. Right before we reached the cabin we came to the bridge Bunny warned us about. She'd actually underplayed its bad condition. That wooden bridge was a wreck. If we had to bring the trailer up tomorrow and it appeared we would, we'd have to park it on this side of the bridge and somehow drive Rawhide this direction. We could do it with enough riders and both the dogs. But, that was tomorrow's problem. We had to capture him first.

"Let's split up here," I said, after we waded through the creek. The water came up to the horses knees, high for this time of year, but they forged it with no problem. I pointed to my left. "That'll probably be the best route. Stormy knows what he's doing. Just listen to him."

"Yes, ma'am," he said without a bit of sarcasm.

I quickly tried to call the others on my cell phone, but got dead air. Bunny warned us that there was only sporadic access at MudRun. It frustrated me that they were all still searching the hills for the bull we'd found, but I didn't have time to ride around trying to find a signal. We had to capture Rawhide before he escaped again.

We spotted him around the back of the barn, drawn to that load of onions dropped off a few months ago. Even with the expert help of our experienced cow ponies and Buck, who like all well-trained and natural cattle dogs, was in heaven when he was herding something, it still took us an hour of feints, darts, and almost-wrecks before we managed to drive one very agitated, frustrated bull into the corral. During that time, a light, but steady rain started. When we finally locked the gate behind Rawhide, Hud and I, both the horses, and Buck were soaked and exhausted. And it was almost dark. We took the horses inside the small barn, unsaddled them and gave them water. Then we dashed into the cabin which looked like it had not been used since Joe died.

I tried my cell phone again. No signal. "Dang, I hope everyone's okay. We need to let them know we found Rawhide. And that we're okay."

Hud leaned against the stone fireplace, crossing his arms over his chest, his hair plastered against his head. "You're right," he said simply.

I looked at him thoughtfully. He'd been quiet, respectful, helpful, and just generally nice to work with during the last few hours.

Something was drastically wrong.

"Are you feeling okay?" I asked.

He shifted from one foot to the other, his round-toed roper boots squeaking from the water, his expression genial. "Sure, why?"

It was beginning to look like we were going to have to spend the night here. I closed my eyes, picturing Gabe's expression when he realized that. I quickly opened them. The truth was, he didn't even know if I was okay. If I didn't get a hold of him, I knew my protective husband. He'd have the National Guard out looking for us. Or he'd kill himself trying to rescue me.

"I have to get in touch with Gabe," I said, looking around the room. Inside a closet I found a green army surplus rain poncho and a working flashlight. I shook out the cobwebs from the poncho and pulled it over my dripping hair. "Maybe by climbing a little higher, I'll find a signal."

"I'll saw some hay in the barn," Hud said. "I'll see if it's decent enough to feed to the horses."

The ever-faithful Buck had decided that, now that the bull was corralled, I was his sole responsibility, so he insisted on coming with me.

"You are an excellent dog who deserves a steak sandwich," I told him as we picked our way up the hill through the wet mixture of sand and clay this area was known for. With every step, my boots sunk a half inch into the mud and made a loud sucking sound when I lifted them. It was a slow one step forward, two steps back. If I remembered right, this road led to a small rise about a half-mile up that Daddy told me they started calling "the phonebooth" because it was one of the few places cell phones worked.

I trudged through the rain, so much mud stuck to my boots it looked like I was wearing overshoes, praying the whole way that when I reached the top of this road, I'd get a signal. Not only was I concerned with setting Gabe's mind at ease, I wanted to find out how everyone else was.

By the time we reached hilltop, the rain relaxed into a light drizzle, but a brisk wind kicked up. Around me, the evergreen trees dipped and waved, the air smelled like a wonderful mixture of rich soil and lung-cleansing pine pitch. The sky was a black as charcol, the clouds obscuring any stars. My flashlight beam made eerie patterns against the swaying pine trees.

I tried Gabe's cell phone with no luck. After a few disconnects and a whole lot of static, I finally broke through to the ranch office's landline.

"Shawna!" I yelled over the wind. In the sky, a jolt of lightening warned me I probably shouldn't stay up here in the open much longer.

"Benni?" she yelled back. Her voice sounded like a tiny chattering in my ear. "Are you and Hud okay? Where are you?"

"MudRun. We're fine. We got the bull. Is everyone okay?"

"What? You found Rawhide?"

"Yes and we're okay! Tell Gabe I'm okay!"

"Got it," she yelled back. "The others are back already. We were worried about you two."

"Tell Gabe not to look for us. Don't let him . . ."

The connection broke. I continued trying for the next fifteen minutes but had to eventually concede defeat. I'd been lucky to get through at all. Since the bottoms of my jeans and my boots were thoroughly soaked and the lightning was still crackling every so often, I knew I'd better hightail it back to the cabin. Loyal to the end, Buck stuck to my side, though he was covered with mud to his belly, all of his tan and black legs now a solid, brown-gray.

"C'mon, Buckaroo," I said. He grumbled deep in his chest and pressed himself against my leg. "I know, you're cold and hungry. So am I."

It took me about thirty minutes to slip-slide my way back down to the cabin, the dark path lit only by the single beam from my flashlight. At the cabin, Hud was nowhere to be found. But a fire was roaring, the Coleman lantern was lit, and I smelled something cooking on the little camp stove. Something meaty and delicious. Next to it was percolating coffee. I felt like pouring the hot, nutty-smelling liquid over every inch of my freezing body.

"Come on, Buck," I said, hanging my slicker up on a nail by the door. "I need to dry you off." I searched through the drawers until I found some old towels, sopped up some of the water in my hair and then started drying Buck.

"You're a good, good boy," I said, rubbing the towel vigorously over his shivering body. His thick undercoat actually kept his skin dry, but he loved the attention and the praise. I wet one of the towels with some bottled water, cleaned each of his legs and checked his toes for cuts. When I finished, he made a quick reconnaissance of the two-room cabin, found an old leather chew stick and plopped down in front of the snapping fire.

The door flew open, banging against the log walls and a powerful gust of wind blew rain in, soaking the sagging wooden floor in front of the door.

"You're back," Hud said. He wore a slicker similar to mine and held another armful of wood. "Figured I'd better stock up for the night before it gets too damp to burn."

"What're you cooking?" I did not want to acknowledge that I'd be spending the night with Hud alone in this cabin.

He dropped the load of wood in the box next to the stone fireplace and nodded over at an unfinished door. "Old Joe had apparently been in this predicament before. There's a bunch of canned foods and bottled water in the pantry. Not to mention enough sterno to last a year.

Canned chili seems to be his preference." He took off his slicker and hung it on a hook next to the door.

"Is there something for Buck?"

He smiled down at the dog. "I didn't forget him. Found a can of dog food, too. Did you get in touch with your husband?"

"No, but I talked to Shawna on the ranch's landline. The others are back and I was able to tell her we were okay." Involuntarily, I shuddered. My wet clothes were started to chill me. "The connection broke before I could tell them much. I'll try again once the storm breaks."

"Doesn't look like that's going to be anytime soon." He'd pulled off his wet boots and socks, then faced me, his back to the fire.

Outside, the rain started coming down harder. Not wanting to completely give in to what fate had in store for me, I said, "Maybe I'll check the creek. If it's not too high . . ."

"Already checked it," Hud said, turning his back to me and holding his hands out to the fire. "As close as I could get anyway. It's pretty high and fast right now. A real Texas gully-washer. And the horses couldn't get through this wet mud on a bet. It's like glue. They'd be ankle-high after two steps. If they could take two steps." He bent over and picked a log from the pile and worked it into the fire. Then he turned to look at me and grinned. "Maybe they should call this place MudWalk, not MudRun."

I stared at him a minute. Spending the night in a tiny cabin during a storm with Detective Ford Hudson. Why did I feel like I was smack in the middle of a really corny soap-opera episode? To complete the cliché, all we needed was a crazed killer outside trying to get in.

"Gabe's going to be worried sick," I said, looking away.

"Come over here by the fire. At least take off your jacket. It'll dry faster hung over a chair." He pointed to one of the ladder back chairs surrounding the rough pine table. His soaked denim jacket was draped over one.

I reluctantly pulled off my jacket, slinging it over a chair. I went and stood in front of the fire. From my knees down, my jeans were soaked and muddy.

"If you take off your boots and socks and lay them on the ledge they'll dry quicker."

I pulled off my boots, but kept my socks on. At this point even bare feet seemed dangerously suggestive.

"You hungry?" he asked.

"Yes," I said.

"Homemade canned chili coming right up."

I fed Buck, then Hud and I ate and drank in silence, listening to the storm build in power.

"Hope this roof holds," I said. "How did the barn look?"

"Better than this place," he said.

That made me smile. "Of course." Joe Darnell had been a good rancher and a good rancher always made sure his animals were given the best accommodations.

He just looked at me curiously, but didn't comment. "There's not much to do here," he said when we finished eating. He picked up our empty bowls and set them on the floor for Buck to clean out. "Apparently Joe and his crowd weren't big readers. Didn't find one book."

"I'm sure there's a deck of cards somewhere." Poker was definitely favored over reading here.

He went through a couple of drawers. "Aha, pay dirt!" He held up a grimy-looking deck that was one of those freebie giveaways at Nevada casinos. He read the name out loud. "The Lucky Tiger Casino, Reno, Nevada."

I glanced at my watch. A little past six-thirty. It was going to be a long night. Though I was feeling a lot warmer than a half hour ago, the drying mud was starting to uncomfortably stiffen the bottoms of my jeans.

"Poker?" Hud suggested.

"My brain is too tired. You'd slaughter me."

"War, then. A no-brainer."

We played the card game for the next half hour until I was bored.

Now it was a little past seven. I was never going to make it through this night. Over in front of the fireplace, Buck slept deeply, his whole body relaxed into what almost appeared to be a boneless shape.

"Lucky dog," I said, resting my chin in my hand.

Hud glanced over at him. "Yeah, wish I could sleep that peacefully."

I stood up and stretched, then went into the pantry and found an old towel. After sitting down on the sofa, I put it under my feet and started chipping away at the drying mud.

"That looks fun," Hud said, still sitting at the table.

"I'm tired of cards. I want to go home."

Hud studied the deck of cards in his hand. "For once we agree on something."

"I hope someone at the ranch thinks to call your grandfather," I said, continuing to pick at the mud on my jeans. "He'll be worried about you."

"I'm sure they did. If not, he'd call over at the ranch to see what kept me. PawPaw's not one to sit and wait for people to come to him."

I smiled at my feet. "I like your grandpa."

"Yeah, he's takin' quite a shine to you too."

I looked up at him. "Seems like he's enjoying himself."

Hud tilted his wooden chair back balancing it on two legs, his back against the unfinished pine wall. "It's good seeing him laugh again. It's been tough on him with MawMaw gone."

"Your mother died? Hud, I'm so sorry."

He shook his head. "No, MawMaw was my grandma. Mama's still in the loony bin, happy as the proverbial bluebird."

I didn't know how to respond to that. He'd confided in me last year that his mother was mentally ill. After years of his dad's beatings, she'd retreated into a fantasy world, one that hadn't included her parents or Hud, her only child, for a long time. It bothered me to hear a mental hospital referred to in that manner, but I wasn't about to correct him. "When did your grandma die?"

"About ten months ago. A stroke took her just like that. No one expected it, least of all PawPaw. He's kind of at loose ends. I finally talked him into visiting me to try and cheer him up." His face grew more relaxed, less edgy as he talked about his grandfather.

"I bet he adores Maisie." Maisie was Hud's little girl. I'd met her once at a Mardi Gras festival.

"She has him wrapped around her pretty little six-year-old finger. It's still tough for him though."

"I know how he feels." Those first months after losing your spouse are almost surreal. You keep expecting them to walk in from another room or through the front door. Every time the phone rings, your heart leaps with hope that it was all a huge mistake.

"I imagine you do. He's thinking about moving out here with me. Mama, Maisie, and I are his only kin now. We'd have to find a place out here for my mother. I'd have to talk to her doctors about how she'd take that."

"How is she doing?"

He shuffled the cards like a pro, the soft whir of them mingling with the snaps and pops from the fire. "As well as can be expected. Drugs work for awhile, then for some inexplicable reason, they stop working. When they do work, though, she's her old, normal self. You'd like her. She's an amazing woman. Thanks for asking after her."

The room became quiet once we ran out of the only neutral conversation in our repertoire. He continued shuffling the cards and I kept scraping mud off my jeans. In the background, the fire spit and crackled and the wind rattled the cabin windows.

He finally broke the awkward silence. "So, who do you suspect let the bull out? Think it's the same person who was trying to get rid of the bones?"

"What?" I lifted my head to look at him, abandoning the mud on my jeans.

"That ornery bull who gave us the runaround for the last three hours. Don't tell me you've forgotten about him already."

"You think someone let Rawhide out on purpose?" Geeze Louise, I hadn't even considered that possibility. I was so used to things like this happening on a ranch. They *always* occurred at the most inopportune times, so it hadn't aroused my suspicions. Frankly, I'd noticed as I'd ridden around the ranch that many of the fences were in bad shape, so a bull breaking through one of them didn't seem unbelievable.

"Things like this happen all the time on a ranch," I said defensively. The fact that I hadn't thought about it being sabotage embarrassed me.

"Don't beat yourself up. You would have thought of it sooner or later," he said, his words deceptively kind, but I could hear a tinge of superiority. His front chair legs hit the floor with a thump. He leaned forward, resting his elbows on his knees. "It makes complete sense. It has us paying attention to something other than who was digging up those bones. Granted, it's not an incredibly sophisticated way of diverting our attention, but it worked."

I hated admitting it, but he was right. I went over to the fire, holding my hands out to warm them. A flash of lighting, then seconds later a distant rumble of thunder echoed above. Before I went to sleep, I'd have to brave the elements one more time and check on the horses.

"Whoever did it would have to be a little knowledgeable about ranching," I said. "Someone who would know that something like this would take a lot of time and attention."

"Yet it wasn't *too* destructive. Just time-consuming." He waited for a moment, then asked, "So, who do you suspect and why?"

I turned my back to the fire and faced him, keeping my hands behind me. He watched me, face easy and open, waiting for my reply, not a trace of superiority coloring it. Maybe I'd just imagined it in his voice a few minutes before.

In the flickering blue-yellow glow of the Coleman lantern and the fire, I realized what attracted me to this man, what he did that my own husband found difficult. He trusted my opinion. Though Gabe said he did, in reality, there was always this thread of condescension that tinged any conversation we had concerning his job. Sure, he trusted me when it was ranch work or horses or even family situations. But anything to do with a crime, he fell back on his trite remark about me playing Nancy Drew, something he knew annoyed the heck out of me. Heaven knows I loved Gabriel Ortiz to my utter and complete distraction, but it was nice having a man consider me at least as smart as he was.

"Shall I rephrase the question, darlin'?" Hud asked. "Too many big words?"

I could almost hear an audible thump when my ego hit the ground. That's what I got for giving Hud the benefit of the doubt.

"Who do you suspect?" I countered, frowning at him.

"No way. I asked first."

"Frankly, it doesn't matter to me. I just want to get through this next week, keep everyone happy and hopefully, help Broken Dishes get a good review from The Secret Traveler."

"The Secret Traveler? That column in the *Tribune*?"

"In the *Tribune* and two hundred other papers across the United States. A good review will be like winning the lottery for the Broken Dishes. A bad one could harm them enough that they could lose the ranch."

"Okay, lesser mystery. Who do you think *that* is?"

Here was a safe topic. It certainly beat having Hud snoop around and zero in on Victory Simpson. Revealing that I suspected one of the most beloved quilt teacher/designers might be involved with something shady at the Broken Dishes would not encourage other quilt teachers to come there, something I hoped would result from this first session.

"There's lots of possibilities," I said. "I'm leaning toward Mrs. Kitty Katz from Long Island. She seems the most well-traveled."

He smirked. "What is it with people and their crazy names?"

I shifted from one foot to the other, stifling a yawn. "Ford Hudson?"

"Okay, okay. So her parents were as nutty as mine. Anyway, she's too obvious."

"True, but you know from your years in law enforcement that it, more times than not, is the most obvious one." I gave a small laugh. "Gabe gets so annoyed with cop shows. He's not very sympathetic to creative license. Just the facts, ma'am. That's his motto."

"Is that why you call him Friday? For good ole tight ass Sergeant Joe Friday?"

I didn't answer. Friday was my special nickname for Gabe. I didn't want to share that with Hud.

"How about the Alaska lady?" he asked when he realized I wasn't going to talk about Gabe. "What's her name? Donna something. I walked in on her taking pictures of the kitchen. Not exactly your typical tourist photographs."

"You did?" Donna Kaufman had gone on all the excursions, a quiet observer in the background. She and I had only had two quick conversations, once about hand-dyed fabric—she'd been creating it and selling it at the Anchorage Saturday Market for years—and the other about Rich's recipe for mocha flan. I told her she'd have to ask him, but that I thought he'd share it.

Hud scratched the side of his neck. "She said she was thinking about buying a ranch up in Alaska, doing the same kind of thing as Shawna and Johnny, but she looked pretty embarrassed when I walked in on her."

Buck muttered in his sleep and his front paws moved in a running motion. Was he gathering cattle in his sleep? I resisted the temptation to reach my foot over and stroke his side, not wanting to disturb his pleasant doggie dream.

"It certainly sounds like she's a possibility." I'd have to start paying more attention to her.

"Back to the bones," Hud said. "Who among the guests seem to show an inordinate amount of interest in them?"

"Very unsubtle transition, detective," I said, finally giving in to a yawn. "What did the forensic people find out?"

"Not much."

"But something?"

"I can't really say."

"I can't really say," I replied, mocking him.

"Very mature, Ms. Harper."

I didn't answer, but stood up and went over to the sink. There was a gallon of bottled water so I poured some in a dish pan, added some soap, and started washing our bowls and spoons.

"You know I can't tell you anything," he said, coming up beside me, taking the soapy dishes and rinsing them with the bottled water.

"Hope that's not all the water here," I said.

"There's more in the pantry. Okay, if you're going to pout, I'll tell you one little thing."

I turned to look at him, trying not to appear too eager. For an experienced cop, he was sure easy to wear down.

"You realize, I'm only this much of a sucker for you, don't you?" he said, raising one eyebrow.

I snorted in disbelief. "Oh, sure."

"It's true and you know why." He was close enough for me to see his eyes were not a solid flat brown, but held hints of dark amber and burgundy, as variegated and changing as a handful of rich Arkansas delta soil.

I looked back down at the soapy water, my face warm with embarrassment, remembering suddenly that I was alone in this cabin with someone who might not, no, make that probably, didn't have the most honorable intentions. Not that I was afraid of Hud. For some reason, maybe not an especially logical one, I trusted him. He would never force himself on me. Remembering the moment between us almost a year ago in my office at the folk art museum, when we almost kissed, maybe it was myself I didn't trust.

"So, what were you going to tell me?" I asked, attempting to move the conversation back to safer ground.

"Someday we're going to have to talk about it, you know. We can't just keep ignoring this thing between us."

I handed him the last dish to rinse off, determined not to let the conversation move into any personal area. "Yes, we can, detective. We can do just that. Now, what were you going to tell me? If you don't want to spill it, then I'm going to turn in."

"Okay, okay, don't be such a spoilsport. I did a background check on everyone at the ranch."

"What? Even the guests? Isn't that an invasion of privacy?"

"You live with a cop, Benni. You know I have a perfectly legitimate reason to do it so, no, it's not an invasion of privacy." He rinsed off the last bowl and set it with the rest on a threadbare tea towel spread out on the gray formica counter.

He was right, but it seemed so unfair. These poor people came to spend a pleasant holiday at a guest ranch and end up having their backgrounds scrutinized. Of course, I'll admit, I was curious about what he found out.

"So?" I said impatiently.

"They are a pretty average bunch of people," he said. He grabbed a paper towel and wiped off the wet counter. "No criminal records on any of them. And those Georgia cousins. Mercy, they are rich. Old, old Georgia families. All their daddies are brothers. These ladies weren't just born with silver spoons, they each have place settings for a hundred. Not to mention quite the reputation for enjoyin' a good time."

I leaned against the kitchen counter. "What did you find out that might have to do with the bones?"

"It's your pal, Whip Greenwood."

"Whip? What about him?"

"How well do you know him?"

I calculated in my head. "He's a couple of years younger than me. I think he came to live at the DIS when he was around twelve or thirteen. Mrs. Olney, whose family owns a ranch over on Highway 46, was a social worker. She talked Joe into taking him in. Whip's always been a nice guy. Kind of quiet, but devoted to Joe and loves the Broken Dishes."

"For the record, he was thirteen when he came to live with Joe Darnell." He crumpled the paper towel and tossed it in the trash can. "Apparently his dad once worked for the Broken Dishes. Whip was about eight years old at the time."

"I didn't know that. Whip never mentioned his father or his mother. At least not to me."

"Good reason not to. His mom abandoned him as a baby and

Mr. Greenwood was a drunk, a criminal, and a flake, so he didn't last long working for Joe Darnell. Lived, or rather barely existed up in San Miguel. One day he just disappeared. Left thirteen-year-old Whip high and dry. That's when Social Services stepped in. Whip mentioned to his social worker about living at the ranch when he was a young boy and how it was the only time he was happy. She contacted Joe and he took him in, just like that. Your Mr. Darnell was apparently a real nice guy."

"I told you he was." Then my eyes widened. "If Whip's dad worked at the ranch, maybe the bones . . .?"

Hud shook his head no. "Nope. Found a record of Lew Greenwood's death in Carson City, Nevada. Died in jail of liver failure waiting for his trial for a liquor store holdup. Small time crook and con man."

"Oh," I said, deflated.

"So, my question is, what else do you actually know about Whip?" He leaned back against the front door across from me and folded his arms over his chest. The room was quiet now, the only sound was the occasional pop from the fire and sleepy muttering from Buck.

"I know he's a good hand. He's a hard worker and a nice guy. He's been a big help to Shawna and Johnny since Joe died."

"Did you know over the last twenty years Mr. Greenwood's been arrested three times for public intoxication, once for battery, and once for trying to evade a police officer?"

I shook my head slowly. "So, he's a little rowdy when he goes into town. A lot of cowboys are. What's that got to do with those bones?"

"His first arrest was when he was two days short of seventeen. Joe Darnell bailed him out. That wasn't the first nor the last time he did."

"I still don't see what this has to do with the bones."

"He has a small problem with staying in control, it sounds like to me. And Joe Darnell had a habit of rescuing his little social project."

"So?" I knew what he was driving at, but didn't want to consider it. I'd always liked Whip, though I admit, I didn't know what he was like outside of the ranch. And I didn't even want to think about Joe helping Whip cover up something like killing a man.

"No convictions, but our quiet Mr. Greenwood is more of a loose cannon than he initially appears. Guess the road apple doesn't fall far from the bull."

"Not always," I said, pointedly, thinking of his father.

He considered my words for a moment. "Okay, you're right. Not always. Did you also know that he and Shawna were an item for a little while when she first came to live with her father? Something her daddy wasn't real thrilled about according to gossip."

"Yes, I knew that."

"So why didn't you tell me?"

I shrugged. "It's over and everyone's fine with it."

"According to who?"

"Shawna. And what does this have to do with those bones?"

He just smiled. "Maybe nothing. Maybe something. It's just interesting at this point. So, who do you suspect, Detective Harper?"

I made my face as bland as I could. "I don't suspect anyone."

"I don't believe *that* for a minute."

I moved away from the fire and grabbed my still damp and muddy boots, waking Buck, who jumped up as instantly as alert as a Marine Corps guard. "I'm going to check on the horses and then go to bed." Like a true Marine, always faithful, Buck followed me out to the barn, sticking close until I was back inside and banging on one of the bottom bunk's mattresses to scare away any lurking critters.

Hud was still sitting at the table shuffling the cards when I finished. "Who do you suspect?" he asked again.

"I have absolutely no suspicions at all," I said, pulling off my boots and setting them near the fire.

"You're an irritatingly stubborn woman, Benni Harper."

"So I've been told." I looked in a closet and found four striped wool camp blankets in a large plastic bag. "Two for you, two for me." I tossed his on the bunk across from mine.

"Guess I'll join you," Hud said, performing the same ritual on the bunk bed on the cabin's other side. "I'm a light sleeper so don't worry about the fire. I'll add wood during the night."

"Good," I said and settled down under the blankets. "Wake me up when room service delivers breakfast."

About fifteen minutes after he'd extinguished the lantern, when I was about two seconds from falling asleep, Hud's voice startled me awake. Its rich, full tone seemed to fill the corners of the small room.

"I can't sleep." The light on his wristwatch lit up, a greenish-blue glow in the semi-darkness. "It's only eight thirty."

"Try," I replied in a groggy voice.

"I'm bored."

"For cryin' out loud." My eyes flew open and I stared at the bunk bed slats above me, completely awake now. "You sound like a five year old."

"Tell me a story." I could hear the laughter in his voice.

"Once upon a time there was a stupid Texas cop who wouldn't go to sleep so the cranky cowgirl shot him dead and left his body for the buzzards. The end."

"Tell me about yourself. What's your favorite movie? Who gave you your first kiss?

"Shut up."

"Tell me something that you've never told Gabe."

"In your dreams."

"Want me to tell you about my dreams?"

"Not especially."

He shifted around in his bunk. "Okay, then I'll tell you about myself."

"Your favorite subject." I rolled on my side, my back to him.

"I'm a trivia buff."

"Arrggg," I replied, wrapping my pillow around my head to try and drown out his voice.

"I can't help it. I have a steel-trap mind when it comes to trivia. You don't ever want to play Trivial Pursuit with me."

He was a mosquito. A 170-pound Texas mosquito. "Trust me, Hud, I don't ever want to play anything with you. Now, be quiet."

He got up, padded over to the fireplace and stabbed at the logs with the metal poker. "A vampire bat needs blood every three nights."

"You are determined to torture me, aren't you?" I said, turning over to watch him add another log to the fire.

He turned and grinned at me, his features indistinct in the flickering light. "The name of Popeye's boat was The Olive."

"After Olive Oyl?"

"Give the girl a cigar. Zane Grey's real name was Pearl Grey."

"Do not, under any circumstances, tell my daddy that."

"Saint Nicholas is the patron saint of pawnbrokers. The Galapagos Islands are the only place on earth that has both orange groves and penguins."

"So I'm assuming the penguins never get colds."

"Milk is heavier than cream."

"So my gramma's saying that cream and grease always rise to the top is true."

His laugh rumbled low in his chest. "More times than you can imagine, ranch girl. Llamas are native to South Dakota. Shave a polar bear and you know what you have?" He climbed back into his bunk.

I couldn't resist. "What?"

"A bear who's blue all over."

Okay, that made me laugh.

He propped himself up on one elbow and looked at me for a long minute, his shadowed face serious. "Tell me something your husband doesn't know about you."

"I told you no."

"One little thing. What can it hurt?"

"Forget it."

"I'll harass you the rest of the night if you don't."

"You're not kidding, are you?"

"You're very sharp for someone so heartbreakingly pretty."

"Make like a polar bear and turn blue."

"One teeny-weeny thing that Gabe doesn't know."

"Impossible. He knows everything about me."

"Now *that's* impossible. C'mon, you know all this incredibly personal stuff about me and I don't know anything about you. That's not fair."

"Ain't nothing fair in this ole life, detective. Thought you, of all people, knew that by now."

He inhaled deeply, a melancholy expression passing quickly over his face. "Yes, I do know that."

For some reason that remark sobered him and he was quiet for a time. I was almost asleep again, when his voice reached out in the darkness.

"Benni?"

I waited a few seconds, then said, "What now?"

"About what I said before . . . I mean, about your daddy . . ."

Blood rushed up to my head, throbbing loud in my ears. Each breath I took seemed to struggle out of my lungs. I did not want to talk to this man about my father. Not here. Not now. Not ever.

"I'm sorry," he said. "I didn't mean to . . ."

"Forget it," I snapped.

"I can't. The expression on your face when I . . ."

"I said *forget it*. I'm not going to talk about this, Hud. I mean it."

He was silent for a moment. "I just wanted to say I know how it is. How it feels to not know your father. I'm sorry. That's all I wanted to say."

Though I wanted to turn over and yell at him to shut up, mind his own business, to take a flying leap into a pile of manure . . . I couldn't. I knew too much about him and his father, about the physical scars hidden under his starched cowboy shirts. Fathers were not an easy subject for him either. Were they for anyone?

"Good night, detective," I finally whispered.

"Good night, ranch girl."

Soon he was softly snoring and I, of course, was now wide awake.

I lay there in the dark listening to the rain march across the cabin's tin roof like so many determined soldiers. Buck grumbled and growled every so often, more dog dreams. Hud talked in his sleep, muttering about two-penny nails. I watched the flickering shapes the dying fire made on the cabin's low ceiling, wishing I was home in my own bed.

Though I resisted, because of Hud's words, my mind whirled around the subject of my father and his possible role with the bones. I thought about all the things I didn't know about Daddy. Would it have been easier for me if I'd had siblings to share this with, to complain about his emotional distance, his dogged reticence? Though off and on during my life, I'd vaguely wondered what it would be like to have a sister or a brother, mostly I didn't think about it. With Elvia and her brothers being so close to me from the time I was in second grade, it was almost the same thing.

Their relationship with Señor Aragon was so different than mine with Daddy. Señor Aragon was so open with his emotions. His children never had a doubt about what he thought or felt. In fact, they often grumbled among themselves that he told them *too* much about what they should do with their lives, what he thought about who they dated or married, what they should do with their money, where they should live. Elvia said he talked openly about his own stumbles in life, saying he showed his broken life to his children because then they would not make the same mistakes he did. Did it help? Maybe. Maybe not. The Aragon boys and Elvia had all made plenty of mistakes of their own because don't we all stubbornly want to make our own mistakes despite the warnings of those who've gone before us?

My mind drifted to a sermon I heard Mac give one Father's Day about our relationship to God. He posed the theory that whatever problem we had with our earthly father is the problem we would always struggle with God the Father. If that was true, I could see why Hud had a hard time believing in any sort of a loving God. And why I always wondered, deep inside, if God truly loved me like the Bible claimed. Have I always wondered that about Daddy? I could imagine what he would say if I asked him if he really loved me.

"I haven't ever left, have I?" he'd say and that would be that. Blunt, practical, no room for discussion.

I haven't ever left.

I will always be with you even unto the ends of the earth. That was somewhere in the Bible, though I couldn't remember where. One of the Psalms? Somewhere in the New Testament? Was it part of the Great Commission? My hyped-up brain clicked along like a merry little train, lights blinking, horn blaring. I felt like screaming in frustration. I would never fall to sleep if I didn't turn it off. And lack of sleep was a sure-fire guarantee for getting into a wreck tomorrow when we tried to herd Rawhide into the trailer.

I deliberately moved my thoughts from my father to what Hud suspected about Whip. Could Whip be involved with letting Rawhide out? Or with those bones up on the hill? Was it a situation where he lost his temper and got rid of the evidence? Victory's possible relationship with Joe Darnell seemed like small potatoes now. Tomorrow, before everyone arrived, I was going to try to pry out of Hud what the sheriff's department planned on doing about Whip. I was almost certain that Shawna knew nothing about his background and that, maybe, Johnny didn't either. I couldn't imagine them keeping Whip on after her father's death if they did. Then again, if he were blackmailing them with something . . .

Now I was reaching. What started out as a typical, hard-drinking, cowboy's personal life had turned into a blackmail plot involving the whole Darnell family. I really, really needed to get some sleep. The last thing I remembered was trying to imagine a polar bear without his fur. Would his skin be bright blue, robin's egg, or sky blue?

I was in a deep sleep when something jarred me awake—a loud boom, a crackling sound, then a flash, another boom. A gust of wind rattled the cabin windows. The rain had stopped, but apparently we were having thunderstorms. What time was it? I'd left my watch on the table across the room and didn't want to crawl out of the warm pocket my body had created in the blankets. Far off, I heard coyotes call out with their weird, mournful yipping. They seemed particularly agitated tonight, maybe smelling Buck's presence? They came closer to the cabin, howled to him in challenge, like gangbangers flashing provocative hand signs to rivals. Buck jumped up and dashed to the front door, his growl a deep, primitive rumble in his chest. I was glad I'd kept him inside. He was tough, but no match for a pack of coyotes.

"It's okay, boy," I called softly to him. "That'll do."

He padded back over to me, nosed my cheek, asking for a scratch. I accommodated him and then told him to lie down.

Hud muttered in a sleepy voice, "What's going on?"

"The coyotes are restless," I whispered. "Probably the weather."

I drifted back to sleep and what seemed like hours later was awakened again by a sudden jolt, a sharp rattling of the windows, followed seconds later by a sensation of rolling waves, sort of like when you walk really fast on one of those moving airport sidewalks.

"Shit!" Hud cried, jumping out of bed, his legs tangled in the blankets as he did a weird, awkward dance trying to free them. "Oh, crap." He stood in between the set of bunks, his eyes wide and flashing, like an out-of-control horse. His agitation upset Buck who started running to the door and back, barking, loud and sharp.

Like a seasoned Californian, I lay there for a moment, trying to decide if the earthquake was bad enough for me to climb out of my warm bed. The rolling wasn't unpleasant and meant we probably weren't at the epicenter. Besides, there wasn't much to hurt us way out here. I watched Hud's semi-hysteria for about thirty seconds before dragging myself out of my cocoon.

"Calm down, you big wuss," I said, sitting on my bed, rubbing my eyes. "It's just a little earthquake."

In the light from the dying fire, his fearful expression flashed into an angry one.

Whoops, I thought. Not the right moment for a joke.

The quick jolt of an aftershock caused me to grab the side of my bunk bed. Hud's face panicked again and it occurred to me that this was probably his first earthquake. Buck resumed his spirited barking.

"That'll do," I yelled at Buck. I jumped up, dashed across the room and grabbed Hud's forearm. The muscles were tight under my cold hand as we stood inches from each other, each holding onto the wooden bunk bed while the wooden floor rocked and pitched.

"Don't worry," I said in my most calm voice. "We're safer out here than in a city. I promise." I ran my hand up to his biceps and squeezed it, trying to reassure him. His muscle was hard under my hand, his skin warm and smooth.

When the rolling finally stopped, I let go of his arm. "I'm sorry for making fun of you."

He inhaled deeply, then let it out. His face relaxed slightly and he gave a nervous smile. "Guess I am a wuss. Just never felt anything like that before. It's a little . . ." He was at a loss for words. A first for Detective Ford Hudson.

"Disconcerting?" I filled in. I picked up one of the wool blankets from the floor and wrapped it around myself. The fire was glowing embers now and the cabin's temperature had to be a good thirty-five degrees.

He laughed nervously and nodded. "*You* didn't even get out of bed. Now I know why people think Californians are nuts."

I laughed too, glad he wasn't upset at my unkind behavior. I hated it when someone made fun of my fears. I've always felt people should respect other people's fears even when they don't understand them. Something I'd just failed miserably at with him. "We are, I guess. But don't you think it's all in what you are used to? I mean, if I saw a tornado, I'd probably either run in circles screaming or pass out in fear."

"With good reason. They aren't anything to mess with."

"The earthquake's probably why the coyotes were so restless."

"Isn't animals predicting earthquakes an old wives' tale?"

I shrugged. "So they say, but I've seen agitated animals too many times before one not to give it some serious consideration."

His face suddenly became alarmed. "Maisie . . ."

"How long has she lived here?"

"Since she was two."

"Then she's an old hand at earthquakes. She probably didn't even wake up." I pulled the blanket a tighter around me. "It wasn't that big. I'll guess a five or so. Probably didn't even knock her stuffed toys off the shelf."

His tense face started physically relaxing in front of my eyes.

I unwrapped myself from the blanket. "I'd better go check on the horses. Earthquakes can make them nervous."

"I can do it," he said. He sat down on the sofa, turned both of his boots upside down checking for uninvited guests and started pulling them on. "It'll give me a chance to do something macho and salvage what's left of my shredded manhood. How about you pretend you're a girl and make us something hot to drink?"

I laughed and said, "You got it."

I stoked the fire and added wood until it was blazing again, then put the small teakettle on the camp stove to boil water. In the pantry there were packages of instant hot chocolate. Just the thing we needed, sugar, chocolate, and warmth. By the time he came back, I was pouring the water into the mugs. I took mine and sat on one end of the sofa and watched him peel off his damp slicker. While he was gone, the rain had started again. In the distance, there was a flash and thunder rumbled again. I picked up my watch and checked the time. Three thirty in the morning. I yawned, wondering if either of us would be able to go back to sleep.

"At least we can't lose our electricity," Hud said, standing in front of the fire, palms held out.

"That's true. Wish I could fall back to sleep as quickly as Buck." Once the excitement was over and the fire was blazing again, Buck had sprawled right across the rug in front of the fireplace, a study of complete relaxation.

"No kidding," Hud said, looking down at the sleeping dog. After a few minutes, he sat down in the easy chair opposite the sofa where I was reclining. "I suspect I won't be able to sleep for the rest of the night, but feel free to go back to bed. I'll wake you when it's morning."

"That's okay," I said, trying not to yawn. "I'll stay up too. It's warmer here near the fire anyway." I was still feeling guilty for teasing him about his genuine fear so the least I could do was keep him company.

"Great," he said, obviously relieved. "Want to play cards?"

I shook my head no. Before he could suggest something else, another aftershock shook the little cabin. As was sometimes the case with aftershocks, it seemed to feel stronger than the initial quake. Buck bolted up and started pacing. Hud's eyes narrowed slightly as he tried to hide his nervousness. His Adam's apple moved convulsively as he physically tried to swallow his fear.

"Smashed pennies," I blurted out, sitting up.

That threw him for a loop, making him forget the shaking ground for a moment. His face screwed up in confusion. "What?"

"I collect smashed pennies. Well, I think the technical name might be something else, but it's those machines where you put in fifty cents and a penny and it smashes it into some kind of commemorative flat, you know, penny thing." I smiled at him. "Are you getting what I'm saying?"

"You what?" His dark brown eyes widened in surprise, his fear temporarily forgotten.

"I have over a hundred," I added as the ground rolled beneath us.

"Smashed pennies?"

I nodded. "I even have a smashed dime. From Memphis. It has Elvis's picture on it."

"Gabe doesn't know this about you."

Instantly, I regretted my impulsive good deed. "I'm going to tell him as soon as I see him so don't get any grand idea that you're special."

"But I knew before he did." He grinned at me.

"I'll deny it."

"Smashed pennies, huh?" He shook his head and laughed.

"Hey, quit laughing. I was trying to be nice." Now that the room had stopped shaking, I yawned again and laid back down on the sofa.

"Tell me some more trivia. Maybe I can impress Dove the next time we play Trivial Pursuit."

He looked at me for a long moment, then said softly, "Thanks."

"Trivia, please," I said, leaning my head back and closing my eyes. His expression was a troubling mixture of gratitude and some other emotion I sensed was much more dangerous to both of us at this particular moment.

The last thing I remember was something about there being no actual sand in sandpaper, then it was morning. At some point in my sleep, I'd been covered by another blanket, the ends tucked in around me. The fire was still going strong, but Hud's chair was empty. Even Buck was gone and for an instant, cold slivers of fear raced through my veins. Had they left without me? Minutes later, the front door flew open. Buck dashed in with Hud right behind him.

"Isn't breakfast ready yet? I've already watered the horses and checked the road. It's dry enough to ride on. Creek's low enough to wade."

I sat up, sleep in my eyes causing them to feel scratchy and irritating. "Is Rawhide still there?"

Hud nodded. "Looking a little less testy than yesterday. I think all the hullabaloo might have calmed him down some."

"Tired him out anyway."

He grinned. "Sometimes that's all you can do with us men, just wear us out."

"I should try and call Gabe."

"Like I said, the creek is back down. Hasn't rained for the last two hours. We should be able to get out of here pretty easy now. The mud around here seems to dry fast."

"Yeah, it does. We just want to make sure and escape before another rainstorm hits. I don't want another night like last night."

He cocked his head at me. "You mean you didn't enjoy our first night together? And me trying so hard."

I ignored his innuendo and asked, "Did you ever get some sleep?"

He shook his head no. "But I had a real fine time watching you."

"Oh, go saddle the horses," I said, too cranky from lack of sleep to banter.

While he went out to the barn, I walked to the "phone booth" to try and reach Gabe again. It was much easier going this morning, the mud slightly harder since it hadn't rained for a few hours. At the top of the hill, after walking around and around looking like some kind of person on speed, I finally caught a signal. I tried Gabe's cell phone first, but didn't even get his voice mail. I finally made it through to the ranch's landline.

"The road's fine," I yelled. "And the creek is down. Have them bring the stock trailer as close as they can."

"They're already on their way," Shawna called back through the crackling line. "Gabe's been up pacing all night. He, Whip, Lindsey, and Sam left about forty-five minutes ago on horseback. Chad and David are coming up behind them with the truck and trailer."

That Gabe had been up all night certainly didn't surprise me. "I'll keep trying to call him on his cell phone." I noticed that she didn't mention Johnny and I didn't ask. Did he ever make it home last night? Things were really starting to look bad for Shawna and Johnny's new marriage.

I tried Gabe's cell a couple more times with no luck. But, if they left when Shawna said that meant they'd probably be here within the next hour. Back at the cabin, Hud had both the horses out and saddled. White air blew out of their noses and they were restless to get started, sensing they'd be working again. Rawhide also sensed something was about to happen and was starting to stomp around the corral uttering angry little snorts.

"I'm going to walk up the road and wait for them on the rise," I said to Hud. "We can see them from a long way off. Besides, the sun hits there first so it'll be warmer."

"Good idea," Hud agreed. "I'll join you."

At the top of the rise, about a quarter mile from the cabin, there was a small patch of sunlight that was just coming over the sharp blue-gray edges of the eastern hills. We stood there not speaking, hands shoved deep in our jacket pockets, exhaling powder puffs of frigid air. Right now, all I wanted to do was wrangle this bull into the stock trailer, ride quick as possible back to the ranch and take a long, scalding hot shower.

We were both standing there when Gabe first appeared over the hill. He rode Jet who was obviously behaving himself today. Gabe wore a split-leather, sheepskin-lined jacket, jeans, and boots, looking like something out of a Robert Redford movie. In the early morning sunlight, his black hair gleamed the same color as the stallion's coat. He sat straight and proud, but easily; one of those natural riders who seemed to mold themselves into the horse. He knew that and was proud of it, which was why yesterday, when Jet was out of his control, he'd been so embarrassed. This moment made up for that.

An undeniably handsome man in any situation, right at this minute, he looked magnificent—like a character in a Remington painting, the ultimate Western man, every woman's fantasy of the brooding alpha male, a romance writer's dream character come to life.

As he rode toward us, the other riders far behind him, I involuntarily gave a small sound halfway between a sigh and a moan. "Wow."

With his hands on his hips, Hud watched Gabe's approaching figure.

"Wow, indeed," he finally said, giving a small chuckle. "You know, ranch girl, I'll have to kill you if you repeat this, but I can see why you're in love with him. Shoot howdy, if I was a woman, I'd probably fall in love with him myself."

CHAPTER 12

$\mathscr{I}$ SWUNG AROUND TO STARE AT HUD, MY MOUTH DROPPING open.

He just grinned at me, completely guileless. "I just call 'em how I see 'em."

Then I started giggling. Maybe it was fatigue, maybe it was relief. Maybe it was just the sheer unpredictability and silliness of what Hud said, but by the time Gabe forged the creek and rode up to us, I was laughing so hard I could barely catch my breath.

Even the irritated frown on Gabe's face couldn't stop my laugher.

"I mean it, Benni," Hud said, under his breath, right before Gabe was within earshot. "I'll skin you alive if you tell anyone I said that."

"What's so funny?" Gabe asked seconds later, swinging down off Jet. His expression roared that this wasn't exactly the scenario he expected to find.

"Nothing," I finally gasped. "It's . . . it's just a stupid Texas joke that Hud told me right before you rode up."

Gabe looked over at Hud, his eyebrows moving together, demanding an explanation.

Hud, as quick on his feet as a barn rat, said, "What do you have when you have a pair of cowboy boots with a Stetson on top?"

Gabe's annoyed expression didn't changed one millimeter.

"A Texan with the crap kicked out of him."

Okay, that set me to laughing again. I'm sure it was just pure exhaustion.

Gabe frowned, shook his head and thrust Jet's reins at Hud.

"Are you okay?" He turned to me and placed his hands on my shoulders.

I nodded, my laugher dying away when I realized how concerned he really was. "Shawna told you we were fine, didn't she? I mean, last night. I got through on the cell phone for about fifteen seconds."

"Yes, but that earthquake was pretty strong. Broke quite a few dishes at the ranch."

I smiled at his unintentional play on words.

"That little burp," Hud said. "Shoot, we barely felt it."

His Texas bravado had finally kicked back in. I didn't dare look at him afraid I'd give his secret fear away.

"We were worried about a mud slide," Gabe said, ignoring Hud. "That cabin sits directly over a fault and apparently the hill behind the corral is not very stable. It's given away before. That's why they have a new barn. The slide stopped just short of the cabin the last time they had a quake."

I glanced over at Hud whose eyes widened slightly.

"We came through it fine," I assured Gabe. "And we didn't see any indication of a mud slide." Of course, that was because we hadn't looked. It hadn't even occurred to me, something I didn't think I'd share with Gabe at this particular moment.

He looked at me for a long, silent moment, piercing me with his blue-gray eyes. Then he bent his head and kissed me hard. After fifteen seconds or so, he pulled back, his message firmly delivered and absolutely clear. He was marking his territory.

"That was extremely juvenile of you, chief," I said in a low voice. "And entirely unnecessary."

"So arrest me."

As the others approached, he said in a louder voice, "Let's get this bull down the hill. There's some emotional reassurance that needs to be done with the guests. They weren't counting on an earthquake as part of their vacation."

"Did you tell them we didn't charge extra for it?" I asked flippantly.

"I don't think any of the guests are quite ready to joke about earthquakes yet."

"You know," Hud said, handing Jet's reins back to Gabe. "That was my first earthquake."

I glanced at him, surprised. That was something I was sure he'd keep to himself.

"Is that right?" Gabe said, his face neutral.

"Yep," Hud said, flashing a deceptively innocent smile that should have warned me. "It's also the only time I've spent the night with a woman where both the sky lit up *and* the earth moved."

He started back down toward the cabin. "I'll go fetch our horses," he called over his shoulder.

"*Pendejo,*" Gabe said under his breath, his bottom lip disappearing under his mustache.

"Oh, Gabe," I said. "He's just yanking your chain. You know nothing happened."

Minutes later, the rest of the group rode up—Bunny, Sam, Whip, Lindsey. Chad and David were farther down the road with the truck and the ranch's battered stock trailer. I tried not to stare at Whip, but knowing what I did now, I couldn't help studying him when he wasn't looking.

Bunny devised a game plan to drive the bull out of the corral, down through the creek and back up onto the road. With the dogs and all of us on horseback, it would be difficult, but not near as time-consuming as what Hud and I went through to capture him yesterday.

For a change, things worked in our favor and we weren't forced to rope him, something that Sam and Chad might have found fun, but the rest of us would just as soon not have to attempt with so little sleep under our belts. With our collective experience, good horses, well-trained dogs, and sheer luck, we managed, in a little less than an hour, to drive Rawhide through the creek, down the hill and into the waiting stock trailer.

On the ride back, I asked Bunny, "Where's Johnny?"

She tsked under her breath, looking more like a mother at that moment than a ranch manager. "Stupid boy never came home last night. Shawna is just beside herself."

"That's too bad. I hope their marriage survives this." And that Whip wasn't classless enough to try and move in on Shawna when she was feeling so vulnerable. I looked at Bunny for a moment, wondering if she knew all this information about Whip. She must, being the ranch manager. Joe would have no reason to keep it from her. This was getting more and more complicated as time went on.

"Me too." She rested one hand on the saddle horn as our horses ambled carefully down the still slightly muddy trail. "Whip sat up with Shawna all night waiting for him."

"That's not a good thing," I said, ducking to miss a low tree branch.

"No, it isn't. If Johnny doesn't watch it, he's going to lose Shawna before their first anniversary."

"He's young," I said, remembering how emotional and irrational my own first husband had been when we were twenty and newly-married. Everything is so dramatic when you're that young. Sometimes you make rash decisions you end up paying for your entire life.

"If they can make it through this, they've got a pretty good chance, I'd say. This kind of responsibility and stress would be hard enough on older folks. At their age . . ." She let her voice drift off.

"That's for sure," I agreed. What would Shawna do? Was she willing to give up her land, her only legacy from her father to save her marriage? Would Johnny force her into making that choice? Would she be dumb enough to run to the arms of another man, one who might not have her best interests at heart, just because her husband was acting like a fool? Right now, I wouldn't trade places with her for all the cattle in San Celina County.

When we arrived at the ranch, Lindsey offered to unsaddle Patrick for me.

"Thank you a million times over," I said, handing her the reins. "I feel like I haven't taken a shower for a month."

She took Patrick's reins with her free hand and started walking him and her horse toward the stables. "Sounds like you and the detective had quite a night. It's the talk of the ranch."

I stuck my hands in my back pockets and frowned. "Please, don't say that. Trust me, there was nothing romantic about my night up at the cabin. I was cold, wet, muddy, and cranky. Not to mention I didn't get to brush my teeth. And there was an earthquake."

She shook her head and stroked Patrick's neck. "The quilting ladies were all abuzz about your, as the Georgia cousins put it, wicked good fortune. Guess they all have quite a crush on Detective Hudson."

"He's all theirs as far as I'm concerned."

"Just wanted to warn you. You'll be quizzed within an inch of your life, I'll bet. Especially by the cousins."

I was on my way to my cabin when Shawna called out to me from the front porch of the lodge. Glancing at my watch, I went over to her. "I'll be able to serve lunch with no problem. I just need to take a shower first or whatever scrumptious vittles Rich has prepared will be overwhelmed by the scent of mud, horse sweat, and manure."

"Don't worry about that. I served dinner last night with Rita and we did fine. If you're too tired, I'm sure she and I can handle lunch."

"No, I can do it. I actually did get some sleep last night despite rain, lightning, thunder, and earthquakes."

The mention of the quake caused a small grimace on her face. "I know. Can you believe we had an earthquake? Is there anything else that can go wrong? Luckily, most of the guests were pretty good-natured about it, but nerves are on edge, just the same."

"Don't worry, Elvia and Emory are coming tonight. She's talking about Western books and trust me, Emory's personality will completely take everyone's minds off our unstable earth. He's the original camp counselor. He'll have everyone playing charades and, what's more, *liking* it."

"I hope you're right," she said. "And Meg Matthews is doing her cowgirl poetry reading too. She's going to give a little lecture on ranch poetry this afternoon during teatime and encourage any of the guests who are game to try their hand at writing a poem about their ranch experience. Anyone will be welcome to share their poems tonight after dinner."

"Kind of a cowboy karaoke?" I said, laughing.

She smiled slightly, looking a little less haggard. "I'm sure the Georgia cousins will provide us with some amusing moments."

"Without a doubt," I said. "So, is there anything you need?"

She tapped her temple with her fingertips. "Oh, yes, I wanted to tell you I found another box of old pictures and documents about the ranch. They were in my dad's room under his bed." She swallowed hard. "I really haven't gone through any more of his stuff since you helped me a few months ago. Seems like there's just always something to do around here."

"I understand. Remember, there's no time limit or rules about when you have to do that. I only went through my late husband's things a few months back and he's been gone almost three years. When it's time, you'll have the strength to look at your dad's things."

Her eyes were moist with unshed tears. "Anyway, I did find some pictures and stuff. I put the box in your room. Maybe you can use it in a talk or something."

Or, I thought, see if there is anything in them that would connect someone with the bones.

"Have you heard anything about our friend up there?" I pointed up at the Luna Lake trail.

She shook her head no. "That detective has been nice, but not very helpful with information. He's starting to make me nervous the way he hangs around all the time. Do you think the guests have noticed?"

"We *know* the Georgia cousins have," I said, hoping to relieve her worry a little.

"Yes, and I know they don't mind. But I'm worried the other guests might think he suspects them."

Which he does, I thought. But I knew what she was implying. "In that way the earthquake might have helped. It will be what everyone talks about for the next few days. With the activities we have planned tonight, Isaac's photography class tomorrow, and the barn dance tomorrow night, we'll keep them all so busy they won't be able to worry about whether Hud is spying on them or not."

"I sure hope so." She glanced over at the road leading away from the ranch. I knew what she was thinking. All of this to worry about and a husband who hadn't come home last night.

❖

THE BOX OF PHOTOGRAPHS AND DOCUMENTS SAT NEXT TO MY twin bed, tempting me to start going through them immediately. I resisted because lunch was only an hour away and I didn't want Shawna to have to serve again. She had enough to worry about. After a deliciously hot shower I was pulling on a clean flannel shirt when the front door of the cabin opened.

"Honeybun, are you here?"

"In the bedroom, Dove," I called.

She came into the room and sat down on the bed, her face screwed up with annoyance. Outside, I could hear Socrates' lonely honking. He really hated her being out of his sight.

"I'm ready to squeeze the snot out of that Sissy Brownmiller."

"That's real Christian of you," I commented, buttoning my shirt. "Oh, and I'm fine. Thanks for asking."

She waved a hand at me, unconcerned. "Oh, I knew you was. Shoot, you had water and shelter. Gabe just had his hackles raised 'cause you was spending the night with that detective."

"I don't really like people referring to it that way."

"Does a husband good to worry a little. Long as there isn't actually anything he needs to worry about." She gave me the eye.

I raised my hands, palms up. "I'm completely innocent."

"Just you be careful. People aren't always what they seem."

I turned around and dug through my suitcase for a pair of jeans. I didn't want her to see the expression on my face, because there wasn't a thing on this earth I could hide from Dove. I didn't want to tell her what was going on with me and Daddy. Did she know her son any better than I knew my father? I had no idea. As open as my and Dove's relationship had always been, the subject of my father, except for everyday things, was something we didn't discuss.

I glanced over at the pasteboard box. Maybe I could look at them after lunch. Then I yawned. If I didn't fall asleep first.

"Have you found out how Sissy is cheating yet?" I took the clean pair of Wranglers and shook them out, trying to snap the suitcase wrinkles out of them. Sissy Brownmiller's foibles were always a good way to avoid talking about more intimate subjects.

Outside, Socrates gave a loud honk, then a hiss. It was followed by a distinctly male voice spilling a wagonload of curse words. His voice faded away, Socrates obviously again successful in his life's mission to protect Dove.

"Whoops," I said. "Sounds like someone with the XY chromosome walked a little too close to our door."

Dove didn't even crack a smile. "I don't know what to do. Sissy's basically a good woman."

"Except for being a cheat and a gossip," I added. "And stingy and . . ."

"You can start pointing fingers when you walk on water, missy."

"Okay," I said slowly, not knowing exactly what she was in here seeking, but realizing I'd best shut up and just listen. Then again, I was Dove's granddaughter so that would likely prove impossible.

"Have you talked to Mac about this?" I suggested. One of the things I loved most about our pastor at First Baptist was how diplomatic and wise he was. Surely he could bring some peace into this conflict.

"We don't need to be bothering Mac with something this petty. He's a busy man."

"Then how about someone who isn't actually a member of the domino game? How about Miss Heil?" Jo Ellen was the senior women's Sunday school teacher and was known and loved for her tolerant and gentle personality. She was always the judge at the church's pie competition every autumn, the only person in our congregation whose pie-tasting integrity was not suspect.

"We don't need to bring more people into this than need be. I don't want it to become bigger than it already is," she said, her face genuinely worried. "For some reason, Sissy feels the need to win so bad she has to cheat. Makes me feel sorry for her. Like we're not doing enough to make her feel cared about." From the other side of the door, Socrates let out another mournful honk.

I suddenly felt ashamed. Where was my charitable soul? "Then maybe you should just let her win. I mean, what difference does it make? It's not like you play for money." I pulled on my jeans and tucked my shirt in.

Dove's face suddenly brightened and she abruptly stood up. "Thanks for your input, honeybun. I'll see you tonight."

Before I could say another word, she was out the front door.

❖

HUD WASN'T AT LUNCH, THANK GOODNESS, SINCE I WAS GETTING a little weary of the feint and jab he and Gabe were doing. Whip sat next to David Hardin, but didn't say much during the meal. Because of what I knew about his background and his former relationship with Shawna, I tried to pay particularly close attention to what he did say. The trouble was, Whip never talked much.

Before lunch, Rich had told me that Johnny came back late this morning, hungover and cranky. He'd come into the kitchen for some coffee.

"He's feeling real low about leaving Shawna in the lurch with that bull loose," Rich said while he folded whipped cream into a chocolate mixture for the chocolate-mocha mousse that was this evening's dessert. "Wanted me to tell him what he could do to make it up to her."

"What did you say?" I asked.

He flashed me a mischievous smile. "That in my long marriage begging and groveling always worked wonders for me."

Though at the other tables the conversation was loud and lively, it was subdued at the employees' table. The strain of keeping this guest ranch going, the specter of the bones floating above us, and the tension between Shawna and Johnny was starting to take its toll.

"What are you doing this afternoon?" Gabe asked when I sat a bowl of homemade peach ice cream in front of him.

"Probably go through the new box of photographs and stuff that Shawna gave me and see if I can use any of them. I was thinking about putting together an album of the ranch's history to keep in the recreation room, containing things like old photographs, pay stubs, and lists of what things cost through the years. I've seen that done at bed and breakfasts. What are you going to do?"

"Work Jet some more. Is there anything you need me to help with?" He was feeling much more relaxed since Hud was nowhere in sight.

"Eventually with decorating the barn. We can do it after dinner, while Meg is doing her poetry reading."

"Okay, I'll be in the back corral if you need me."

❖

THE CABIN WAS WARM AND QUIET, TEMPTING ME TO CRAWL under the fluffy red comfortor and take a nap, but I forced myself to continue going through the box of photographs. What I'd told Gabe was the truth, I was considering making an official Broken Dishes Ranch history album, but I was also hoping that somewhere in these photographs there might be a clue about the bones and who tried to dig them up.

There were so many photographs, more than in the boxes I'd looked at before, that I needed a system to keep them straight, so I started dividing the photographs into piles—those showing people I knew, such as pictures of Joe and David Hardin when they were young, pictures of the ranch's buildings, pictures of people I didn't know. I was only about one quarter of my way through the box when the front door opened and Elvia's strong alto voice called out from the living room. The clock next to the bed said three o'clock.

"Benni?"

"In here," I called to her.

She walked into the bedroom, followed by my cousin, Emory, who even after almost a year of marriage to my best friend, still had a dazed I-can't-believe-my-good-fortune look to his handsome face. They were dressed in their best cashmere-and-denim, Ralph Lauren weekend-in-the-country clothes, which meant that neither of them would likely be getting within five hundred feet of any actual cow pies. Elvia's denim jacket not only had a fake mink collar, but fake mink cuffs.

"How many little polyester minks did you have to kill to make that jacket?" I teased her.

"Oh, pipe down," she said, sounding a little more like my cousin, Emory, every time I saw her.

"We saw Gabe out at the corral wrangling a very good-looking piece of horseflesh," Emory said, plopping down on the bedroom's one overstuffed chair. "He said you were working on the ranch's photograph album."

I gestured to the piles on my bed. "It seemed like a good idea when Shawna brought me this box, but it's becoming more work than I anticipated." Not to mention I hadn't found one suspicious thing in the photographs. If Victory had any connection to the ranch before now, so far, it hadn't shown up in any of these pictures.

Elvia picked up a photograph of an early Parkfield rodeo queen. "Look at that hair. I guess big hair has always been in style with you Westerners." Elvia had worn her glossy black hair in a conservative shoulder-length, straight style since we'd graduated from college in the early eighties.

"Hard to improve on perfection," Emory said with a grin. "There's something to be said about big-haired women."

"Which you can just leave unsaid," Elvia retorted, tossing the picture back down on the bed. "Can you put this aside for a little while? I need help setting up my book table before Meg gets here."

I looked back down at the photographs, reluctant to stop. "Sure. I can do this after dinner. Whoops, forget that. We have to finish decorating the barn after dinner."

"I'm going to be working on it this afternoon so you shouldn't have much to do," Emory said. "So, what's this we hear about you finding a dead body on a trail ride?"

"Bones," I said. "And it wasn't me, but one of the ranch dogs who found them." I reached for my denim barn jacket and slipped it on. "Since I'm assuming you heard about the bones from your old friends at the *Tribune*, tell me, have you heard anything I don't already know?"

Emory, before he opened up the west coast division of his father's smoked chicken business, worked for the *San Celina Tribune* and still had good connections there.

"I have no idea," Emory said. "What do you know?"

"Actually, nothing of consequence," I admitted. "The detective on the case has kept real quiet about what forensics has told him about the bones."

"I heard your buddy, Detective Hudson, is on the case," Emory said, standing up. He slipped his arm around my shoulders and Elvia's as we walked toward the main lodge. "Tell me, how's the chief taking it, you working with your old partner again?"

I bumped my hip against his. "He's not my buddy or my partner, razorback-face. Gabe is just fine with it. It's not even an issue."

Emory threw back his head and laughed. "You are so amusing and that is such a bold-faced lie, sweetcakes. This weekend may turn out to be more fun than I anticipated."

I looked around his shoulder to Elvia. "Please control your husband or I will be forced to smack him upside the head."

"Be my guest," she said.

"You two are a regular LaVerne and Shirley," Emory said, smiling big as could be. He loved it when we teased him.

We were almost finished setting up Elvia's display of western-themed and local books, including all of Meg Matthews' and Isaac Lyon's books, when Isaac himself burst into the room, slamming the door behind him. Outside, we could hear Dove's indulgently scolding voice.

"Hi, Pops," I called across the room. "I see you've met the infamous Socrates."

"Where did that demon bird come from?" my step-grandfather asked, his large, wrinkled face awashed with a mixture of irritation and amusement. One of his huge, bear-paw hands compulsively gripped the Nikon camera that almost always hung around his neck. His other hand pointed to the lodge's double doors. He was a powerfully built man, one who, in his younger years, always had problems with men wanting to fight him, knowing that if they felled this redwood of a man, they'd command respect from their buddies. As far as I knew, no man ever did. But Socrates was not just any male.

"We don't know where he came from, but we know where he's decided he wants to live—at Dove's side. Oh, and he hates men."

"So I gathered," Isaac said, dropping his hands to his side. "I couldn't even get within ten feet of her. You know, that beak of his went straight for the old apple orchard."

I grinned at him. "Yeah, somewhere he learned exactly how to intimidate other males. Don't feel bad, you aren't the only one whose family jewels have been in mortal danger."

"What bird? What are you talking about?" Emory asked.

"A goose who's fallen in love with Dove will not let any man get within, as Isaac pointed out, ten feet of her. He showed up the first day Dove arrived."

"I love your gramma," Isaac said, running his hand over his white hair, pulled back in a long braid tied with a piece of leather. "But I think, under the circumstances, she'll just have to do without me this weekend."

The door opened and Dove squeezed in, leaving Socrates out on the porch. Pitiful-sounding honks filtered through the thick door.

"Now you can kiss me," Dove told Isaac.

He accommodated her, then said, "I guess we'll have to sneak around to be together, Mother Goose."

"Enough of that. I'm still calling around trying to find his home."

"Have you thought of giving him to Rich?" Isaac said. "With some nice spring potatoes . . ."

"Oh, hush," she said, looping her arm through his. "Are you all set for your class tomorrow?"

"I am. I was just coming in here to see if Benni would consent to being my assistant. The class has fifty people in it and I'll definitely need some help, especially during the fieldwork."

"Sure," I said. "What do you need me to do?"

"Just be a general gofer, pass out paper and pencils, run the projector, give the students handouts, be in charge of water. I'm going to lecture in the morning and after lunch we'll be going on a nature walk to put into practice what I talked about in the lecture. I thought we'd go take some photographs at that cemetery I passed on my drive here."

"The Parkfield cemetery?" That was perfect. I'd wouldn't mind taking another look at the grave Victory had been so interested in, see if I could figure out anything else about it. "I was just there with the quilt ladies. Lots of interesting headstones. So, your lecture is in the barn, right?"

"Yes. Can we have about fifty chairs and maybe a movie screen?"

"I'll check with Shawna and make sure everything is set up. I saw a portable screen in her office, I think."

"You're a doll." He turned to Dove and said, "So, think we can sneak out the back way and avoid your new friend's bunker-buster beak?"

"We can try," she said. "There's another exit in the kitchen through the pantry."

A few minutes later, we heard Isaac's voice yelling a not-very-polite adjective followed by the word *goose*.

"Apparently Socrates is smarter than they realized," I said, laughing.

"I'm staying far away from Dove this weekend," Emory said. "Elvia and I do eventually want to have children."

At four o'clock, the books all set up for this evening's performance,

I left Elvia and Emory on their way to work on the barn decorations. I still had an hour before the tables needed to be set for supper, so I headed back to my cabin to work on the pictures again. Unfortunately, my cousin, Rita, got there before I did.

She was laying on my bed reading *Country Weekly* magazine. Half her suitcase of bugle-beaded cowgirl couture was spread all over her bed. My organized little piles of photographs had been unceremoniously dumped back into their original pasteboard box.

"What did you do?" I said, staring down in the box at my once organized piles.

She calmly turned a page, then pointed a foot at me. "Polished my toenails. I'm waiting for them to dry." Her toenails were a shade of greenish-blue that seemed to glow.

"I meant why did you mess up my photographs?"

She laid her magazine down and looked at me, her spiky eyelashes blinking in innocence. "I put them right on top of each other in the box. What's the big deal? I mean, it's not like I flung them all over the room." The magazine went back up.

I started to snap a reply, then stopped. It would do no good to point out that she wasn't the only person living in this cabin. She would always be one of those people who "don't get it." Her world revolved around what Rita wanted at the moment she wanted it.

"Any word from Skeeter?" I asked, hope always springing eternal in a desperate soul.

She gave a wet raspberry from behind her magazine. On the cover, Alan Jackson gave me an understanding smile from under his white cowboy hat. "He's an ass. He's Tiffany Ann's problem now."

"Tiffany Ann?"

Another raspberry came from behind the magazine. "She's the buckle bunny who I caught behind the grandstand in Reno with her skanky tongue halfway down my husband's lyin', cheatin' throat."

I grimaced. There was a picture I'd just as soon not have in my permanent memory banks. But, remembering how much it hurt when I thought Gabe was in love with another woman, I felt a stab of pity for my young, albeit irritating, cousin. "I'm sorry, Rita. Is there anything I can do?"

"Nope," she said, turning a page. "He's pond scum. But I'm going to get him back. Then when he least suspects it, I'll leave *him* buck-ass naked in the dust, just like he did me."

Another mental image that stunned me for a moment. "Well," I said, trying to be encouraging, "at least you have a plan."

"You bet I do." She tossed the magazine aside. "And it just might include that cute detective, Chevy."

"Ford," I automatically corrected.

"Huh?"

"Never mind," I said quickly. It'd be good for his ego to realize she didn't even remember his name. "Are you and he . . . uh . . . whatever?" I *thought* he'd just been pulling my chain.

"Not yet," she said, sitting up and touching a finger to her bright blue toes. "But I'm considering it. He is kinda old, though. Maybe I'll look for someone like, more cool and younger, to piss off Skeeter."

That made me smile. "I think you should mention that to Detective Chevy. I'm sure it's something he'd like to know." Then my smile melted slightly. I hoped she didn't mean Sam.

She shrugged. "Whatever."

I picked up the box of photographs and started for the sitting room.

"Hey, I forgot," Rita said. "I think I, like, figured out who that secret travel person is."

I turned to stare at her. "You have? Like, how?" Hearing my answer, I felt like groaning out loud. Great, I'd only shared a room with Rita for a few days and I was already beginning to sound like her. Next thing you know I'd be painting my nails neon pink and wearing a shredded T-shirt that said, "I Kissed the Lead Singer."

"I think it's one of the Georgia cousins. The one with the big mouth."

"Hey," I said in a low voice, pointing at the open cabin window. "Rita, don't say it so loud. Those ladies are paying your salary. Which one are you talking about?"

"The one who's always telling everyone what to do. I think she's the travel person. The dark-haired one."

"You mean Reba?"

"Yeah, though she's no Reba McIntire, that's for sure."

I wasn't even going to ask what Rita meant by that.

"I'm leaning more toward Kitty, the lady from New York," I said. "Or maybe even Karen Olson. No one would suspect someone from Iowa."

"Nah," Rita said. "It's Reba. I can see it in her eyes."

Then try and make sure she has butter once in awhile, I wanted to say. "We'll see, I guess."

"I'm telling you, it's Reba."

I took the box of photographs into the living room and tried to think of a place I could go where I could spread out without someone messing my system up. There wasn't one place I could think of since privacy for the hired help was not a priority. Then I got an idea. Envelopes. I'd separate them in those 8½-by-11-inch manila envelopes. There must be some in the ranch office. I could separate the photographs here in the cabin's living room with a minimal need for space. Sure enough, when I went over to the office, Shawna had a box of them.

"Take as many as you need," she said.

"Thanks," I said, grabbing a handful. "This should do for now."

Back at the cabin, I had only sat down for ten minutes or so when Rita came out of the bedroom wearing sprayed-on blue jeans and a pink-and-white camouflage-print T-shirt that declared in black letters across her chest, "If I got smart with you, cowboy, how would you know?" I had to admit, that one made me smile.

"It's five o'clock," she said. "You'd better put that away and help me get the tables set for supper." She flounced past me triumphantly, obviously thrilled she was telling *me* what to do, leaving in her wake a trail of musky Tabu-scented air.

"Well, shoot," I said, not caring that she felt triumphant just as long as she served dinner on time. But it was frustrating that every time I started on this, something interrupted me. I looked down at the picture in my hand. It showed Joe Darnell, Dave Hardin, and a thirtyish-looking man I didn't recognize standing on the front porch of the two-bedroom adobe house where Shawna and Johnny now lived. It was the only picture I'd found so far of the adobe. On the back was penciled—Joe, David, and Brownie—April 1963. I slipped it in an envelope I'd labeled, Misc People. I wondered who Brownie was. Most likely one of the ranch hands that had come and gone during the many years the Darnells owned the ranch. It was a common occurrence in the early and middle part of the century. Now there usually wasn't enough work on small- or even medium-sized family ranches to hire extra hands. There were also not that many experienced cowboys left to hire.

Remembering Rita's tenacious declaration about The Secret Traveler, I tried to casually observe Reba while I served her Rich's molasses-baked ham steaks, new potato salad, fresh corn-on-the-cob, and chocolate-mocha mousse.

"Anyone want seconds on dessert?" I asked.

All the cousins groaned in unison.

"Anything else I can offer you?"

They gave great, full womanly laughs and pointed over at the employee table where Iry was eating, but Hud's chair was empty.

"Where's Detective Hudson?" asked Reba.

"I have no idea, but when I see him, I promise to tell him you all are looking for him."

"We heard you spent the night with him," Pinky said, arching her eyebrows.

"We're green with envy, girl," Reba said.

"It wasn't like *that*," I said. "I'm a married woman."

"Too bad," Gaynelle said, looking genuinely sorry for me.

"Is he coming back?" Loretta asked. "I honestly don't think we've all been questioned enough." The other cousins nodded, laughing and elbowing each other.

"The next time I see him, I'll tell him that you all have lots more to tell him," I said, smiling at their obvious enjoyment of the situation and each other.

"You do that, honey," Reba said. "And we'll be *forever* in your debt."

Good, I thought, mentally patting myself on the back. If Rita was right, then maybe a few more minutes with Hud would secure a good report from Reba. If Reba wasn't the columnist, well, they'd still remember their good time here and possibly tell all their affluent Georgia friends.

After dinner, everyone retired to the Annie Oakley Room where Meg would give her poetry reading. She'd already taught her class on ranch poetry this afternoon and, from what Rich told me—he'd come out of the kitchen to listen to some of it—there was going to be some pretty hilarious poetry written by the guests, mainly the Georgia cousins. Most of it centered around saddle-sore behinds.

Shawna came up beside me as people were starting to find seats. "Are you still game to help decorate the barn?" She held a hot mug of tea between her hands, bringing it close to her face for warmth. "Elvia, Emory, and I started this afternoon, but didn't finish. There's still a few strings of lights to be put up."

I stuck my hands in my back pockets. "Is it a two-person job?"

"Not really," she said. "I suppose I could do it alone."

I shook my head. "No, I meant I could do it. Why don't you sit here, drink your tea and enjoy Meg's performance? I've heard her many times so it's not as special for me. Gabe will help me if I need it."

She sipped at her tea, looking at me with grateful eyes over the rim of her mug. "Are you sure?"

"Positive. After I'm through, I'll go back to the box of photographs and documents you put in my room."

"Are you finding anything interesting?"

I nodded. "Lots of pictures of your dad and different buildings around the ranch. There's only one of the adobe so far. I was hoping to do a section of the album with just ranch buildings, then and now. It shows him, Dave, and another man standing on the front porch of the adobe. The date on the back was 1963."

"Must have been one of Dad's ranch hands. I wasn't even born then."

"And I was five. The guy's name is Brownie."

She took another sip from her mug. "Never met him. Except for a few birthday cards that Mom let me have, I've only been in touch with Dad for a little over two years. Everything that happened on the ranch all those years is a mystery to me. Guess they always will be now."

There was nothing I could say that would be appropriate. Losing both your parents within two years of each other was a situation beyond words.

"I'm dividing up the pictures into categories," I said. "Then we can go through them and work out a theme for this family history album." Maybe working on something like this would help ease her grief about her dad.

"That sounds wonderful. It'll be a really special addition to the guest ranch." Her generous mouth turned straight. "Providing that we have a ranch when this is all through."

"You will," I said with conviction. "All these kinks will work themselves out. And, trust me, people will remember the fun stuff they did, not the occasional stumble." At least, that's what I was counting on.

"I hope you're right," she said, echoing my thoughts.

I found Gabe sitting in an easy chair in the TV room off the main hall. Or more accurately sleeping in an easy chair. His day working with Jet and his night worrying about me had obviously caught up with him. His head drooped to the side and his book, about the battle of Gettysburg, lay across his lap. I didn't have the heart to wake him. There couldn't be that much more work to do decorating for the barn dance. If I didn't finish it tonight, I'd set my alarm and get up early to do it.

The barn's decorations, as Shawna promised, were almost finished. They weren't real elaborate, mostly tiny white Christmas lights strung around the rafters, some appropriately placed hay bales, some old farm implements hung on the gray, weathered walls. A long row of folding utility tables was stretched across the back, covered with red-checked tablecloths. A couple of punch bowls sat on one end and a huge, silver coffee urn, the kind that serves a hundred, sat on the other. There were four flower arrangements, one for each table, that featured red carnations and white daisies with red gingham ribbon and pale shocks of wheat cleverly arranged in the flowers. Elvia's touch was apparent. Old Western paperbacks by Louis L'Amour and Zane (Pearl!) Grey were stuck inside the arrangements, which would be given as door prizes.

It was obvious where the last strands of lights needed to go, around the arbor where the band would set up. I found a ladder and was on the next to the top step stringing them through the wooden arbor when someone cleared their throat. The loud and unexpected sound echoed up into the barn's rafters, startling me. I dropped the strand I was holding and grabbed the ladder to keep from falling.

I carefully turned around to see who was there. Hud stood a few feet away, grinning.

"Geeze Louise, you want to knock or something?" I said.

"I cleared my throat. What more do you want? And why are you so jumpy?"

"Lack of sleep. A possible murderer running loose. Crazy Cajun detectives sneaking up behind me. Take your pick." I climbed down off the ladder. "What do you want?"

"Saw you leave the poetry reading and was curious where you were skulking off to."

"I didn't see you there." As the cousins had so pointedly noticed, he hadn't been at dinner tonight, though Iry was, regaling our table again with hilarious Cajun jokes, especially the Boudreaux/Thibodeaux ones which were, according to him, a Cajun form of the Hatfield and McCoys.

"Been working."

I waited for him to elaborate.

He took a hand out of his pocket and scratched his nose. "Yeah, been reading reports all afternoon." He pulled off his jacket and tossed it on a hay bale. Then he picked up the strand of twinkly lights

I had dropped and started wrapping them in a large circle. "Why don't you let me put these up? Shawna doesn't need you breaking a leg. Who would take the guests on their trail rides?"

"What reports were you reading?" I knew he was teasing me with his statement. He'd gotten back some information from the forensic lab and was dangling it over my head like a string of yarn.

"Oh, just some reports." He started up the ladder with the lights.

I was silent for a moment, determined not to lose my temper. It was starting to wear on me, the tension at the ranch, the restless and half-night's sleep I'd been getting, the bickering between him and Gabe, the still troubling feeling that Victory was involved somehow. And my father. Always that worry about my father and his possible role in this. I put my fingertips to my left temple and started rubbing. A headache that had been hovering around the edges of my brain for the last twenty-four hours had blossomed in the last ten minutes.

Hud turned around and looked down at me. "You're being unnaturally quiet."

"I have a headache. Look, if you're going to finish this, then I'm going back to my cabin." I turned and started for the barn door.

"I can't believe you're giving up that easy," he called after me.

"Believe it," I said over my shoulder.

"Did anyone ever tell you that you were high-strung?"

I continued walking toward the door.

The aluminum ladder fell with an ear piercing clatter, causing me to turn around. Hud headed toward me at a fast walk.

I held up my hand for him to stop. "Hey, I thought you were going to finish decorating."

"I will, but first, don't you want to hear what the reports said?"

There was no way I believed that he would tell me what he'd found out. Not without a catch. "Right, you're just going to tell me."

He nodded.

"Without me begging or harassing you?"

He nodded again.

I folded my arms across my chest. "Why?"

He shrugged. "Because I'm a nice guy? Certainly nicer than you who has told me exactly nothing."

I didn't answer, because he was right. But all I had were suspicions. He possessed hard facts. And right now, I just wanted to hear what was in those forensic reports. "I keep telling you I don't know a thing. What do the reports say?"

He inhaled deeply. "Maybe I shouldn't. I could get in big trouble for telling you this."

I turned around and started for the door.

"The bones are of a male, over twenty-one years old, more likely, according to measurements, someone quite a bit older. Late thirties, early forties. Head wound consistent with severe trauma. In other words, someone bashed our friend a good one. Enough to kill him, most likely."

I turned around slowly, listening.

"He'd been in the ground at least thirty to thirty-five years. They figured that out from soil samples, vegetative growth, animal activity. Maybe a little more or less. No matter what they show in the movies, forensic science is still a lot of guess work. Kristen told me they considered doing a mitochondrial DNA test to determine the family he's linked to, though this type of DNA is not individual. It tracks the family tree through the mother's line."

"Did they?"

"No, they didn't get the okay. These labs only do what the department authorizes and my superiors aren't convinced this is worth the time and money the test would cost."

"In other words, the sheriff is still trying to figure out whether it will help his career."

"Don't forget, him's a her now. Actually, not this sheriff. She's a pretty straight-shooter, not as politically motivated as the last one. A real cop, from what I can tell."

"So, why not do all the tests they can?"

"Money, *chère*, pure and simple. There just ain't enough of it in the budget. Since those bones have been found, there's been a lot more pressing work come into the lab, things where public safety is a problem, like rapes and homicides. Fresh ones."

He was right. We'd gone over this ground before. A homicide like this wouldn't be a top priority, no matter how unfair that was. Nobody's life was in danger because of these old bones. A crime was committed and perhaps, it would only be up to God to hand out justice in eternity. We here on earth will just have to wonder.

"So, they aren't going to try and see if he's related to . . . uh . . . anyone connected with Broken Dishes?" I couldn't even say Joe or Shawna's names.

"They might eventually. Right now it's relegated to the unsolved homicide file. They did a missing person search for the time span when these bones were supposedly buried. No reports of anyone matching this description turning up missing in this area."

"Then I guess that's that," I said, hugging myself. The temperature in the barn had suddenly grown frigid. I wouldn't have to worry about whether I'd have to tell Hud about Victory's possible connection with the ranch. Whatever it was, even an illicit relationship with Joe Darnell, it didn't really matter now. And I could try to forget that my father might have been involved.

"Could be," Hud said, his expression enigmatic.

"Seems kind of sad, this person never being identified. Being buried without a name."

"Happens every day of the year. Every city has a potter's field." He gestured over at the lights. "I'll finish up here. Go canoodle with your husband." He walked back toward the ladder and the lights he'd dropped.

At the barn door, I turned around, unable to stop myself from asking, "You're just going to give up on it? Whoever did this will get off scot free?" I don't know why I was pressing the point. With Daddy possibly involved and the ranch's reputation on the line, I wanted to walk away. But something in me wouldn't. Something couldn't.

"I don't want to," he said, holding his hand out in an apologetic gesture. "But my job doesn't stop while I'm working on this case. There are other crimes to investigate." He gave me a sardonic half-smile. "Besides, I thought you were all for letting the Big Guy handle stuff like justice and revenge at the end of this craziness we call life. You've preached those very words at me ad nauseam."

I clamped my lips together, irritated at first. Then I gave a small laugh. He was absolutely right. I was always going on and on about how I believed that God's eternal justice will eventually prevail. So why all of a sudden did I feel so compelled to ferret out the truth in this situation? Especially when I should be trying to protect my own father?

Because it did matter. No one should get away with murder and deep down inside, unlike the other time when Hud and I had to let someone go because there was nothing else we could do to bring the person to justice on this earth, this time everything hadn't been done.

"Because we haven't exhausted every means," I said, looking at the ground, feeling more than a little embarrassed and slightly queasy. "I think God would expect us to do that before leaving it up to His justice."

He bent down and picked up the strand of lights again. "Spoken like a true detective. The first sentence, anyway. So, now that I've told you everything I know, how about letting me in on what you've discovered? And don't deny that you haven't figured out something. I can tell you have by the dog-puddle-in-the-kitchen look in your eyes."

"I don't know anything." It wasn't a lie. I suspected a lot, but didn't *know* one dang thing. Besides it appeared right now that it didn't matter one way or the other.

"Have you talked to Mr. Wonderful about any of this?" He looped the strand of lights over his shoulder.

My five seconds of hesitation told him what he wanted to know. He chuckled. "Well, I'll be. You really aren't an easy girl to play with. Of course, that's why I find it so much fun. But *he's* going to pop his cork when he discovers you've been holding out on him."

"I have to go," I said, turning to leave.

"I know I don't have to tell you this," he called after me. "But *lache pas la patate.*"

I stopped, but didn't turn around. I wanted to keep going, but it would drive me crazy if I didn't find out what he'd said. "What?"

"Old Cajun saying. Don't drop the potato is what it literally means. But what it's really saying is, don't give up, *chère.*"

"Grab the dogs," I yelled at some guests while I ran toward the stable. "Lock them in the horse trailer."

Whip stood in front of the stables, holding a bunch of wet towels. "Here," he said, thrusting them at us. "Cover their eyes and lead them out. There's four inside. The rest I pastured last night."

A horse screamed in panic and Lindsey visibly flinched.

"Put one over your mouth," he said, then headed inside the stables.

I followed him inside with Lindsey at my heels.

"Benni, you take Stormy," Whip yelled. "Lindsey, take Tanya. I'll try to get Jet."

Inside, the smoke was already thick enough that we had to feel our way down the aisle. With a towel over my mouth and nose, I unlatched Stormy's stall door. Then I pulled the towel aside and called out his name a calm voice. "Stormy, good boy. It's okay, now. We're going to get you out of here."

He reared back slightly, his ears pinned back, the whites of his eyes a bright glow in the thickening smoke. Every time another horse screamed in panic, his nostrils flared and he screamed in reply. I threw my towel over my shoulder and grabbed the halter hanging by the stall door. Talking to him the whole time, I eased my way closer. When I touched his shoulder, he bolted and darted away from me.

"C'mon, Stormy," I crooned, willing myself to stay calm so he wouldn't sense my own fear. "It's okay, buddy. We're going to get you out of here. C'mon, buddy. It's all right." I choked on the last sentence, the dense smoke already burning my lungs.

I moved toward him, touching his shoulder again, grabbing his mane when he tried to dart away. "Stormy, calm down," I said in a firmer voice. Then I started coughing. I pressed my face into his side. His skin quivered with fear.

Coughing and spitting, I managed to slip the halter around his neck and buckle it. Forget trying to get it over his nose, there was no way I could manage that. He still reared up, jerking away from me, not wanting to leave his stall, the place where he felt safest, no matter how dangerous it actually was.

CHAPTER 13

*L*ATER THAT NIGHT, I WAS STARTLED OUT OF A DEEP, DREAMLESS sleep.

"Fire!" a voice outside our window yelled.

"What?" Rita mumbled in her sleep.

Like any rancher worth her salt, that word snapped me into instant consciousness. I sprang out of bed, pulled off my pj bottoms, dragged on a pair of jeans and boots. In less than a minute, while Rita was still struggling to sit up, I was out the cabin's front door with Lindsey close behind me.

Elvia's voice yelled, "What's going on?"

"Where is it?" Lindsey cried.

In front of us, the lodge and adobe ranch house looked fine.

"The barn or the stables," I said.

We ran around the cabin toward the stables where smoke was pouring out of the entry. Inside, the sound of screaming horses turned my heart to ice.

People started emerging from their cabins. Somewhere in the din someone screamed, "Call 911!" The two ranch dogs ran to the smoking building and back, barking shrilly.

I threw the wet towel over his head, covering his eyes, hoping it would cover up some of the smell and heat from the fire. Horses were often easy to trick and, right now, it was the only one I had up my sleeve. The smoke felt like needles in my lungs. I didn't see any flames, something I wasn't sure was good or bad. All I knew is we had to get out of there. My eyesight blurred and Stormy suddenly became a big brown blob.

He balked as I led him out the stall door into the aisle.

"It's okay, Stormy," I encouraged while leading him at a fast, but firm walk. "You can do this. You can do this."

In the smoke ahead of me, I could see Lindsey struggling with Tanya, who kept pulling back on her lead. Tanya reared back and let out a terrified scream. That caused Stormy to start pulling away from me in a panic. I grabbed a handful of mane and held on.

"Cover her face with something," I yelled to Lindsey.

Lindsey took the towel she'd been attempting to hold over her own mouth and threw it over Tanya's face. In seconds, we had both the horses outside and away from the barn.

"Here!" I yelled at Isaac, thrusting Stormy's lead rope at him. "I gotta go back in."

"Be careful," he yelled.

I ran back inside. In the aisle, Johnny and Gabe struggled with Granite, who was refusing to come out of his stall. My chest burned every time I took a breath.

"What can I do?" I screamed at the men, my voice harsh and foreign-sounding to my ears.

"Get out!" Gabe yelled back. "This is the last one."

I hesitated, not wanting to leave Gabe.

"Go!" he commanded.

I obeyed him and ran out of the building. Outside, I bent over, holding my knees as I coughed and hacked and tried to inhale clean air.

"Honeybun," Dove's voice said behind me. I felt her hand gently patting me between my shoulder blades.

"Is Gabe . . . are all the horses . . . ?" I started.

"He's fine. They're all fine. Fortunately, most of them were in the far pasture." She pointed toward the parking lot.

I looked back at the stable. Johnny and Gabe had finally gotten Granite out and were leading him toward the pasture.

"The dogs?" I managed to squeak.

"They're fine too. Now, be quiet and catch your breath." She rubbed a small circle, patting me gently when I gave into a coughing fit.

Rich used every hose available fighting the fire and started a bucket brigade with most of the guests filling pots with water and passing them down a long line. I joined the line between David and Shawna, passing buckets of water. Tears streamed from my eyes from the smoke and from the futility of our battle. It was obvious the stables could not be saved.

Fortunately, it was a still, cold night with no breeze and the area around the stable was clean of brush, so, following Rich's orders we managed to keep the fire contained and away from the other buildings. Finally, Rich told us to stand back, that it would be better to let the flames burn themselves out. We stood silently and watched the flames licking up the old wood, unwillingly mesmerized by the brilliant yellow and orange blaze, as if we were watching some kind of horrible reverse aurora borealis, bent on destroying rather than enchanting.

By the time the two Paso Robles fire trucks and the paramedic van arrived, the flames were almost out. With Rich's expertise as a fire fighter and thanks to the recent rain, which had dampened everything, they were able to contain it to the stables. Hud and his grandfather, as well as half of the inhabitants of Parkfield, followed the fire truck. Rural folks did that for each other. More than one time in my life Dove, Daddy, and I dropped what we were doing and rushed to help friends fight a fire.

Whip came over to where I stood with Dove and Gabe. His face was dusky from the smoke, the whites of his eyes bright red. "I did a head count. Looks like all the horses are safe."

Shawna walked up beside him, tears streaming down her face.

"Oh, sweetie," Dove said, pulling her into her arms. Gabe, Whip, and I watched while Shawna sobbed into Dove's soft shoulder, helpless to do anything about this latest disaster.

"Well, shit," Whip said under his breath and strode away. Like most men, he handled sadness better by becoming angry. I watched him walk toward the pasture, where the horses were bunched together in a tight pack, tail to nose, tail to nose, gaining comfort from the herd.

"Where's Johnny?" I asked. It seemed to me that he should be here comforting his wife.

Gabe pointed over at the fire truck. He was deep in conversation with one of the firefighters. His auburn hair stuck up in all directions and his hands moved wildly as he explained something to the fireman.

What was he telling him? This fire wouldn't be easily explained. Unless they discovered faulty electrical wiring chewed by mice or internal combustion because of alfalfa hay that had been baled too wet, I knew there was a good chance someone deliberately started it. Possibly the same person who let Rawhide out and who was digging up those bones. I scanned the crowd, looking for Victory. She'd been right there in the middle of the bucket brigade, her gray hair tied back in a ponytail. If she was involved, would she go this far to get people's minds off the bones? As far as I knew, no one knew except me and Gabe, who I told last night right after I talked to Hud, that the sheriff's department had decided to close the investigation of the bones. To the person who was trying to divert our attention from the bones, Hud was still a threat, someone he or she needed to throw off track.

Gabe slipped an arm around my shoulders. "How are you feeling?"

I cleared my throat, trying to dislodge what felt like a lump of coal stuck in my esophagus. "Okay. What about you?"

"I'm fine. I wasn't in there as long as you." He drew me closer to him and I could smell the smoke permeating his damp sweatshirt. He rubbed his lips back and forth on top of my head. My hair couldn't smell too good right now, unless he liked the scent of burnt pine.

"Why did this have to happen now?" I asked, my voice sounding gravelly in my own ears. It hurt to talk.

"I don't know, *niña*. I don't know."

We watched Rich talk to the fire captain in charge. They both walked around the charred building, accompanied by one of the firefighters who was, Rich has told Gabe, studying to be arson investigator. The paramedics insisted that all of us who rescued the horses take some oxygen. When we refused to go to hospital, one of the paramedics asked us to sign a release stating we'd chosen to forgo that route of care.

"Will there be any permanent damage to his lungs?" Shawna asked, standing next to Johnny, gripping his hand as he inhaled oxygen. Her cheeks shined with tears.

"Probably not," said one of the paramedics, a jovial, red-headed young man named Jack with a killer white smile. "But I'm not a doctor, so you might want to check with your physician. Sure wouldn't recommend any of you entering a marathon in the next few weeks."

After a few minutes of oxygen, I wandered over to where Bunny and Whip stood talking to the arson investigator. Whip was quiet as Bunny answered the man's questions about what kind of hay they stored in there and how much.

"That hay's been in the barn since late summer," Bunny told him. "If it was going to burn, it would have long before now. It might be the electrical system, but it's doubtful. We had the wires completely replaced only a year ago. I supposed mice could have chewed the wires . . ." Her voice sounded doubtful.

"Then there's a good possibility it was deliberately set," the investigator said. "We'll wait until it cools down a little more and take a closer look. You'll need the investigator's report for your insurance claim."

Bunny nodded. "I'll talk to the owners about it." The she glanced up at the grayish-black sky. "What time is it anyway?"

The investigator checked his watch. "Four o'clock."

In four hours we'd have fifty people here waiting for a continental breakfast and in fourteen hours we'd have two hundred people here ready to dance and have a carefree Saturday night.

"We'd all better get back to bed then," Bunny said. "It's a full day tomorrow . . . well, later today, that is." Ignoring her own words, she started toward the pasture to check on the horses. I knew Bunny wouldn't rest until she'd physically run her hands over every single horse herself.

"Hey, sweetcakes," Emory said, coming up to me. His Ralph Lauren jeans were soaked with water and black with dirt. "How are you breathing?" Elvia clung to his arm, her black eyes glassy with worry.

"I'm fine," I said, then had a short coughing fit.

"Sounds like it," Emory said.

"I'll be okay," I said, finally catching my breath. "I just hope Shawna and Johnny will be."

We looked over to where they stood with the investigator, heads bent over some form he was writing on.

"Those poor kids," Elvia said.

I wandered over to where Victory was standing with David. They stood silently watching the smoldering pile of burnt wood that used to be a stable, identical looks of sadness on their faces.

"You two okay?" I asked the question that everyone had been passing around like a baton in a relay race.

"Yes," Victory said. "But I'm just sick for Shawna and Johnny."

"We all are," I said.

"How could it happen so fast?" she asked.

"Probably didn't," David answered. "If this had happened during the day when people were awake, we would have caught it before it destroyed the whole building. Who knows how long it smoldered without anyone knowing?" His sober face told me he didn't, for a minute, think it was faulty wiring, mice, or bad hay.

"I hope they have insurance," Victory said, pushing back a strand of silver hair that had blown across her face.

"I'm sure they must," I said. As she walked toward her cabin, stopping every so often to speak to someone, I watched her, trying to fight the thought, could she have set the fire? The thought chilled me.

As people started wandering back to their rooms to either rest or clean up, Gabe came back over to me.

I undid my messy ponytail. It tumbled down around my shoulders sending up a scent of acrid smoke. "I need a shower."

"We all do," Gabe said. "The water pressure will probably be pretty low the next couple of hours."

I sighed. "It's going to be a very long day."

"Looks like caffeine may be the drug of choice the next twelve to fourteen hours."

"No doubt. I heard the fire investigator talking to Bunny and Whip. He said there's a good possibility it was arson."

Gabe nodded. "Always a possibility."

"Maybe it was the electrical wiring," I said, not wanting to believe anyone would deliberately put horses in danger.

Gabe just said, "We'll have to wait and see."

"I sure hope whoever The Secret Traveler is, they didn't hear that rumor. That's not exactly the image Shawna and Johnny would like for the ranch." Then I yawned. "I can't believe people will be here in less than three hours for Isaac's seminar. I'd better get cleaned up and try to take a nap."

"Me too," he replied.

We kissed and agreed to meet before breakfast. I watched Gabe walk to the bunkhouse and go inside.

I was on my cabin's doorstep, when Hud called my name. I'd seen him and his grandfather in the crowd that arrived shortly after the Paso Robles fire trucks, but with all the commotion, we'd not talked.

I watched him stride toward me.

"Are you okay?" he asked.

"Yes." I brushed a strand of sticky hair from my face.

"I heard most of the horses were in the back pasture."

I nodded. "There were only four in the stalls, thank goodness."

"Don't you find that oddly convenient?"

I didn't like what he was implying, even though I'd thought it myself. "We've left horses in the pasture overnight lots of times."

"Who told you there were only four horses in the stable?"

I looked into his cloudy, bourbon-colored eyes. "Whip."

He glanced down at my pale blue, soot-stained pj top. "I think my daughter has those same pajamas."

I looked down at my ruined top. They were my favorite flannel pjs covered with cowgirls on bucking broncos. Now they felt itchy and damp and stunk of smoke. Embarrassed, I crossed my arms over my chest.

His amused expression turned intent, a coon dog on the scent. He wore faded Levi's and a gray sweatshirt that said Tulane University. I'd heard of it, but for the life of me couldn't remember where in the south it was.

"I heard you were one of the first people to hear about the fire."

"Me and Lindsey were. But the others were there within minutes."

"Who set off the alarm?"

What he was implying was obvious and something I'd tried not to think about. The emotions of the last few hours started getting to me, and I felt tears sting my eyes.

"The horses could have died," I said, looking at the ground, not wanting him to see me cry. "I don't believe Whip would go that far." A small bouquet of butter-and-eggs, a simple wildflower whose name usually made me smile, became a watery blur.

I didn't want it to be Whip. In spite of how he'd acted the last few days, I'd always liked him. I admired his ability with horses and cattle. He respected them and, I thought, loved them in that gruff, unspoken way of ranchmen. And with what I knew about his background, it seemed like he received a raw deal in life. Would he risk the lives of these horses out of jealousy of Johnny or anger at Joe? Or was this connected with those bones? Those blasted bones that I wished Buck had never found.

I looked back up into Hud's face. A smudge of soot streaked his left cheek, like he'd scratched himself without realizing he had dirt on his fingers.

"Why would he sound the alarm if he was the one who started the fire?" I said.

"You know why. So he'll be the one least suspected."

I blinked my eyes rapidly, trying to relieve the scratchiness behind the lids. "Except that didn't work. You do suspect him."

He lifted one hand, palm up. "Ah, but I'm a contrary Cajun." In the misty gray air just before dawn, his face took on a harder edge. He smiled at me, but the smile never reached his dark eyes.

"Do the Abbotts have a lot of insurance?" he asked.

I squeezed my arms tighter across my chest. I liked that implication even less. I knew the ranch needed cash, but I refused to believe Shawna or Johnny would burn one of their own buildings, put their horses, friends, and employees at risk just to collect a claim. "Why don't you ask them?"

"I intend to. And just to throw a little more kindling on the fire, did it ever occur to you that even if neither of the Abbotts thought that insurance money would help the ranch, maybe one of their workers might."

"Like who?" I said hotly.

"David Hardin has a good reason for this ranch to keep going. He's in his sixties, no money saved, very little social security. If this ranch goes under, where will he go?"

Behind him, one of the fire trucks pulled slowly away. "Don't cops ever get tired of suspecting everyone they meet?"

His smile did reach his eyes this time. "I don't, but why don't you ask your husband? Maybe he has more Christian compassion than I do. But I doubt it." He reached over and gently swiped a finger across my cheek. "*T'est blam comme in mort, catin.*"

His touch caused me to flinch and take an uneasy step back. "What did you say?"

"You're pale as a ghost. Go take a shower and put on some blush. Let me see to Mr. Greenwood and the others. You stick to your horseback rides and quilting."

His words raised my hackles. "That remark is not only condescending and sexist, it is contradictory. Didn't you tell me just last night not to give up?"

His hand reached out, palm up, like he was about to hand me something. "That was before it started getting ugly. It would break my heart in a million pieces to see you get hurt."

His words took me by surprise. Before I could respond, he turned and walked toward the lodge. "I've got work to do. See you tonight, *chère*. Save a dance for me."

CHAPTER 14

I WATCHED HIM WALK TOWARD THE LODGE. I WAS ANNOYED BY
his condescending attitude and uncomfortably touched by his concern.
They were the same confused feelings he'd stirred up in me from the
first time we met. But right now I was just too tired and troubled to try
to figure them out. Over in the lodge I could see Kitty through one of
the windows, her head bent over her sewing machine, obviously unable
to go back to sleep. From my own experience I knew it was not the
first, nor last time quilting helped a person through a troublesome time.
At least when you quilted, something useful came out of your fear.

My hot shower felt wonderful, but it also woke me up enough that
I knew there'd be no sleep for me. Rita, though she'd woken up,
watched the whole spectacle, and even passed a few buckets of water,
hadn't been personally affected enough to keep her from going back
to sleep. She snored away in our bedroom like she'd just watched the
filming of a low-budget disaster movie. Lindsey's door was closed so
I assumed she and Elvia were both trying to nap before our long day.

It was five thirty, which gave me an hour before I needed to be at
the lodge to set up for both the continental and regular breakfasts.
Now would be as good a time as any to continue sifting through the
box of photographs and papers Shawna left here yesterday. The small

sitting room in our cabin was quiet. Doing this would be the next best thing to taking a nap.

Within a half hour, I hit pay dirt when, at the bottom of the box, I found a black leather King James Bible, its edges worn rough and brown from use. The gold-leafed presentation page read *To: Joseph William "Will" Darnell From: Your loving mother, Charlotte Darnell, on the occasion of your graduation from high school in the year of our Lord 1951. Broken DIS Ranch, Parkfield, California.*

I was willing to bet that Shawna had not seen this Bible. It was just what she needed right now, this concrete connection to her father.

The family history section was partially filled out and I noticed that Joe had a sister named Clarissa who died when she was eighteen. He never mentioned her in all the years I knew him. Then again, I was a kid and she'd died so young. The Bible said she died in 1965. I must have met Clarissa Darnell because my family had known the Darnells since I was a toddler. But, there was a lot I didn't remember before age six or seven. I could barely remember my own mother, much less a woman I'd probably only seen a few times.

I flipped through the Bible to see if anything else had been written or underlined in the pages. The parts a person marked in their Bible often told a lot about a person. My pastor, Mac, customarily borrowed a person's Bible right after they died and used some of the underlined passages to compose the person's funeral service. He would have had a hard time with Joe Darnell. Though the Bible looked well-used, there were no verses marked. Whatever struggles Joe had, he kept them between himself and the Lord, with no evidence left behind for others to peruse. It reminded me of Gabe, who was also reluctant about putting any feelings down on paper. He claimed that all his years he'd worked as a homicide detective made him wary about putting secret thoughts and feelings in a permanent record.

"Eventually, someone will read it," he'd once said. "I don't like the idea of anyone, even after I'm dead . . . maybe, especially after I'm dead . . . knowing my secret thoughts."

"Good thing others don't feel the way you do," I answered, long a fan of old diaries and letters. "Or we'd have no personal history to reflect back on or learn from."

I set the Bible aside to take to Shawna. This would mean something special to her. A few more minutes of digging through the photographs yielded a couple more showing the ranch in its early days. There were two more showing Joe and David. At the bottom was one that particularly interested me because part of it was neatly cut off. It showed the front porch of the ranch house again, obviously a favorite picture-taking spot, and four people—Joe, David, and a young woman who looked enough like Joe to be his sister, and part of a booted leg in stained chaps.

On the back of the photograph written in pencil was, *July 4, 1963—Joe, Clarissa and B—*. The rest of his name was missing. It sparked a memory of something I'd seen earlier. I set it down and looked through the photographs I'd separated. Here it was, the one of Joe, David, and someone named Brownie. Could this be that Brownie again? Why had someone cut him out of the photograph?

I stared at Clarissa's round, smiling face. She wore a polka-dotted, belted dress and flat shoes. Her hair was very blond and in a classic sixties flip hairstyle, as perfect as if she'd just come from the beauty parlor. She held a small American flag in her hand. There was something about her eyes that struck me. I wasn't sure what it was. She stared directly at whoever was taking the picture, but it seemed to me like she didn't see them, like she was staring off into space, almost like that so-called thousand-yard stare I saw in some of Gabe's old Vietnam photographs. The men in the photographs, Gabe included, looked like they were seeing something we couldn't.

Joe smiled easily at the camera, his eyes squinting against the sun, looking exactly as I remembered him except younger.

I stuck the photograph inside the Bible. In all my searching it was the only one I'd found of Shawna's aunt Clarissa. Did Shawna even know she'd had an aunt?

I continued sorting through the pictures, finding more of Joe, David and Isabel, Shawna's mother, but not another one of Clarissa. Was that the only photograph of her? That might explain why, if someone was mad at this Brownie person, they would just cut him out of the picture rather than toss the whole thing out.

I glanced at the clock above the fireplace when Lindsey came out dressed for the day. "Shoot, it's a quarter to seven already."

Inside their bedroom, I could make out Elvia still snuggled under the red paisley comfortor. Music played softly on the radio between the two beds. I didn't worry about Elvia getting up early, she didn't really have to do anything until the dance tonight.

Lindsey stretched and gave a wide yawn. "I'm going to check and see if Bunny needs me to do anything. Catch you later."

"Hey, Rita!" I went into the bedroom and shook the lumpy bundle. "Wake up. We have to serve two breakfasts in an hour."

"I'm getting up," she mumbled, not moving a muscle. "I had a rough night."

I gave her one more vigorous shake and headed out of the room. "You'll miss Rich's cinnamon rolls if you don't get moving."

"Cinnamon rolls?" I heard her say as I closed the front door.

The minute I stepped outside, the acrid odor of the stable fire permeated the crisp morning air so that even when you weren't in sight of the charred building, you still knew there'd been a fire. I purposely avoided the area, not ready to think too much this busy morning about all the possible scenarios that could have happened last night. Before going to the kitchen, I dropped the old Bible off in Shawna's office with a note. I had a feeling she'd like to see this right away.

Only Sam was in the kitchen standing in front of a long line of cinnamon rolls. The room smelled heavenly. I'm sure cinnamon must be one of God's favorite flavors. Sam was slapping white frosting on them at warp speed.

"Hey, stepson, you're certainly the ambitious one this morning," I said, heading for the coffeepot.

He turned to look at me, his pastry knife dripping white icing on Rich's clean floor. The panic on his face made me stop in my tracks.

"Sam, what's wrong? Where's Rich?"

"Migraine. He went back to the bunkhouse about ten minutes ago. He can barely see and he's barfing his guts out. He told me to get started and that you'd help. What do I do now?"

A migraine. It was probably set off by all the smoke or maybe the stress. Who knew what set off headaches like that? I just knew that when a person had one, they were often incapacitated for at least a day. Poor Rich. And poor us. What a time for him to have one.

"Okay," I said, forcing myself to sound calm when what I wanted to do was run in circles and scream. "You and I can do this, Sam. Just keep working on the cinnamon rolls. Isaac's class is expecting a continental breakfast and we're going to give it to them."

His young face twitched in anxiety. "I was supposed to set up the tables in the garden, but I've been trying to get these rolls done. Shawna's out there trying to put them up. And I haven't even started breakfast yet."

"Don't panic. I'll scout around for some help. Just keep icing those rolls."

I went out into the dining room, where the tables for breakfast still needed to be set. Out in the garden, Shawna, Johnny, and Isaac were unfolding long tables.

"Rich is sick," Shawna said, her face one incident away from a hysteria that would match the horses' a few hours ago.

"I heard," I said. "I'll set the inside tables and then help Sam."

"Dove's gone for reinforcements," Isaac said, smoothing a blue-and-white paisley tablecloth over a folding table. "If you're needed here, I can handle my class alone."

"That should be no problem," I said. "By the time your class begins, everyone will have been fed and I can leave the cleanup to Rita."

"I'll help her," Shawna said.

Back inside the dining room, Dove had the WMU ladies setting the breakfast tables.

"Bless you, sisters," I said. "I'm going to start cooking breakfast."

Just then, Kitty walked out of the quilting room. "What's going on?" she asked me.

"We just had another slight mishap. Our chef has a migraine. But don't worry, breakfast will be on time."

She tsked under her breath. "Dear, dear, I know how migraines are. They never come at a convenient time, do they?"

I smiled and shook my head no.

"Do you need any help? I spent my childhood working in my parents' coffee shop at the Jersey shore. I'm a whiz at eggs and pancakes."

I hesitated. Asking a guest to work in the kitchen? That wasn't exactly the best advertisement for a guest ranch. What if this was a trick? What if she was The Secret Traveler?

Karen Olson and her husband, Dennis, came up behind her.

"What's going on?" Karen echoed Kitty's words.

I explained the situation again.

"Oh, for goodness sakes, I have four children and more grandchildren than fingers," Karen said. "And I've organized more church and scouting pancake breakfasts than I care to remember. I can help too." She gestured to her husband. "And Dennis fries a mean strip of bacon. We'll have breakfast on the tables in twenty minutes."

"Well, okay," I said, figuring I had nothing to lose. Any chance for a good mention in The Secret Traveler's column was barbecued moose meat now. "Strap on aprons, folks, and join me and Sam in the kitchen."

Leaving Dove and the church ladies to finish setting the tables, I organized Karen, Kitty, Dennis, and Sam into separate tasks. We changed the pecan waffles and individual cheese omelette menu that Rich had originally planned to a simple pecan pancakes and bacon breakfast with each guest getting a half a grapefruit.

"We'll have to figure out something for lunch," Kitty told Karen as they team-worked the pancakes.

"How about BLT sandwiches?" Dennis suggested. "They're easy."

"Perfect," Karen said. "What about dinner?"

The kitchen doors flew open and Marty Brantley barreled in. "Heard that our sweet little chef is under the weather and you folks needed some help."

"Grab a knife and start cutting those grapefruits in half," Kitty ordered. "Put two raisins and a cherry on each one for eyes and a mouth." She winked at me. "Adds a little humor, something we'll likely be needing today."

Sam looked up from his cinnamon-roll assembly line and grinned at me, his face relieved. "Rich better watch out. These people might take his job."

Everyone laughed and I stood there for a moment and marveled at the human capacity to adapt to change and the incredible kindness of strangers. These people had paid a lot of money for this holiday and would have had a right to be irritated at all the troubles we'd been having. Instead, they not only rolled with the punches, but jumped in and started slugging away, fighting fires and making their own breakfast.

Breakfast was served on time and received rave reviews from everyone. Outside, the continental breakfast that came with Isaac's class also went smoothly with not a cinnamon roll crumb left for the birds.

"You'll have to clean up," I told Rita. "I have to help Isaac with his class."

"Alone?" she whined.

"No, Shawna said she'd help you. But she's had a pretty rough night, Rita. A rough year actually. Can't you just suck it up this once and pull a little extra weight without complaining?"

"Oh, all right," she said, giving a dramatic sigh.

On the way to the barn where Isaac's lecture was to take place, I stopped by my cabin and shoved a bunch of the photographs into a envelope. Maybe while he was lecturing, I could find time to go through them. Then I stopped by Dove's cabin to tell her what was going on.

"Me and the ladies will help serve lunch if Rita needs help," Dove said. "Don't you worry. Just be a good assistant to my sweetie."

I started out of the room, then thought of something. "Did you ever meet Joe Darnell's sister?"

Dove shook her head no. "She died before I could meet her. Your daddy and mama spoke of her a few times. Said she was a sweet woman, but she wasn't quite all there." Dove tapped on her temple.

"What do you mean?"

"I think she was slow."

"Oh," I said. "That explains the picture."

"What picture?"

"One I found in a box Shawna gave me. Her name was Clarissa. The Bible says she died in 1965. Something didn't look quite right in her expression."

"I was so busy with your mama and you I didn't know too much of what went on with other folks. Why are you asking?"

I shrugged. "Just curious. I don't know if Shawna knew about her or not."

"Know about who?" Edna McClun asked, coming out of the bathroom.

"Joe Darnell's sister," Dove said.

Edna made a small clucking sound. "Such a tragedy."

"What was?" I asked.

"His sister." Edna looked at me meaningfully. "She wasn't quite right in the head."

"So Dove tells me. Did you know her?"

Edna nodded. "Oh, yes. She was a friendly little thing, but oh my, sometimes she could have a temper. Joe just doted on her. Brought her to all the social events. He wasn't a bit ashamed of her."

Good for Joe, I thought.

"She was born that way," Edna said. "They didn't even really realize it until she was past the age of eight. She just never matured after that. In her head, that is."

"How did she die?" I asked. "According to their family Bible, she wasn't very old."

"I think it was her appendix, if I remember correctly. Just burst on her. They lived so far from town. Like I said, a tragedy."

"Why do you want to know about Clarissa Darnell?" Edna asked.

"I just saw her name in the Joe's Bible and was curious."

"Joe did a real good job taking care of his sister once his parents passed away," Edna said. "And it couldn't have been easy. Like I said, she had about the brain of an eight year old or thereabouts. I think their mama died when Clarissa was twelve or so and their daddy not long after. Joe was her only family and real protective of her."

That had to have been hard way out here, especially for a bachelor like Joe. "How much older was Joe?" I asked.

Edna scrunched up her face trying to remember. "Oh, maybe fifteen or so years. A good little bit. Clarissa was a late baby. Maybe that's why she was born that way."

So a twenty-seven-year-old bachelor was left with the responsibility of his mentally handicapped sister when she was twelve, just going into puberty, out here almost fifty miles from even a small town like Paso Robles, which was even less populated in the late fifties when Clarissa was a teenager. That really was a tough row to hoe. But that was Joe as I remembered him. He had the softest heart I'd ever seen in a man and was never one to give up on people he loved.

Because I'd always been fascinated by oral history more than traditional history, I couldn't help wondering about the minuscule details of Clarissa's life at the ranch. What did she do all day? Who helped her get dressed, do her hair, take a bath? And all the feminine stuff like her monthly periods? I couldn't imagine Joe taking care of personal things like that. But even if he had hired some woman to stay out here with Clarissa, and there was no indication he had, it still would have been hard. Was he relieved when she finally died? Or did he miss his only sibling, the last person in his family? I'd never know the answers to those questions.

"Well," I said, straightening up and sticking my hands in my pockets. "Doesn't matter now. Right now, we have to help those kids save this ranch."

"You run along and help Isaac," Dove said, shooing me with her hand. "Don't even think about another meal until tomorrow."

I went across the room and threw my arms around Dove, hugging her enthusiastically. "Gramma, to quote Sam, you're the bomb."

"I have no idea what that means, but I'll assume it's good." She hugged me in return, then smacked me affectionately on the butt. "Get along with you now."

Down at the barn, most of the students had already taken a seat and were chattering among themselves. Isaac was having a rough time getting the screen to stay up so I rushed over to help him. After setting up the screen and the projector, I sat in the back and listened to Isaac talk about taking photographs. Though I'd heard him speak on this subject many times before, every time I learned something new and he inspired me to look at the world in a different light. This time something he said particularly struck me.

"I believe art—even at its most beautiful—is at the core, motivated by pain," he said in his melodious voice. "That is because art is made by human beings and as human beings, pain is what motivates everything we do. We are either causing it or running from it or facing it, but pain is always there, bracketing what we do. To get more mystical, we are born in pain, we live in pain, and we die in pain. There is, in my opinion, no way to make authentic art and in our case, pure and moving photographs, without feeling and showing pain—sometimes ours and sometimes that of our subjects."

He went on to discuss how that is true even in nature photography where more often than not there weren't human subjects.

"Even mountains can feel pain," he said. "Anyone who has observed strip mining can attest to that. And sometimes the pain we show is that which is in the future."

After his lecture, we took a short break and then he announced that we'd all be driving to the Parkfield cemetery to take our first set of photographs.

"Let's carpool as best we can," he told the class. "There isn't much parking." I drove Isaac and his equipment in my truck, giving him a short break from the eager intensity of his students.

"Have you heard anything more about the fire?" he asked.

"Only that Detective Hudson thinks Whip might have done it. Or

David Hardin. Or Bunny. He even suspects Shawna and Johnny! He seems to suspect almost everyone of ulterior motives."

Isaac pulled at his seat belt, then impatiently unhooked and hooked it again. "That's his job, kiddo. Both Whip and Johnny are young men in a lot of pain. And pain in young men often redirects itself into destructive anger."

"I know," I said, not wanting Hud's suspicions to be true. Not for Johnny, because I knew it would hurt Shawna. And after hearing about Whip's childhood, I didn't want it to be him. It did seem like he was dealt a lousy hand in life, certainly worse than Johnny. Then again, as I'd pointed out to Hud in the cabin the other night, life wasn't fair, and Whip had been pretty fortunate that Joe had taken him in. Not many foster kids were that lucky. Whip certainly could have had a much worse life than growing up on the Broken DIS Ranch.

Isaac rolled down his window and rested his elbow on the ledge. "Something's going to have to come to a head soon. I have a feeling that detective is getting a little tired of hanging around the ranch playing games."

"Could be," I said, shrugging my shoulders. Yes, something had to come to a head soon. But what would make that happen? The ranch itself burning down?

At the cemetery, while the students wandered around looking for that perfect shot, I headed straight for the headstone where Victory had lingered. "God's Precious Lamb." It told a painful story, all right. One that was obvious to anyone. It had to have been a child not old enough to name. A miscarriage perhaps? There wasn't even a date, though the stone looked weathered. Out in these harsh elements, though, it would be hard to tell how long it had been there. Before I said anything to Victory, I'd made up my mind I was going to question David Hardin. He'd lived at the ranch the longest.

We ate lunch sitting under a couple of pine trees. The students, ranging from teenagers to senior citizens, crowded around Isaac, listening to whatever words came out of his mouth as if they were drops of liquid gold.

While he talked to them, I went back to the truck and started going through the photographs I'd brought. There wasn't much of interest until I came to one of Joe and a man wearing jeans and a San Francisco Giants baseball cap. There was something familiar about his face, but I couldn't put my finger on it. Then again, I'd looked through so many pictures of people these last few days, he might have just been someone in one of the other photographs. Though Joe Darnell hated going to town, he loved big gatherings at his ranch and was a generous host. I slipped the photograph back into the envelope. Over at Isaac's tree, people were starting to stand up and walk toward the cars. It looked like we'd be heading back to the ranch. I glanced at my watch. It was three o'clock. The session was only supposed to last until four to give us time to get the barn ready for the dance. From what I could gather, most of the people who came to the photography class were also staying for the dance so there'd be lots of people hanging around, speculating about the stables' charred ruins.

On the short drive back to Broken Dishes, I asked Isaac, "Don't you ever get tired of answering the same questions over and over?"

He pulled at the silver ring in his ear and chuckled. "Sometimes. But I remind myself that all they are doing is trying to understand."

"What's not to understand? The things you teach are pretty clear."

"One can understand here, kiddo." He tapped my temple. "But not here." He tapped his chest. "What I'm asking them to do is dare to show through their photographs their feelings about things, give their view of life, the good and bad of it. I'm asking them to be vulnerable. They understand it intellectually, but what they're trying to figure out is how do they make that jump, how do they take that chance. Often the distance between their vision of themselves and the truth of who they really are is the crucial leap they have to make. Most won't, to be honest. The price is too high."

I thought a moment about what he said. Their vision of themselves.

"What you're saying is the person they show the world and the person they really are might not be the same person."

"Right."

Like my father. And a lot of people. Even, if I was going to be honest, myself. "Isn't that all of us really?"

He leaned his head back on the headrest and closed his eyes. "Of course it is. Who we are and who we want people to think we are aren't ever the same thing. But the truest artists draw aside that curtain for just a moment and we see truth, the truth of *them* anyway. But human nature prevails and they become scared and the curtain drops back down. Truth isn't easy and it isn't always pretty. And to be honest, most people just want to look pretty and therefore make their pictures, the representation of themselves, pretty too."

"So do you think we can't ever truly know another person?"

"It's hard. We might be able to know parts of them. Then again, it's only the parts they allow. You know, we're all afraid if someone saw the real us, they would turn away in utter disgust. And maybe they would. As I said, who we really are isn't always beautiful. It's something artists deal with all the time, this laying out of themselves. It's probably why more than one artist has killed themselves. They just couldn't take the raw vulnerability anymore."

"So why do they do it then?"

"Because they sense . . . we all sense deep in our souls, that real truth is a good thing. Truth shouldn't be hidden. And something in them compels them to show it, even if it is painful, to them or to their viewers."

Isaac's words tumbled through my mind the whole time I helped get the barn ready for the dance. His words struck a chord inside me, though I couldn't put my finger on what it was exactly. It had to do with everything that had happened this last week. Somewhere hidden under all the hurts and anger and confusion resided the truth. I didn't believe that things happened in life with just some slap-dash random pattern, like pellets from a shotgun. It couldn't have been an accident that all these things came together right at this moment, these people,

the discovery of the bones, Joe's death and the future of the ranch. I
sensed before Shawna and Johnny could go on to make a life,
whether here or somewhere else, that the truth, whatever it was, had
to be revealed. Even if it ended up being about my own father.

After I finished dressing for the dance in my best black Wranglers
and a bright green cowboy shirt with black snap buttons, I decided to
drop by the bunkhouse to check on Rich. Next to the stables, I ran
into David. No one else was around, good fortune for me. This might
be my only chance all night to ask him about the unnamed headstone
at Parkfield cemetery.

"Hey, David," I said. "Are you ready for the dance?" It was obvious
he was because he was wearing a crisp white cowboy shirt, a black-and-
turquoise oval bolo tie, and new black jeans. I looked down at his feet.
"Shoot, I could blow-dry my hair in the spit shine on those boots."

He grinned at me. "I cleaned up a little."

"I have a question for you."

He nodded, then glanced over my head, his eyes suddenly lighting
up. I turned around and saw Marty walking toward us, her hand
raised in greeting.

"Are you ready to cut the rug?" she called to both of us though her
eyes were only for David. There went my small window of opportunity to talk to him alone.

"I sure am," I called back. "And I'm guessing the good Mr. Hardin is
also." I turned around to smile at him, but his eyes were only for Marty.

"The good Mr. Hardin looks very nice tonight," she said, smiling
at him.

He actually stammered a little before saying, "You do too, Marty."

"I'll see you two later," I said. "I'm going to check on Rich."

"I just came from the bunkhouse," David said. "He's asleep."

"Good. Maybe when he wakes up his migraine will be gone."

We discussed the agony of migraines on our walk over to the barn.
We were all in agreement that Rich's headache might have been
brought on by a combination of stress and the fire's smoke.

"Another arson investigator came out today," David said.

"Really?" I said. "I was gone all day with Isaac and his photography class. What did the investigator say?"

David's face became grim. "That it wasn't faulty wiring or bad hay. They found solid evidence that it was set deliberately."

We were all quiet for a moment.

"That's awful," I said, not voicing what we were all obviously thinking. That it was especially terrible because that meant someone here at the ranch did it. I looked up at David, trying to see if there were any signs of deceit on his face. Certainly none that I could tell.

Those thoughts were whirling through my mind when I took my assigned place behind the punch bowl. The dance had been going on for about a half hour and I'd already had to refill the punch bowl once.

"Hey, gorgeous," Gabe said, coming up beside me and slipping his arm around my waist. "You look great, but you also look sad."

I leaned into his comforting bulk. "Thanks, I'm just tired."

He nuzzled the top of my head. "Did the photography class go well this afternoon?"

"Isaac was wonderful. Like always."

"*Querida,* what's wrong?"

I pulled away and looked up at him. "I told you, I'm just tired."

He looked out over the crowded dance floor. The band was playing a Merle Haggard song, "Okie from Muscokee." A group of men stood next to the band belting out the words. "You know, everything's going fine here. I don't think anyone would miss you if you snuck away and went to bed early."

I punched him lightly on the chest with my fist. "No one?"

"You know I would. But I would rather see you get some sleep."

"You know, for once, I'm going to admit you're right. As much as I'd love to be here, I'm just exhausted."

"I'll walk you back to your cabin."

"No, don't. Your presence here will keep things from getting too rowdy and make the guests feel more at ease. Shawna and Johnny don't need one more unforeseen incident to give The Secret Traveler something to write about."

He shook his head. "I'd guess they'd better kiss any kind of a good review from that person good-bye."

"Please don't say that."

"It doesn't necessarily mean the guest ranch won't succeed."

I stirred the pineapple and ginger ale punch, watching the cactus-shaped ice cubes move round and round like the dancers on the floor. "You're right. But it would have been great if they could have gotten a good national review like that." I gazed out over the dancing couples. "At least it does look like the guests are having a good time. I'm going to stay here behind the punch bowl for little while longer. I want to show as much support for Shawna and Johnny as I can." I nodded over a table near the band. Shawna and Johnny sat with the Georgia cousins and they were all laughing at something. It was good to see them looking young and carefree, if only for a little while.

"Okay, but promise me you'll try to leave in the next hour or so."

"Sí, papacito. Now, go mingle with your cop buddies. I notice quite a few of them made it. Thanks for spreading the word about the dance. Please try to talk some of them into dancing with the Georgia cousins."

At the table with Shawna and Johnny, it was obvious the cousins were trying to have fun, but they kept giving longing looks at the two-stepping couples.

He gave them a dubious look. "I'll try, but those women are pretty intimidating. Too pretty, too smart, and definitely too confident."

I laughed out loud. "Can a woman be too much of any of those things?"

"For us cowardly men? You bet." He winked at me.

I watched my husband weave his way through the crowd toward his buddies, not missing the interested glances tossed his way by many of the women.

"He's a regular Moses, isn't he?" Hud said, walking up to the table. He was dressed in a starched navy blue western shirt with white pearl snaps and wore a pair of merlot-colored ostrich cowboy boots that probably cost more than my first truck.

I shrugged and didn't answer.

"He parts the waters," Hud explained.

"I know what you meant."

He picked up the punch ladle and started stirring the pale yellow liquid. "This spiked?"

"Only with ginger ale. We've had enough trouble around here. Out-of-control drunks would be about the last straw."

He nodded and continued playing with the punch. "Want to dance? I know Mr. Wonderful doesn't dance so you must get a hankerin' for it every so often."

"Please, quit playing with the punch and no, I don't want to dance."

"Liar."

Not in the mood for one of our verbal sparring matches, I said, "Do you really know what you could do that would make me extremely happy right now?"

He leaned across the table. "Darlin', you know I'd give half my fortune to see a smile on those lips."

"Please dance with the Georgia cousins. You are a wonderful dancer and, heaven only knows why, they think you are cute as a corncob pipe. It would make their night and I'd be eternally grateful." Then I added quickly, "But just *dance* and nothing else. No one-night stands."

He stood up and placed a hand on his chest, feigning shock. "Me? You would think I'm *that* immoral? That insults me deeply."

"I'm serious, Hud."

He cocked his head at my sincere tone. Then he turned and looked over at the cousins. One of them, the short blonde named Gaynelle, caught his eye and waved enthusiastically. He sent a cautious wave back, then turned back to me, his face just a tad unsure. "They look kind of desperate."

I looked over at them. All I saw was a bunch of attractive, confident women in their late thirties who looked ten years younger. Tonight they were dressed to the nines, each wearing a Manuel western-style dress though in different jewel-tone colors. I knew they had money now. Manuel was the top designer of country-western clothes worn by many Nashville superstars.

"They are really nice, Hud. And I'm sure they have tons of rich friends who might be potential customers for the ranch. Do it for Shawna and Johnny. You know what they've been through this week."

He didn't answer for a moment, then said, "If I dance with the fair Georgia cousins, you'll owe me one. A big one."

I closed my eyes for a split second, knowing this was a mistake, but deciding to opt for the greater good of the ranch. I opened them and stared right into the dark depths of his brown ones. "Yes, I will."

He gave me a small salute. "Ma'am, you've bought yourself a dancin' gigolo. I promise, this will be a night they won't forget."

"Thank you. It's just tonight, I promise. You'll never have to see them again."

He glanced over at them. "Good, because I gotta tell you. They're kind of intimidating."

"That's funny. That's exactly what Gabe said. Deep down inside, you guys really *are* afraid of strong women, aren't you?"

He raised his eyebrows. "Only en masse, ranch girl. Singly, we love you tough, feisty women."

I pointed to the dance floor. "Dance, you fool."

"Yes, ma'am."

He kept his word. Within the next hour he not only danced separately with each of them, he was now showing them how he could, after requesting the lively Cajun tune "Jolie Blonde," dance with two of them at once. It was pretty amazing. And he talked his grandpa into dancing with them too. It was pretty obvious from whom Hud inherited his dancing gene. At least for the Georgia cousins, tonight would be something to remember.

Now that the cousins were happy, I decided to take Gabe's advice and sneak out. I found my cousin Emory and Elvia over by the souvenir table where they were doing a brisk business selling Broken DIS T-shirts and ball caps as well as Isaac's, Meg's, and Victory's books.

"I'm calling it a night," I told them, picking up Victory's latest book. It showed not only the patterns of old quilts, all of which she reinvented into unique interpretations, but it told the history of the quilts' names and famous quilts made of each pattern. The title of the book was "Old Quilts—History and Mystery."

"It's only eight thirty!" Emory said, taking a fifty-dollar bill from a man who held two T-shirts and a ball cap. "Be right with you, sir." He handed the money to Elvia and pulled out a plastic bag for the man's purchases. "But I can see why. You look like big helpin' of homemade sin."

"Thank you very much," I said, squeezing the back of his neck. "Elvia, I thought being married to you would straighten this Southern turkey out."

"Blame it on my mother," she said. "She thinks he can do no wrong."

"Señora Aragon is a highly intelligent, perceptive lady," Emory said in a fake haughty voice.

"She is and she likes you anyway," I said.

Elvia handed the man his change while Emory put the merchandise and a Broken DIS Guest Ranch brochure in a bag. "Thanks, sir," Emory said. "Y'all come back now, you hear? Preferably with all your friends."

"We intend to," the man said, pocketing the change. "My family's having our annual reunion in May. Fifty of us. We're seriously considering having it here. If we like it, we might come back every year."

"That's wonderful," I said. "They'll have a ball. I promise."

After he left, I said to Emory and Elvia, "Isn't that great? Hope other people are considering the ranch for things like that too."

"This dance was a good marketing idea," Elvia said. "We've put brochures everywhere. I think things will work out fine for Shawna and Johnny."

"I hope so," I said. "We've certainly had our rough spots these last few days."

"Speaking of rough spots, sweetcakes," Emory said. "We *still* haven't heard the details of your night with Detective Hudson."

Elvia came over and stood next to Emory, her hand on his shoulder. "He's right, *mi amiga*. What happened?"

"Nothing, nothing, nothing," I said, exasperated. "And please don't refer to it as my 'night with Detective Hudson.' "

Emory looked up at his wife. "She seems agitated. Think anything naughty happened?"

Elvia laughed. "No, *cariño,* not our Benni. She's a good girl."

"Did you at least think about it?" Emory asked. "I bet you did. You did, didn't you? You bad girl."

"You, dear cousin, are just as annoying and obnoxious as you were when you were ten. I'm leaving now."

"Inquiring minds want to know," his laughing voice called after me.

On the way out, I spotted Victory at a table with some of the quilters. I took my book over there for her to sign.

"You should have just let me give you one," she said, signing her name and date on the title page. "Nature never clashes. Take a chance!" she wrote, a statement she'd told the quilters more than once and was her theory about color. She handed the book back to me and smiled.

"I couldn't do that," I said. "I not only have to support quilt designers, I have to support my friend's bookstore."

"Well, thank you," she said.

I flipped through the book on my way through the barn, glancing at the quilt histories, my own particular interest. I flipped back to the front and read the dedication page. This one was not only dedicated to her husband, as many of her books were, but showed their wedding photograph. I'd never seen a picture of her husband. Garland Simpson was a very handsome man.

He also looked familiar.

I stared at the picture for a moment, my mind twisting to remember something. Then it came to me. The photograph of the man in the Giants cap. The man with his arm flung around Joe's shoulders.

It was Garland Simpson.

CHAPTER 15

I STEPPED OUTSIDE, WHERE NO ONE COULD SEE MY SHOCKED expression. The air was about fifteen degrees cooler than inside the barn and felt good on my burning face.

Victory's husband had known Joe. It was an answer to a big question, but now there were so many other questions it created. Questions only Victory could answer.

The clouds had all cleared away and the stars looked close enough to slip in my pocket. I leaned my head back and just soaked in the vastness of the universe. What was I going to do with this information? There was only one real answer. I would go back to the dance and find my husband and tell him everything. He'd be annoyed at me for not telling him sooner, even though he'd been adamant about not being involved. But he'd also take over and do the right thing with this information, even going to Hud with it if he thought that was warranted. I completely trusted Gabe's integrity in doing the right and proper thing when it came to his job.

"Beautiful, isn't it?" David's voice startled me.

I turned to look up at him. "It sure is."

He took off his cowboy hat and bent his head to look up at the sky.

"In my whole sixty-seven years I've never gotten tired of looking at the stars out here."

In the distance, I could hear the yipping of coyotes calling to each other. "I was just headed back to my cabin. I'm bushed."

"It's been a rough day for everyone."

"I'm glad I caught you. I have a question."

"That's right, you did," he said. "We were interrupted earlier. Shoot."

"I was at the Parkfield cemetery today with Isaac and his photography students. There was this headstone, one that didn't have a name or a date. It just said 'God's Precious Lamb.' You've lived at the Broken Dishes the longest. Do you know anything about it?"

A small breeze came up, blowing my hair across my face. A scent of charcoal rode on the breeze. How long would that smell linger? Until a new stable was built or even longer? The uncomfortable minute of silence that followed told me that there was something important about this particular grave. And his words, when he finally spoke, told me even more.

"I can't answer that," he said.

"You can't?" I said, disappointed.

He wouldn't look at me, but kept staring out at the dark hillside, the black dots of oak and cottonwood trees just barely visible to our eyes. "Benni, it's not my story to tell. I think . . ." He stopped and I heard him take in a chestful of air. "I think you need to talk to Victoria Simpson about that."

She *had* been at the ranch before.

"Did you know Garland Simpson?"

He looked over my head at the hills behind me, obviously reluctant to answer.

I watched his face and waited. If Daddy had never met Victory, like he told me, and he was at the DIS Ranch fairly often, how would she have met David? He had been with Joe a long time though, since they were very young men. Whatever connected Joe, Victory, and David must have happened before Daddy came into Joe's life. David and

Victory had done a good job hiding their acquaintance from me and even more importantly, from Hud.

"How did you know Victory and Garland?" I asked again.

"Like I said, it's Victoria's story to tell." He cleared his throat. "I have to get back. Told Marty I was only coming out here for a minute."

"Wait," I said, hating myself for doing this, for not trusting my father.

He turned, gave me a quizzical look.

"My father . . . did he know Victory and Garland?"

David's eyes grew thin and wary. "Not that I know. Victory and Garland never came to the ranch as far as I know except . . ." He stopped. "Benni, why don't you ask your father?"

"I will," I said quickly, relief flooding through my chest like a gulp of hot coffee. Maybe Daddy had been telling the truth when he said he didn't know Victory. Then again, that didn't mean he didn't know about the bones. "Thanks."

He nodded and went back inside the barn.

I started walking away from the barn, toward the direction of the lodge. The further I walked, the more muted the music became until it was almost a soft tinkling, like the chatter of the creek up at MudRun. Now that I knew that she'd known Joe, I knew I'd have to speak to her.

But what would I say? Hey, Victory, I've found out you have a past with this ranch, with Joe Darnell. By any chance were you up the hill the other night digging up bones? Oh, and hey, was my daddy involved too?

Digging up bones. The phrase reminded me of an old country-western song. I couldn't remember who sang it—Randy Travis? He was singing about an old love affair and claimed in the song that some things were better left alone. Was that true in this case? Are there some things better left unspoken? Would what came out benefit the people still living or just cause more pain? How could I or anyone know if we didn't know what the truth was? Or was seeking the truth just my rationale because I was curious about things that were none of my business?

If the bones hadn't been discovered would any of this had come to light? That incident propelled the truth, or the search for the truth, to the surface, a force to be reckoned with. If David knew Victory before and she'd been involved with someone here at the ranch, and somehow she was mixed up with those bones up on the hill, Hud would eventually find out. He was a good investigator and, heaven knows, as tenacious as one of those Catahoula hounds.

Walking through the ranch compound, I convinced myself it would be better for Victory if I talked to her first. After all, I was the catalyst that brought her here. If I hadn't come up with the idea of a quilting weekend, none of this might have happened. But how would I start? With the question about the unnamed headstone. That would be the opening I'd need. That and the fact that she'd been to the Broken Dishes before. I'd wait on the front porch of the lodge and when I saw her leave the dance for her cabin, I'd go talk to her.

Go get Gabe, a tiny voice inside me insisted. But I ignored it. And I knew why. I didn't completely trust what David said. If in the course of talking to Victory I found out my father was involved, I wanted to hear that alone. I didn't even want Gabe there. As much as I loved and trusted my husband, if my father had done anything wrong, I wanted to hear the details first, to have time to absorb them and try to live with them.

I was passing the dark ranch office, when I spotted a quick flash of light inside. Then it was black again. I stopped, not sure what to do. The area around the main lodge and the office was empty. Everyone was at the dance. Or so I thought. There were so many people in the barn, I hadn't spotted everyone, including Rita or Chad. But, then, I'd been preoccupied and wasn't exactly taking roll call.

I cautiously sidled up to the window and tried to peek inside. The blinds were partially closed, blocking my view. The front door was open a crack. Should I try to see who was inside before going for help? I didn't want to make a bigger deal of this than it was. And by

the time I ran back to the dance, found Gabe and we returned, whoever was in there would be gone. I wasn't crazy enough to try and
capture them, but I was crazy enough to at least want to see who it
was so I could tell Gabe.

I crouched down and slipped past the window, sneaking toward
the cracked door. If I was lucky, the person would walk by and I
could identify them, then take off for the barn.

I had just made it to the top step of the porch when the front door
swung open and a tiny bright light hit me square in the face. Instinctively, my hand flew up to shield my eyes.

"What the . . .?" I heard Whip's voice say.

Before I could answer, I felt his hand close around my wrist and
pull me inside the room.

"You!" Whip growled, raising the flashlight like he was going to
strike me.

I opened my mouth to scream.

He dropped the flashlight and grabbed me, slapping his hand over
my mouth. I struggled to get away, but he was strong and outweighed
me by at least seventy pounds. Remembering what I'd learned in a
self-defense class, I suddenly stopped struggling and let myself become
a dead weight. That surprised him enough to hesitate and I broke out
of his grasp. I bolted for the door, too intent on escaping to even
scream, when Johnny and Shawna burst into the room.

"What's going on?" Shawna cried.

Johnny launched himself toward Whip, throwing his full weight
into him. They landed with a thump on the floor and rolled around,
knocking against the office chair, trash can, and glass-shaded desk
lamp. The glass shattered across the wood floor.

"Stop it!" Shawna screamed.

"Go get Gabe!" I said to Shawna, pushing her toward the door.
"Go!"

She hesitated a moment, then took off running.

I turned to watch the men roll around the floor, knowing there was
nothing I could do. They had each other in a bear hug, each trying to

gain advantage enough to throw an occasional punch. There was no doubt Whip had the advantage in weight and fighting experience, but Johnny was young and mad and full of adrenaline. I glanced around and picked up a stapler, the heaviest object I could find. If I had to, I could hit one of them over the head. I hoped it wouldn't come to that.

After a five minute eternity, I finally heard Gabe's voice, calling my name. I ran out onto the office's front porch. Gabe was coming toward me at a sprint. Hud and Shawna were about twenty feet behind him.

"Get in there!" I screamed at him.

He stopped when he got to me, his breath coming fast and hard. "Are you okay?"

"Yes, but Whip is going to kill Johnny!"

"Any weapons?"

"Not that I could see."

Inside, we heard a loud crash.

Gabe and Hud pushed past me into the small office. Within minutes, they had Johnny and Whip separated and across the room from each other.

"You little asshole!" Whip yelled, blood dripping out of his mouth, as Gabe held his arm behind his back.

Johnny, struggling to get away from Hud, screamed back, "You crazy son of a . . ."

"Stop it! Stop it!" Shawna cried. "I can't take this anymore. What is wrong with you two?"

I gazed around the room at the mess. The petty cash box was out and open, the cash Shawna kept on hand for emergencies was gone. It appeared that Whip was taking what he could and was going to run. Was it because he had set the stable fire?

"Oh, Whip," Shawna said, her eyes filling with tears, obviously coming to the same conclusion as me. "Why would you do that to me? The horses could have been killed. Someone could have died."

Whip stopped struggling against Gabe, his face suddenly so stricken, so defeated that it would take a stone-hearted person not to feel some pity for him. There was not a one of us who couldn't say we might not have felt the same things he was feeling, even done the things he'd done, if we'd been dealt his hand in life.

"I'm sorry, Shawna," he said, staring at the floor, unable to look at her. Gabe loosened his grip slightly. "I didn't think it would spread that fast." Sympathy softened the tenseness in my husband's face.

Hud, holding Johnny back, asked in a firm voice. "You going to behave?"

Johnny nodded and Hud slowly let go of his arm. Johnny brought his arm forward and rubbed it.

"Arrest him for arson," Johnny said coldly. "You'd better believe we're pressing charges."

"Johnny," Shawna said. "Let's talk about this first."

"No!" he snapped at her. "There's nothing to talk about. He tried to ruin us and was getting ready to run. He deserves to be in jail. Shit, for all we know he killed someone and put those bones up there. He's a loser, Shawna, and prison's the best place for him."

"No," a voice said from the doorway. We all turned toward it.

"I don't know about the fire," Victory said. "But he didn't put those bones up there, and he didn't dig them up. I did."

CHAPTER 16

SHE SURVEYED OUR SHOCKED FACES. "I WAS JUST COMING from the dance and I heard the commotion . . ."

We all stared at her, still startled silent by her declaration.

She brought a hand up to her cheek. "Actually, I didn't put the bones there. I just tried to dig them up. Obviously, I failed." Her eyes became glossy with unshed tears. "Please, don't blame Mr. Greenwood for something I did. Oh, it's all so complicated. I don't know how to start."

When no one said anything, I did.

"How about with why?" I asked.

She inhaled deeply and stepped into the office. "Have you ever made a promise that you later regretted?" She looked at me as she talked, as if focusing on one person would make it easier to tell her story.

I nodded. "Sure." Hadn't everyone?

Her voice shook with agony. "I couldn't say no. I mean, it was his dying wish. How could I refuse my husband his dying wish?"

"Your husband?" Hud interrupted. "Your husband asked you to dig up those bones?"

She nodded her head yes, tears still glittering in her eyes.

I waited for her to go on, but when she didn't, I asked again, "Why?"

She clasped her hands in front of her, the white knobs of her knuckles straining against the skin. Her voice dropped to a hoarse whisper. "He wanted the . . . bones . . . the person . . . properly buried. He said he couldn't die in peace unless I promised him that I would do this."

I felt myself let out the breath I'd been holding. So many questions rushing through my mind—who, why, when?

"Mrs. Simpson, would you like to sit down?" Gabe said, his deep voice kind. I gave him a grateful look.

"Yes, thank you," she said.

I uprighted one of the office chairs and helped her sit down.

Gabe whispered something in Whip's ear and I saw Whip nod. Gabe let loose of his arm. Whip didn't move from where he was standing, not even to rub his arm.

"Go ahead, Mrs. Simpson," Hud said.

The words poured out of her as if they'd been stuck behind a thick dam for years. "Garland was very sick those last few months. And so depressed. I couldn't convince him to talk to me, to tell me what he was feeling. I knew something was bothering him, something deep and hurting, but he wouldn't share it with me. I think maybe he didn't want me to have to bear this burden any longer than necessary. Maybe he was protecting me in the only way he could in those last days when he was so helpless, like a baby. He hated that. *Hated it.* Garland was very masculine, loved to hunt and fish. And those last days, he . . ." Her voice choked over the thickness in her throat.

I reached over and touched her shoulder. "Would you like something to drink?"

She shook her head no. "He and Joe were old friends. They served in Korea together. Garland said that sort of friendship bonds you for life. That unless you'd been through battle with a man, you didn't really know his mettle, you didn't really know if you could trust him."

I glanced over at Gabe, who probably understood that better than any of us. He gave an almost imperceptible nod at her statement.

"He always said war had been hard, but that there were things in his life that were infinitely harder," she continued. "He would never tell me what he meant. Not until two days before he died. It took hours, but he finally told me the whole story. What that man Leon did to Clarissa. What Garland and Joe did."

We all waited while she paused, the only sounds besides our breathing was the far off sound of the band, the distant twang of the electric guitars.

"I should start with the beginning," she finally said. "With Clarissa. That's where it really starts."

"Joe's little sister," I turned and said to the others. "She died from a burst appendix."

Gabe and Hud both looked at me, surprised. Then Hud frowned.

"Dad had a sister?" Shawna said. "I had an aunt?"

I nodded. "Clarissa. I found out about her when I read your father's Bible. I left it for you here in the office with a note." I turned and looked at the desk. I dug around until I found it buried under a pile of pink invoices.

"I saw your note and set it aside to read later," Shawna said. "We've been so busy and there was the fire . . ." Her face flushed at the mention of the stable fire. Johnny shot an angry look at Whip.

"She's buried in Paso Robles," Victory said.

"Next to Joe?" I went to his funeral and did not remember seeing another Darnell buried next to him.

"No," Victory replied. "She's in another part of the cemetery. Not even next to his parents. I guess they weren't that organized in buying plots."

"Who was Leon?" I asked.

Her voice hardened. "Leon Brown."

The last name sounded familiar. "Brown? Brownie?" I said. The man in the cut-up photograph?

"That was his nickname. He worked for Joe. Back in the sixties."

"What did Brownie do?" I had to ask, though it was becoming obvious what it could be. My stomach churned at the thought.

"He took . . . advantage . . ." She paused and licked her dry lips. "Sexual advantage of Joe's sister."

"He raped her," Gabe said.

I felt a cold chill race over my body.

"Yes, Chief Ortiz, you're right. I shouldn't soften it. Taking sexual advantage of an eight-year-old is rape in any civilized society."

"He raped a child?" Shawna said, her voice choking.

"Physically, no," Victory said. "She was in her late teens, but not in her mind."

One of Shawna's small hands flew up to her mouth in horror.

"This Brownie," I burst out. "What happened to him?"

"Did your husband kill him?" Hud asked.

Her pale face looked startled. "Of course not! He only helped Joe bury him. He said he always felt guilty for that, felt like they had done a horrible thing. But Joe asked him for his help and he gave it. Joe and Garland hadn't been in touch for years, but for who knows what reason, fate, maybe, Garland was here in San Celina County on business. He'd met Joe in Paso Robles that night for dinner. They were coming back to the ranch. Garland was just going to spend one night, catch up on old times. They came back earlier than Joe had told Brownie and walked in on Brownie and Clarissa. Joe had trusted Brownie. He was supposed to have been watching out for Clarissa." She paused, swallowing hard. "Garland was a very loyal man. He would not have run out on Joe when he asked for his help."

"Joe killed Brownie," I said.

It made sense, though I still couldn't imagine the Joe Darnell I'd known, soft-hearted and full of silly jokes, killing a man in cold blood.

Victory's eyes blinked rapidly. Her words came out in a stutter. "Oh . . . oh . . . no, that's not . . . No, I'm sorry, I'm making a mess of this. No, Joe didn't kill Brownie."

"Clarissa did," Hud said.

Shawna gasped and a small sob rose up from her chest.

"Clarissa?" I repeated.

Victory nodded, tears gleaming against her cheeks now.

"Why didn't they just call the sheriff?" I asked. "It was self-defense, right? He raped her . . ."

"I don't know the whole story. I guess no one but Brownie and Clarissa really ever did. But when Joe and Garland walked into the living room and Brownie was lying face down on the floor. Clarissa was just sitting there, holding one of the fireplace pokers, her clothes a mess, blood everywhere. Joe rushed over and grabbed the poker out of her hands. Of course, then it had his fingerprints on it too."

Something came to me right at that moment. "David Hardin. He worked for Joe then." Had he lied to me?

She shook her head. "David was gone the weekend it happened. No one was here but Joe, Garland, Brownie, and Clarissa. Garland and Joe buried Brownie and never told anyone. I don't think Garland ever saw Joe again. Garland said he understood why Joe did it, to save Clarissa from the publicity, from the scandal. And if Joe said he did it or they pinned it on him, who would take care of her? Garland said they both agreed it was the best thing for everyone. Everyone except Garland. My husband suffered from that day forward. In the end, he couldn't think of anything else except giving Leon Brown a proper burial. It was the thing that kept him alive, I think. When I finally promised I would do it, he allowed himself to die."

"But your husband died two years ago." I left the rest of my question open. What took her so long?

"I called Joe shortly after Garland died and told him what I knew, what Garland's last wishes were. He absolutely forbade it. Said Leon Brown had the grave he deserved, that he deserved to be buried with animals because that's what he was. He wouldn't even allow me to come to the ranch. That's why I couldn't believe it when I heard through the grapevine you were planning this quilt retreat. It seemed the perfect opportunity for me to carry out Garland's wishes. And Joe was gone too, so he couldn't object." She put a trembling hand up to her forehead. "I just panicked in the middle of doing it. It turned out to be harder than I thought."

"How did you even find it?" That, alone, was incredible.

"Garland made up a very elaborate map with all the details. Don't forget, I grew up on a ranch. Finding his burial place was the easiest part."

"But Brownie's family or friends. Didn't they ever wonder what happened to him?"

"He didn't have any family. At least any that cared enough to put in a missing person's report. And men like Brownie moved around a lot. His friends probably just thought he'd gone off to work on another ranch somewhere."

"So, what happened after they buried him. How did Clarissa manage?"

Victory's eyes burned dark now with suppressed anger. "If Garland hadn't been so sick when he told me this story, I would have let him have it. Can you even imagine a girl, much less one with Clarissa's emotional maturity, surviving the trauma of rape and killing someone, with no one to talk about it with? Why couldn't they have told me? At least I could have talked to her, helped her." She wiped the tears from her cheeks with both hands, her voice high with agitation. "And to go through that miscarriage alone. It just breaks my heart. I was so close. They should have trusted me. They should have told me." She slammed a fist on her knee.

"Miscarriage?" I said. The unnamed gravestone. God's Precious Lamb. "That headstone you were looking at in the Parkfield cemetery. That was Clarissa's baby."

Her anger seemed to dissipate as quickly as it came, her face gray with exhaustion. "Joe said Clarissa was only about three months along when it happened. She didn't even realize . . ." A sob stuck in her throat. "He said it was probably for the best. That it was better to not even give the baby a name."

"David Hardin. He knew. He told me to come talk to you."

She inhaled deeply. "Apparently Joe told him at some point in their lives. I guess he had to confide in someone. When Joe died, I called David and told him about Garland's request. He said what Joe told him right after I called was, if anything should happen to him . . ."

A small agonized sound escaped from Shawna's chest.

Victory looked over at her, her eyes shadowed with fatigue. "Joe said to not let me move Brownie's bones to a real cemetery. So David said he couldn't help me, that he'd promised Joe. But he also said he'd never stop me if I found a way to do it. I guess, like me, he was both trying to honor the request of someone he loved and do what was right."

She looked over at Shawna, then down at her clasped hands. "I'm so sorry, Shawna. Your quilting weekend seemed to me like a sign from God to carry out Garland's request. I figured I had two weeks. I was going to do it little by little, put the bones in my trunk and take them to some out-of-the way cemetery and bury them. No one would ever know. It was just a lot harder than I expected." She covered her face with her hands, her body shaking with silent sobs.

Shawna stared at her for a moment. Then, without a word, she went over, put her arms around Victory, and cried with her.

CHAPTER 17

$\mathcal{B}$EFORE THE DANCE WAS OVER, THE UNMARKED SHERIFF'S CAR Hud called for arrived, and the deputies took a handcuffed Whip back to Paso Robles. None of the guests even knew what had taken place.

"We'll find you a good attorney," Shawna told Whip when Hud helped him into the car. Whip wouldn't even look her in the eye.

"We will not . . ." Johnny started.

She turned to him, her delicate face determined. "We owe him something, Johnny. No, he'll never work here again and he might go to jail, but we owe him something. He was like a son to my father and Dad didn't treat him right. It's up to us, to *me*, to correct that."

He tightened his lips and didn't protest, his young face obviously struggling with what she said. This would be, I could see, a subject they'd return to more than once in their marriage. But the way they looked at each other, the silent communication passing between them, I also suspected that they'd overcome this, the first of many treacherous mountains that had to be climbed in every relationship.

Compared to the first week, the second was as smooth as Rich's dulce de leche pudding. By the last night everyone was in a relaxed, jovial mood. We never explained where Whip had gone and when people asked, we said he preferred to keep that private. That raised a few eyebrows, but no one pressed us for details. The locals would eventually hear or read about the fire and the story behind the bones in the newspaper. We could only hope they would judge Joe and Whip by the whole of their lives, not just one incident. Those who weren't local, we could only hope if they did hear about either situation, they wouldn't hold it against the Broken Dishes.

Victory continued on with her classes, a trooper to the end. No one even guessed what a traumatic time she'd been going through. Hud made arrangements for the Leon Brown's remains to be released to her once the case was officially closed. She was going to honor her husband's last wishes and have him buried in a proper cemetery, a plot she purchased in San Celina.

The dance ended up being an overwhelming financial success and Shawna and Johnny were thinking about doing it again. The brochures were already bringing in lots of inquiries and it looked like, even if the Broken Dishes didn't get a positive review from The Secret Traveler, whom we still hadn't flushed out, they would get enough business to keep them solvent for a while.

With Whip gone, Shawna and Johnny, along with much sound advice and help from Bunny and David, were getting organized for the next group of guests, due two weeks after the first group left. We'd managed through all our connections and two good employment agencies in San Celina and Paso Robles to find waitresses, wranglers, and enough other help to make the next round of guests' visit a little less bumpy.

By the end of the second week, Shawna and Johnny seemed more in tune with each other and enthusiastic about the ranch's future. They still had a long, difficult road ahead, but they seemed ready to face it. Victory graciously offered to come back and teach a couple more quilting sessions, encouraging their hopes.

During the week, I came up with an idea, hoping to add a little silliness and fun to the session. "Let's have a talent show on the last night. It will star the guests and the staff. We can call it 'Star Search at the Broken Dishes.' We could make a video to show future guests."

"I don't know," Shawna said, her face doubtful.

"Let's ask everyone," I said.

My idea was met with enthusiasm from the Georgia cousins and the quilters and a little bit of moaning and groaning from the staff.

Confirming our belief that the Georgia women had more money than was probably good for anyone, a day after we announced the talent show, FedEx delivered a top-of-the-line karaoke machine and an expensive video camera. It was their gift to the Broken Dishes ranch, they announced, for showing them such Southern hospitality out here in the wild West. And, as the cousins pointed out, it would make it easy for everyone to participate in the talent show.

Before the talent show that last night in the Annie Oakley Room, Rich served his famous cinnamon rolls and coconut-chocolate-chip cookies one final time. To break the ice, he and Sam started the show with a duet they'd worked up of old western trail songs. They'd been practicing their act for three days in between kneading bread dough and making chicken pot pie. And it sounded like it. Hearing them butcher the lyrics to "I'm an Old Cowhand (on the Rio Grande)" was hilarious. Gabe, who joined us that last night, videotaped it himself and planned on torturing Sam with it for the rest of his natural life.

"I don't think I've ever had such an exciting and fun vacation," Karen said, coming up to stand next to me near the tea cart. I had told her in confidence about the old crime. If she was The Secret Traveler, I could only hope she wouldn't hold it against the ranch. "Dennis and I are going to come back next year. We're going to talk our kids into coming."

"That's great," I said feeling hopeful. "Start a family tradition."

On the last day, I passed out the photographs we'd been taking for the last two weeks. Everyone had a great time looking through their recent memories. But photographs and sore behinds weren't the only souvenirs they were taking home from Broken Dishes. Marty Brantley had an even better souvenir. David Hardin.

"Am I hearing wedding bells?" I whispered to Shawna.

"Could be," Shawna whispered back. "She says there's no hanky-panky going on, but that they just want to see if he likes living in southern California part time. He told Johnny if they decide to get hitched, they might consider buying a place over in Paso Robles. Sort of a compromise between big city and the country."

"But he'd still be close enough to come out here, smell the sage, and visit you all," I said.

"Right," Shawna said. "I just think that's wonderful. David finally finding love after all these years."

"Speaking of love, did you hear the latest about Socrates?" I asked.

Shawna laughed out loud, a real, true belly laugh. "No, what's going on?"

"Dove finally found his owner this afternoon. It's an old guy who owns a cabin outside of Shandon. Apparently he's been looking for Socrates for a couple of weeks. He was anxious to get him back. Especially in time for Easter, if you get my drift."

Shawna's face was uncomprehending. Then it dawned on her what I was saying. "Oh, no, you mean . . .?"

"Yep, Easter dinner was in Socrates' future. And not as an invited guest."

"Was?" Her voice sounded hopeful.

"Over Isaac's very loud protests, even my country-born-and-bred gramma couldn't let a goose who was so smart and loving end up in a roasting pan. So, with the exchange of hindquarter of Harper beef, Socrates now has a new home as head security goose at the Ramsey Ranch."

Shawna giggled behind her hand. "Does your dad know yet?"

"Nope," I said, grinning. "But it will definitely give him and Isaac something new to bond over, their joint fear of Dove's goose."

We turned to watch one of the Dennis Olson take the makeshift stage we'd set up in the corner of the room and start fiddling with the karaoke machine.

"Aren't y'all just having the best time?" Gaynelle, one of the cousins, said to me and Shawna. She picked up another cinnamon roll and took a bite. "Bless my mama's pearls, he could make a mint selling these in Atlanta."

"You know," I replied as we listened to Dennis commence with an unbelievably out-of-tune rendition of "The Thunder Rolls" by Garth Brooks, "though, this performance might classify as an assault with a deadly weapon. That means you and your cousins could be arrested as accessories."

She gave a merry laugh. "Probably not the first time someone has wanted to do that." She winked at us.

About a half hour into the talent show, Hud showed up. His grandfather, Iry, had come for dinner a few nights, but Hud had stayed away this last week, something that frustrated the Georgia cousins to no small degree even though I explained to them that he wasn't our personal sheriff's detective and was probably working on other cases.

"*Bonjour, Madame Ortiz,*" he said, coming up to where I stood alone next to the tea cart.

"Hi," I said. "Is everything taken care of with the . . ." I'd started to say bones, but didn't actually know what to call them now.

"Yes," he'd said, picking up a miniature chocolate-chip cookie and popping it in his mouth. "Old Brownie will get his right and proper burial. This was a weird one, ranch girl. No doubt about that."

I stuck my hands in the back pockets of my jeans and nodded in agreement. "No kidding."

"You know, I'm still pissed at you for keeping me out of the loop about Mrs. Simpson. You should have told me what you knew." He licked a bit of chocolate off his thumb and narrowed one eye at me.

"I didn't *know* anything so I wasn't about to run around pointing a finger at possibly innocent people. That's *your* job."

He just took off his cowboy hat and inspected the brim, rebending it slightly in front, a hint of a smile on his face. "That's okay, I know the real reason why you didn't tell me or your husband."

"What do you know about what I did or didn't tell Gabe?"

"Darlin', it was obvious by the annoyed expression on his face when you said you knew about the existence of Clarissa Darnell and

Brownie that he was as much in the dark as I was. It was also obvious that you'd suspected Victory was involved."

Actually, the subject had come up with me and Gabe. I'd gotten his same old, yadda-yadda "I'm-a-cop-you're-not-you-could-have-gotten-hurt" speech. I could have repeated it with him word-for-word. I gave Hud the same explanation I did Gabe a week ago.

"I know you cops. If I'd have told you what I suspected about Victory, you would not have been able to contain yourself. You'd have somehow pushed her or made her feel uncomfortable or made her feel like a criminal. What if she *hadn't* been involved with the bones? It could have hurt Victory, Joe, Shawna and Johnny, and the Broken Dishes."

"But she was involved. Besides, give me some credit. I wouldn't have been that obvious."

I rolled my eyes. They were almost the exact same words Gabe said.

"Look," I said. "I was being a good investigator and biding my time until I acquired enough facts to make an informed decision before telling my . . ." I almost said superiors, then thought better of it. Hud would latch onto that word like a starving crocodile and I'd never hear the end of it. "Telling someone," I finished.

He laughed again. "You have an answer for everything, don't you?"

"I do my best," I said, smiling in spite of myself.

"Like I said, I understand why you didn't want to tell me or the chief."

I looked at him warily.

"Your daddy," he said, settling his hat back on his head. "You were afraid he was involved and it was tearing you up. For your sake, I'm glad he wasn't."

I looked away, toward the fireplace. "I called him the morning after Whip was arrested. I wanted him to hear about Joe from me, not the ag grapevine."

"What did he have to say?"

I continued staring at the stone fireplace. The fire danced and flickered reminding me of both the fire at MudRun and the fire that destroyed the stable. One time it kept two people warm, the other it could have killed. For some reason I couldn't articulate, that seemed important to me.

"He thanked me for telling him." I heard my voice crack. "Then he asked about the cattle. Wondered how many heifers Shawna and Johnny planned on breeding this year."

"That's it?" Hud said, spitting the words out. His mouth drew tight in anger. "Typical."

I shook my head no. "Daddy's not like . . ." I almost said your father, but that would have been too cruel. Hud didn't need to be reminded what kind of father he had, not with what scars he literally carried on his chest and back from his dad's bullwhip.

"Benni, there's more than one way to scar a person." The hardness in his voice was uncompromising.

I inhaled deeply, not wanting to go there with him. It was something I could barely discuss with Gabe, who had a father who had actually been the most open and loving person in his family. "Daddy doesn't talk much. That's just the way he is."

My father's reaction still confused and hurt me. Had he known all along about the bones? Had Joe told him in a vulnerable moment? If he had, why hadn't Daddy trusted me enough to tell me? Or had Joe kept Daddy, whom he always claimed to be his best friend, in the dark also? Was Daddy hurt about being left out of the most important incident in his best friend's life? So why didn't he tell me so?

I looked Hud directly in the eyes. "I'm sure he's hurting inside."

"I'm sure he is, *catin*," he said softly, his anger dissipating as quickly as it came.

"Okay, Detective Hudson," Pinky said, coming up to us. "We've got a little surprise for you and your grandpa. And I'm here to tell you, we are more than a little aggrieved that your sweet self has been scarce as Confederate dollars around here this last week and you are going to pay for it."

"Save me," Hud mouthed silently as she lead him away.

"Have fun," I said, wiggling my fingers at him and laughing.

In the next five minutes they had Hud and Iry sitting up on the make-shift stage for their talent show's number. They turned on the karaoke machine and proceeded to serenade the two men with the song "Fever" by Peggy Lee. You have not truly experienced that song until you've heard it performed by four very confident Southern women wearing black satin cowgirl shirts and skin-tight Wranglers. I didn't know Hud could turn that shade of red.

"I think, for once, he's out of his league," I said to Gabe, who came up and put his arm around me.

"Serves him right," Gabe said.

I gave a low laugh. "Don't get too cocky, mister. There's a rumor that the cousins are zeroing in on you next."

The momentary panic on his handsome face was worth the points I lost in heaven for that little lie.

After the cousins' performance, everyone mingled, enjoyed Rich's goodies and said their good-byes, exchanging business cards, phone numbers and e-mail addresses. It was amazing how quickly a group of people could bond in two weeks.

There was only few more problems that hadn't been addressed. I found Dove in the kitchen haranguing Rich about catering her next historical society brunch. For free, of course.

"Can I steal her for a moment?" I asked Rich.

"Please, do," he replied, looking relieved.

"You're not off the hook yet, young man," Dove said, playfully shaking a fist at him.

"What do you need, honeybun?" she asked out in the empty hallway.

"What happened with Sissy and the dominos?" I'd noticed that Sissy had been pouting all night, her arms crossed over her chest like she was guarding the crown jewels.

Dove beamed. "I took your advice and it worked."

"My advice? What advice?" I didn't remember suggesting a thing and had, without meaning to, put the whole domino debacle on the back burner with all the other more immediate problems at the ranch.

"We all got together and started cheating ourselves," Dove said. "It drove her crazy!"

I stared at her like she'd gone nuts. "I might have been distracted these last two weeks, but I'm fairly sure I never told you all to cheat."

"No, no, you're hearing me wrong. We cheated so that she'd win. Every single time. It's driving her so crazy that she's refusing to play anymore. We're just going to let her sit and stew about it awhile, until she figures out why we did it. Maybe that'll make her mend her ways."

In a cockeyed way, it was the ultimate gesture of grace. They confronted her sin without out-and-out humiliating her.

"Maybe you should change your name to Solomon," I said, giving her a hug.

"Oh, pshaw," she said. "Where's Rita and Skeeter?"

"Left this morning," I said. "There's a rodeo in Tucson in three days."

"She'll regret taking him back," Dove said. "Men like him never change."

"Maybe not," I said. "But she looked pretty doggone determined this time. And she has a plan." Such as it was.

Dove shrugged, not convinced. "Like Arnold, she'll be back."

Last night, right in the middle of dinner, we were interrupted by the sound of a truck badly in need of a muffler. The horn blared the first few bars of "Dixie." The Dukes of Hazzard live on.

"What is *that*?" one of the quilters had asked as I served her chili and cornbread.

"An answer to a prayer," I replied, looking up at the ceiling. "Thank you, Lord."

"Skeeter!" Rita squealed, apparently forgetting all about the skanky Tiffany with the uncontrollable tongue.

"Make him work for it, cousin," I said, as she tore off her apron. "Remember the Alamo."

Her expression was as empty as her bank account. "Huh?"

"Tiffany," I said with a big sigh. "Remember Tiffany."

Slowly, the light came on. "You're right," she said, tying her apron back on. "Benni, you go tell him I'll see him when I'm through working. He can just sit his cheatin' butt on the porch and wait for me."

"You go, girl," Reba called out, her cousins loudly agreeing.

"Gladly," I said, grinning. It was the most out-and-out satisfying thing I'd done in two weeks.

I was contemplating the tea cart of goodies, listening to Dove and the WMU ladies harmonize on "Moon River" when Hud walked back over to me. His face was still a little pink from the cousins' serenade.

"You're still eating, Miss Piggy?" he said.

"Hey, Inspector Clouseau," I said. "You looked a little frazzled there. Didn't think that was possible. All those female hormones a little too much for you?"

He gave an uncertain laugh. "Those Georgia ladies are lethal. Thank goodness they're going home tomorrow. Don't know if I could keep up with them."

"Ha! He's finally met his match."

"Note that it takes four women."

"Your ego is only surpassed by that of my husband's. You two are more alike than you realize." I glanced over at Gabe who, my white lie coming true, was now being collectively charmed by the cousins. And he didn't look a bit intimidated. At least not yet.

Hud's face turned serious. "Are you doing okay?"

I shrugged. "I'll be fine."

His dark eyes studied my face for a moment. "You called me Inspector Clouseau."

It was my turn to be embarrassed. The name Gabe had derisively called him slipped out before I realized it. "I'm sorry. I was just kidding. I didn't mean to make fun . . ."

He held his hand up to silence me. "No, I like it. Kinda puts me up there near Joe Friday."

"I . . . don't think so, Hud. You're a . . . you're a nice guy. But . . ."

"But what if I'd gotten there before him? Tell me that I had a chance at your heart if I'd shown up in your life first."

I didn't answer right away. Hud's question caused too many confusing thoughts to rush through my head. It was weird, how comfortable I felt with him. He felt sort of like an old friend, or maybe, like Victory had said about Joe and Garland, like someone with whom I'd gone through battle. This was the third time he and I had been involved in a strange crime situation. Were we destined to spend our lives like this, forever crossing paths in this odd way? His words made me wonder, just briefly, what might have taken place between us had he come into my life before Gabe. Would it be Cajun French, not Spanish, being whispered to me in the dark, making my blood run hot, my crazy, unpredictable heart swell with desire?

He cocked his head. "What's going through that shifty little mind of yours?"

"Nothing," I said, glad he couldn't read my thoughts.

He watched me a minute, then gave a slow smile. And I knew that he knew. That I wondered. That I would always wonder.

"I have something for you." He pulled something out of the front pocket of his jeans. "Hold out your hand."

I hesitated for a moment.

"Oh, c'mon, don't be such a wuss. It's not a bug."

"I'm not afraid of bugs," I said, cautiously opening my palm.

It was a smashed penny. I looked at it closer. "Olaf Johnsen's Llama Farm, Red Owl, South Dakota."

"For your collection," he said, grinning. "Does Gabe know yet?"

"Yes," I lied, smiling in spite of myself. In all the hullabaloo, I'd completely forgotten to tell him about my secret collection.

Hud's eyes laughed at me, as if he knew what I was thinking.

"Benni, Hud, get over here!" called Pinky. "We need your voices. Since we're the first set of guests, we're videotaping a group sing for the future guests of Broken Dishes." They were all gathered around the karaoke machine, following the words. Gabe had a cousin on each side and was starting to look a little dazed by their overwhelming attention.

"Happy Trails to you," everyone started singing.

"I know some trivia," I said to Hud as we started toward the stage. "Did you know that Dale Evans wrote that song? Everyone thinks it was Roy Rogers, but he just sang it. She was the one who wrote it."

"I did not know that particular piece of information," Hud said.

"Well, Clouseau, now you do," I replied. "Let's go sing."

CHAPTER 18

THE SECRET TRAVELER IS "HOME ON THE RANGE"

What do rolling, oak-dotted hills covered with blue lupine and neon orange California poppies, wild pigs, barn dances, quilting seminars, five-star home-style cuisine, gentle horseback rides, and hospitality that is bigger than all outdoors have in common? The Broken DIS Guest Ranch in San Celina County, is what. This traveler just spent the most incredible two weeks in an atmosphere of warmth and friendliness and good, old-fashioned neighborliness at the "Broken Dishes" Guest Ranch in the beautiful Cholame Valley in California's beautiful Central Valley . . .

*T*HAT'S TWO *BEAUTIFULS*, LORETTA," REBA SAID FROM OVER ON the china blue brocade divan. "Someone fetch that woman a thesaurus."

"There's one right here inside my laptop," Loretta said. "If I could just find it. You'd think if we paid three thousand dollars for a computer, it'd write the dang column for us."

"We need a secretary," Gaynelle said, her voice a languid drawl.

The writing session for their column was at her house this time, a Southern plantation-style mansion outside of Atlanta that had been in her family since before the War of Northern Aggression, as her grandpappy still called it. She was serving espressos with peppermint schnapps and the chocolate-mocha mousse recipe she talked Rich into giving her. She'd been liberal with the schnapps and it was beginning to show.

"We need to get this column in," Reba said. "And if y'all have one more of Gaynelle's espressos, we'll never finish this by deadline. Now, *concentrate*, you decadent Southern trelles." That was Reba's not very clever combination of tramp and belle, a description she thought fit the cousins to a tee. To be fair, she thought it up when they were all ten years old.

"How about gorgeous?" Pinky offered from over on the red silk fainting couch. "And speaking of decadent, am I the only one here who's had erotic dreams about that cute little Cajun sheriff?"

"Oowee," Loretta said. "He was something on that dance floor, wasn't he? I'd love to wrap his cute little bootie up and take it home."

"Do y'all think his rhythm translates to other, more interesting, places?" Gaynelle asked, giggling again.

"Now there's something I'd like to concentrate on," Loretta said, setting the computer aside and reaching for her espresso cup.

"Girls, girls! The column, the column!" Reba said, exasperated.

"Da plane! Da plane," Pinky cried, causing all of them to start laughing uncontrollably, something not hard to do with the cousins.

"We'll never get this done," Reba moaned, giving in and taking her third chocolate-mocha mousse. "Not to mention I'll be walking that treadmill for the next twelve hours straight if y'all don't stop forcing me to eat this divine mousse."

"You know, this has been the most fun trip yet," Gaynelle said. "And we're doing a good turn for a nice young couple on top of it. Sure hope everything works out for Shawna and Johnny."

The cousins nodded in agreement.

"So, where'll we go next, dear cousins?" Reba asked, digging into the mousse with a solid silver spoon that Gaynelle's many-times-great grandma had hidden from the Yankees. Twice.

"Thinking about hot Cajuns, how about something down Louisiana way?" Loretta suggested. "We haven't been there for a good long while."

"I am not going to another Mardi Gras with y'all," Reba said. "My ankle still throbs when it rains."

"No one forced you to swing off that balcony," Pinky said.

"Those beads were really pretty," Reba retorted.

Gaynelle stood up and stretched. "You know, a certain sheriff's detective mentioned to me that he was flying back to Baton Rouge with his grandpa over Mardi Gras to help him pack for his move out to California."

"Didn't Iry say his cousin owned a restaurant there?" Reba said, cocking her head.

"King Varise's Cajun Palace and Dance Hall," Gaynelle said. "He gave me a card. Said they always have a big Mardi Gras celebration."

"Mardi Gras in Baton Rouge," Reba said. "Could make a fascinating column."

"Detective Ford Hudson, you sweet thing," Pinky said, holding up her tiny cup. "Put on your dancin' shoes. The cousins are coming to Baton Rouge."